Down Range

Down Range

A Novel

Taylor Moore

HARPER LARGE PRINT

An Imprint of HarperCollinsPublishers

DOWN RANGE. Copyright © 2021 by Robert Taylor Moore. All rights reserved. Printed in the United States of America. No part of this book may be used or reproduced in any manner whatsoever without written permission except in the case of brief quotations embodied in critical articles and reviews. For information, address HarperCollins Publishers, 195 Broadway, New York, NY 10007.

HarperCollins books may be purchased for educational, business, or sales promotional use. For information, please e-mail the Special Markets Department at SPsales@harpercollins.com.

FIRST HARPER LARGE PRINT EDITION

ISBN: 978-0-06-309018-7

Library of Congress Cataloging-in-Publication Data is available upon request.

21 22 23 24 25 LSC 10 9 8 7 6 5 4 3 2 1

*Like the pioneers before us, Texas pilgrims today share
the age-old desire for a future as bright as our stars.
Being Texan isn't a birthright, it's a state of mind.
It's to the trailblazers of past, present, and future
that I dedicate this novel.*

Down Range

Prologue

At ten years of age, Asadi Saleem didn't know much, other than that he was in danger, maybe even about to die. His clearest memory of the attack was falling face-first into the snow outside the house. That was when the coldness crept into his bones.

He was certain the killers were the same men he'd seen before. The skinny one had a lizard's face, pointed and smooth. The giant was scruffy, with a reddish-blond beard that dangled like a goat's.

Now Asadi was their prisoner.

With only a T-shirt and underwear as insulation, he could feel the icy metal floor of the van biting at his skin. He tried to rise, but his hands and feet were tethered. Asadi yanked at the restraints but his body was nearly frozen and his muscles quivered like jelly. He tugged harder, just as the brakes squealed and the van came to a stop.

The creaking of hinges preceded two sharp clanks. Soft footsteps and calm voices gave way to shouting and a scuffle. The violent outbreak was followed by silence.

Tears burned in Asadi's eyes, but just as he began to weep, the voices outside grew loud again. As grief morphed into panic, Asadi turned to the black windows. Although it was difficult to make out any definite shapes, he could tell there was someone holding a flashlight.

A border crossing? A policeman?

With a glimmer of hope, Asadi screamed, but only a whimper escaped through the rope cinched over his cracked lips. He swallowed hard against the metallic tang of blood and cried out again as a key zipped into the lock on the rear of the van.

The doors swung open, revealing two silhouettes. Asadi's heart sank as one moved closer with a syringe. Clamping his eyes shut, he curled into a ball, and sobbed a desperate prayer. The prick to his neck sent a shock wave of pain through his body as the image of his captor echoed in his brain.

His only shred of hope came from the familiar neon sign in the distance—the one he remembered from two days before—of a smiling bandit atop a galloping red stallion, blazing like fire. Its legs pulsated in an alternating pattern that changed by the second.

Sliding back into the fog of his frozen nightmare, Asadi's mind clung to the vision of a man and his horse, racing to save him. He'd be rescued by his friend—*the cowboy*—the one who'd promised—*you'll always be safe with me.*

PART ONE

The hardest thing on earth is choosing
what matters.

—LARRY MCMURTRY, *LONESOME DOVE*

1

Three days earlier . . .
Nasrin, Afghanistan

Garrett Kohl kept looking back at his dusty white Land Cruiser, nestled between the foothills about forty yards down the ridge. A little rough and dirty math showed he was nearly out of the safe zone and drifting farther from it by the second.

He tried to squelch the chiding voice in his head, but with every step he took into the mountainous Taliban terrain, it grew more persistent. By the time he was nearing the edge of the escarpment overlooking the small Afghan village, an old line of caution boomed in his head like a honky-tonk serenade.

If you get your ass in, you better get your ass out.

Had Garrett been sipping on a Shiner Bock beer at the Stumblin' Goat Saloon he might have enjoyed the melody. But the warning was no beer joint poetry dripping from the mouths of Sturgill Simpson or Robert Earl Keen. It was a little hard knocks wisdom imparted five years prior by a seasoned instructor at the DEA Academy in Quantico.

A Georgia-born gunslinger named Joe Bob Dawson ended every tradecraft lesson and war story with one of several sayings. First among his favorites was *I didn't get this old by accident*, which was followed by a close second: *I want to meet Jesus, just not today.*

Either way, the message to his deep-cover officers was clear. The kind of work they did was as dangerous as it gets.

As a former Green Beret turned DEA special agent, Garrett had, over the years, become a devoted disciple of more than a few old hands who had been there, done that, bought the bloodstained T-shirt. And he treated their lessons like gospel. He'd been in a few tight spots more than once, and their wisdom had saved him on several occasions.

Slowing his pace, Garrett dropped into the prone position and inched over a blanket of powdery snow to the edge of a crag overlooking the valley. Finding good cover behind the serrated stump of a fallen gray cedar, he lay flush against the cold granite, struggling to catch his breath as adrenaline surged and lactic acid pumped into his aching thighs.

After a short rest, he rolled to his side, unzipped his brown Carhartt jacket and jerked at its fleece lining to let a little cool air flow in. Garrett nudged the black Filson watch cap up on his forehead, raised the camera's viewfinder, and made a slight adjustment to the lens. Once the snowcapped mountain peaks were in focus, he shifted his gaze downward to a narrow but powerful mountain tributary.

The meadow lining its banks was emerald green, reminding him of photos he'd seen from Ireland and Scotland. But the crown jewel of the whole view was the sky-colored water swirling over jagged gray fangs of rock. The image was surreal, like some lost valley from an ancient storybook world.

In fact, it would have been a postcard-worthy shot were it not for the two dozen heavily armed tangos bunched around at the creek, about sixty yards below his position. He didn't recognize them, but they were dressed in black *shalwar kameez* and carried Kalashnikov rifle variants with polymer stocks. Their modern rifles and tactical chest rigs made them look more like paramilitary troops than straight-up Taliban or ISIS.

Of course, it was growing nearly impossible to identify anyone by guns and gear. Since the pullout of NATO forces, terrorist organizations, drug runners, and warlords were thriving, in large part due to proceeds from the opium trade. For that reason, Garrett and his DEA team were deployed to Afghanistan. The jihadi movement had grown bigger than ideology. It was about money and power. And selling the drug large scale bought dump trucks full of both.

The call to morning prayers caught Garrett's attention, and he watched the tangos drop to their knees on small maroon rugs laid out on the chalky stone. With heads wrapped in black turbans, they bowed and rose, mumbling in a low steady cadence that carried on the wind. The hunter in Garrett liked the sound cover provided by the gale, but the rest of him cursed the damn bite of it.

Garrett adjusted the lens, zoomed in on the creek, and captured a few photos of weapons and equipment. There were three Toyota Hilux pickups and a red Nissan four-by-four pickup with a Dushka machine gun mounted over the cab. But nothing out of the ordinary for a warlord's convoy.

Several more snaps with the camera and he checked his six. No one in sight, but a deep uneasiness set in, a burn in his stomach he recognized from over a decade of war-zone tours and undercover assignments. Garrett didn't normally travel alone, but the rest of his unit had relocated from Camp Tsavo to another Forward Operating Base (FOB) southwest of Kandahar. This elite squad of expert counternarcotics and counterterrorist fighters made up of former operators from Army Special Forces, Rangers, Navy SEALs, and Force Recon Marines had shifted their efforts to tackle opium production in the fields.

Garrett was left standing to continue running their confidential sources. Cultivation and trafficking were two separate parts of the same serious problem, and DEA headquarters didn't want either getting worse. Unfortunately, Washington's allocation of resources wasn't consistent with its expectations. He and his team did the best they could with what they were given, but it was only a matter of time before something big fell through the cracks.

At the sound of a cranking engine, Garrett eased the camera back around and brought the lens into focus on the Nissan. He was repositioning for a better view when a stinging gust of wind tore across the valley—chilling him to the bone. He grabbed a black-and-gray *shemagh* scarf from his pack, wrapped it around his face, and tugged the coat's hood over his head.

With hair past his collar, a thick beard, and sleeve-tattoos inked over sinewy arms, Garrett came across as a hell of a lot more outlaw than lawman. It was a look and persona he'd affectionally dubbed *redneck crank dealer*, developed while working deep-cover operations in the meth trade around North Dakota's oil fields and interstate truck stops. He'd later perfected the guise smuggling cocaine for Mexican cartels in the border hinterlands of Texas, New Mexico, and Arizona— mostly along the Rio Grande.

Surviving in this world meant playing the part. And Garrett played it to a T. On top of the assortment of tattoos that included death skulls and screaming Comanche warriors, he wore trucker hats, pearl snap shirts, faded Wranglers, and Twisted X boots. Between the look, swagger, and a whole mess of battle scars, there wasn't a square inch of him that didn't look rodeo cowboy gone horribly off the rails. If someone ever questioned his authenticity, they sure didn't do it to his face.

Garrett focused in on the red Nissan pickup that had moved parallel to the creek. In addition to the Dushka machine gun there were two RPGs lying on the tailgate. Lots of lead and gunpowder but not what he was looking for. No drugs. No money.

According to his source, a Russian arms dealer named Vadik Sokolov, the Taliban in the area were delivering a good-size shipment of opium to an Uzbek buyer that morning. It was a payload estimated in the millions of dollars. Garrett debated the reliability of the intel, knowing full well it could be garbage, but Vadik had never steered him wrong. And because of that fact he was freezing his butt off up in the mountains and hoping like hell he could stay out of sight.

Getting caught out there alone was a surefire ticket to a miserable death. He'd be mutilated and murdered or murdered and mutilated. Either way, it was a helluva bad end. But serious money bought serious weapons, and a cash infusion of that magnitude to the Taliban, ISIS, or any other terrorist organization posed a major security threat. Reporting of loose SA-24 surface-to-air weapons systems had upped the ante. Russian missiles capable of hitting a jet at over ten thousand feet posed a grave risk to U.S. forces operating in-country, not to mention civilian airliners if smuggled overseas.

Looking over at the opposite bank from where the Nissan sat, Garrett watched as a group of black-clad men herded a crowd of villagers, including women and children, into the icy shallows. Nearly forty or fifty friendlies at a rough count. There was a fair amount of yelling and screaming from both sides, but it was unclear to Garrett exactly what was going down or why. Tribal disputes were common, particularly in this part of the country, but they usually resulted in little more than threats and some bruised egos on behalf of whoever was on the receiving end.

Which is why it came as a gut punch when the armed men raised their rifles and let loose a barrage of machine-gun fire that sent the villagers tumbling back into the water. A few seconds passed, and those who hadn't drifted with the current met a second volley that finished the job.

It was a scene more horrific than any Garrett had ever witnessed on the battlefield—and that was saying plenty. As a combat veteran, he'd seen men shot and blown up, and he'd held them while they died. But there was nothing so horrifying as the slaughter of women and children.

Unlike Hollywood's depiction of a quick, painless death by shooting, the reality was deeply unsettling. Panicked villagers gave in to their baser instincts. They clawed, scratched, and climbed over each other to flee the onslaught of bullets. Shrieks of pain and grief rose above the echoing gunfire in a deafening discord of pleas from the dying.

Garrett was stunned by how quickly the firing squad had acted. Forcing himself back into the moment, he contemplated a plan to put an end to the bloodbath, but at this point, there wasn't much left to stop. Beyond that, taking on this many men alone would be suicide. There was nothing to do but capture it on film, head back to Tsavo, and send a report to headquarters.

Satisfied he'd taken enough photos to capture the horror, Garrett was about to turn and head down the slope when he saw five villagers swim the creek. But before they made it to the other side, waiting soldiers either shot the poor souls or finished them off with their knives.

Garrett took a deep breath and contemplated his options. With only his LWRC M6 rifle and a couple extra mags on his gun belt, he could punish a few of the bastards, but then what? The rules of engagement were clear. Weapons were for defense not revenge. If he engaged first, he'd be looked upon little differently than the murderers below.

Aside from that, he was in a region off-limits to Americans pursuant to a treaty negotiated between the Afghan government and the Taliban. Washington and Kabul were trying to keep the peace, and Garrett's violation would be upsetting the applecart with a stick of dynamite.

For his infractions, the CIA base chief would have him on the first flight home to face a firestorm of political and legal scrutiny. At best, it would end his career. At worst, he'd go to prison. And that was assuming he made it out alive in the first place. Although rage flowed through him like an electric current, he quickly tamped down his feelings and made the rational decision to exfil.

Easing back over the edge for a last look, Garrett raised his rifle and peered through the magnified optic to find three black-clad fighters charging up the ridge. His hair stood on end in momentary panic until he realized they weren't after him but a village boy no older than ten. They were about forty yards out and closing fast.

Garrett's pulse raced but the world around him decelerated into slow motion. With his senses kicked into overdrive, the click of his rifle's selector from SAFE to FIRE seemed loud enough to give away his position. He glanced behind him at his Land Cruiser, his instincts screaming at him to haul ass and jump inside, but for some reason he couldn't move. Whether it was a duty to stay or the guilt of leaving, Garrett wasn't sure. He only knew that a whisper from God superseded his flight response. Over and over he heard. *Not. Just. Yet.*

Garrett returned to the scope and found the kid again, the boy's eyes streaming with tears, chest heaving as he gulped in panicked breaths. The kid had gained a decent lead on his pursuers, but a slip on some loose rocks caused him to stumble and fall. Popping up with a skinned knee, the boy tried to run, but the nearest attacker, knife gripped in one hand, extended the other and clutched his foot. The child wailed in pure terror, crying out for his mother.

That pitiful scream moved Garrett more than any threat of torture or death. And it was in that microsecond that he tuned out every bit of wisdom he'd ever heard and followed the voice speaking to his soul.

The *crack* of Garrett's rifle signaled the launch of three rounds that slammed into the attacker's chest, cutting short the swing of his blade and sending him tumbling backward in a cloud of gray dust. Sliding his crosshairs right, Garrett lined up on an orange-bearded freak who lumbered up behind the boy. His face was tensed, neck muscles clenched as he raised the dagger to strike. But a single shot from the M6 punched a tiny hole below his left eye, killing him instantly.

Immediately shifting upward, Garrett steadied the crosshairs on the third fighter, and landed a bullet center mass, crumpling him into a pile of black rags atop the chalky white stone.

Garrett flinched as a 7.62 round cracked by, rolled left, canted the rifle to access the offset red dot, and shot at a half dozen marauders sprinting for cover behind the Nissan. Downing one and hobbling another, he shifted fire to a group caught out in the open.

Emptying his rifle, Garrett dropped the mag, snatched a reload from his belt, and jammed it in the magwell. He hit the bolt release and went back to work. In a matter of seconds, his last round was spent, and there was nothing left but the lingering echo of gunfire and a pile of dead bodies.

In a lull of return fire, he peered over the ridge to find the kid still thirty yards out, clawing his way upward. The gravel beneath his feet was making progress difficult.

Garrett rose to help, but a fusillade of rounds ripped overhead and pinned him flat. He popped in a new mag and was acquiring a target when two fighters behind the Nissan leapt into the bed and swung the Dushka in his direction. The gunmen were in his crosshairs, but the machine gun belched first, unleashing a buzz saw of Soviet-era firepower as the bullets climbed the ridge.

Since it wasn't *if* but *when* the massive projectiles connected, Garrett dumped three rounds into the Nissan's engine compartment, then took a couple of potshots at the Dushka operators as he scrambled to his feet.

He looked over the edge to where the boy had been but only churned-up earth remained. Even over the cacophony of gunfire and strafing rounds, Garrett could still hear the cries. It was only in his mind, he knew, but it would scar his soul nonetheless. Yet another life he could not save.

With a heavy heart, Garrett aborted his rescue and tore a path down the embankment in the opposite direction, fighting for purchase atop loose gravel. He was within fifteen yards of his vehicle when gunfire sounded from behind. At five yards, the *tingting* of bullets rang out as they hit the armor-plated doors. He dove headfirst under the engine block and low-crawled to the passenger side as rounds cracked overhead.

Garrett kept beneath the windows as he climbed in and slid to the driver's side. The steel doors had held so far, but a heavy-caliber round or RPG would be the end. Once behind the wheel, he cranked the engine and was about to throw it in gear when he witnessed what had to be an adrenaline-fueled hallucination.

The boy had not only escaped the knife-wielding mob and Dushka machine gun, he was standing outside. Garrett opened the door and yanked him in with a swift tug.

Swiveling back, Garrett jerked the Glock 17 from his holster and blasted twice, hitting the closest pursuer center mass. The marauder stumbled, fell forward, and slid under the chassis.

A cloud of white dust wafted into the cab as Garrett pulled the door shut and slammed the Toyota in drive. With a wall of earth to his right and a swarm of fighters to his left, he mashed the gas, kicking up a burst of gravel that pinged and thudded in the wheel wells.

As the knobby tires rumbled over the dead body, Garrett redlined the tachometer, forcing the engine into an angry roar. Launching deeper and deeper into hostile territory, he shot a glance in the rearview, but the 7.62 rounds dinging off the armored plating told him everything he needed to know. Going back the way he'd come in was not an option.

They hadn't driven more than a half mile when the valley opened up to a fork in the road. With an established route to the left and a goat path to the right, it wasn't a hard choice. But his decision to stay the course rattled the hell out of his young navigator.

"*Right! Right! Right!*" the kid screamed in Dari.

Against his better judgment, Garrett followed orders. At first, they dipped into a moderate slope, but in a matter of seconds their escape route became more mountain than mound. He jammed his boot on the brakes, just as an RPG slammed into the road ahead, pelting his hood with rocks and flame.

Forty yards to the left of his original trajectory, a half dozen fighters opened fire, raking the driver's side and *thwacking* the windows in a tight group of successive rounds. With the ballistic glass spiderwebbed to zero visibility, Garrett mashed the gas, punching through a hail of dirt clods and thick black smoke, plowing over a short cedar as they zigged and zagged down the steep mountain trail.

At the mercy of the terrain, he took his foot off the brakes and let momentum take over. He jerked the wheel left, missing a boulder, then right to avoid a tree, but lost complete control when the Toyota hit a dry creek bed and launched into the air.

With his stomach in his throat, Garrett threw out an arm to brace the boy but couldn't get a hold before the weightlessness of midair suspension ended in a teeth-rattling touchdown. Fortunately, the ground leveled out and they rolled to a stop at the edge of a wheat field.

The interior went dark as a cloud of billowy dust engulfed them, but Garrett could see that his young companion was alive and uninjured, just scared to death. The skinny Afghan boy looked to him with desperate eyes, his horror-stricken face caked in muddy tears. And it was at that moment that a stark reality settled in. For the sake of one kid, too stubborn to die, Garrett had made a reckless decision.

Not only had he jeopardized the mission, his career, and possibly his freedom, he'd violated an international agreement that could have ramifications on a global scale. And because of this, his fate now rested with the people he trusted least. His life was in the hands of the CIA.

2

Back at Camp Tsavo, Garrett sat outside the CIA base chief's office, going over and over the events of the massacre in his head. It was late and he was exhausted, but if he was going to take an ass-whoopin' from Kim Manning, he'd rather get it over, done, and behind him.

He'd dealt with her a few times before and she'd always been kind of a hard-ass control freak—a sort of my way or the highway kind of gal. And there was a good chance she'd want to nail him to the wall over his actions in Nasrin.

Garrett didn't know exactly what to expect, truth be told. Intelligence officers were unpredictable, measuring success with a whole different yardstick than law enforcement. There was also a chance he could walk into her office and be greeted with an attaboy and a big sloppy kiss. But that was wishful thinking.

Preparing for the worst, he carefully rehearsed how he'd tell the story from start to finish. Given what he knew about Kim, she'd want every detail, even beyond what he'd included in the Intelligence Information Report (IIR) he'd written earlier. She was a woman who lived in the weeds, a workaholic perfectionist with a near photographic memory.

There'd be no highlights here. She'd want the play-by-play. She'd also demand to know why he was out there alone without coordinating with her first, which meant he'd better have a good reason right off the bat. Of course, *good reasons* were open for interpretation. Priority for DEA and CIA were often two different things.

Garrett and his team made criminal cases, while the CIA made craters. It was a hell of a lot easier if problems, or in some cases *people*, just disappeared. They'd send in a drone, or a hit team, or pay off some black-bag assassin to knife you in a dark alley, whatever it took to solve the problem. If the Agency wanted you gone, you were gone. Plain and simple.

Having crossed paths with more than a few bottom feeders that *needed killin'*, Garrett didn't necessarily disagree with the CIA's tactics. In fact, he'd have done it himself without qualms, but DEA wasn't operating under a *presidential finding.*

Of course, there was no sense in bitching about it. CIA had a direct line to the National Security Council and that was that. If the DEA developed a good intel source, you could bet your ass the Agency would either poach them or kill them before you could say boo. Two Agencies. Same team. Different objectives. It was a match made in hell, but policy makers back in Washington expected everyone to sing kumbaya for the good of the country. *Yeah right.*

Although he didn't work for Kim directly, Garrett was obliged to confer with her before making any drastic moves. And the act of shooting up a village and absconding with a child was pretty much the definition of a drastic move. DEA operations were supposed to be deconflicted through the CIA base chief first. No exceptions.

That also meant Garrett's *shoot first—ask permission later* policy in Nasrin was bound to ruffle feathers. And Kim's feathers were already ruffled given the blistering verbal assault she was delivering to the poor bastard inside her office. She was known around Tsavo for slicing and dicing with a quick wit and a razor-sharp tongue. But sometimes her razor was followed with a mallet. Whoever was in there was getting flayed and beaten all at the same time.

Looking around at the empty desks inside the skiff made Garrett uneasy. It was evening, true, but the Sensitive Compartmented Information Facility (SCIF) was almost never vacant, which led him to believe it was void of witnesses for a reason. Not a good sign.

The portable building, which housed CIA's base of operations, was spartan at best, a rickety headquarters comprised of particleboard walls and cheap vinyl flooring. It was a hodgepodge of computer monitors set atop smudgy plastic tables. Millions of dollars in equipment kept in a structure little better than a lawn mower shed.

Garrett was toeing at a rat's nest of multicolored cables beneath his chair when a piece of silver duct tape became affixed to his boot. He leaned over and ripped it off, as the diatribe in Kim's office ended. A newbie CIA operations officer blasted through the door looking queasy and disheveled. The guy made brief eye contact but didn't break stride. Another bad sign.

"Garrett Kohl!" Kim bellowed from inside her office. "Get your ass in here! Right now!"

He walked in to find Kim sitting behind her desk, glaring at the monitor, and pecking away at her keyboard. She worked for at least a minute and a half uninterrupted while Garrett stood there at the door like an idiot. It was a power move for sure, but what could he do? She had power and he didn't.

He'd have been more pissed had he not been reminded of an inside joke with his friend Carlos Contreras, a die-hard old operator who ran the CIA's Ground
Branch paramilitary team at Tsavo. The former SEAL
and self-proclaimed Puerto Rican ambassador to Afghanistan always referred to Kim as "the Dragon
Queen," a reference to the poised but brutal Daenerys
Targaryen character from *Game of Thrones*.

The description was as comical as it was accurate.
From her blond hair to her slight frame, Kim was a
miniature-size dynamo of fire and fury. She couldn't
have been taller than five foot three or weighed more
than a hundred pounds, but she somehow managed to
fill a room with her presence and intimidate even her
toughest foes.

After mouthing the last few words to whatever she
was reading, Kim clicked a coffee-stained mouse,
shoved her keyboard forward, and looked up. "Ah . . .
Special Agent Kohl. A bull *in search* of a china shop."
With unnerving calmness, she added, "Sit down,
cowboy."

As the son of a Texas rancher, Garrett was all too
familiar with the nickname. He'd heard it his entire
career. Normally, he took it with pride, but not in the
field. In the field *cowboy* meant reckless. And that
wasn't a reputation you wanted in a war zone.

As Garrett walked to her desk, he noticed the only place to sit was a splintery wooden chair that looked like something you'd see next to an elementary school Dumpster. It was clear she wasn't going to begin until he was seated, so he dropped into the wobbly chair, much lower than hers. She was already starting with the dirty CIA mind games, and he suspected next she'd find a way to lean over the table and show her cleavage, which was surprisingly ample for her tiny frame.

In his experience with her, she'd never been shy about using every weapon in her arsenal to assert control. And Garrett couldn't say he blamed her. No way it was easy to get the edge on a bunch of type A Neanderthals like himself, so she made use of what the good Lord gave her. It may have been a disgraceful trick, but damned if it wasn't effective. And the longer he was in-country the better it worked.

Kim eased back in her chair looking cheerier than he expected. "Sounds like you had quite an experience while I was over in Kabul. Am I right?"

"Yes, ma'am, it was that for sure." Garrett's voice was gravel and molasses. His sentences arrived when they felt like it. He punctuated this one with a friendly smile.

"I read your report." She tapped a file on her desk with her index finger. "Mass murder. A big shootout. Very interesting stuff."

He lifted the secure lock bag, stowing his report, a map of the area, and the horrific images caught on camera. "I brought photos, if you want to take a look."

Kim raised her hand and waved him off. "Not necessary. Already have them." From drones to satellites, she always had eyes in the sky.

As soon as Garrett launched into his version of the story, she stopped him and gave her own recounting of the events he'd laid out in the report. It was a line by line summation, all off the top of her head, and without missing a single detail.

As Kim spoke, he bobbed his head in a way he hoped looked earnest, seeking to foster some goodwill. When she finally wrapped it up, Garrett responded with a tone of finality.

"Yep, I guess that about covers it."

He rose to leave, but she raised a hand and pushed the air.

"No wait, there's more. There's the part about how you brought one of their children back here for us to deal with."

Garrett eased back into his creaking chair. "There is *that*."

"Everything else I could cover up. But with the kid in our possession, we've got to come clean. Let the Afghans know we were in a restricted zone."

Garrett held back as much as he could. What was he supposed to do? Let the kid die? "Well, you weren't there, Kim. You didn't see what I saw."

"Doesn't matter what you *saw*. This is a sovereign country, Kohl. What matters is DEA doesn't have the authority to play judge, jury, and executioner over here."

You do it all the time, Garrett thought but didn't say. He removed his cap, hung it on his knee, and stared at the Lone Star Dry Goods patch with the bison silhouette, which made him long to be home. Realizing he'd better get his head in the game or run the risk of losing it, Garrett mustered up a little contrition to make his case.

"Look, Kim, I know this puts you in a tough position. But if you'd have been there in the moment, heard the screams, seen the blood, you'd understand why I did it." He looked up and locked eyes. "They butchered these people like animals. I had to do something."

"I agree you had to do *something*. But that *something* was gain proof of what happened, then come back here and report what you saw. I don't have a problem with you being there. I have a problem with vigilantism, as will Afghan authorities if this gets out. And if it does, the ambassador will have a hell of a lot of explaining to do. We've already had enough bad press over what those trigger-happy contractors did last year."

Your contractors! Garrett again kept quiet. He didn't know the details, but there'd been a big hullaballoo over a case of mistaken identity leading to the deaths of several Afghan civilians. Kim was deputy at the time. The base chief was sent home early.

"And in case you weren't aware," she continued, "your weapons are issued for self-defense, not so you can go *Punisher* on everybody's asses out there. This is not the movies. You *do not* get to take the law into your own hands."

Garrett leaned back in his chair, contemplating her response. Legally, he *was* in the wrong. There was no arguing it. The rules of engagement were clear. He engaged the enemy first without being under attack. Guilty as charged.

Realizing the ramifications for his actions, Garrett did his best to calm himself. Fighting her was a losing battle. "I know, Kim. You're right on the ROEs. I messed up. Big time."

After a few awkward seconds passed, she rolled her eyes to the ceiling. "So . . . here's the part where I'd normally be telling you I'm shipping you back home. From there, the DEA will let you go immediately, and you'll spend the rest of your days back in *Nowhere-*

land, Texas, busting teenagers smoking weed behind the Piggly Wiggly. *If* you're lucky." Her eyes drifted back down as she spoke. "That sound appealing to you, Kohl?"

He let out a huff. "No. It doesn't." After a pregnant pause he added, "I feel like I hear a *but* coming though. Am I right?"

She met his gaze. "*But* that wouldn't do either of us any good. You go away with a ruined career and I lose someone who owes me a big favor."

Garrett relaxed, but only slightly. Repaying a favor to the CIA could be a cure worse than the disease. "Okay . . . what's on your mind?"

Kim picked up a manila folder and waggled it at him. "Did some reading on you today."

"Kind of figured you'd done all your snooping on me a long time ago."

Ignoring the comment, she opened the folder and studied the first page. "Says here you were an instructor at the Special Forces Advanced Mountain Operations School at Fort Carson."

Garrett shifted in his creaking chair. "What of it?"

"Tactical mountain operations, wilderness survival, high-alpine medical emergency training." She looked up wearing a curious expression. "Kind of a stretch for a kid from the Texas High Plains, wasn't it?"

Garrett had to laugh. The part of the Texas he was from was called the *Llano Estacado*, Spanish for Staked Plains. Legend had it that this expanse of rolling grassland, larger in size than New England, was so flat and barren that Comanchero traders centuries ago had to drive stakes in the ground just to keep their bearings. It was in every way the opposite of the battlefield he'd come to know.

Kim's question was reasonable enough, but still he wondered where in the hell she was going with this one. "Spent some time in the mountains when I was younger. Mostly New Mexico. Got a feel for it, I guess. My best memories growing up were elk hunting, fly fishing, and camping out under the stars with my dad and brother."

"Nature boy, huh?"

Garrett gave her a half smile. "The outdoors suits me better than anywhere else, I suppose, but that wasn't what got me interested in mountain warfare."

"Then what was it?"

For the first time in their conversation, he felt at ease. They were finally on a subject he didn't have to qualify, couch, or justify first. "Horses."

Kim repeated the word *horses* and looked at the file. She ran her finger up the page as if following the time line backward. "DEA. Criminal Justice degree from

West Texas A&M University. Tenth Special Forces Group. High school in Canadian, Texas." She tossed the folder on her desk. "Nothing in here about horses."

The Kohl family's remuda was as good as it gets, and that wasn't just personal bias. By genetics alone, quarter horses were gifted sprinters—breed favorites in the quarter-mile race and competition rodeo. But it's not just bloodline that makes them superior. It's having a good trainer. And Garrett's father was among the best.

Garrett shook off the intelligence gap. "Your people probably didn't find it particularly important." He leaned back again, feeling more comfortable by the second. "Not surprising. Most people think horsemanship is a useless skill for soldiers these days."

Kim narrowed her gaze. "You weren't one of those Green Beret horse soldiers, were you? The ones who dropped in here after 9/11?"

"A bit before my time, but they were the reason I joined the army. When I read about what they did, I knew exactly how I wanted to serve my country. So, I made up my mind I was going Special Forces and I did everything in my power to make it happen."

"I admire the hell out of those guys." Kim's face registered a genuine appreciation. "Tip of the spear."

She was heading down a path, but to where Garrett didn't know. Feeling as though she was buttering him up right before she went for the jugular, he cut to the chase. "But you're not interested in horses or history, are you, Kim?"

She shook her head. "What I want to know is the next part of your story. The part where you left Colorado, came over here, and started running and gunning with a specialized unit near the Pakistani border. The part where your whole team was wiped out and you became a candidate for the Medal of Honor."

Garrett had been the only survivor of a specialized JSOC mountain unit operating on horseback. While mounting a raid against an ISIS cell in Pakistan, Garrett's team was ambushed, and all but he and one other were killed. Injured by shrapnel, Garrett managed to escape with his comrade, who later succumbed to his wounds during the harrowing escape.

Of course, Kim probably already knew all this. Or at the very least, she knew that digging into his work with the Joint Special Operations Command was off-limits. Even for someone with her security clearance it was a big no-no. She was testing him for a reason.

But Garrett figured he'd play along to see where she was going. "What about it?"

"The review process for the award was over before it ever began." She looked a little frustrated. "Who shut it down?"

He nodded at the file. "Why don't you tell me."

Kim thumbed through the papers. "Doesn't say." When she got to the last page, she focused in on something. "My guess is you were either operating somewhere you weren't supposed to be, or you were doing something you weren't supposed to do. Which was it?"

Garrett let her statement hang in the air for a while. When it was clear she wasn't going to let it go, he gave her a little nugget. "Maybe a little of both."

She cocked her head and smiled. "Good enough for me."

It was clear to Garrett she was driving toward something. Kim already had leverage given what happened in Nasrin, so it wasn't blackmail. It was as if she was looking deeper, wanting to know how far he'd push the boundaries to get the job done. "Is there a problem here?"

"Not at all." Kim looked as though she'd gotten what she wanted. "I've made an entire career being in places I wasn't supposed to be and doing things I wasn't supposed to do. Off-the-books is where I live. The key is being able to keep your mouth shut—which, given our conversation here, you're clearly able to do."

Garrett let her words sink in carefully. A few minutes earlier she was reading him the riot act over breaking the rules of engagement and being in a restricted zone, and now it appeared she was opening up. It was exactly what CIA operations officers do when they're evaluating a potential foreign asset for recruitment. She was seeing if he could be trusted and gauging his willingness to be brought into the fold. Garrett decided he wasn't going to make it easy.

When he sat like stone without a reply, Kim continued. "The group who massacred those villagers today. This isn't the first time they've done it."

Now she was offering a secret to get information in return. Garrett decided he'd play along. "Okay, it's the first I've heard of it. Although I know ISIS, the Taliban, some of the traffickers take—"

She waved him off. "It's not any of those groups. Nothing to do with Islam or drugs. It's something completely different."

Garrett was tempted to ask more questions but decided to get to the point. "What does this have to do with me?"

"The boy you brought back here. He's the only witness to what happened today."

"So?"

"We think they might come after him."

"Who might come after him?"

Kim clucked her tongue. "That's what we're looking into."

"But you think he's in danger?"

A single nod. "We need somebody to look after him until we can get to the bottom of what's going on. And we need somebody who can keep quiet about it."

Garrett could finally see what she was angling for and he didn't mind. Discretion was his middle name. And if watching over the boy would make all his problems go away, what she wanted was an easy fix. "Protective-custody assignment?"

She leaned back in her chair looking satisfied. "You could handle that, couldn't you?"

The truth was, Garrett didn't know much about kids, but whatever it entailed was bound to be easier than any backlash he'd receive for the mess in Nasrin. Knowing he could put the boy in front of some video games or cartoons and feed him hamburgers, the notion gained some appeal.

"How long we talking? Couple days? Week?"

"I'll let you know more once you get there."

Garrett cocked his head, unsure if he'd heard correctly. "Get where?"

"Back to the States."

"Whoa, wait." He pointed toward the right wall of her office, the direction he imagined the U.S. might be. "You want him out of Afghanistan?"

"He's not safe here."

Garrett raised his hands to his sides, palms up. "We're in the middle of a heavily guarded U.S. military installation surrounded by HESCO barriers, razor wire, and some of the most elite war fighters in the world. Where on God's green earth could we be safer?"

"Anywhere else," she answered, without elaborating.

"So, back home?"

"We don't know exactly who we're dealing with yet. But we think it involves corrupt factions within the Afghan government who are making a territory grab in the restricted zones. If we can prove it, the men behind these massacres will go to a war crimes tribunal, which means we're going to need a witness. And it looks like *he's* it right now."

It wasn't a huge surprise. Although things in Kabul had gotten better, there was still a fair amount of tribalism. And if someone high up in the government was diverting money and resources to their own hit squads, it would explain the upgraded equipment in the hands of the men who butchered the villagers.

In fact, it raised another question. Had the equipment been purchased with U.S. tax dollars? Is that what all this was about? Before he wasted too much time on the subject, Garrett let it go. International intrigue was the CIA's department. His job was to stop bad guys from doing bad things. The Agency could clean up its own messes.

"What about me? I saw everything."

"Let's not forget, *you* were never there. And we've got your own war crimes to sort out. On top of that, I think a ten-year-old village boy will generate a hell of a lot more sympathy than a machine-gun-wielding narc who looks like the Rob Zombie version of Jeremiah Johnson."

Garrett took a moment to ponder the comment. Jeremiah Johnson he'd heard before, and he didn't necessarily mind being reminded of his resemblance to the legendary mountain man played by a young Robert Redford. However, Rob Zombie was a new one. And he couldn't say he was pleased. Suddenly he didn't feel so bad about Contreras's Dragon Queen comparison.

"What about the photos?"

"They're exactly what we need," Kim conceded, "but we'll have to find someone else to claim credit. One of our assets can fill that role when the time comes. Aside from keeping the shootout off the front pages of the *New York Times*, you're not going to want anything to do with this, Kohl. As soon as we mention your involvement, consider your cover blown and your career over. No matter how many assurances you get, some politician somewhere will sell you out. Trust me. CIA has learned that lesson the hard way."

She was right. No point in arguing. Last thing he wanted was more attention. In fact, too much attention was the reason he'd taken the assignment in Afghanistan. There'd been a rumor floated among DEA sources that he was in the crosshairs of a Mexican cartel. And true or not, Garrett's superiors didn't want to take a chance. Despite his protests, headquarters forced him to pull up stakes and move on—leaving a lot of unfinished business south of the border.

There was a part of Garrett that wondered if Kim was being truthful. Was there really a tribunal or was this some made-up story to buy time before the CIA started making craters? If the boy wasn't safe at Camp Tsavo, it meant this whole thing went deep and was about to get ugly. And if Kim was worried these Afghan officials could carry out a successful hit inside a secure base, that meant it went high up the political chain. Possibly to the top. There were more than a few local contractors who would do the bidding of some bad actors for the right price.

Of course, there was another alternative Garrett had to consider. The U.S. had historically used surrogates to *take care of* some nasty business—the Contras in Central America, SAVAK in Iran, and the Mujahideen right there in Afghanistan to name a few. These organizations used methods that were not for the faint-hearted. Imprisonment. Torture. Even executions.

Hell, his own organization had its skeletons. The takedown of Pablo Escobar in Colombia was just one example. Shadow wars like that had been waged by most world powers at some point in time. Garrett didn't necessarily have a problem with it. Years under-cover with drug dealers, gangs, and cartels had taught him that sometimes you have to get your hands dirty.

But those endeavors were never without collateral damage, and more times than not, they left a bloody wake. If this poor kid had seen something he shouldn't have, then maybe someone back in Washington didn't want him talking. And if that were the case, this boy would never live to tell the tale. Of course, *he too* was in the exact same boat. As loose ends go, he was a big one, which meant he might be standing in the CIA's next crater.

3

Before Garrett could dig further, Kim had sprung from her chair and was heading for the door. Without so much as a word, she left her office. It was as if she knew he had reservations and wanted to get the process started before he could back out of the deal. He was contemplating whether Kim had a touch of psychic ability when she returned to the doorway in a huff.

"You coming or what?" She had a manila folder clamped under her arm.

Against his better judgment and curious as hell as to what was in that file, Garrett rose from the wobbly chair and followed her out into the SCIF. She was nearly halfway through the maze of desks and filing cabinets by the time he caught up. He could tell they were headed toward the office belonging to Bill Watson, deputy chief of base.

As Garrett walked beside her in silence, he couldn't help but dwell on the negative, still thinking about what might happen once they left Tsavo—if they'd ever be heard from again. Kim wasn't a monster, but she was as ruthless as they come. And he'd known some bad hombres, so that was saying a lot. He also knew paranoia was getting the better of him. Year after year of deep-cover work with the cartels had instilled a strong distrust of most people. It wasn't spiritually healthy, but it kept him alive.

As Kim approached Watson's office, she slowed her pace, almost tiptoeing, and Garrett followed suit. He was about to ask what was going on when she put her finger to her lips and spoke in a voice just above a whisper. "He's asleep."

Garrett's first thoughts were of the deputy chief. "Watson's still here?"

Kim shook her head and laughed. "No. Asadi."

"Who?"

She looked at Garrett like he'd lost it. "You know. *The boy.*"

Garrett walked forward and peeked inside. There was a small out-of-season plastic Christmas tree in the corner being used as a night-light. He scanned to the left, to an old tan couch missing the back cushions. The boy, Asadi, was lying atop it, zipped tight in a royal blue sleeping bag. His breathing was heavy enough to hear from the door.

Garrett adjusted his voice to match Kim's whisper. "He's living in the SCIF?"

"For now." She gave a curt nod, pulled the folder from under her arm and thrust it at him. "A list of safe houses in Virginia and Maryland."

Safe houses? This thing was getting weirder by the second and Garrett had the same sinking feeling he'd had earlier when he was climbing that ridge before the massacre. Time to end this goat rope before it went any further.

Garrett waved her off. "Don't need it."

"Why?"

"Not doing it."

Kim hurled the same question, this time with more indignation. "*Why?*"

"Because there's something you're not telling me."

"There's a whole hell of a lot I'm not telling you. But even if I could, would you really want to know?"

It didn't take long for Garrett's curiosity to give way to self-preservation. He gave a shake of the head.

"I'm in a dirty business, Kohl. You know that. And with it comes collateral damage. I just don't want him to get caught in all that. Do you understand?"

As Kim's eyes rested on the boy, her face softened. She looked kind, almost maternal. Apparently, the Dragon Queen had a soft spot after all. There was even a slight curl to her lips. "I just need you to keep him safe and out of sight until I have a solution. That's all."

Garrett pulled the cap from his head and ran his fingers through his hair, looking around the empty SCIF for some reasonable person who would jump in to save him. But he had no one in his corner and no real option but to comply with what was essentially extortion by guilt. "Well, God help you if I'm your solution." Already regretting his decision, he let out an exaggerated sigh. "If I do this, Kim, I'm doing it my way. Not staying in some roach motel in West Baltimore."

Kim cocked an eyebrow, as if she could sense his reservations about getting into her world any deeper than he was already. "DEA digs that much better than ours?"

He shook his head. "No, I just got a place in mind."

Kim returned the map to her folder. "I don't care where you go, so long as you keep him out of sight until this thing blows over. Just check in and let me know how he's doing."

At first, Garrett had fully expected her to argue, but the truth of the matter was that spies like her respected good tradecraft. She'd be tracking him wherever he went, so trying too hard to stay off the CIA's radar was an exercise in futility.

Kim tilted her head in Asadi's direction. "While you're gone, we'll get to the bottom of who was behind the massacre and clean things up."

There was that phrase he'd heard her use in the past. *Clean things up.* Garrett shifted his stance, uneasy with the ambiguity of the phrase. Did she mean clean up his role in the incident, clean up the bodies, or clean up the ones responsible for the massacre? Garrett would have asked, but figured it was probably better not to know.

Still though, there was a question nagging at him. "So, what's going to happen to him?"

Her forehead wrinkled in confusion. "What do you mean?"

"I mean . . . when this is all over. Once you've *cleaned up.* There weren't any survivors in the village. My guess is his whole family was murdered."

"Oh." Kim was clearly caught off guard, as if she hadn't thought that far in the future. But that couldn't be the case. She was always a few steps ahead. "I'm sure he has relatives in the village over or something. If they're out there, we'll find them." Her face lost any luster it might have had before. "If not, there are other options."

He didn't want to ask but felt compelled. "Like what?"

"You know. Organizations that look after kids like him."

"You mean an orphanage?"

Kim seemed amused by his concern. "A place to help him get resettled."

"Oh." Now, Garrett's face fell. He focused on the word *resettled*. The government had a dolled-up term for every bad circumstance you could imagine.

Kim leaned against the wall and rubbed exhausted eyes. She dropped her hands, studied him, and asked with genuine compassion, "You sure you're up for all this, Kohl?"

The truth of the matter was that Garrett hadn't thought her offer all the way through. He was fine with a protective-custody assignment. Watching over the kid wasn't a problem. The problem was that he hadn't had time to fully process the fact that Asadi might've been better off had he not intervened. He hated to think that way, but it was the truth.

Even if Kim made it safe for Asadi to come back, what the hell was there to come back for? His family was dead, and his home destroyed. And the best alternative was some rat-infested orphanage where he'd live a miserable life until he was released into a world with no opportunity. It would make him a prime candidate for the extremist madrasas, which meant there was a good chance he'd be strapped into a suicide vest before he could even shave.

Garrett's heart sank at the realization he was snake-bit, doomed to move from one tragedy to the next, ruining everyone's lives. First, his family, then his team, and now the boy. If this was a curse, it was one he had to break. And the only way to do it was to return to the place he'd been running from for years. His only option was to head back home.

4

Garrett put an arm around Asadi and pulled him to his side. Although the doors and windows on the UH-60 Black Hawk helicopter were closed, it was still brisk. Fortunately, the hop from Tsavo to Bagram was a short one—less than half an hour, tops.

Kim had done her best to scrounge up a fresh set of clothes and a thin jacket for Asadi, but something warmer was definitely in order. The Texas High Plains got bitterly cold in January, and to blend in, the boy would need something a little less refugee and a lot more down-home on the ranch.

By the look on Asadi's face he was scared, exhausted, and utterly traumatized. The plan was to keep him good and distracted. The kid may be grieving, but boys were boys, and Garrett himself still broke into a smile every time he heard the whine of the engine spooling up and felt the thumping *whomp* of the bird's massive rotors, beating through his body like a bass drum.

Looking down at Asadi, he asked, "Well, what'd you think?" He pointed to the window. "Ever think you'd see your country from way up here?"

The boy looked up, his big brown eyes staring back blankly. He wasn't as impressed as Garrett had hoped. Of course, they were a good four hundred feet off the ground and there wasn't much to see in the darkness anyhow but a few scattered lights.

After a second, Asadi rose in his seat, glanced out the window, and curled his lips slightly. It wasn't quite a smile, but Garrett counted it as a win. He reached down and mussed the kid's hair. "Wish it was daytime. Be more to see."

That was only partially true. Even in daylight there wasn't much there but a whole lot of dirt. Of course, the land where Garrett grew up wasn't that different. The Texas Panhandle was within an area once known as the Great American Desert, an endless sea of grasslands so boundless that the buffalo that once roamed it by the millions made only a speck.

Fortunately, the Kohl Ranch was located by the Canadian River, a near thousand-mile tributary originating in the Sangre de Cristo Mountains of Colorado that meandered lazily through New Mexico and Texas until it finally met the Arkansas. While much of the High Plains was desolate, Garrett's boyhood home was nestled directly beneath the Caprock Escarpment, a beautiful caliche ridge jutting out from the flat plains a thousand feet high.

On top of scenic views and a natural spring, Garrett's ranch was teeming with whitetail deer, pronghorn antelope, and aoudad sheep, which shared the grazing with cattle and horses. For a man whose two greatest passions were hunting and riding, it was paradise on earth.

Garrett was about to persist with Asadi when he noticed that the crew chief behind the pilot, an African American woman in her late twenties, kept glancing back at them. He was certain that she, like everyone else at Tsavo, had probably been given the requisite briefing on Secret Squirrel operations.

Don't talk to the operatives.

Don't ask them questions.

And you damn sure don't repeat what you saw. Because you didn't see anything anyhow.

But her passengers weren't just unusual for a special ops mission. This was a Rob Zombie meets Mowgli from *The Jungle Book* kind of bizarre. Who could blame her for staring?

Garrett shot her a smile to let her know it was okay and the crew chief returned the gesture. "Got one about his age back home."

Garrett detected a sadness in her eyes. "Where's that?"

With each syllable her southern accent grew more apparent. "Little town outside a Birmingham, Alabama. Place called Toadvine."

It was obvious she was homesick. Garrett knew the look. He'd seen it in the mirror about a thousand times before. "Got much longer here?"

The crew chief didn't answer. She was still staring at Asadi, her face etched in worry. "Boy needs a better coat."

Garrett detected a mild tone of judgment. But when he saw that Asadi was shivering, he understood this mother's concern. "Yeah, well, I'll have to do a little shopping when we get where we're going." He pulled the kid in closer, a token gesture to make sure she knew he cared. "Weren't a whole lot of options and we left in kind of a hurry."

"Where ya'll—?" Catching herself on the fly, she flipped her question into a statement. "You go shopping, buy goose down or wool. My gramma always says, 'You can't outdo what God gave us.'" The crew chief chuckled. "But she's old school. Grew up on a farm."

"Me too." Garrett yanked the wool watch cap from his coat pocket and dangled it for her to see. "And your grandma's right. Can't beat the basics."

With a smile, the woman looked out the window, clearly reminiscing on a moment that meant nothing at the time but everything far from home. "My boy says wool's too scratchy." She chuckled again, this time to herself. "Throws a *big ol'* fit every time I make him wear it." Turning back to Garrett a moment later, she was a little misty-eyed. "I guess I'd just rather him be itchy than catch a cold. Know what I'm sayin'?"

Garrett nodded and shoved the hat back into his coat pocket. He didn't know how to respond, so he just kept quiet.

The crew chief looked down, unzipped the pack beside her, and pulled out what looked to be a folded green blanket. She balled it up and tossed it over. The military-issue nylon poncho liner, affectionally dubbed the *woobie*, was heaven-sent. Garrett unfolded the garment and draped it over the boy. He even pulled some onto his own lap, craving a little warmth himself.

Content to see Asadi nestled under the blanket, the crew chief smiled and turned back to the window. Her mothering was done, and she went back to soldiering.

On the approach to Bagram, Garrett was taken off guard by their entry on the back side of the base. The bird swung in low, landed at the dark far end of the runway near an awaiting Gulfstream jet. The CIA was for being spooky, but this took the cake.

Garrett had assumed they'd be flying Uncle Sam Airways, but the plane didn't have the worn-out look of government aircraft. This G700 was fresh off the line—a hell of an expensive flight, but odds were the CIA wasn't paying a dime. Some billionaire in a place like Dubai owed the Dragon Queen a huge favor, and now she was cashing in. For once, Kim's heavy hand had turned out to be a blessing.

When the Black Hawk landed, there was no one there to greet them and no instructions over the headset. Their newfound friend simply got up, moved over, and gently unbuckled Asadi's four-way harness.

Garrett wadded up the poncho liner to hand back, but the crew chief waved him off.

"Keep it," she said with a smile. "A gift for the little man till you get to where you're going."

Garrett nodded a thank-you, led Asadi to the door, and helped him onto the tarmac. In the frigid night air, intensified by the rotor wash, they ducked low, sprinted to the clam-shell stairs, and climbed aboard.

Only a few steps into the fuselage Garrett felt immediate warmth.

As they moved through a cabin of planked walnut,
Casablanca marble, and white leather sofas, Asadi's
eyes went as wide as saucers. New-car smell had nothing on a seventy-million-dollar luxury jet. The Black
Hawk might not have impressed him but the G700 certainly did.

They had barely leaned back into their plush chairs
and buckled the seat belts when the jet taxied down the
runway and shot them out of Afghanistan at just under
Mach speed. It was obvious to Garrett that Kim wanted
them gone before midnight and she'd done everything
in her power to make it happen. The mission, thus far,
had been rush-rush, which made him suspicious.

What the hell was she *not* telling him?

The assignment was one for the books, or off-the-
books, as the case may be. Garrett had done some bab-
ysitting before. That was nothing new. But this wasn't
guard duty over some drug dealer ratting out his buddies. This was taking care of a child who'd experienced
a tragedy and Garrett didn't have a clue as to how to do
that. He'd barely survived his own.

Asadi hadn't said a word since the attack, which for
the moment Garrett didn't mind. He needed a little time
to think. Going back home was going to be awkward. It

had been three years since his last visit, and he'd left more than a few things unsettled. History hadn't been kind to the Kohl family and he and his father didn't always see eye to eye. Not only that, Garrett was on bad terms with his brother, who'd in the past been his closest ally.

Other than his dad, nobody knew Garrett was DEA. Given his deep-cover status, he'd kept his work a secret. As far as his brother and sister knew, he was employed by an international offshore drilling company, a perfect cover since he'd worked oil field jobs growing up. It also explained why he was gone for long periods of time and couldn't readily be reached. They believed he'd been working off the coast of Bahrain for the past year and a half.

At first, Garrett worried his dad might spill the beans, but Butch Kohl was basically a hermit, who only left the ranch to get feed for the horses and cattle or make a grocery run. And even if he had flapped his gums about his son being a deep-cover DEA officer, no one would believe it. The old man was a borderline crackpot who hated the government. Anyone he told would have believed it to be another of his half-baked conspiracy theories.

Garrett's oil field cover was the same one he used with the narcos. Because he'd done the job, it gave him credibility. Not only did he look the part, he could walk the walk, working the narcotics supply chain from source to buyer. Like drilling equipment, he could move dope across any border on the planet, which made him lots of friends in the world of smuggling.

Three hours into the flight, the adrenaline had finally worn off and Garrett was feeling the effects. Unlike Asadi, who'd closed his eyes and started snoring the moment his head hit the couch, Garrett sat ramrod straight, staring out the window at the dark abyss. But the dim lighting and the soft whine of the Rolls-Royce Pearl 700 engines eventually worked their magic and sent him adrift in a place somewhere between sleep and consciousness.

Moments later he was shaken from it by a scream and the realization that Asadi was in the throes of a nightmare. Garrett jumped from his plush swivel chair and stumbled across the aisle atop wobbly legs, still sore and aching from the climb earlier that morning. After catching his balance, he took the few steps to where the boy was thrashing under the woobie, sat, and woke him as gently as he could.

"It's just a dream," Garrett assured him. "It's only a dream."

Garrett used a voice loud enough to rouse Asadi but quiet enough not to frighten him, rubbing his back with the palm of his right hand, making slow clockwise circles between his shoulder blades. It was what Garrett's mother had done when he'd had nightmares as a child.

As Asadi came to, he lashed out and tried to push away. It was obvious he was fighting off the murderers from his village—his cries were the same. The poor boy was calling out for a mother who'd never again answer. It was the same dream and heart-wrenching pain Garrett had known most of his life.

Asadi looked up, his face wet with tears, and Garrett did his best to convey a look of peace through his eyes. "It's okay, buddy. You're safe now. You don't have to worry about them anymore."

Garrett nodded, hoping the gesture would convey to Asadi the meaning of his words. After a few seconds, the boy quit squirming and stared back. His body went limp and it was clear what had happened. Asadi had broken out of the awful dreamscape only to realize his reality wasn't any better, and nothing would ever be the same.

Looking around, Garrett searched for help that wasn't there. Other than the flight crew, who'd been holed up in the cockpit since they arrived, it was only the two of them. And for the first time in a long time, he felt lonely. Powerless. The kid was damaged goods and needed more care than Garrett could provide.

He glanced down as Asadi closed his eyes. Unsure what to do, Garrett cradled him gently and reclined back into the couch. After a few seconds, the boy was breathing heavily, fast asleep in his arms. Not wanting to wake him, Garrett tilted his head back and rested it against the window. With eyelids too heavy to hold up, he gave in to the darkness, searching for answers to some age-old questions.

At this point in his life, he was well beyond *why bad things happen to good people* and had moved on to *why do they keep happening to me.* Was it a test from God? Was there something he should've done but didn't? It seemed the faster he ran, the closer his ghosts followed. And he shuddered to think what would happen when they finally caught up.

5

Making their descent into Texas, Garrett stared out the window of the Gulfstream jet, even though they were above the clouds and there was nothing to see. Anything was better than looking at Asadi, who monitored his every move, and smiled whenever they made eye contact.

On undercover assignments and during past military deployments, Garrett typically kept to himself during his downtime, and preferred others do the same. But it was abundantly clear the kid wanted his attention. He wondered if he could survive this much one-on-one time if the job lasted more than a couple of weeks.

After landing at the Naval Air Station in Fort Worth, Garrett and Asadi were met by a nondescript white van beside a remote hangar. Their driver, who looked to be a plainclothes military police officer, made the two-and-a-half-hour drive west, and dropped them off at the closest thing Garrett had to a home—the thirty-three-foot Airstream Classic he kept parked at the Mesquite Falls RV park on Possum Kingdom Lake. The travel trailer, Skeeter bass boat, and black GMC Sierra HD pickup were the only possessions to his name.

For Garrett, these things were all he needed or wanted, and he found this Jimmy Buffett kind of life-style to be one of the better perks of living undercover on the DEA's dime. As a single man with few expenses, he indulged himself the best he knew how. And lake living on Possum Kingdom was to him what the Fortress of Solitude was to Superman, a place to disconnect from the ugliness he faced on the job and recharge his soul. He got there a lot less than he wanted, but when he did it was magic. His boat, a fishing pole, and an iced-down cooler full of Shiner Bock beer was about as good as it got.

He was tempted to stay a night in the Airstream before heading off to the ranch but figured it'd be going against better judgment. Guests at Mesquite Falls tended to be nosy, as was the lady who ran the place. Over the years, she'd learned to give him some distance, but that didn't mean she wouldn't spread gossip whenever she had the chance. And him showing up at the lake with a ten-year-old Afghan village boy would be the biggest thing to happen to the RV park in years. So, he wasted no time in charging his truck battery, packing up, and shoving off before alerting the neighbors.

Garrett had expected the drive from Possum Kingdom would take about six and a half hours, but according to reports, the northwest part of the state was already getting pelted with an incoming Blue Norther. In his opinion, there was no weather phenomenon more beautiful or more deadly. Depending on her mood she could be heaven, hell, and everything in between.

The rolling wall of blue-black clouds could plunge temperatures by sixty degrees in a matter of only a few hours, and even result in a full-on blizzard if conditions were right. Expectations for this storm weren't as dire, but still to be considered. Garrett would have to take extra caution.

Proceeding northwest at a quick clip, Garrett and Asadi shot through Wichita Falls on their way to the heart of the Panhandle. It was a tour through the old country where Garrett's Comanche ancestors once reigned supreme, terrorizing anyone who'd dared venture onto their land. This route even took them through Quanah, named after Quanah Parker, son of Comanche Chief Peta Nocona and wife Cynthia Ann

Parker, a settler's daughter kidnapped at the age of ten who ultimately assimilated into the tribe.

Garrett turned north off 287 to cut across Interstate 40 just shy of Goodnight, thus named after his boyhood hero. On top of being a superlative cowboy, Indian fighter, and Texas Ranger, Charles Goodnight had famously blazed a trail as far north as Wyoming with herds of livestock.

The farther Garrett drove, the more he remembered how much he loved this part of the state. From Palo Duro Canyon to the Oklahoma border, the land looked and felt like the Wild West. It was the old stomping grounds for buffalo hunters, scouts, and gunfighters like Bat Masterson, Billy Dixon, and Kit Carson. This rough country drew in tornadoes and wildfires like flies to honey. And the people inhabiting it now had as much grit as the ones who'd settled it.

Large ranches that encompassed dozens of square miles were cut in half by deep valleys and sharp ravines, exposing soil so red in places it looked drenched in blood. On the vast plains, massive center-pivot irrigation systems a quarter mile long ran parallel with the horizon, while rusty pump jacks bobbed on the scrubby ranchland.

Cattle hunkered behind windbreaks made of corrugated tin to get out of the blowing snow, fighting for prime real estate around feed bunkers teeming with grain. Others, not as lucky, wove paths through thorny mesquite brush, nuzzling through inches of powdery snow to scare up what was left of the short-shorn winter wheat.

Over centuries, this stretch of land spanning several million acres had gone by many names. Texas High Plains. Llano Estacado. And Comancheria. But one thing never differed. It was rough and unforgiving country—both an island and a fortress, forming a natural barrier to those not welcome. If Mother Nature didn't kill you, Indians or outlaws probably would.

With the exception of its inhabitants, not all that much had changed. Most who lived there still preferred isolation. It was a great place to hunker down, escape, or hide. And like outlaws of ages past—many still did.

Garrett pulled the black Ray-Ban Aviators from his face and tossed them on the dash. He looked over at Asadi, buckled in the passenger seat beside him, and pointed to the Flying Bandit Travel Stop off in the distance. Towering over the building was its trademark sign—a neon cowboy atop a galloping red horse. The motto for every franchise location was the same.

You're in cowboy country, pardner. Enjoy the ride!

There was something about the image and slogan Garrett had always loved. It made the Texas High

Plains seem rugged and untamed, like it had been two hundred years ago. And apparently, he wasn't the only one who felt this way.

Asadi was grinning, mesmerized by it too. He turned, pulled out imaginary six-shooters from his belt, and made *pewpew* sounds with his mouth.

Garrett pulled a hand from the wheel, clutched his chest, and let out a howl. "Okay, Outlaw! You got me! I give up!"

Asadi laughed, blew pretend smoke from his fingertips, and returned the guns to their holsters.

Happy to see the boy in good spirits, Garrett checked his watch and saw it was well past noon. "You hungry?" he asked, glancing over. "Want something to eat?"

Asadi smiled but didn't respond. He was too enthralled with the massive eighteen-wheelers gassing up at the truck stop pumps to pay much attention to anything else.

Feeling his own hunger pangs, Garrett tapped the brakes, turned the steering wheel right, and eased into the parking lot. He pulled into a spot by the door, held up an index finger, and gave a head tilt toward the store. "Wait here. I'll be back in a flash."

Getting an understanding nod from Asadi, Garrett hopped out, charged into the store, and grabbed two bottles of Mountain Dew and a couple of Bandit burritos from under a heat lamp. The whole process took about a minute, if that. With the gold standard of junk food in hand, he stepped outside and raised the loot in a display of triumph. But his pulse raced when he realized Asadi was no longer sitting in the passenger seat.

Darting to the driver's window, Garrett looked inside the cab but found nothing. He circled around the truck bed, passed the tailgate to the passenger side, and breathed a sigh of relief when he saw Asadi standing in the next parking spot over. He was wrapped in the green woobie, looking up at the Flying Bandit sign, captivated by the cowboy and his neon horse.

Garrett felt a little guilty that his first reaction was to give Asadi a good scolding. The poor kid just wanted to get a little air and stretch his legs a bit. They should've done that a hundred miles back.

Feeling his heart rate return to normal, he moved beside Asadi and stared up with him. "If you like that one, you're gonna love the real ones. We've got the best around." Garrett made a sweeping motion with his arm that spanned the snowy plains before them. "Lots of room to ride and beautiful scenery to boot. Especially above the.caprock."

The Caprock Escarpment wasn't easily explained. This two-hundred-mile-stretch of caliche canyons and mesas jutting from the earth a thousand feet high in some places was either beauty or a blemish depending on your stewardship.

Created by millions of years of runoff from the Rocky Mountains, this geological oddity, with its serpentine creeks and rocky ravines, scarred the smooth flatlands with exposed rock ranging from desert tan and pale gray to blood red. Garrett had traveled all over the world but had yet to see a work of God's hand that was anything like it.

When Asadi looked to him, puzzled, Garrett steepled his hands and drew them into a ninety-degree angle. "It's kind of like a one-sided canyon or a plateau." He racked his brain trying to think of the right words in Dari but came up short. "Ah hell, forget it. You'll see soon enough."

He opened the passenger door and helped Asadi back inside. Roads were getting icier the later it got. And the last thing he wanted was to go off in a ditch and get stuck in a snowbank this close to home. His old man would have a field day with a move that boneheaded, and Garrett didn't want to start things out with a fight.

Of course, Butch Kohl was a cantankerous old son of a bitch, so avoiding a run-in with him was like avoiding the IRS. Somehow or another, they always got you in the end.

6

Garrett continued on for another hour before pulling off the highway and turning onto the dusty caliche oil field road leading to the ranch. Atop the hardened white surface of natural cement, it was a bumpy fifteen-minute ride—one he'd cursed a million times. But it was a welcome change from the smooth hum of the asphalt. The chuckholes and growl of rock beneath felt and sounded like home.

He was finally back to a spot that filled nearly every childhood memory, and there was a peace that settled over him. It was the feel of belonging to the land, being grounded, connected to something unchanged. For better or worse, the Kohl Ranch was a place where time stood still.

The first property they passed on the way to the house was Shanessy Farms, a place owned by the same family for over a century. They grew alfalfa hay under four center-pivot irrigation circles and used the rest of the land for grazing their registered Hereford cattle. A small single-story home with chipping white paint, green trim around the edges, and a chimney that puffed smoke nearly year-round was the centerpiece of the farm.

Garrett's favorite thing about their place though was the large cottonwoods surrounding it. If trees were gold in the Texas Panhandle, then this was Fort Knox. He could make out the dim lamplight coming from the west window, which gave him hope the owner, who'd been widowed for as long as he could remember, was at least still alive.

The farm had always been a showplace, but it was clear now those days were over. The children had never taken much interest in it and money was tight. Kate got around to fixing things whenever she could.

Like the Kohls, she had plenty of oil beneath the surface but didn't own a drop. During a drought in the 1950s, the mineral rights were legally severed from the surface, and the royalties sold to a wealthy family out of Amarillo with the last name Kaiser. All but a few of the heirs had moved to Connecticut and New York, and probably couldn't point to this place on a map.

The Kohl Ranch was fourteen sections of ranchland, just shy of nine thousand acres, or fourteen square miles, and there were at least a dozen drill sites on the property. That meant they had the hassles of dealing with energy company operations, but hardly any of the benefits. But that's just the way things were and there was nothing to be done about it.

Over time, Garrett had learned to accept it. And truth be told, he'd rather have the land than the minerals. Everything that meant anything to him was right there before his eyes. It was all his best memories and what made him the man he was. He could see, touch, and smell what they owned. And you couldn't put a price tag on that.

Garrett opened the window to get a whiff of home, but quickly reversed course as a flurry of icy snowflakes blew in and pelted his face. With a full-body shiver he adjusted the temperature controls, resulting in a blast of warm air from the vents. The farther north they traveled, the colder it got, and the more the wind howled.

The old joke around the Panhandle was *the only thing between us and the North Pole is a barbed wire fence*, and Garrett was apt to believe it. Gusts were over thirty miles per hour and the temperature gauge on his truck read fourteen degrees, which meant with the wind chill it was somewhere around five.

As they pulled up to his house, he was a little disappointed. With its chipping white paint and sagging porch, the place looked shabbier than he remembered. Of course, everything was covered in snow, making it difficult to tell for sure. Like Kate at the Shanessy place, there was a good chance his dad was letting things slide. On top of getting old, Butch Kohl was rough as a cob, and had pushed away pretty much everyone. Managing the property all on his own couldn't be easy, even for a man half his age.

Garrett watched his dad open the front door, step out on the porch, and scowl. He was wearing a red flannel shirt, blue jeans, and his house slippers. His white hair all tussled looked like a tumbleweed. If the old coot was cold, he didn't show it. Instead, Butch just stood there, sullen as a man about to get a prostate exam, a procedure he'd testily refused for decades.

Pulling up by the front porch, Garrett slowed, put the truck in park, and stepped outside. He left the diesel engine running and the heat on, not knowing how long the awkward homecoming process might take. Before he could even get out a hello, his dad fired the first salvo with his growling voice.

"What are *you* doing here? Obama send you to take my guns?"

Garrett shook his head. What the hell else could he do? He hadn't seen his father in over three years, and this was the old son of a bitch's idea of a welcome wagon. "Obama's been out of office for years now, Daddy. And I work for the DEA. Don't have nothing to do with your guns."

Butch grunted and leaned left. Beneath his ratty old slipper, a board creaked. "If you say so." He peered around Garrett and eyed the truck for a good ten seconds. "Who's that?"

"Just a kid I need to keep out of sight until things get sorted out."

Butch chuckled to himself. "You knock up one of them senoritas down in Old Mexico?"

Garrett turned toward Asadi, who was looking a little nervous. "He ain't mine, and he ain't Mexican. He's from Afghanistan."

Another grunt from Butch. "They all steal, you know." The old man spit a stream of tobacco juice off the porch and turned to walk back inside. "Keep him out of my stuff."

Garrett didn't know if the stealing comment was referring to Mexicans, Afghans, or kids, and wasn't about to ask. He'd been baited into too many asinine no-win quarrels with his dad to get roped into another. Instead, Garrett stepped back a few steps and took in the view of their old farmhouse in its entirety. There was a long row of eight-inch icicles dangling from the roofline.

He turned back to Asadi and raised one finger to indicate he'd be a minute. The boy nodded, seeming to understand. From there Garrett crunched through the snow and walked inside to find it in the exact condition he expected. It was a little grimier than his last visit, but the place was still bare bones. No photographs on the wall. No knickknacks on the table. Only a few necessities. If loneliness was a picture, this would be it.

"Daddy, what exactly are you worried about him stealing? That old mop you never use or them magazines you never read?"

Butch ambled over to a faded green La-Z-Boy recliner in the living room where Fox News was blasting at full volume. He plopped down, carefully maneuvered into the grooves of the cushion, then jerked the lever on the side with the force and intensity of a fighter pilot in a dogfight. "Make all the fun you want, but this is like a palace to *those* people."

He clicked on a reading lamp that shared the end table with about a half dozen yellowing issues of *Field*

& *Stream* and *American Rifleman*. There was a Bible there too, covered in a layer of dust.

Garrett would never concede it, but his dad was right. He'd seen the village where Asadi was from. No electricity. No running water. In some ways, this was a palace.

"Well, it'll do for what we need. If you'll allow us to stay."

Butch sighed. "Suit yourself." He picked up one of the magazines, just to prove a point, and narrowed his eyes on an article about mallard ducks. "This is still your place too. At least until the government takes it. Puts us all in one of your work camps or shoots us."

Again, Garrett knew better than to take the bait, lest he get sucked into a fight. But he almost would've welcomed the distraction, as he sunk into sadness thinking back on how things used to be when his mother was alive. Warm and bright. The smell of fried chicken. Vegetables from the garden lying out on a chopping board. Fresh-cut flowers in the spring. At one time, it was a real home. But after she passed, his dad threw out everything that reminded him of her. Apparently, bare walls and an empty house were better than painful reminders.

His dad had struggled immensely and getting rid of her things was the only way he could cope. The problem wasn't what he'd done, it was the fact that he hadn't bothered to ask Garrett, his sister, Grace, or his brother, Bridger, if they wanted any keepsakes. That incident marked the beginning of the downfall.

As usual, Butch had taken it upon himself to fix what needed fixing. And in this case, the fixing involved cutting short the grieving process by ridding the family of his wife's memory. He also aided the recovery process through some liquid healing with his old buddy Jim Beam, leaving his sons alone to fend for themselves. Grace had already graduated and moved off to Stillwater to go to Oklahoma State University.

Garrett was about to thank his dad for the invitation, half-hearted as it was, when something caught his attention. Something damn strange and way out of place in the lonely home of a sad old man. It was a sight Garrett hadn't seen in years. Butch Kohl was wearing a smile.

Garrett found his room how he'd left it, albeit dust covered and a little musty. The twin beds were still made up in camouflage goose down comforters and there was a full-size American flag hanging on the wall between them. Every other square inch of the shared space was covered in high school memorabilia and old posters of *Sports Illustrated* swimsuit models like Tyra Banks and Heidi Klum.

Bridger's side of the room was crammed full of football trophies and rodeo buckles, and plastered with academic awards. Garrett's was mostly bare, save a few pairs of deer and elk antlers, some old photographs, and three Catalena custom cowboy hats hung on nails.

But his prize possession was displayed prominently in a twelve-by-fourteen-inch wooden box with a glass lid. It was sitting atop the end table by his bed. The case had been a Christmas present from his mother, custom-built to hold his collection of hunting knives. He blew the dust off and opened the lid. Inside was a treasure trove of memories, as each blade held some special significance. He had everything from Case to Kershaw, but Moore Maker out of nearby Matador was always his favorite.

He pulled out the eight-and-a-half-inch stag-handled Damascus bowie knife and unsheathed the blade, which was still sharp as a razor. His mother had given it to him as an early birthday gift just a couple of weeks before she died. For opening day, she'd said, always proud of his ability to bring home wild game. She'd never said it, but he always wondered if it had something to do with her Comanche ancestry. Garrett looked more like her than anyone else and he always figured he was kind of a reminder of his grandma. She had died when he was a baby.

Garrett studied the knife a little more, sheathed it, and stuck it in his belt. He grabbed a Moore Maker pocketknife and slid it in his pocket. He probably would've sat there all night had he not remembered why he was there in the first place. Asadi needed a fresh set of clothes.

He set the box back on the nightstand, knelt by a trunk at the foot of his bed, and opened it. It took a little digging, but he found what he was looking for, a black-and-gold Canadian Wildcats jersey and his blue-and-silver Dallas Cowboys jacket. Both he'd worn when he was about Asadi's age, maybe younger.

They might be a little big, but they'd keep him warm and help him blend in. Nearly every kid in the Panhandle wore football paraphernalia of some kind, so it was at least a good start. Garrett fished around some more and found his green John Deere stocking hat with the yellow ball on top. The iconic running deer logo was emblazoned across the front. It was a little dated looking, but it'd work for now.

He grabbed the gear, went back outside, and stood on the porch. Asadi's uneasy eyes were trained on the door. Of course, Garrett couldn't blame the kid for being anxious. In the past forty-eight hours, he'd lost everyone in the world who mattered and now he was sitting in a foreign land with Rob Zombie as his chaperone and Archie Bunker as the innkeeper. Who wouldn't be worried? But when Garrett approached the truck, clearly bearing gifts intended for a young boy, Asadi donned a big toothy grin.

The reaction warmed Garrett's heart. He walked to the truck, opened the door, and handed over the coat and hat. "Hope you're a Cowboys fan and a John Deere man."

Apparently, Asadi was both, given his satisfied look. Garrett helped him out of the cab, where his feet landed in about four inches of fresh snow. No sooner had he hit the ground than he took off through the powder hooting for joy. The boy was clearly ready to play and appeared to be coping with all the changes better than expected.

Feeling the chill, Garrett zipped his Carhartt jacket and pulled up the fleece-lined hood. He rotated his body to keep the frigid north wind from blowing down the front. Although he wanted to get inside to warm up, he knew he'd better let Asadi play awhile. It was exactly what he did with his horses on a cold morning—turn them out, let them run, buck, fart, and get the hump out of their backs before getting down to business. The kid had been sitting in a truck for nearly seven hours, so there was no doubt he had some pent-up energy to spend.

After about ten minutes, Garrett could tell Asadi wasn't going to wear out or get cold enough to cry uncle, so he called it himself. "Hey, Outlaw!" The boy, kicking a valley through a two-foot snowbank, looked up and smiled. "How about we go inside and get some grub?" Garrett pointed to the house and made the gesture of holding something to his mouth.

For the first time since the day at the village, Asadi spoke. "Grub?" He walked over to Garrett wearing a curious expression.

When the boy got closer, Garrett could see he was shivering. His little brown hands were a pinkish-red. "Yeah, grub. Something to eat." He made a chewing gesture. "Food."

Asadi glanced at the house, clearly worried about Butch. The old man was harmless but wore the sourest of expressions no matter the occasion. If something impressed him, he never showed it. Been that way for years.

"Don't worry about him." Garrett smiled. "He ain't as mean as he is ugly."

Asadi, who appeared to mull over Garrett's words, gave a little laugh and turned toward the house. He stepped onto the porch, opened the door, and walked right in like he owned the place. At the sight, Garrett couldn't help but laugh. If nothing else, the kid had balls.

And he figured he'd better grow a pair himself. If they were living with Butch, he was sure going to need them.

Garrett walked back into the house and stomped the snow from his boots on a mat in the kitchen. He looked into the living room to find his dad dozing in the La-Z-Boy. The old man probably hadn't had visitors in over a year and there he was buzzing and snorting like a Briggs & Stratton with a bad carburetor.

Asadi was sitting on the couch staring at Butch in awe. It was hard to imagine how one little old man could create so much racket with his nose. Garrett took his boots off and tossed them by the door, creating a louder than intended thump that echoed through the house.

Butch's eyes popped open and he turned toward the kitchen groggily. "Oh. It's you."

Garrett made a big show of looking around. "Who the hell else would it be?" He walked into the living room and sat by Asadi. "I'm guessing you don't do a whole lot of entertaining these days."

Butch picked up the TV remote and lowered the volume. "I get enough company."

"Who?" Garrett protested. "Grace and Bridger?"

Butch shook his head. "Don't see Grace much. She's still down in Midland with that *banker*." He said the word *banker* like a regular person might say *pedophile*. "Your brother comes out though."

"Bridger!" Garrett howled. "When's the last time he's stepped foot inside this place?"

Butch abruptly changed the subject. "Expect you'll be wanting to get over and say hello, given how you pissed him off last time you were here." Before Garrett could counter, Butch continued. "Plus, you'll want to see your nieces before they get married, move off, and start having kids of their own."

"The twins are in middle school, Daddy."

A grunt. "Well, with the frequency you visit, I'd shake a leg." Butch paused, seeming to ponder something. "Think they're cheering at a basketball game tonight. If you're interested?"

"Cheerleaders, huh?" Garrett remembered their mom cheering back in high school, but she was better known for her accomplishments as a barrel racer. Bridger first met her on the rodeo circuit and things blossomed from there.

"Sophie and Chloe as good as riders as Cassidy was back in the day?"

"Oh yeah, they're hell on wheels." Butch's pride in his granddaughters was more than apparent. "Going to be pretty like her too, I expect."

Cassidy Kohl defined Texas beauty. She had long blond hair and deep brown eyes that complemented a year-round tan. Her body was lithe and lean from riding and hard work on her family's farm near Shamrock.

Butch chuckled a little. "Bridge said he's got his shotgun oiled up and ready. Guess the boys are already taking notice."

"Well, that's living proof God's got a sense of humor. If anybody deserves grief, it's him. I know he's made a few quick getaways with birdshot nipping at his ass."

Thinking back on good times made Garrett eager to see Bridger and his family, but it wasn't going to be easy. The last time they'd spoken they'd gotten into a huge argument. There was no way he was going to ask directly, but Garrett thought he might do a little fishing—see if his brother was still mad at him. "Other than getting his rightful comeuppance, he's doing okay?"

"He's all right." A beat passed and Butch lost his grin. "Good as can be, I reckon."

Garrett knew his dad well enough to know the old man was holding back. And Butch Kohl never held back. "Well, what is it?"

"What is what?"

"Don't hold out on me now, Daddy. Bridger still pissed off or something?"

Butch shook it off. "Nah, it's not that."

That was good to hear, but it only meant something else was going on. Garrett always suspected Bridger would do something to screw up his marriage. Perfect was never good enough. He always wanted more. "What is it then? Something to do with Cassidy?"

"No, he's been good to her as far as I can tell. Truth be told, I don't know what's wrong. Last time I saw him he just seemed real nervous. Said he had some problems."

"What the hell kind of problems does he have? Too much money? Wife too hot?"

This was classic Bridger. When life was too good, he went looking for trouble. In life and love, big brother shined like the harvest moon. He was the champion quarterback and rodeo star. But Bridger had a wild streak, a temper, and a tendency to break rules without getting caught.

Growing impatient with his dad's reluctance to spill the beans, Garrett leaned forward and locked eyes with him. "Dammit, Daddy, you gonna tell me what's going on or am I going to have to sit here and guess all night?"

"I don't know," Butch bristled. Simmering a moment, he looked Garrett in the eye. "He just seems rattled. That's all."

Garrett couldn't ever recall seeing Bridger rattled. Other than running low on beer money and a couple of close calls in the baby department, his brother guzzled life from a silver chalice. Butch could pshaw the idea of his brother stepping out all day long, but if money were on the odds, Bridger was two-timing Cassidy and in danger of getting caught.

"All right," Garrett grumbled. "You want me to press him a little, see what I can find out?"

Butch didn't answer, but that meant yes. His only two responses were silence and tantrum.

It had been Garrett's intention to work up to reconciliation with Bridger over the course of a few days. But Butch seemed anxious, and that wasn't normal. The old man's cure for everything from skinned knees to aneurysms was *rub some dirt on it.* If he was worried, there was a reason.

Garrett rose from the couch with a groan. He'd just gotten comfortable and didn't fancy the notion of going back out into the cold, but if Bridger was really in some sort of trouble, then he'd better get to the bottom of it. He walked to the dining room table and grabbed the well-worn silverbelly cowboy hat he'd retrieved from his room.

A quick glance at his watch and Garrett saw it was just after four. Bridger would still be at his office. He thumbed over at Asadi, who had gotten up from the couch a few minutes earlier and was staring out the window. Fitting the hat to his head, he turned back. "I'll need to keep him out of sight while I'm here."

Butch was the only one outside Garrett's chain of command who knew he was DEA. And to the old man's credit, he had been good about keeping it to himself and not asking questions. Of course, it could've been because he just didn't care. Either way, Garrett could depend on his discretion.

Garrett lowered his voice, an implied way of saying this is between you and me. "Think you can watch Asadi while I'm out?"

A look of panic spread across Butch's face. "Well . . . uh . . ."

Garrett didn't wait for the forthcoming pathetic excuse. "Won't be more than a couple of hours, I expect."

"What the hell am I supposed to do with a kid? He don't even speak good English."

Garrett decided not to touch that one. "Well, teach him something. *Hell.* You're always talking about how much you know about everything. Here's your chance to prove it."

"Like what?"

"I don't know." Garrett shrugged, loving every minute of his dad's state of panic. "You'll figure it out."

By the look on his face, you'd have thought Butch was trapped in the house with a Bengal tiger. "But the kid don't know nothing. Probably piss in the wind if I ain't watching him good."

The old son of a bitch had walked into a trap.

"Well, Daddy, one thing we got out here is lots of wind. And he just finished a big bottle of Mountain Dew." He nodded in Asadi's direction. "Sounds like you got your whole afternoon cut out for you."

His dad started to argue but Garrett interrupted. "And see if he wants something to eat. I got him a burrito at the Flying Bandit earlier, but he hasn't had anything since."

Butch looked disgusted. "You feed him that crap, he'll be wanting the commode before he wants another meal."

"He liked it," Garrett argued.

"Nobody likes Bandit burritos unless they're drunk off their ass or in a real big hurry. Which one was he?"

Garrett was already getting roped into one of his dad's stupid arguments. Before continuing down that road, he communicated the best he could to Asadi that he'd be back in a couple of hours. It involved a lot of pointing to the numbers on his watch, but as usual, the boy seemed to get the message.

Convinced he understood, Garrett grabbed his coat from the table and turned back to his dad. The old man was cussing at the screen, yelling something about *estate taxes* and *government waste*.

Garrett chuckled to himself thinking about the ride over from Afghanistan on the seventy-five-million-dollar Gulfstream. It was one secret he would have love to let slip, just to rile the old man. But rather than provoke a fight, Garrett took off out the front door and climbed into his snow-covered pickup. He was feeling more than a little squeamish about leaving Asadi there with his dad, but at the moment meeting Bridger took priority.

Despite past differences, repairing their relationship was something Garrett had to do. And the reason for this was Butch Kohl. He was turning into a lonely old curmudgeon, and even worse, letting the ranch fall to ruin.

Blood and soil mattered a hell of a lot more than Garrett had thought they did. And he was going to see to it that he took care of both.

7

After texting his brother, Garrett agreed to meet at the Cattle Exchange for dinner. He'd hoped to keep a lower profile, but a crowded public venue had its plusses. And keeping Bridger's notorious temper in check was a big one. With a little time to kill, Garrett tooled down the backstreets of Canadian and hung a right on Main by the old Women's Christian Temperance Union turned public library.

At one of the highest points in town, Garrett tapped the brakes, bringing his truck to a crawl, which wasn't an issue on a street with no traffic. He digested the familiar sights in slow motion. Returning home was like settling into a hot bath—only tolerable if dipped into an inch at a time.

Passing the redbrick Hemphill County courthouse, he gazed between the two-story skyline of the sleepy downtown and took in the view. There were a couple of banks, a coffee shop, and a single-screen movie theater, all within a minute's walk of each other. A few antiques shops and boutique clothing stores had popped up, but other than that not much had changed.

His eyes finally rested on the snowy horizon that glimmered orange in the dipping sun. With its ice-crusted foothills and rolling prairie, the vast emptiness beneath a roofless sky gave the impression of a frontier that had no end.

As a kid, Garrett had sworn he could see all the way to New Mexico, but it was probably only about ten miles. Even so, it was glaringly obvious why Canadian was called the "oasis of the high plains." As the crow flies, it was nearly three hundred miles west of Tulsa with not a damn thing in between—and three hundred more to Santa Fe with a helluva lot less.

No one passed through it. If you got there you were going there. And nobody did that.

Although tranquil and isolated, Canadian was a town with secrets. Some dark. Some deep. And some the subject of titillating scandal. Of course, scandals ranged from offenses as trifling as showing too much cleavage at the church picnic to as egregious as knocking up the preacher's daughter and running off with the collection plate.

But every so often, there was a stark reminder that people are people no matter where you go. And this small town had its scattered bones and shallow graves to prove it.

On the right-hand side of Main was Bridger's law office, a one-man operation decorated in an Old West motif. Garrett always thought the place looked more like the set of *Gunsmoke* than anywhere you'd do legitimate business, but he kept that to himself. With the lights on and people milling around inside, it was obvious that whatever client meeting his brother was obliged to attend that afternoon was still in full swing.

With no signs of it wrapping up early, Garrett turned right onto Second Street and to the old Canadian River Wagon Bridge on the outskirts of town. He veered left off the highway, taking a side road to the riverbed where he parked at one end. There were a couple of pickups by the historical marker—one a silver Ford dually, fresh off the line, the other a white fleet truck with a Renegade Oil & Gas Services logo emblazoned on the side. It was nearly five o'clock, which meant a couple of buddies had probably kicked off early and were out on the footbridge knocking back a couple of cold ones.

With just a sliver of lingering sunlight, Garrett jumped out of his pickup and took in the scene before him. In the near darkness, yellow lights hanging from the beams of the giant iron framework cast spoked shadows on the walkway like ribs off a giant skeleton. As kids, he and Bridger would dare each other farther and farther out until a rustle from beneath sent them sprinting back to safety.

Of course, it wasn't hard to spook a couple of kids, but the idea of ghosts beneath their feet wasn't entirely unfounded. More than a few men lost their lives building that bridge, especially the ones lowered into the concrete pillars to reinforce the foundation. Many went in, but not all came out, and their bodies still lay entombed inside.

Garrett had hoped for a tranquil return, but raucous voices coming from the silhouettes ahead were already fouling up the winter air. Loud as they were, it was clear whoever was out there was knocking back more than a couple. In fact, there was a good chance these guys were three sheets to the wind.

Wanting to avoid any drunks, particularly ones who might be old acquaintances, Garrett turned to head back. But a cry for help stopped him dead in his tracks.

He instinctively reached for his Glock only to find a bare hip. He'd yet to retrieve his pistol, still stuffed inside the Eberlestock pack on the truck floorboard.

As he stood calculating how long it would take to get there and back, a second shriek pierced the night, and he sprinted toward the scuffle wondering what the hell he'd do if he came face-to-face with a loaded gun. The closer he got, the clearer it became that weapon or not, the aggressor in this fight owned Garrett in size by at least three inches and a good forty pounds.

Careful to keep a healthy distance, Garrett slowed his pace. With all the authority he could muster, he issued the command, "Let him go! *Now!*"

Giving little regard to the warning, the aggressor glanced casually over his right shoulder, then turned back to the skinny guy whose neck was within the grip of his left hand. With an easy but powerful shove, he sent his victim tumbling backward onto the planks.

It wasn't until Garrett moved within a few feet that he recognized the notorious ne'er-do-well before him. Bo Clevenger turned and lumbered forward until the shaved head sitting atop his bull neck came into the full glow of the light above.

"I'll be damned. *Garrett Kohl.* That you, ol' friend?"

Ol' Friend. They'd never been friends. Not by a long shot.

Bo had been an all-state middle linebacker in high school, and probably good enough to play college ball. But after a possession with intent to distribute charge, no recruiter would touch him. He turned to bulldogging and had done fairly well on the rodeo circuit, but apparently jumping from a horse full speed atop a four-hundred-pound steer and wrestling it to the ground never satisfied Bo's demons. He was always chasing another. And when he broke the necks of three animals in consecutive competitions his infamy grew.

Whether or not the killings were intentional, nobody knew for sure. What wasn't disputed was that Bo was sadistic and mean. Always had been.

Drawing in a frigid breath, Garrett locked eyes with his *ol' friend.* "What the hell's going on out here, Bo?" When he got no answer, he turned his attention to the one who was still lying on his back. "You all right?"

The guy was clearly scared out of his mind, and Garrett couldn't blame him.

Bo laughed. "*Ah hell,* this ain't nothing but a little mix-up." He turned back to the guy on the ground. "But we got it all straightened out. Didn't we, Smitty?"

Unlike Bo, who wore the same menacing smile he always had, the guy on the ground looked downright sick. Other than a few vigorous nods he didn't move a muscle.

Garrett peered around Bo and locked eyes with Smitty, whoever he was. "Why don't you go on and get out of here then."

Scrambling to his feet, Smitty stuffed a crumpled paper bag into the inside of his coat and gave them a wide berth as he darted by. It didn't take long for the tap of Smitty's work boots to give way to the whistling breeze.

Not wanting to take his eye off Bo, Garrett kept his focus straight ahead. If he had to guess, this was a dope deal gone bad. Of course, he wasn't about to blow his cover over a low-level hustler and a couple ounces of crank. There were bigger fish to fry out there than these two.

Bo breezed on with the conversation as if nothing had happened. "So, what brings you back to town, Kohl? Last I heard you was out on a rig. Making them big bucks in the sandbox."

Since Bo had moved on, Garrett figured he would too. "Bigger than they're paying around here these days."

"Depends on how you fit into the sector."

Bo was referring to the role you play in the energy sector. *Upstream* was the extraction of crude oil and natural gas, and *downstream* was refining them into something usable. *Midstream* was the transfer of raw production, usually by pipeline or trucking. Even when prices were down, there was always a way to make money.

Garrett suspected he already knew the answer but asked anyhow. "And where do you fit these days?"

Amused by what appeared to be his own inside joke, Bo's smile grew wider. "I just get things where they need to go."

Before he could dig, Bo asked, "You seen Tony yet?"

It wasn't surprising Bo asked about Deputy Tony Sanchez, Garrett's best friend since childhood. They'd practically been joined at the hip since kindergarten and didn't part ways until Garrett joined the army and Sanchez the marines. They hadn't spoken in a while, which was entirely on Garrett. It was yet another fence to mend while he was home.

When Garrett didn't answer, Bo gave a slight tilt of the head as if Sanchez was right behind him. "He told me you'd done forsaken us all for greener pastures."

If Bo wanted to be cagey, Garrett would return the favor. "Nah, I haven't forsaken anybody, Bo. Just been on a big bear. That's all."

"*Big bear*, huh?" Bo shook off the answer. "This hitch ain't lasted no couple months. You've been gone for years."

Garrett shrugged. "Time flies when you're having fun, I guess."

"Or maybe you been hiding from something?"

Given his DEA cover, Garrett maintained a heightened sense of awareness. And alarm bells rang loud when talking to someone in the drug game. "What would I be hiding from?"

"The truth."

Garrett's pulse quickened. "And what's that?"

"Bad blood between you and your brother."

Family feuds were some of the best fodder for gossip in small towns. No doubt, his blowout with Bridger had been big news. But why it would concern Bo was anybody's guess.

Fishing for a bigger catch, Bo cast his line a little further out. "Something to do with him working for Kaiser, I heard."

By Kaiser, Bo was referring to Preston Kaiser, a kid they'd gone to middle school with until he was shipped off to the New Mexico Military Institute over in Roswell. He'd gone on to Vanderbilt, like most of the Kaisers, but came back to Amarillo to work in the family business.

There were more than a few Kaisers around the Panhandle, but Preston was the heir apparent of the wealthy clan. He had worked in their banking operations since graduation and had only taken over Mescalero Exploration after his father died five years prior.

The family had an oil refinery in Borger and a feed-lot in Hereford, but the real moneymaker was Kaiser Bank.

"Can't see how me and my brother are any of your concern."

Bo moved toward Garrett with a startling sudden-ness and stopped short within a couple of feet. He raised a massive arm, dropped a hand on Garrett's shoulder, and wrapped his fingers around it like a vise. "Well, it ain't my concern, exactly. I'm just saying Kaiser money makes the world go round is all." Bo's next words came out more threat than question. "And you can't fault a man for wanting a piece of that, can you?"

Garrett was sizing up his opponent, determining exactly where to ram his fist, but Bo barged past with-out warning, making little effort to sidestep him as he lumbered away.

Moving from light to shadow beneath the skeleton framework, Bo vanished at the end of the footbridge. Left with the solitude he'd come seeking, Garrett no longer wanted it.

His ghosts were back and he hadn't even been home an hour.

8

Garrett settled into a booth in the Cattle Exchange restaurant at the far corner by the window, his back to the wall and far from the main entrance. He was already on edge after his run-in with Bo, and this place was a who's who gathering spot for wheeler-dealer types around Canadian. Showing up here for lunch or dinner meant there was a good chance you'd see somebody you knew. One unexpected reunion was bad enough for the evening.

Fortunately for Garrett, his beard and long hair provided good camouflage. Anyone who hadn't seen him since his army days would mistake him for an oil field roughneck or feedlot cowhand, unworthy of a second glance.

He pulled his hat brim low and scanned the crowd. It was right after five o'clock and the usual assortment of diners were trickling in and assembling themselves by profession around their customary tables. Oil field hands in coveralls, cowboys in boots and spurs, and farmers in brown Carhartt workwear were scattered about the restaurant, intermixed with bankers, attorneys, and local proprietors whose attire fell anywhere between business and business casual.

Garrett had been tempted to suggest another restaurant, somewhere more private, but didn't want to argue for a venue change against his brother the lawyer. That'd be a no-win fight. In the end, he was glad they'd settled on a place he'd been missing. Mounted trophy deer, Old West portraits, and big Texas flags adorned the walls. The restaurant was characteristic of the region in decor and clientele, hence the crowd in business suits.

When oil was discovered back in 1955, many of the ranchers struggling to survive in the fickle and oftentimes brutal climate found themselves awash with cash. And those who didn't piss it away on racehorses, vacation homes, and private jets figured out a way to make their money grow. There were more than a few in the area whose net worth was north of fifty million.

Though like Garrett's family, most eked out a living and that was that. Some had a lot. Some had a little. No different from anywhere else.

Booms came and went but one thing never changed. There was plenty of petroleum under their feet. The Anadarko Basin is one of the deepest in the country, and no matter how much you drain it there always seems to be more. In fact, the largest gas well ever drilled in America was in what became known as the Buffalo Wallow oil field. It started producing in 1969 and still yields dividends to this day.

Garrett drummed his fingers on the table, as his mind shifted from his family's deteriorating ranch to Asadi, and the fact he'd left him alone with his dad. Butch would take good care of him, that wasn't the issue. For all his faults, too numerous to count, the old man was as good a grandpa as it gets. Bridger had assured him of that on many occasions.

But Garrett and Asadi hadn't been separated since their journey began. For better or worse, *he* was the only constant in the boy's life. He was half-tempted to call and check in when Bridger walked up to the booth and stared. "*Damn*, Bucky, I almost walked right past you."

Garrett didn't even have to look up. Only two people in the world ever called him Bucky, and the other had been dead for over two decades. Having buck teeth at an early age had been the subject of fun for everyone but him. His mother had said it with affection, as more a term of endearment, but coming from Bridger it was a kick to the gut.

Nevertheless, Garrett ignored it and slid out of the booth as Bridger threw out a hand. There was a time when his brother would have pulled him into a full bear hug, but too much time had passed. Bridger was still pissed, even if his Clint Eastwood smile didn't show it. He followed up the trademark smirk with a skeptical glare.

"They don't have a barber out on those rigs or what?"

First *Bucky*, and then a shot across the bow. If nothing else the name-calling and banter gave him a familiar feeling of home. He'd play along. *For a while.*

"Well, they got 'em out there, Bridge, but I was holding out for more of a . . . *stylist.*"

Garrett gave Bridger the onceover and determined he didn't look any the worse for wear. The golden boy was still golden and looked every bit the part of a successful lawyer. Perfectly tailored suit. Designer tie. And Lucchese boots. He was the golden boy in both the literal and figurative sense.

Bridger had inherited their dad's blond hair and blue eyes, traits of Butch's German and Scottish ancestors who'd migrated to the Panhandle after the Civil War. Unlike Bridger, who was six foot three and belonged on a Wheaties box, Garrett, like his mother, was smaller in stature, a shade under six foot, and ropier than the corn-fed kids around Canadian.

Bridger chuckled as he slid into the booth. "A stylist, huh?" He gave a shake of the head. "I ought to style your ass good with some sheep sheers. How long's it been since your last trip?"

Things were a bit frosty, but his brother's joke was a good start. Like their mother, Garrett preferred to breeze past any awkwardness. Or even better, avoid it altogether. Mena Kohl would have had Genghis Khan to supper, so long as he washed his hands. Bridger, on the other hand, had inherited Butch's sharp temper and penchant for grudges. Letting bygones be bygones just wasn't in their DNA. Of course, Garrett was one to talk.

At any rate, he followed his big brother's lead and slid into his seat. Pretending to ponder a question he already knew the answer to Garrett dragged out his response. "Three years, I think." Another pause for effect. "Christmas, if memory serves."

"That's right, it *was* Christmas," Bridger confirmed. "You brought the girls those pretty scarves. Where were they from again?" The question had an almost disbelieving tone.

"Indonesia." Garrett hoped like hell he'd told the right lie to protect his DEA cover. It was getting harder and harder the more places he traveled.

"That's right," Bridger said with a slow nod. "They still wear those things all the time. Make a big deal to all their friends about how exotic they are, and how they got them from their *cool* uncle, rambling around the world like some roughneck gypsy."

"Glad to hear it." Garrett grabbed his menu and scanned the back. It was starting to look as if Bridger was going to let things go. And then he struck.

"It wasn't their fault, you know?"

"What wasn't?" For some reason Garrett felt the need to play dumb, maybe hoping his brother would buy the charade. But he never did.

"What happened between you and me."

"I *know* that," Garrett protested hotly. None of it for show this time.

"Then why'd you write them out of your life, along with me, Cassidy, and everyone else around here." Bridger cut his eyes outside the booth, clearly aware of his fiery timbre. He worked to lower his voice. "You want to be mad at me, fine. But the girls didn't deserve to be abandoned by their favorite uncle. They worship the ground you walk on."

The words stung, and any blistering retort Garrett

was formulating flew right out of his system. There was nothing he could say to refute that. And this wasn't just another of Bridger's Jedi mind tricks he used as a lawyer, it was the cold hard truth.

"You're right, Bridger." Garrett took a deep breath. "You're right. They didn't deserve that and neither did Cassidy."

"You saying I did?"

"I'm saying I still don't agree with *what* you did."

"Working with Kaiser?"

Bridger narrowed his focus on Garrett. "Look, I know you hate Mescalero, and I don't blame you. And you have every reason to given what happened. But the rest of us who stayed here had to move on. You understand that, don't you?" Garrett didn't answer, so Bridger pressed on. "It's the biggest oil and gas operator in the entire Panhandle. It provides jobs for people in six counties. Banks are full of Mescalero money, and so are the pockets of just about everyone sitting in this restaurant in some way or another."

"Including you," Garrett noted.

"Including me," Bridger admitted.

Given his brother's seemingly humble admission, Garrett considered easing up on him. *Considered* it. He wanted to let it go but couldn't. "Listen, Bridge, the fact that the Kaisers' pockets are deep doesn't justify what they did to our family."

Bridger looked around and leaned forward. "In case you haven't figured it out yet, agriculture in this part of the world doesn't exactly keep the lights on like it used to."

He gestured toward a group of four cowboys guzzling frosty mugs of beer a few tables over. "Those guys get to keep their heritage because there's about fifty pump jacks and a few new oil derricks sitting on the ranches where they work. That's the truth. Oil runs this place, whether the price is high or low. It's what keeps us going. Period."

"So?"

Bridger's volume dialed up in response to the single syllable. "*So*, what you said to me last time was out of line and I expect an apology."

Years ago, they were both a few beers in when Garrett told his brother that working for Mescalero was like pissing on their mother's grave. The comment was as vulgar as it was hurtful, but it had felt good at the time. And it felt good because it struck a nerve. Made it hurt. They hadn't spoken since.

"You know how I feel about the Kaisers and you work with them anyhow."

"I work with Preston. He's different from the old man."

"The apple doesn't fall far from the tree, *they say.*"

"They do say that," Bridger conceded. "Which means they could say the same thing about us. You want to live in Butch Kohl's shadow for the rest of your life?"

It was time to relent, Garrett thought. He wasn't conceding he was wrong about the Kaisers, only that his brother was right on a few points, particularly the one about his nieces. His thirst to punish Bridger had put innocent people in the cross fire. It was time to bury the hatchet.

"Bridger, you know I don't want that. And more than anything else I don't want the twins caught in the middle of this." Garrett swallowed hard before eating the crow. "And the comment I made to you about Mama was way out of line. I'm sorry for that."

Bridger shook it off, but whether his brother actually forgave him was still up in the air. Their mother taught them from early on that when one brother offers an apology, the other accepts. It had put the Band-Aid on more than a few knockdown drag outs and that's all that mattered. But something was off with Bridger, and it wasn't just their feud. Rarely serious at all, his brother had a nervous edge that was out of character.

Garrett set the menu aside and stared Bridger in the eye. "Everything else okay, man?"

Bridger looked surprised. "Yeah, why?"

"Daddy mentioned you haven't been yourself lately."

"Well, did he say who I've been?"

Ah hell! Was he really going to play this game? If he had to pull it out of him like he had with Butch, it'd piss him off all over again. Garrett didn't pay the lame joke any attention, just pressed ahead like he did with an evasive informant.

"He just said maybe you were stressed about something. With oil prices down, I thought maybe money was a little tight or something?"

Bridger shook it off. "Nah, things are good. Practice is flush. Still doing enough title opinions for Mescalero to keep me up to my eyeballs in work."

"Everybody's health okay? The girls? Cassidy?" Garrett chuckled out, "You don't have six months to live, do you?"

Bridger didn't laugh at the joke, which made Garrett think he was on to something. But he didn't let on, hoping his brother would fess up on his own.

"No, we're *all* in good health. Thank God." Bridger glanced around, seeming to make sure there was no one in earshot. "But . . . there's been a few things got me pacing at night."

Garrett's mind immediately went back to marital problems. "What kind of *things*? Something to do with Cassidy?"

Bridger shook it off. "No, she's fine. We're fine." A beat passed. "For now."

"What do you mean *for now*?"

Bridger looked around again. "Got a problem with some cases I worked a while back." He looked nervous and jumped a little when the waitress walked up to the table. After ordering their beers and steaks, they sat in uncomfortable silence as his brother waited for their server to not only leave but go back inside the kitchen.

Bridger looked out the window and stared at nothing. "There's been some weird stuff going on around here, that's all."

"Well, what, Bridge? What kind of weird stuff are we talking about?"

The waitress placed their beers on the table and scampered off. Bridger gulped down about half the beer in a swallow and answered with a single word. "Well, it's *drugs*."

The confession made the hair on Garrett's neck stand on end. He was intrigued for obvious reasons, but there was a part of him that suddenly felt like his cover was blown. That said, drugs in the Texas Panhandle were nothing new. They were as big a part of the energy business as the oil itself. His incident with Bo Clevenger was proof of that.

"Yeah, well that's the oil field. Rig hands take meth like kids drink Kool-Aid. It's just how it is."

"I'm not talking about meth, Garrett. We've had that here for years. I'm talking other stuff. Like opiates."

Now that *was* surprising. Opiates were rampant everywhere but hadn't been as rife in the oil field as stimulants. Rig workers and truck drivers were typically looking for something to keep them going. *Work hard—play hard*, and all that crap.

Garrett hadn't seen a big demand for drugs like heroin with those types. But with oil prices depressed, the money wasn't flowing like it once had in all parts of the country. A lot of people had lost their jobs. Maybe they were looking for something to kill the pain.

"Well, it seems kind of unusual, but tastes change, even in the drug world, I'm told."

"I'm not talking about what they're *using*, Garrett. I'm talking about what they're *selling*. Transporting across state lines." Bridger looked frustrated, almost panicked. "And now they're making threats."

9

Asadi didn't know what to do but was sure he didn't want to stare out the window all day. He wanted to explore. The more he sat, the more he thought about his family, and what happened at the village. And the more he dwelled on it, the sadder and more homesick he became. He screwed the green top back on his soda bottle and walked into the living room where Garrett's father, *Booch*, sat dozing in front of the television.

After standing there a few seconds and being ignored, Asadi plopped down on the sofa, which shot out a plume of dust from beneath the cushion. The old man pointed to the spot and spoke in a low gravelly voice.

"Nobody ever sits there, so it's a little . . ."

Asadi didn't comprehend a word but could tell he was embarrassed about the mess.

Butch switched the channel to a news show and stared at the man on the screen with intense disgust. He let the words *Doppler Dan* drip from his mouth slowly, like venom, then added with a scornful tone, "This guy couldn't predict a tornado if it flew up his cornhole." A grunt and grin preceded his next line. "More like Doppler *Dumbass*."

Asadi wasn't sure what Butch had said but laughed anyway. He knew *ass* was an American profanity. His older brother, Faraz, had taught him several. Although neither of them understood what the words meant, they laughed nonetheless and repeated them to each other while out in the garden, well beyond earshot of their parents.

Butch snorted. "You like that one, huh?" There was a gleam in his eye. "Well . . . everyone hates a weatherman, I suppose. From here to Timbuktu, they don't know nothin'. All they do is talk a bunch of trash."

The old man's dramatic fussing made Asadi laugh even harder, a reaction that made Butch grin wide. "Hot dog, sonny, you must be as disgusted with these people as I am." He slapped his thigh. "Well, if you hate this turd, wait until you see the rest."

The old man reclined farther into his chair, until his body was nearly as flat as the floor. He slapped his thigh a few more times and laughed. Part of Asadi felt guilty, as if it was a sin to be happy after what happened in the village. But the rest he was just glad to forget, even if only for a moment. He was near to sinking back into the sadness when Butch suddenly flung his legs forward and returned his flat chair to its upright position. He sat on the edge and turned to Asadi.

"Well, we can't sit around all day laughing at these idiots. We got horses to feed."

At the word *horses*, Asadi smiled. He'd never seen one up close in his life. Sure, they had them in Afghanistan, but not in his village, and none like the ones he'd seen on the drive up. None with cowboys atop them for sure. He could barely contain his excitement.

Butch ambled over to the dining room table and grabbed the cold weather gear Garrett had laid out for Asadi. "All right, sonny, time to earn your keep."

After Butch dressed him in his new shirt, coat, and hat, Asadi went to the mirror in the hallway leading to the bedrooms and stood there taking in the sight. He felt like he was looking at a stranger, like someone he'd seen in a book or magazine. He looked like an American kid.

He had been admiring himself for less than a few seconds when Butch called his name from the back door. As he turned the corner out of the hallway, Asadi was met with a blast of frozen air that chilled him to the bone. The coat and hat did little to stop the cold and he shivered hard even before setting foot outside. Nevertheless, he bounded through the entry, off the back porch, and jumped into a layer of fresh snow.

Asadi was about to grab a handful of the white powder when he looked over to find the most beautiful sunset he'd ever seen. Across the endless prairie, the sun exploded in hues of orange, yellow, and pink as far as the eye could see. And it was all captured between a layer of purple storm clouds above and a snow-white blanket below.

Butch didn't even look at it. Instead, the old man trudged through the snow to the barn behind the house. Asadi followed closely as they walked in, disappointed that it was only slightly warmer. The back of the structure was open to the outside. Under an awning a crowd of massive beasts waited behind the fence, huddling for warmth as they munched lazily on hay.

Butch pointed and mouthed the words *core-der horses* several times, seeming insistent on noting the importance. He even went into great detail, using not a single word other than *horse* that Asadi could understand.

At first, Asadi was terrified when five of the large creatures rumbled over, having never seen an animal that big up close. But it became clear they were not a threat and were more interested in food than they were in him.

The old man tapped his chest with the palm of his hand and said *Booch*, then pointed to each horse and rattled off their names. Asadi wanted to remember each one but it was hard to focus. He was too enamored of the beasts themselves.

Never had he seen something so impressive—beauty and power all at once. And he could tell Butch felt the same. It was in his eyes, a warmth that showed through as the old man rubbed their big foreheads and scratched their noses. He looked at them like family.

Asadi had been timid, hesitant to approach the horses until Butch led him over by the hand. Although he couldn't grasp the old man's words, he could somehow feel the lessons as they were conveyed to him. They were about trust, moving slowly, and being calm.

Butch pulled from a brown sack a handful of pellets and poured them into Asadi's upturned palms. A few cascaded over and landed on the ground. Asadi worried he was wasting them, and his face must have shown it. But Butch just laughed it off.

"Plenty more where that came from." He pointed to the horses. "Now go over there and make yourself a friend or two."

Asadi understood the word *friend* and knew what to do. He carefully walked over with the feed and slid it between the slats. But he was startled by two competing horses that butted heads and accidentally dropped them to the ground. One waiting in the wings swooped in between them and nibbled at the scattered pellets. Asadi looked back again, worried he'd done something wrong.

The old man slapped his thigh and hooted laughter. "You've heard of horseplay, haven't ya', sonny?"

He didn't know what Butch said but assumed the old man had made another of his jokes, so Asadi laughed too. The old man ambled over with his brown sack of feed and handed him a second scoop. "Give it another go!"

Asadi took the gesture to mean try again. And so, he did. This time successfully. And now that he had the hang of it, he kept up the feeding, doing his best to dish out the pellets evenly, and make sure all the horses got fed and none grew jealous.

Of course, he learned quickly, it was impossible. Some were ruder than others, nosing their way to the front and taking more than their fair share. They were just like people in that way. Some were greedy. Some were kind. But they were all magnificent.

He didn't know their names, but Asadi had labeled them by the way they acted. And he'd already made his list of favorites. Assuming they could be ridden, he wanted to ride the one in the back, the one too shy to barge up like the others. He was black, with a white splotch on his forehead that looked like a star.

Asadi liked the gentleness of the creature and felt like they could be friends. Wanting to get to know him better, Asadi threw a pile of pellets to the ground a few feet away and watched the group rush toward it—all but the one in back.

With the rest of the group out of the way, Asadi moved to the side, grabbed a handful of feed and held it out to the black horse. After a few seconds, the big guy rumbled over. He extended his nose timidly to Asadi's hand, took a few big whiffs, and raised his upper lip.

Turning his palm to the sky, Asadi unfurled his fingers and let the horse nibble at the pellets. He was nearly finished when the others realized what was happening and rushed over.

At this commotion, the black horse eased away and again took his place behind the others. But as the horse looked back, he let out a gentle whinny, a sound Asadi took to mean he had made a real friend.

10

Before Garrett could get more details about the threats to his family, the waitress came back at their table with the steaks. And as far as he was concerned, it wasn't a moment too soon. After taking a second to gather his composure, Garrett dove right in. "Bridger, if somebody's threatening your family, you need to go to the sheriff if you haven't already."

"If I go anywhere, it won't be the sheriff's department, especially with Crowley at the helm."

"Why not?"

Bridger hesitated, as if searching for the right answer. "He's . . . just not the right guy."

"How is the head local lawman not the right guy?"

"Because the only thing that exceeds his incompetence is his stupidity."

Fair enough. Garrett had run into a few in law enforcement that fit that description. But Bridger still should have reported the incident to get it on record.

"Crowley's more *politician* than lawman," Bridger scoffed. "You want anything done in a serious way you gotta break out of his circle."

As sheriff, Crowley should have been the top of the local law enforcement food chain. But in small towns, these guys are all beholden to donors. Families like the Kaisers hold more sway than the mayor or county judge.

The thought of doing an end run on Crowley and having Bridger talk to Sanchez crossed Garrett's mind. But if his brother hadn't thought of that already, there was a reason.

Wanting a little more time to think on it all, Garrett let it go. "Well, you know who's worth their salt around here a hell of a lot better than I do. But my guess is that if you're going up the law enforcement chain then this thing goes deeper than some local yokels?"

Bridger again looked over his shoulder. Content that they were out of earshot, he picked up his fork and knife and spoke as he sawed into his steak. "About a year ago, two hotshots got stopped near the Oklahoma line on I-40 by the Texas highway patrol for speeding. Trooper got a weird feeling and called in the dogs.

Didn't take long before they'd pulled out about eight pounds of heroin hidden in a compartment under the trailer."

"Eight pounds?" Garrett made an extra effort to feign ignorance for the sake of protecting his DEA cover. Hotshot drivers were responsible for quickly moving oil field equipment from one spot to another. "I'm guessing that's more than you need for a fun little road trip."

"A *lot* more. It's why I was surprised when I got asked to represent these guys."

"Who hired you?"

"Oil field services outfit based out of the Eagle Ford. Company called Renegade."

Garrett immediately remembered the Renegade Oil & Gas Services truck he'd seen out by the bridge. He'd seen them all over town.

After a quick look around Bridger continued, "I mean . . . I've done some light criminal cases around here in the past. You know, DWIs and rodeo cowboys doing dope. But nothing like this. I gave some referrals in Amarillo for criminal defense attorneys who knew a hell of a lot more about that stuff than I did."

"And?"

"Renegade still wanted me as their man. You know, local guys, so they wanted a local lawyer. But what was really at the heart of it all was keeping the whole thing quiet. Said it was in everybody's best interest that it stayed under the radar, so it didn't reflect poorly on the company's reputation. And since they're tied so closely with Mescalero, it would have given both companies a black eye. You know how people gossip."

Garrett didn't need any reminders about that. Renegade's reaction was understandable but rare. Most employers want nothing to do with anyone conducting criminal activity on the job. In fact, they're usually so pissed they turn out to be the prosecutor's biggest allies. But with oil prices low as they were, a lot of these service companies had gone under. Losing a customer as big as Mescalero in a down market would hurt like hell.

"Okay, so, what'd you do?"

Bridger threw up his hands. "I defended them."

"Why?"

"Kaiser had agreed to provide legal counsel as part of some clause in his master service agreement with Renegade. Aside from that, he had a good working relationship with them and didn't want to start over with another company on account of a bad egg."

The more Garrett thought it through, the more it all made sense. Even for a company like Mescalero, one with investors, it was easier to just make the problem go away rather than deal with bad publicity. "Well, how'd it all turn out?"

"Good for Renegade and Mescalero, I guess. It never went to trial, just like they wanted. Whole thing was resolved quick and quiet."

"And the hotshots?"

Bridger let out an exasperated laugh. "Hell, these guys had a list of priors long as my arm and they wouldn't cooperate with law enforcement. *At all.* The DA offered a lighter sentence if they rolled over on their buddies, but the two turned it down flat. They pled guilty and went straight to prison. Do not pass go, do not collect two hundred dollars."

Garrett leaned back in his booth, taking it all in. He signaled the waitress for two more beers. "No names? No nothing, huh?"

"They wouldn't say a thing, Garrett. These guys were scared. They took the first plea deal and got the *big bitch* given their previous convictions. Twenty-five to life. Caught chain to TDC lickety-split. Over and done."

"Twenty-five to life?" Garrett shook his head. "I'm thinking these are the kind of guys who would throw their own mama under a bus to get out of trouble. Am I right in thinking that's a little strange?"

"That's strange, all right." Bridger leaned in and lowered his voice. "What's even stranger is I got a thirty-thousand-dollar bonus check from Renegade for the *fine* work I did."

Garrett took a moment to process all Bridger had told him. "A bonus for what?"

"They said it was for my *discretion* on the matter." Bridger shook his head and laughed. "Discretion is part of the job. All I did is what I was supposed to do. And I didn't talk about the case to anyone other than who I had to but that's nothing out of the ordinary. At least for me."

"Then what kind of discretion were they talking about?"

Bridger shrugged. "Got a feeling there was more to the story. Like maybe I might get some questions later on. And low and behold about a week later, a couple Texas Rangers paid me a visit out at the house. One was out of Lubbock, the other from down on the border at Weslaco. Had a lot of questions about Renegade. So, I told them what I knew, which wasn't much, then they left me a card and thanked me for my time."

"Anything come of it?"

"Nothing from them." Bridger looked around again and lowered his voice. "But about six months later, two more Renegade hotshots heading west toward Albuquerque got nailed for dope at a truck stop near Adrian about three o'clock in the morning.

"The driver went inside to take a leak and the other idiot got into an altercation with some lot lizard hopping rig to rig doing her thing. Apparently, he wasn't satisfied with *the job*, and when she tried to collect, he refused to pay. Kicked her out of the truck right onto the concrete. Sheriff's deputy happened to be there filling his coffee and saw it all go down."

"How'd they happen upon the drugs?"

"The one inside the bathroom took off running, so the deputy knew something was up. They tore the truck apart, finding double the amount of dope they did before."

Garrett was genuinely intrigued and having fun. After all these years he and his brother had something in common besides their dysfunctional family. "How'd you handle this one?"

"I didn't," Bridger stated flatly. "Renegade's lawyer called me up again and wanted me to do the same thing."

"And?"

"I refused."

"Why?"

Bridger laughed. "I know you'll find this hard to believe, but some lawyers *do* have a conscience. And these guys were looking at some serious prison time. I'd learned my lesson from the first one. Stick to what you know. They needed a real criminal lawyer and I told them that very thing."

The waitress came back and set a couple of fresh beers on the table. Bridger took a hefty swig and continued after she left. "A few days later, I get some visitors at my office. A couple of local rednecks. One big sumbitch. The other a worm. They asked me if I'd reconsider Renegade's offer and started with questions like whether or not I'd thought about the welfare of my family. Veiled threats but a clear message."

Garrett didn't like where this was going. "They mention the girls?"

"*By name.*" Bridger clenched his napkin in his fist. "That's when I threw their white trash asses out in the street and called up Bo Clevenger."

Garrett was tempted to tell him about his earlier run-in involving Bo and the Renegade employee but didn't want to interrupt until Bridger got to the end. "Why him, Bridger? What's Bo got to do with this?"

"Works for the Renegade regional office here. Runs a contract crew of hotshots."

Now it was coming together. And it might explain Bo's brand-new top-of-the-line Ford F-350 Platinum parked in the lot. A truck running north of $80,000 would be hard to justify if it wasn't a moneymaker. Of course, given what Garrett had just seen on the Wagon Bridge and was hearing from Bridger there was a chance his old *friend* wasn't just a low-level hustler anymore.

Garrett leaned forward. "All right. What'd *he* say?"

"Said he had no idea what I was talking about. Acted like it must've been some buddies of the guys arrested and said he had nothing to do with it. But he didn't back down either. Asked me if I'd reconsider working a deal like I had before."

"And?"

"I stuck to my guns. Told him I couldn't take the case and that was that."

"But let me guess, *that* wasn't *that*."

Bridger looked out onto the dark street, seemingly at nothing, lost in his thoughts. "Last month, our dog was killed."

"*Scooter?*" Truth be told, Garrett had just assumed the gray-muzzled black Labrador had probably already died. Still, it hurt to hear the news.

Bridger looked back and nodded. "We'd had him since the girls were just babies. You came with us to pick him up. Remember? Over in Dalhart."

Garrett felt sick to his stomach. He had a vivid image in his mind of the twins dressing the dog like Santa Claus, with the little red hat, beard, and all. The good-natured thing just sat there and let them without making a fuss.

"I know what you're thinking, Bridger, but around here dogs don't always have the longest life spans. How many did we lose out at the ranch over the years? Between rattlesnakes, coyotes, and oil field trucks. I bet we—"

"It wasn't a *damn* truck, Garrett. The dog had arthritis so bad he never left the house." Bridger looked straight ahead with a thousand-yard stare. "When the girls got home, he was lying near dead on the front porch. Beaten and bloody. Barely able to breathe." Bridger paused and swallowed hard. "We couldn't even move him an inch. The second you touched him he'd whimper and cry. So, I sent the girls back to town and took care of it myself."

"*Dammit*, Bridge! Who would do something like that?" Garrett looked around to make sure no one heard him. He hadn't meant to react the way he did, but he was shocked, saddened, and outraged. "What the hell's going on here?"

"What's going on?" Bridger answered in a quiet voice, "What's going on is I'm doing penance for my sins. Being punished for the things I never should've done in the first place." He looked back out the window, into the darkness. "And now everyone I love is going to suffer."

PART TWO

For they have sown the wind, and they shall
reap the whirlwind.

—HOSEA 8:7

11

As Garrett drove the dark back roads returning to the ranch, he slowed below the speed limit. The roads were getting icier as the temperature dropped, and the thick snow clouds blotting out the moon and the stars didn't do much for visibility. Not only that, he was distracted. In all his life he'd never seen Bridger that worried.

Garrett had pressed for more answers, but ever the skillful lawyer, his brother had parried him with ease. There was more to the story, that was certain, but Bridger was holding back. Given what had happened to the dog, someone was sending a message. The question was what to do now.

At the academy, Joe Bob Dawson used to say *crooks don't recruit model citizens, they recruit other crooks.*

And if the theory held, it meant his brother was into this thing a hell of a lot deeper than he was admitting. The question was *how deep.*

No matter what his brother had gotten himself into, Garrett wasn't going to let threats stand against his family. Blood was blood, and despite their differences, Bridger had been there for him after their mother died, their sister abandoned them, and Butch turned to the bottle. At one time, his brother was the only real family he had.

Turning off the highway and back onto the white caliche road leading to the ranch, Garrett worked to distract himself by looking over at Kate Shanessy's place. There was something about it that looked warm and inviting. Of course, with the dancing snowflakes swirling in front of his headlights anything indoors sounded pretty good. He looked forward to the fire his dad no doubt had raging back at the house.

If Butch was good for nothing else, he was a master at that. Despite his shortfalls, the old man had always liked to see his family enjoy the warmth he provided. *Mama made the meals. Daddy made the fire.* That was how it worked.

Deep in thought, Garrett jerked the wheel hard to the left, nearly missing his turn. His truck rumbled over the cattle guard. The only good thing about Bridger's dilemma was that it took Garrett's mind off Asadi and the whole mess back in Afghanistan. He hadn't heard from Kim and didn't expect to, at least not for a few days. The wheels turned slowly in South Asia, and any investigation they had launched into these corrupt government officials was going to take time.

Garrett parked as close to the house as possible, wanting the shortest distance from his truck to the front door. The snow was falling harder and the wind blew even angrier than it had when he'd left. His dad would complain he'd parked on the grass, but who cared. If it wasn't that, the old man would find something else to gripe about.

After shutting off the engine, Garrett flipped the coat hood over his head and made a dash onto the porch and inside the house. To his surprise, there was no roaring fire and Fox News wasn't at full volume. He called out for his dad, then Asadi. When no one answered, a sinking feeling came over him. He shouted again, and the blaring silence made his hair stand on end.

Garrett stepped quickly to the back of the house and noticed the light on out in the barn. There was a trail of steps not yet covered by the fresh white powder. One set big, one set small. As he trudged through the snow, he realized he should have known all along where they'd be. His dad cared more about those horses than anything else in the world. And other than blood, it was about the only thing the two of them had in common anymore.

Garrett swung the barn door open, all the while cursing the cold, to find Butch sitting in a lawn chair by the heater, his old blue heeler Pato sitting on his lap. The dog wagged its tail at the sight of a visitor but didn't bother to get up.

Asadi didn't acknowledge Garrett's presence at all. He was standing inside an open stall, shoveling horse manure into a blue wheelbarrow. Beads of sweat gathered on his brow.

Garrett turned to his dad, who was grinning from ear to ear as he scratched Pato's head. "Daddy, I didn't bring this boy halfway cross the world so you could make a slave of him."

"*Slave*, hell! The boy likes to work."

Butch tapped Pato's butt and the dog jumped to the floor. He scampered to his bed in the corner of the barn, where he slept on a pile of old blankets under a heat lamp.

Garrett walked over, offered his dad a hand, and helped him out of the lawn chair. "How do you know?"

Butch grinned and pointed. "Look at him go." After a beat he added, "Don't think I ever saw you work that hard. *At anything.*"

Garrett was tempted to argue but seeing Asadi in action led him to believe his dad was right. The boy's face radiated a sense of purpose, maybe even a little pride in a job well done. He didn't know much about Asadi's background, other than he'd grown up on a farm, so it was possible doing a few chores made the boy feel at home.

Garrett turned to his dad. "What'd you two do while I was gone? I assume he hasn't been shoveling horse crap since the second I walked out the door."

Butch cocked his eye at Garrett. "No, I've been instructing him on a few things."

"*Dear Lord*, Daddy! I was just joking earlier. I shudder to think what you might teach a ten-year-old boy."

Butch took a few steps toward the stall and Asadi glanced up. The boy looked eager for a reaction. When their eyes met, the old man gave a single nod of approval. Asadi smiled back and returned to shoveling.

"I've got lots of wisdom to pass on." Butch turned to Garrett. "To those who'll listen."

Again, Garrett let it go. "Well, thanks for looking after him, anyhow."

Butch shook it off. "How'd it go with Bridger?"

"Good," Garrett affirmed, still watching the determined look on Asadi's face. "Better than the last time we were together."

Butch had been there for the big blowout. And although the old man would never admit it, Garrett knew that Butch agreed with him. Getting involved with the Kaiser family was a bad idea. Of course, the truth of the matter was, it was hard to avoid. Mescalero Exploration was as big a part of the Texas Panhandle as wind and isolation. If you didn't like those things, you might as well pack up and leave, which a lot of people did.

"So, what'd you find out from Bridger?" Butch's voice went low, clearly reluctant to show his concern. "Everything okay?"

"Nothing to worry about. He's got his ups and downs, like everyone else. But he says the girls and Cassidy are doing well. Busy as hell with work, but that's all right, I suppose."

Garrett didn't want to reveal anything about any potential threats to the family until there was more to go on. He kept things vague and changed the subject. No sense in worrying his dad unless it was absolutely necessary.

"I might meet with Tony Sanchez for breakfast tomorrow if that's all right with you?" Garrett thumbed over at Asadi. "If you don't mind watching the boy again?"

Butch sighed as though it was a big chore. "I guess he can help me cake the cattle." The old man cracked a smile. "Glad you keep in contact with Sanchez." He always pronounced it *Sandchiss*. "He's the only lawman I know that's worth a damn."

Garrett didn't know if the remark was a blatant insult or an attempt at humor. Either way, he moved on. "You see him often?"

Butch nodded. "He checks in on me about once a month. Always got good county gossip. Brings his mama's tamales by around Christmastime.

The thought of his dad looking forward to a visit from a sheriff's deputy made Garrett sad. Sure, the old man was the cause of most of his problems, but nobody deserved to be abandoned. Not even a cantankerous old rattlesnake like him.

Garrett looked around, feeling a little embarrassed it had come to the point where a stranger had to look in on his own father. "Well, I'll be sure to thank him when I see him. You know, for the tamales and such."

Butch nodded again but didn't say anything. He looked a little uncomfortable himself, which was an admission to his loneliness.

Garrett changed the subject once more to keep the conversation moving along. "Canadian seems about the same. I guess the downturn in oil prices hasn't killed this place like so many others."

"Yeah, I don't get to town much. But from what I can tell, things are humming along." Butch looked reluctant to make his next admission. "For all their *ways*, the Kaiser family kept this area afloat." As almost an afterthought, he added, "Honestly, I don't know how they do it."

At first, Garrett didn't think much of the comment but given what Bridger had told him earlier he decided to press further. "What do you mean *how they do it*?"

"Exactly that." Butch shot Garrett a confused look. "All the other oil companies around here went bust or dern near shut down to nothing. But not Mescalero. With oil prices where they are, they've got to be losing money." Butch paused a moment before continuing. "Rigs keep running and Preston Kaiser is buying up minerals and leasing everything he can get his hands on." Another pause. "Of course, he's getting it all at a discount since he's pretty much the only game in town now."

"Humph." Garrett let out the sound involuntarily.

"Humph, *what*?" Butch asked.

"Kicking folks while they're down. Huh?"

Butch chuckled. "Ain't nobody put a gun to their heads."

"I know it, but—"

"But what? We got a history with the Kaisers. They did that to us during the drought. Well, I got news for you, son. Nobody put a gun to your granddaddy's head either." Butch let out a sigh. "I know you got your issues because of what happened with your mama. Nobody knows that better than me. But the one responsible for that is dead. And he died a miserable old bastard, I'm told. Maybe even more miserable than me." He chuckled a little. "Don't let all that ruin what you got with your brother. There may come a time when he's all you got left."

Before he could answer, Garrett looked over to see Asadi standing before them, pitchfork in hand, and a big smile on his face. His wheelbarrow full of horse manure sat near the stall door. He said something in Dari and pointed to the wheelbarrow when nobody responded.

Butch elbowed Garrett in the ribs. "He's asking what to do with the mess, you dolt." The old man gave Asadi a thumbs-up. "Good work, sonny. We'll take care of that when it warms up."

Garrett stood in surprised silence. Who'd kidnapped his dad and replaced him with Mr. Rogers? Butch had never told him *good work* once in his life and he sure wouldn't have let him wait until it warmed up to finish a job. He was about to call him on it when his dad patted Asadi on the back.

The boy grinned wide and Garrett decided to just let it be.

12

Awakened in the middle of the night by a scream, Garrett grabbed the holstered Glock on his nightstand. But it took only a moment to figure out what had happened. The boy was having a nightmare, same as before—a desperate plea for his mother.

Leaping from the covers, Garrett moved to the bed and sat next to Asadi, still thrashing beneath the blankets. He rested his hand on the kid's shoulder. "It's okay. It's me." His voice was just above a whisper. "Your old friend Garrett."

Garrett attempted to rub his back, the way he'd done on the plane ride over, but the boy lashed out, still fighting the marauders from his village.

"Whoa, Outlaw. You're safe, buddy. Nobody's going to hurt you."

With the boy struggling against him, Garrett turned on the lamp, hoping a little light would break him free from his violent trance. Within seconds, Asadi had snapped out of it, breathless and sweaty. Having no idea what to say or do, Garrett leaned in and gave Asadi a hug, just like his mom had done when he was upset. The boy wrapped his spindly arms around him and squeezed in response. Asadi sniffled, then broke into sobs.

Since the trip began, there were times when Garrett wished he could communicate more clearly with Asadi, but this wasn't one of them. There was no mystery as to what the boy was dreaming about. And the awful truth was, he'd dream that dream forever. Losing a parent early on left a wound that wouldn't heal.

Garrett would have yelled at God if he thought it'd help. He'd raised a fist to Heaven plenty of times before, but it never did a lick of good. So instead, he asked for a sign. A miracle. *Hell*, any damn clue on how to help this poor kid. But with none forthcoming, he did the only thing he knew to do. He pulled Asadi into an even tighter embrace.

A squinting Butch Kohl shuffled into the bedroom wearing his old moth-eaten pajamas and threadbare plaid robe. His midnight voice was more sandpaper than usual. "What's the matter with him?"

Garrett didn't want to lie but couldn't involve Butch in the details about the massacre. "Well, Daddy, let's just say he's been through about as tough a time as a kid can go through."

Butch stared at Garrett through half-closed eyes, letting a little time pass before answering. "Well, I guess if anybody'd know how to help him then, it'd be you."

Garrett had been waiting for the old man to come up with some kind of nasty retort, and when he didn't, it threw him for a loop. He couldn't help but wonder if his dad's rare vote of confidence was the miracle he'd asked for. He was struggling for a response when Butch turned and ambled into the kitchen. A light went on and there was a clanging of pots and pans.

"Making the boy some hot chocolate," his dad called from the other room. "Want any?"

Given how rarely his dad offered him anything, Garrett readily accepted. He pulled away from Asadi, who had stopped crying, but was still latched on. The boy looked up with puffy red eyes.

"Hot chocolate?" Garrett asked, having figured out the boy understood a little English.

Asadi got out of bed and held out a hand, which Garrett took, and they both went into the kitchen. By the time they sat, Butch already had the milk on the stove and three mugs on the table. Garrett suspected the tub of Hershey's cocoa powder on the counter was probably the last one his mom had ever bought. He was tempted to check the expiration date but knew it'd only get Butch riled. If the old rattlesnake wanted to make hot chocolate twenty years expired, he'd let him. Garrett doubted his dad ever made any for himself. *He kept it because of her.*

While Butch had purged most of her other keepsakes, some memories died harder than others. And in his mother's world, hot chocolate was as close as it gets to a panacea. From broken hearts to broken bones, if a steaming cup of cocoa didn't fix it, it couldn't be fixed. Garrett had sat at that table with a hot mug more times than he could recall.

Butch slid a mug to Asadi and looked over at Garrett. "You know, this kid has the makings of a real horseman."

Garrett looked to Asadi, who was staring at the cup with a cartoon emblem of Texas Tech's masked rider, then turned back to his dad. "Is that right?"

"Yep." Butch walked over and stirred the milk, which was starting to bubble. "Soon as the weather turns, I figured I'd take him out for a ride. If that's okay?"

"Fine by me." Garrett followed his approving nod with a question that made him feel like a helicopter parent. "You been riding enough to keep them gentle?"

"Every chance I get." Butch moved the pot off the burner. "You still ride?"

Garrett repeated his dad's answer. "Every chance I get." He laughed at the absurdity of the truth. There was a time in his life when horses meant everything in the world to him. But he hadn't done much consistent riding since his days at Fort Carson.

"Take it that means *not a lot*."

"To tell you the truth, I can't remember the last time I was on the back of a horse." Garrett shook his head and gave a quiet answer, mostly to himself. "Years, I guess."

His dad turned back to the milk and gave it an easy stir. "Nothing stopping you from it while you're here. Do a little hunting too, if you want. Your gear is still in the hall closet."

Garrett felt a little guilty. He and Bridger had gone on an elk hunt in New Mexico a few years back and hadn't invited their dad. It had made for some hurt feelings, but since Butch didn't mention it, he'd apparently let it go.

"Yeah, I've been meaning to move all that stuff down to my trailer." Garrett let out a chuckle, hoping to keep things light. "Figured you'd be charging me for storage by now."

Butch cocked an eyebrow. "Who says I haven't?" Breezing on, he added, "King's the best hunter. Sure-footed and quiet. Knows how to stalk. Best disposition I've ever seen."

The thought of a hunt put Garrett at ease. He almost couldn't wait. "King that sorrel?"

Butch brought the boiling milk over to the table and poured a little into each cup. The powder rose from the bottom and swirled at the rim. Garrett grabbed a spoon from the center of the table and stirred. Asadi, who'd been watching the process, did the same.

Butch returned the pot to the stove and took a seat. "Yep, that's him."

As strange as it was, sitting around the table with the old man and the boy felt as normal as anything had in years. He didn't know why or how, but Asadi's presence bridged a gap. It created a portal through time, where he and his dad were speaking to each other in a way they hadn't spoken since Garrett was in middle school.

For the first time in over two decades, this house was a home.

13

Garrett awoke before sunrise after a more restful night's sleep than anticipated. He checked in on Asadi before leaving the house and the boy was sawing logs. They didn't get to bed until around two in the morning, and even once they were back under the covers, Asadi was tossing, turning, and glancing over every few seconds to make sure Garrett was still there. He was clearly scared and who could blame him. Nothing in his world was familiar. Not one single thing.

After about a half hour of restlessness, Garrett sat up, grabbed his phone, and pulled up Google translate on the browser. After typing in his sentence, he walked over to Asadi, and showed him the screen. Although not perfect, the crudely translated message in Dari seemed to work a much-needed miracle: Don't worry. You'll always be safe with me.

Asadi smiled, laid his head down, and was fast asleep in minutes. Garrett knew better than to give himself too much credit. As hard as Butch had worked him out in the barn cleaning stalls and feeding horses, the real miracle would be if the boy woke by noon. The old man could work a hummingbird to death.

At any rate, Garrett was glad Asadi was getting some good rest. Now that Butch had a little help, he was probably planning to paint the house or install a new septic system. On a nine-thousand-acre cattle ranch, the possibilities were endless.

As Garrett drove to Miami, pronounced *my-am-uh*, he observed how the clear sky, tall as it was wide, turned from cornflower blue to cobalt the higher it reached to heaven. In summertime, the stretch of tundra between his ranch and town flourished into rolling swells of wheat, bluestem, and buffalo grass that swayed rhythmically like the ocean tide.

The county road was one of his favorites, as was the place he'd agreed to meet Sanchez—a little café called Henry's that had swapped hands about fifty times since they were kids. The place had chipped paint, ripped vinyl chairs, and smelled like a grease trap. But it couldn't be beat for crisp bacon, fluffy pancakes, and a steaming cup of coffee.

If memory meshed with reality, the county judge would be sitting at his regular table, surrounded by farmers, ranchers, and oil field types complaining about bad weather or the *damn* liberals in Washington— whichever was more aggravating at the time. So, when Garrett walked inside it didn't disappoint. He was met with the full force of scraping forks, tinkling spoons, and crinkling newspapers that carried over the dull rumble of wall-to-wall patrons.

Looking around for anyone he might know, Garrett found only strangers' faces. Still preferring to keep a low profile, he seated himself in a corner. He was just resting easy when *she* walked up to take his order.

"All right, what'll it be?"

Even if Garrett hadn't seen her, he would have known that throaty voice anywhere. She hadn't recognized him though, and he hoped it'd stay that way. Lacey Capshaw wasn't looking at him directly, her attention diverted by a surly patron barking about runny eggs.

She rolled her eyes, sighed, and faced Garrett head-on. "Coffee?"

He scooted his mug toward the edge of the table and looked at the menu. "That, and an ice water, please."

She poured his coffee like it was second nature, barely glancing at the cup as she scanned the diner for more empties. "Ready to order or need a minute?"

Garrett pulled his brim lower. "Waiting on a friend, so it might be a few." He glanced at the door searching for Sanchez.

There was a quick gasp, preceding Lacey's inevitable question. "Garrett Kohl, is that you?"

He feigned a look of disbelief and pretended to rub sleep from his eyes. "Lacey?"

She stared at him like he was crazy. "Do I look so old you don't even recognize me?"

Garrett laughed to buy some time, but the truth was she'd never looked prettier. Her icy blue eyes and thick chestnut hair were exactly as he remembered. And any pound she might've gained had found its way to all the right places. Even in her faded Levi's, white V-neck, and New Balance running shoes, this small-town girl could stop traffic anywhere in the world.

Garrett was instantaneously transported back to high school, where he was the squeaky-voiced farm boy with pipe cleaner arms, and she the head cheerleader with a silver Mercedes convertible. Panic set in as he fumbled for the right answer.

"Yeah, of course! You look fantastic!" The words poured out with way more gusto than intended.

"Clearly, I'm not worth shootin' until I've had my coffee." Garrett took a big sip of the steaming cup as if to remedy the problem, burning the hell out of his upper lip in the process. He forced a smile as he fought through the pain.

Lacey looked at him curiously. "What are you doing here?"

He pointed at the menu. "Breakfast."

"No. I mean back home." Lacey lost her look of surprise and appeared genuinely glad to see him. "It's just that I haven't seen you around since you—"

"Got blown to pieces."

To minimize the awkwardness, Garrett had taken to answering for people when it came to what happened in Afghanistan. It was easier to make a joke of it than endure the agony of watching people fumble for the right words. But before he could follow up on his *blown to pieces* remark, she responded.

"So, what are you up to these days besides looking like a desperado?"

It took a couple of seconds for Garrett to process the fact that she was giving him a compliment. She'd always had a thing for bad boys. And now, apparently, he was one. Rather than try and think of something clever, he smiled and moved on. "Been doing some oil field work overseas. Mostly offshore."

She let her shoulders drop and her lips curled into a grin. "Isn't that kind of lonely?"

"A little, maybe. But you stay so busy there's not much time to think about it."

"And your folks?" she asked, writing on her little notepad as if she'd forgotten something about an order. "How are they doing?"

Another awkward moment but this time there was no quick quip to follow. Garrett did his best to respond without bringing up her obvious oversight. "Daddy's doing all right. Stays busy. Horse business is a bit slow. But he keeps things afloat. Good as you can ask for, I suppose."

The panic registered on Lacey's face the moment she remembered the car accident. She quit writing on her pad and looked up slowly. "Garrett, I'm *so* sorry." She looked around the crowd of patrons as if seeking a source to blame. "It's not that I didn't remember, I just got an order wrong earlier and I—"

Garrett cut her off, "Lacey, it's okay. That was a long time ago."

"But still I—" She glanced around again, her eyes a little misty.

"No, I can see you're busy and I totally understand." He mustered the same voice he used to gentle a colt or calm a wounded soldier—a commanding yet gentle whisper with the cadence of a lullaby. "No big deal, Lacey, I promise. No big deal."

Undoubtedly, Lacey was feeling some guilt over the misstep but if he was laying down odds it went deeper, much closer to home. Growing up, she'd been from one of the wealthiest families around, but her father, who was in the oil business, had lost it all in some bad deals. Destitute and depressed, Henry Capshaw put a .38 Smith & Wesson in his mouth and blew his brains out, leaving Lacey and her mother to fend for themselves. Lacey was a junior at Texas Christian University in Fort Worth when it all went down and had to drop out before finishing.

Garrett had heard through the grapevine she'd married a heart surgeon in Amarillo. They'd even opened an art gallery where she displayed her own paintings, which sold quite well. Life was bliss until she found out her husband was running around on her with more than a few women around town. Now, she was a divorced mother of two, apparently slinging hash back here. Her real-life sad story was about as bad as the fake one people made up about him.

In an abrupt change of subject, she asked, "How long you back for, Garrett?"

"Not sure." He looked back at the door for Sanchez. "Maybe a week or two."

He was about to ask if she'd be free sometime for a longer visit when a bell dinged in the background and a man's voice carried over the dull rumble of patrons. She rolled her eyes and jabbed a thumb back at the kitchen.

"Sorry, I've gotta pick up." It looked as if she were about to say something but changed her mind. "It's really good to see you, Garrett. Don't be a stranger."

Lacey spun on a heel and got back to work, stopping twice on the way to the counter to freshen a couple of empty coffee cups. And as she walked away, Garrett let out a sigh of relief. He was about to turn back to the menu when Sanchez sauntered up in full sheriff deputy's uniform that included Stetson hat and cowboy boots that *tock, tock, tocked* on the approach.

Garrett slid out of his chair and gave his childhood best friend a solid inspection. The former Marine Scout Sniper and combat veteran still wore a buzz cut, which made him look slightly jug-eared and a little crazy. Although a good bit shorter than most of the Teutonic Panhandle locals, Sanchez had a rock-solid build. He had more than a few scars on his gnarled head from hooves and fists, a few licks earned breaking horses at the Kohl Ranch, others standing up to bullies in high school.

Garrett stood and feigned a sucker punch. "Well, if it ain't the short arm of the law."

Sanchez laughed, lunged at Garrett and grabbed him by the head, pretending to go in for a choke hold. "Quanah Kohl, the poor man's version of pretty much everything."

Garrett's friend always called him Quanah, given his mixed Anglo-Comanche ancestry. Sanchez was an avid Texas history buff and had been since an elementary school field trip they took to Palo Duro Canyon. He particularly loved the Texas Rangers, claiming to be a descendant of Antonio Sanchez, a member of the famed lawmen from back in the mid-nineteenth century.

After letting Garrett go, Sanchez looked over at Lacey, who was serving a table across the room. "Ahh . . . taught you well, my boy. Always with his eyes on the prize."

Ah hell. Garrett knew his friend had seen him watching her as she walked away. And he could tell exactly what Sanchez was thinking. Lacey Capshaw and her cutoff shorts had been the subject of numerous conversations back in high school, usually while dove hunting out at the ranch with a twelve-pack of cold Natty Lights.

"Now you know what brings me back here, Garrett. What about you?"

"You're the one suggested it."

"I'm not talking about this place. I'm talking *home.*"

Before Garrett could respond, Sanchez unloaded both barrels. "After three years? Not an email. Not a phone call. Nothing. Just show up out of the blue, huh?"

Garrett was a little thrown. Given the warm greeting he figured his old friend was going to let bygones be bygones. He knew it was going to be a little tense, but this was downright hostility. And it didn't sit well.

"Didn't realize I was under any obligation to report to you or anyone else."

"Didn't think keeping up with your best friend was an *obligation*."

Garrett wondered if Sanchez and his brother had joined forces to make him feel like the biggest jerk on the planet. At the very least, they were using the same playbook. He was starting to wish he'd taken Kim up on a CIA safe house.

"Wasn't like that."

"Then what was it like?"

"Look, Tony, when Bridger and I got into it over the Kaiser deal it brought up a lot of old memories. *Bad* memories. Just didn't want to be around for a while. That's all. Nothing to do with you."

"Nothing to do with me? You know what I've been through and I could've used a friend. Someone who knows what it's like coming back home after being over there."

By *over there*, Sanchez was referring to a war zone. And like a lot of veterans, his ghosts had followed him home. The *why me and not them* guilt was both real and devastating.

Sanchez's nightmares began with an insurgent and an RPG. He got the guy, clean through the chest, but not before the attacker had pulled the trigger on a marine fire team. Two lived. Two died. And Sanchez turned to the bottle. It was an elixir that nearly took everything the war hadn't. Fortunately, this marine powered on and came out the other side. No thanks to Garrett.

Having developed a taste for crow over the past twenty-four hours, Garrett dolloped another big helping onto his plate. He leaned back and let out a defeated breath.

"All right, Tony. You win. You were there for me when I needed you and I wasn't there for you when I should've been. I may be late to the party but I'm here now. And if there's anything you need, I'm all in."

Unlike Bridger, who had to follow the Kohl Code of clemency, his best friend didn't shake off the offense and forgive and forget. Sanchez was holding on to his grudge like grim death. He'd been that way since they were kids. It was his only attribute Garrett hated.

——————

It was an awkward breakfast, one filled with pro-longed silences that were fortunately filled by pass-ersby who'd stop by the table to hit up the sheriff's deputy for the latest gossip. But Garrett was genuinely beginning to wonder if their friendship was too far gone. He was almost tempted to give up after all the dull shrugs and one-word answers and decided to lay it all on the table.

"Now after all we've been through over the years, you really gonna punish me for the rest of my life?"

Sanchez's dark leathery face was set, as rigid as a statue.

"I said I was sorry," Garrett persisted. "What the hell else can I do?"

A wry grin crept across the deputy's face as he slid the check across the table. "Well. You can take care of this for starters."

Before Garrett could say a word, Sanchez slipped out of the booth, donned his cowboy hat, and marched out of the café. Grabbing a twenty and a ten from his wallet, Garrett placed the bills under a saltshaker and followed his friend outside.

Sanchez was standing in the parking lot grinning from ear to ear. He didn't say a word, but his look said it all. The breakfast tab was just the beginning.

Sanchez jumped in his white Chevy Tahoe with the Hemphill County Sheriff's Department logo on the side, cranked the engine, and rolled down the window. "I'm thinking this is a good start, Quanah. But while you're here I suggest we drive on down to Amarillo for some steaks and Macallan 18 over at OHMS. What do you say?"

Garrett had to laugh. Buying his way back into his friend's good graces was going to cost him. "I say . . . we play it by ear."

"Just remember." The sheriff's deputy smiled wide. "I know where you live."

He had just put his truck in reverse when Garrett stopped him. "Hey, Tony, what do you know about Renegade?"

Sanchez lost his smile. "Why do you want to know?"

"No reason, really. Bridger mentioned some things in passing. Sounds like they've got a few employees on the naughty list."

Sanchez looked around the parking lot before answering. "Man, nobody's digging too far into that one. Drugs weren't found in the county, so not a whole lot of people are interested in taking on a company that's providing good jobs." Sanchez lowered his voice. "Drilling stops and this place dies. Money like that takes care of lots of problems."

Garrett furrowed his brow. "It also *causes* lots of problems if used the wrong way."

"I hear what you're saying, but I'm just being real with you. Kaiser money makes the rich richer and the poor less poor." Sanchez jerked his thumb toward the direction of Canadian. "Hell, who do you think eats at my mama's restaurant? Oil field, that's who. You can drive by her place at lunch and it's standing room only."

As Garrett was about to counter, his friend interrupted. "Look, buddy, I know you hate the Kaisers. Believe me, I get it. But they're good to the community. Hospital equipment. Courthouse refurbishment. Hell, they even put in a jumbotron at Wildcat Stadium. So, as far as people round here are concerned, if it ain't a local problem, it ain't a problem."

Garrett thought about saying, it's a *local problem* for someone, but didn't see the point. Almost everybody around here was borderline isolationist. It was an argument he wouldn't win.

"Speaking of local problems, I ran into Bo Clevenger last night."

Sanchez nodded. "That's what I heard."

"How'd you know?"

"Small town, Quanah. Things get around."

That didn't answer the question. "Seems he was at odds with some Mescalero employee. Guy named Smitty."

"Well, you know Bo. He's always been at odds with everyone."

The news didn't seem to surprise Sanchez, nor did it draw any concern.

"True enough, I guess. But it was a pretty brazen display. Even for him. Right there on the Wagon Bridge. Made me wonder if things around here are getting out of hand."

Sanchez tapped the badge on his chest. "That a criticism?"

"No. But I did get the impression from Bridger that Sheriff Crowley might be turning a blind eye to some things for the sake of politics."

"So, that's Bridger's take?"

"An observation is all. Between that and seeing what I saw at the river it got me curious."

Sanchez let out a whistle. "You know what they say about curiosity, don't you?"

Garrett understood the politics of crime. From the sheriff's department to the DEA, every law enforcement organization knew when to look the other way. Right or wrong, that was reality. But since Sanchez had provided no help, Garrett had no choice but to find someone who would.

14

Asadi turned over in his little twin bed, kicked the thick comforter from his body, and sat up straight. The aroma that awoke him was straight from heaven. He was certain it was nothing he'd ever smelled before and worried it might be horse. His brother told him there were nomads around Afghanistan who ate them, although he'd never witnessed it personally.

Of course, Faraz was prone to teasing, so who knew if that was true at all. Asadi didn't think Americans ate horse and convinced himself the smell had nothing to do with the wonderful creatures he'd met the night before.

Asadi wanted desperately to go back to the barn and see how they had weathered the cold night. He was particularly interested in visiting his new friend—the black one with the white star on his forehead. Asadi closed his eyes and his mind rested on an image of his family—all there together—happy again.

He'd pushed those thoughts away as best he could over the past few days, telling himself not to worry, that all of this was only a horrible nightmare. Soon he'd wake to find things as they had been. He'd be back in Nasrin, his mother rousing him for school, and his brother snoring in the next bed.

He was near tears when thankfully interrupted by a call from Butch, who was shuffling around in the kitchen. Asadi got up from the warm bed, crept down the hallway, and joined him by the stove. The old man raised the pan where a delightful-smelling meat crackled and hissed in a pool of grease. With a look of pride, Butch pointed to the dish and called it *beh-gen*, and the round breads on the plate *pamcates*.

Asadi sat at the table and ate until he couldn't eat anymore. He'd just finished the last bite when he looked over to find Butch had donned his tan work coat and popped on a dusty brown Resistol cowboy hat over his curly white hair. He held Asadi's football coat in one hand, and the green-and-yellow stocking hat in the other.

The old man had a twinkle in his eye. "Time to work off them pancakes, sonny."

Asadi walked outside to find the winds had died down and the air was crisp and dry—a thick cloud of vapor puffed from his mouth with each breath. Looking around, he could see the ranch was more beautiful than he'd realized. When they'd driven in the day before, the storm clouds had blocked their view. But now that they had passed, there lay before him a blanket of powdery snow as far as the eye could see. Above him was a cloudless sky, the color of ice.

He climbed into the white Ford pickup with a flatbed and Butch cranked the motor. The old man turned to him with a smile. "Ready to feed?"

Asadi nodded, not knowing what he was agreeing to, but certain he would like it. So far, everything on the ranch had been fun. And the distraction hadn't come a moment too soon. He was beginning to dwell on his family, particularly his brother, Faraz. Asadi worried he would be unable to control his tears.

Butch let the truck idle for a minute, then mashed the accelerator with his foot a couple of times. He rubbed his palms together vigorously, cupped his hands and blew into them. Butch placed one hand on the steering wheel, the other on a gear shift and put the vehicle in drive.

They rolled across a winding path that rose and dipped over a set of foothills leading to a tower called a *wim-meel*. Beneath it stood a cluster of several dozen black cows, milling about near a wooden corral. Butch put the truck in park, climbed out, and Asadi did likewise. The old man pointed to a large rectangular contraption on the back of the vehicle which he banged with his fist a couple of times. It made a hollow clang.

"It's broke." He patted a brown sack similar to one they'd used to feed the horses. "Back to basics."

The old man pulled out a pocketknife, slit the top of the bag open, and began pouring out pellets in a line away from the truck. The cattle, which had already gathered around and were bawling, jockeyed for position to get first dibs on feed. After emptying three-quarters of the sack, Butch walked back to the truck, where Asadi was sitting atop the flatbed.

Butch handed the bag to Asadi. "All right, you saw what I done. Now you do the same." He pointed toward a clump of cattle on the other side of the truck, eager for their breakfast.

Asadi froze with fear. Could he wade through the crowd of gigantic beasts and live? He didn't budge from his perch.

Butch smiled. "You can do it, Asadi. Trust me." He pointed again at the same spot and gave a nod in that direction.

Asadi reluctantly moved forward, let his legs dangle over the side, and dropped off the edge. At the sound of his feet hitting the ground, the awaiting cattle were startled and scattered in every direction, a response that frightened him as much as the cows. He retreated until his back was flat against the side of the truck.

Butch let out one of his hooting laughs. "See! They're more afraid of you than you are of them." He pointed at the bag. "You're holding their pancakes, sonny. Now, get to feeding!"

Asadi mustered his courage and marched forward, one foot in front of the other, straight through the herd. To his great surprise, they parted. He emptied the contents of the bag, turned back to Butch. But before he could get a reaction, he heard the shuffling of hooves behind him, and the huff of a big wet nose under his arm.

Although Asadi knew the big black cow was only nosing for food, the sudden invasion killed his confidence. He yelped, sprinted back to the truck, and threw his arms around Butch. The old man roared with laughter, put his gloved hand atop Asadi's head. "Good job, sonny!"

Asadi was laughing too when he heard an *aw hell* from Butch, who was watching a shiny silver truck drive up. It was massive, as big as any he had ever seen.

It was even bigger than Garrett's, and that was saying something. The woman, wearing brown overalls and a dirty white T-shirt underneath, pulled up beside them, rolled down a window, and leaned out. She was the tiniest of creatures, with speckled dry skin that crinkled like paper. Her wiry hair was a reddish-gray, cut short like a man's.

Butch rested an elbow atop the flatbed on his truck as if preparing for a long exchange. Asadi noted he didn't look happy about the interruption but forced himself to be polite. "Kate Shanessy, to what do we owe the pleasure?"

Kate's eyes hid so deep within her sockets Asadi could not tell their color. She didn't return Butch's greeting—just jumped right in—speaking rapid fire in a booming voice that carried over the knock of her big diesel engine.

"Seen a plane flying over a few times last week. Real low to the ground." Kate sandwiched her palms together until they almost touched. "What'd ya' make of that?"

"Government," Butch answered without hesitation. "Probably flying the Canadian to make sure decent folks like us ain't using the little bit a water God gave us."

She spat out the window and gave a little snort. "Wouldn't put it past 'em. But the ones I seen wasn't following the river. Was running a straight shot. South to north, then back again."

Butch looked over his shoulder, as if following the path of an imaginary airplane. "You see any markings?"

Kate shook her head. "Nothing I could identify as peculiar. Just a regular twin engine—no different than any other, I guess."

"Well, Kate, there's folks with money buying up land around here all the time." Butch shot her a wry smile. "*Hell*, might be some rich doctor out of Dallas looking for some hunting property and a new wife."

"Ain't interested." Kate's face crinkled into a frown. "Got a mare about to foal and that damn plane got her stirred up good." She grabbed the bolt-action rifle sitting beside her on the bench seat and raised it to where they could get a good look. "I don't care who it is. Come over my barn again and they'll get a neighborly .270 round up their ass—I'll tell you what."

Butch chuckled. "Ah, truth of the matter is it's probably just a land man scouting where to put their next oil well."

"Them oil companies use helicopters," Kate corrected, "and there ain't nobody drilling around here but that greedy bastard Kaiser."

Hearing the words *ass* and *bastard*, Asadi giggled. Kate turned and squinted at him so hard it looked like her eyes were completely closed. "Who's your helper there, Butch?"

Butch put his gloved hand atop Asadi's head and rested it there. "This here is the latest addition to the Kohl Ranch. Damn good with horses and works a lot harder than my worthless two sons ever did, that's for sure."

Kate craned her neck out the window and pursed her lips as she studied Asadi from head to toe. "Bridger knock up a Mexican or something?"

Butch shook his head. "Nah, ain't nothing like that."

"Must be nice to have some company." Kate kept her eye slits trained on Asadi. And though her lips lay as flat as the horizon, he could tell she was smiling. "Know I could use some companionship myself since Fred died. Girls don't come around much less they need a loan."

"Well, that's unfor—"

"Bridger don't want this boy no more or what?"

Butch looked to Asadi, still struggling to keep up. "No, it ain't that. The boy don't belong to Bridger. He came up with Garrett and he's not—"

"Garrett!" Kate's eyes went so wide Asadi could finally see they were the prettiest shade of green. "Didn't know he was back! And didn't know he had him a woman." She gave a confident sort of nod.

"Well. Good. For. Him. I always thought he was too good a catch to stay a bachelor." For the first time since she pulled up, Asadi was fully convinced Kate was a woman. She patted her heart with a dusty hand. "He still handsome as he used to be?"

"Hell if I know," Butch snapped. "He's covered himself in long hair and tattoos. Looks more like one of the Manson family than one of my own."

"Well, Butch, you the one brought them boys up like mountain men. No sense bitchin' about it now if Garrett turned out looking like one." Kate shook her head and spat in the snow. "Hell, he was never one to make a fuss over his appearance, anyhow. Not even in high school. Hunting and horses were all he ever cared about."

She laughed and popped the door a couple of times with her palm like she was telling her truck to giddyap. "Well, I can't sit around listening to your sorry ass all day. Got crap to do."

Butch looked as though he was about to say something right as she mashed the gas and the massive diesel engine snarled. She was already rolling up the window before he could stop her. Asadi laughed again at hearing the word *ass*.

15

Since it was only a little after breakfast, Garrett assumed the Crippled Crows wouldn't be open. But he hoped he might catch the owner, Ike Hodges, in there early, checking inventory on liquor or mopping up puke—whatever dive bar owners did when they weren't pouring drinks.

Per Garrett's recollection, a few Renegade fleet trucks were parked out front the day before, along with about two dozen Harley-Davidsons and a couple of empty potbelly cattle trailers. The dilapidated establishment welcomed oil field hands, slaughterhouse workers, feedlot cowboys, and the kind of girls attracted to that sort. It wasn't considered family-friendly, as it was home to some less than legal activities: gambling, drugs, and prostitution to name a few.

Garrett pulled into the caliche parking lot at Crippled Crows, glad to see it devoid of all but one vehicle. He didn't know if the red pickup belonged to the owners but had a sneaking suspicion it did. The late-model Dodge Longhorn was parked by a door near the back entrance, which meant it probably didn't belong to a drunk customer who'd left it there the night before.

Garrett nestled his GMC in on the other side of the Dodge, hidden from the main road. Not only did he want to keep a low profile, he thought the owner might be more apt to spill the beans if their conversation was private. Instead of trying the back entrance, Garrett eased around the building and went in through the front door. He suspected he'd be less likely to end up with a shotgun in his face if he came in looking like a boozehound wanting an eye-opener, rather than some goon sneaking in the rear.

He walked in to find it as dark and dank as he'd imagined and stinking to high heaven of stale beer and cigarette smoke. "Oilfield Blues" by Comanche Moon was playing low in the background. Through the dimness Garrett could see particleboard walls plastered with posters of Budweiser girls and Miller Lite ads. A big banner over one of the pool tables was promoting a Saint Paddy's day event from three years ago.

The whole place was constructed of concrete, steel, and corrugated tin. If it ever failed as a beer joint, it might make a decent barn for storing farm equipment or hay. It'd only need a few upgrades. Garrett stepped to the bar and stared at the man behind it who leaned over the counter writing in a notepad.

In a voice as coarse and unfiltered as the Camel cigarette he was smoking, the barman barked out a salutation. "Read the sign, moron, we're closed."

"Looking for Ike Hodges. Was hoping he might help me out with a couple of things."

The guy didn't hesitate in his response. "He ain't exactly the *helping* kind."

"That's a shame." Working to keep his cool, Garrett took a stab at a joke. "I'll probably need a shot of penicillin just walking through the door here. Hate to think it was all for nothing."

The bartender didn't flinch, just took a few seconds to finish up with whatever he was tallying on his paper and looked up. "Ain't you that Snake Eater nearly bit the dust over in Afghanistan several years back?"

Garrett was going to have to work a little harder. He could feel the back of his neck getting hot. "What of it?"

The rangy barman stood erect and leered. He had short salt-and-pepper hair and wore something between a gunfighter's handlebar mustache and about a week's worth of stubble on the rest of his face. He exhaled a big cloud of smoke and added, "Well, if you'd introduced yourself as a *gen-u-wine* hero, before asking for favors, I might've been nicer." The barman smiled. "You're friends with Deputy Dawg Sanchez, aren't you?"

Garrett smiled back. "Been best friends since grade school."

"Well, you can tell that *sumbitch* this ain't no company store, and just because he won't take a bribe, don't mean he can walk his tab."

With that joke Ike Hodges brought the temperature down a few degrees and took the situation from near fisticuffs to some good-natured old-fashioned ball busting. It was a skill Garrett assumed the barman had honed over the years, coaxing broken beer bottles out of the hands of cattle haulers and oil field trash.

Ike sauntered over from behind the bar like John Wayne and cast out his long arm for a handshake. "Welcome to the Crippled Crows. How can we ruin your life?"

Garrett laughed and shook the big calloused hand. "Garrett Kohl."

"I told you, I know who you are. I followed your story real close for a while." Ike moseyed back behind the bar and took two Coors Light longnecks out of the refrigerator, uncapped the bottles, and slid one to Garrett. "This your flavor?"

It couldn't have been more than nine-thirty, but Garrett knew never to turn down a drink when the bartender was buying. "*Cold* is my flavor." He'd have preferred a Shiner Bock but doubted Ike carried anything beyond the redneck holy trinity. Garrett sat on a stool in front of the bar and took a big swallow. "If you don't mind me asking, how'd you recognize me? It's been a while since all that came out in the papers and I don't exactly look like I did back then." He stroked his beard to emphasize his point.

Ike tilted his bottle at Garrett. "A good bartender never forgets a face."

Garrett nodded, truly impressed. "I wouldn't mind that skill."

"Also overheard a couple of roughnecks in here last night talking trash about you." Ike held the Coors between his middle and index fingers and rocked it back and forth. "Curious what I heard?"

"Maybe a little."

"These two young bucks made it clear if you were back in town looking for work with Renegade, you'd better keep looking."

Garrett laughed. "Any reason why?"

"They heard you were kind of a straight arrow. Said something about things running a certain way around here, and they didn't need anybody coming in and messing up a good thing."

Garrett chuckled. "Well, I'll take it as a compliment."

Ike grunted. "The rest, you won't."

"Okay, lay it on me."

"Said you got your ass handed to you by the Taliban. That you'd left all your buddies up in the mountains to die."

Garrett felt the heat on his neck again. "Then I've just got one more question."

Ike smiled. "I know what it is, and it's one you won't get answered."

"Not going to give me their names?"

Ike shook his head. "Nope."

"Why not?"

"Because I know the kind of hurt you can put on them if you got a mind to." Before Garrett could argue, Ike interrupted. "And they're just a couple of dumb kids, that's all. Beating their asses won't change a thing." Ike held up two fists with scarred knuckles. "Believe me, I've tried." He grabbed his Coors and took a hefty swig. "Plus, I have a feeling they won't be so quick to judge anyone who puts on the uniform anymore. At least not in my bar."

Garrett immediately regretted it but had to ask. "How'd you manage that?"

Ike stuck his hand under the bar and pulled out a black billy club, the handle wrapped in a swirl of silver duct tape, the business end gnarled and scuffed. "I escorted them out back and explained in a way they could understand it was time to go sleep it off."

There was definitely more to the story, but Garrett let it go. "Look, Ike, you don't have to defend me. I can take care of myself."

The barman slammed the club on top of the bar with a sharp *clack*. "I wasn't defending *you*, I was defending *us*." He held out his left arm, rolled up the sleeve of his flannel shirt, and displayed a forearm covered in tattoos. Pointing to the profile of an AH-6 Little Bird helicopter dead center, he looked up and locked eyes with Garrett. "Mogadishu. 1993. Saw more than a few guys like you pass on to Valhalla that day."

Valhalla was a term used by special operations forces in a reference to the Viking heaven, a place where warriors live on for eternity. The Battle of Mogadishu was more popularly known as Black Hawk Down. It was clear now, Ike Hodges was a combat veteran himself, most likely flying for the army's 160th Special Operation Aviation Regiment (SOAR). Night Stalkers were the elite of the elite of military helicopter pilots.

Before Garrett could apologize, Ike continued. "And don't try and tell me what I can and can't do in my own bar. I'll take care of business how I see fit. Are we clear?"

If Garrett had learned anything from his careers in the military and law enforcement, it was that sometimes only one answer would suffice. "Yessir." Figuring it was better to change the subject, he moved on. "So, how'd you wind up here in Shangri-La? Assuming you must have pissed off God something fierce to get planted in the middle of the Texas Panhandle with a run-down honky-tonk."

His response was a hearty laugh and the answer of *in more ways than you can imagine.* But he went on to speak for a good half hour about what brought him to his current station in life. If nothing else, his stories were interesting as hell.

Ike was from a ranching community off the Canadian River near Adobe Walls, a place of historical note given two pivotal battles that took place in the area. In the first, famed frontiersman Kit Carson led three hundred soldiers against two thousand Comanche, Kiowa, and Apache warriors. The second battle occurred when Quanah Parker and seven hundred braves clashed with twenty-nine buffalo hunters camped at the outpost. Among the defenders were gunfighter Bat

Masterson and army scout Billy Dixon. Dixon ended the siege with his fabled thousand-yard shot, and later won the Medal of Honor at the nearby Battle of Buffalo Wallow.

After leaving his boyhood home, Ike went on to travel the world with the army, and retired as a chief warrant officer IV, having spent most of his career as a Night Stalker. After retirement he took a high-paying job with Bell Helicopter in Amarillo and worked as a test pilot. He married and had a couple of kids, but after a few years started missing the bullets and bombs kind of lifestyle.

He signed on with military contractor Blackwater during the Iraq War and pretty much made a new life for himself. By the time he came back home to Amarillo, his wife had moved on. It was a story all too familiar in Garrett's world. Deployments and undercover assignments were hell on relationships. In his experience, few survived.

Despite a wrecked marriage, Ike stuck around the Panhandle to help raise the kids. But instead of returning to Bell, he took what money he'd made from contracting overseas and threw it into building "the world's trashiest bar." He also bought a Hughes 500, similar to the birds he'd flown in the army. Ike kept his pilot's license active to do freelance work on the side.

Helicopter hog hunts were big business and made up for much of the income he'd lost after the oil bust.

Ike opened another Coors and pushed it to Garrett using the back of his hand. "Well, now you've heard my sorry tale of a life story. What brings you into my bar at nine-thirty in the morning." Before Garrett could answer, he added, "And don't tell me it's to get drunk because I can see you're still nursing that first beer."

Garrett took down the last three-quarters of the Coors and tossed it in the fifty-gallon drum that acted as a trash can. He grabbed the fresh one. "You know my brother, Bridger, by chance?"

"Not personally, but I know *of* him."

The way in which he said it led Garrett to believe it wasn't in a positive light. But lawyer was a four-letter word to some, and Ike seemed the type to fall into that category.

"He told me he's been having some issues with a couple of Renegade hands."

Ike narrowed his eyes. "Patrons of mine?"

"Maybe." Garrett decided to be as up front as he could without giving away any secrets. Ike seemed like a guy he could trust, and a man who could get information. "My brother's the type of guy who gets in over his head before he even has a clue. So, I'm just hoping to find any trouble before it finds him."

"Bridger seems the capable enough sort. How's this your job?"

"Well, it's not. But I guess I kind of feel like I owe it to him." Bridger's guilt trip over breaking off a relationship with his nieces and Cassidy weighed heavy on Garrett. And now that he knew they could be in danger, he had to make up for it. Of course, he wasn't going to get into all that with Ike. "I guess sticking my nose where it doesn't belong is just one of my bad habits."

Ike took a long drag off his unfiltered Camel. "I wouldn't know anything about bad habits." His smirk faded as it looked like he was solving a puzzle in his mind. "If I'm reading between the lines, I guess you're trying to figure out what Bridger might be up against."

After a beat, Garrett nodded. "When I went into battle, I wanted good intel. Didn't you?"

"*Good intel*," Ike repeated with a smile. "That's hard to come by. In a war zone or on the street. But if you'll settle for good as it gets, you came to the right place."

"I'm not too picky."

Ike took a sip. "What I'm guessing is you already know something that you're not telling me here. Something that's got you rattled. And what you really want to know is if you're walking into a fight with a Ka-bar, when you should've brought your Howitzer."

"Well, you know your ordnance, Ike, what do you think?"

It was clear Ike was thinking hard on the question. "Something about myself you'll come to find out. When it comes to intel, I don't mess around. Been screwed over too many times for that. So, I'll tell you what I *know*, not what I *think*."

Garrett couldn't help but think Ike was referring to the Black Hawk Down incident in Somalia. But anyone who'd spent a career in covert ops had been burned more than once by bad intel. "Fair enough."

The barman took a hefty swig. "We get all types in here. And I believe there's various shades of gray when it comes to illegal activity."

As a law enforcement officer, Garrett had seen criminals use that same logic to justify their actions, from inner-city street hustlers slinging crack to cartel *sicarios* committing murder. Hell, Kim Manning and the CIA were prime examples. He didn't a hundred percent agree with Ike's statement, but he got the point. "Go on."

"Folks come in here *work* for a living. And in my opinion, you bust your ass, you deserve some fun. So, I get roustabouts smoking weed, cattle haulers on crank, and dairymen who just want to touch a tit that ain't swinging under a Holstein, if you catch my meaning?"

"Got it." Garrett gave a nod as he looked around. "A few working girls in the crowd."

"But the ones you don't see in here often are the Mexicans."

Garrett thought about it a minute. There was a time when it might have been true, but Panhandle demographics had changed significantly, particularly with the need for labor. "With all the packing plants over in Cactus and Booker, feedlots around Gruver, large-scale dairies at Dalhart, I figured you'd get plenty of customers from south of the border."

"Mexicans, Hondurans, Guatemalans, Salvadorians, you name it, we got 'em. But them there are immigrants straight off the boat. What I'm talking about are Mexican nationals, ones here to do business."

Now, Garrett's interest was piqued. "What kind of business?"

"The kind of business where they wear slick suits, expensive jewelry, and them pointy-toed roach stomper boots. The kind with guys who throw round some cash." Ike's eyebrows rose. "*Lots* of cash."

Garrett eyed Ike before speaking. Having spent enough time doing undercover work in Mexico with the cartels, he knew exactly the kind of guy the barman was talking about but wanted to make sure this wasn't speculation. "Some of the guys working in these plants have more money than you might think. Maybe they get a few drinks and start acting like big shots."

Ike narrowed his gaze. "You think I haven't seen that before?"

"No, but I want to be sure you're suggesting what I think you are."

Ike's face softened, as though he was hoping Garrett would probe for an answer. "The reason I know something's fishy is because everybody has a place around here." He raised his beer bottle and used it to point out at the tables. "We can talk about this country being a melting pot, but it's really more of a stew. We're all thrown together, but people keep to their own."

"And it's not the case with the Mexicans you saw?"

"Nope." Ike shook his head. "The times I've seen them, which are few, they come in here whooping it up with Renegade oil field trash." He cocked an eye. "No offense to your profession."

Garrett was so fixed on the story and what was shaping up to be a possible legitimate connection to Mexican drug traffickers and Renegade he almost forgot *oil field trash* was his cover. "None taken," he replied, a little off guard. He looked to the fridge behind Ike and waggled his empty beer bottle. "You got another one of these?"

The barman smiled and nodded. "Like I said, don't be caught with a Ka-bar when you needed a Howitzer."

Garrett took the beer and held it a few seconds. The pieces were coming together but he couldn't believe it could go all the way to Preston Kaiser. If there was coordination between the cartels and Renegade, it had to be low level. That was the only way it would make sense. There'd be too much for him to lose if it went all the way to the top.

He stared at Ike, who was wiping down the bar with a rag that looked like it hadn't been washed since the day the place opened. "Just so I can get this straight in my head, you honestly think these guys might be with a Mexican cartel and are potentially working with Renegade?"

Ike scowled as he tossed the nasty rag over his shoulder. "You know the acronym UFO?"

Garrett laughed, feeling the effects of the third beer. "Who doesn't?"

"I'm not talking about the way civilians use it. I'm talking about pilots. Do you know what it stands for?"

Garrett shrugged. "Same as it is for civilians, I guess. Unidentified Flying Object."

"Exactly." Ike pointed at Garrett. "And do you know what that is?"

"I don't know." Garrett chuckled, "A flying saucer?"

"Wrong. It's an *unidentified . . . flying . . . object*. Nothing more. Nothing less." He took a sip of his beer. "I'll tell you what I know, not what I think. And what I *know* is exactly what I saw. Nothing more. Nothing less." With a wry smile, Ike added, "But if you do decide to go poking around with these Renegade boys . . . I'd be damned sure to pack your Howitzer."

Before Garrett could ask any more questions, his cell phone buzzed in his breast pocket. It was an 806 area code number he didn't recognize. He held his finger up to Ike. "Just a second." He pulled the phone out and nearly dropped it when he read the message.

Can you meet for lunch? -Lacey

Before he could think it through, he'd already typed when . . . where?

She wrote back, Chihua's at 11:00.

He glanced at his watch. Perryton was a good twenty minutes from Crippled Crows and most of the roads in Ochiltree County were still iced over. He figured he could make lunch, but he'd have to push the hell out of his truck to do it.

Ike grinned. "Looks important."

Garrett realized the smile on his face must have given him away. Damned if that wasn't embarrassing. Nearly two decades out of high school and he was experiencing the same high he'd felt the time she'd waved at him at Dairy Queen. Turned out she was only signaling for her order, but for a couple of seconds he was on top of the world.

"I've taken enough of your time, Ike. What do I owe you for the beers?"

The barman waved him off. "Told you before, I value good intel. You find out something about these guys coming into my bar, let me know. I like to be on top of what's happening around here." He smiled. "And tell Deputy Dawg Sanchez it's time to pay his tab."

"You've got a deal, Ike." Garrett zipped his coat and turned to leave. "On both requests."

16

Ray Smitty turned his pickup off the highway and meandered down a bumpy oil field road covered in snow. Squinting from the glare of the morning sun, he groped for the four-wheel drive switch on the dash, clicked the nob, and his wheels caught traction. Nearer the Mescalero drill site, he took his foot off the gas and craned his neck forward. Although he was miles from anyone, his heart still raced at the thought of getting caught. Eyes were on him. Even at the edge of nowhere.

Smitty saw the bobbing forty-eight-foot pump jack over the edge of the mesquite brush and stared at it warily. It always creeped him out how the giant iron contraptions came to life on a whim, sucked their fill of oil, then went back to sleep just as suddenly as they'd awakened.

He rounded the corner of the thorny hedgerow to his right and came upon a caliche pad surrounded by barbed wire. Parked behind a white oil reservoir was a metallic blue Chevy Silverado and a sheriff's department Tahoe belonging to God only knows who. Fortunately, the SUV was leaving just as Smitty was pulling up. That was the last thing he needed.

As the Tahoe exited the site and tore off down the road, Smitty eased beside the Chevy and rolled down his window. By accident, he gave a gesture that looked more like a heil Hitler salute than a friendly hello. But if Cade Malek thought anything of it, he didn't let on. Of course, it was always hard to tell what was going on behind those mirrored sunglasses.

In both looks and mannerisms, Malek reminded Smitty of the old Marlboro man. Same style hat. Same etched face. And same no-nonsense attitude. His mouth was a straight line unless he was making a joke, usually at Smitty's expense.

Before he could get out a word, Malek began, "You know, Ray, I'm a little surprised to see your face."

Smitty laughed, hoping Malek was only kidding. "Didn't think I'd show or what?"

Malek's mouth was flat as a board. "Didn't think you were still alive."

It was a strange retort, but one that paved the way for a conversation Smitty needed to have anyhow. "Well, I am for now."

Malek hung his ropey arm out the window and pointed at Smitty accusingly. "What the hell kind of trouble did you get yourself into this time?"

"Didn't do nothing." Smitty shook off the accusation. "Bo just suspects I'm up to no good for some reason. Accused me right to my face."

"And why would he suspect that?"

"Hell if I know." Smitty looked over his shoulder. He always did it when speaking Bo's name aloud. Just in case. "The crazy sumbitch nearly took my head off last night. If some vigilante hadn't showed up, he'd have chunked me off the bridge right into the Canadian."

Malek gave a hearty laugh. "Bo might cripple you a little, but he'll keep you around." He added as an afterthought, "Least for now. The *Garzas*, on the other hand, will kill your ass and smile while they do it."

Smitty wondered if Malek knew the cartel was up to something that he didn't. He was staring at the bobbing pump jack when its mechanical groans faded and gave way to the wind.

"Well, what am I supposed to do, Malek? You're the brains behind this *damn* thing."

Malek tossed a frayed toothpick in his mouth and clenched it in his teeth. "Sounds like you'd better convince Bo you're loyal."

"And just how am I supposed to do that?"

"That's your problem, Ray."

"Yours too if you think about it."

With a consenting nod, Malek asked, "You got a wife and kid to look after, don't you?"

Smitty hated it when Malek mentioned his family. Of course, he'd been the one to bring it up when they'd made the deal, so he'd only himself to blame. "What about 'em?"

"You wanna leave your kin in good standing?"

It was Smitty's turn to nod.

"Then you'd better do your best not to get caught or killed. Either way, it'll come back on them. Just something to keep in mind."

"If it comes back on them, it's because you're the one pushing this thing too hard." Smitty fought to control his temper but it was too late. "It'll be blood on your hands."

Malek gave an easy smile and said what they were both thinking. "You're the one came to me for help. Remember?"

Smitty turned forward and let his eyes fall on the resting pump jack. Fighting to get his emotions under control, he gave a snort. "You don't have to remind me."

"Well, seems that I do." Malek yanked out the toothpick and flicked it at Smitty. "And since you got a debt to pay, I'd suggest you get busy paying it." Smiling wide, he gave the gimme here motion with his hand. "And speaking of paying, you got the money?"

Smitty grabbed the crumpled paper bag he'd gotten from Bo and handed it over. Malek tossed it in the backseat without even looking inside. He never looked inside.

Malek grabbed a fresh toothpick from his console and clamped it in his teeth. "Gonna be out of touch for a couple days. Got business down on the border. Think you can stay out of trouble until then?"

"Grace a God, I suppose."

If Smitty's self-doubt bothered Malek it didn't show. "Shipment still flying in tomorrow?"

Smitty glanced over his shoulder again. Talking about the Garzas made him even more nervous than talking about Bo. "Last I heard. Me and Boggs is supposed to pick it up."

"Good." Malek perked up a little. "Big payday for us both."

His eyes still frozen on the pump jack ahead, Smitty startled when it woke and went back to feeding. "My luck's running thin. I know it." He turned back, this time pleading for an answer. "How much further I gotta dig to get out of this mess?"

Malek's smile went flat. "Digging out from under a dead man ain't easy to do." He eased his head out the window, pulled off his sunglasses and locked eyes. "You really want to put the past in the rearview, then I'd suggest getting a bigger shovel."

17

Garrett gripped the steering wheel, white-knuckled, as his pickup hit a patch of black ice and slid toward the bar ditch. He gave it a little gas to get some weight under the wheels and prayed to God it'd do the trick. The truck still drifted and rumbled off the pavement, but just as the gravel peppered the wheel well, he got it under control and steered back onto the highway.

He exhaled a *dear sweet Jesus thank you* for the miracle, but it wasn't until safely passing by the four-foot concrete culvert in the middle of the gully that he realized how close he'd come to meeting a sorry end. With a dab of sweat on his forehead, Garrett slowly guided his three-quarter-ton GMC back to the center of the road and tapped the brakes.

Fortunately, he'd been able to regain control, but he couldn't help but worry. What would happen to Asadi if something happened to him?

With his stomach already in knots, he was further needled by guilt. His only job was to look after the boy and he'd barely seen him since they got to the ranch. Obviously, there'd been no part of the arrangement with Kim involving "quality time" with Asadi, but that didn't matter. If the kid needed anything right now it was consistency and he sure wasn't getting it from Garrett.

Pulling into Chihua's sparse parking lot, Garrett breathed a sigh of relief. He'd hoped to find an out-of-the-way spot where he and Lacey could converse a little without interruption. Eating in small towns was notoriously difficult. He'd sat through more than a few cold meals after making small talk with a ceaseless trail of passersby. They'd chat for minutes at a time, and usually without a thing in the world to say.

When the hostess asked him if he was ready to be seated, he told her he needed to look around first. Other than a couple of farmers, too occupied with their steaming cheese enchiladas to even notice him, there was no one in sight. It wasn't until he strode the full length of the restaurant that he found her in a secluded corner in a vacant room near the bar. As soon as Garrett walked up, Lacey jumped from her chair and gave him a hug. He was a little surprised by her sudden show of emotion, though by no means disappointed.

As if she could read his thoughts, Lacey explained, "Sorry if I was a little cold at the café earlier. I have to keep my distance with customers around there." She was a little flushed herself. "If I show any attention at all, to anyone, it becomes kind of a *thing*."

Garrett understood. Someone as pretty as Lacey working in a place with lonely cowboys and rig hands had to stay aloof. If she didn't, more than a few would read her charm as a clanging dinner bell. Some of those types were fairly aggressive, others relentless.

"Just took you for a woman with her hands full. That's all." Garrett smiled. "Last thing I wanted to do was get between some old rancher and his fourth cup of coffee."

Lacey laughed and pointed to their table. There was already a basket of chips and two iced teas waiting. "I got us kind of an out-of-the-way spot to avoid the crowd. Hope that's okay?"

Now it was Garrett's turn to look her over and he liked what he saw. Her faded Levi's and a tight gray hoodie revealed every curvy inch of her bodacious figure. She'd lost the ponytail, letting her thick chestnut hair cascade over her shoulders.

Garrett sat and met her ice blue eyes. He could smell the hint of perfume for a moment. "Actually, I was hoping for some privacy."

She looked at him curiously. "Any particular reason?"

"I tend to draw a few stares, I guess." He displayed his forearms bearing the sleeve tattoos. "Some of these little old church ladies don't know if I'm here to eat tacos or rob the place."

Lacey let out a genuine heartfelt laugh. "Well, who cares about the little old ladies. I think it's hot." Her mouth curled into a playful smile. "And I've learned not to care too much about what anybody thinks. If I did, I would've ended up like my dad a long time ago."

Garrett didn't know exactly how to respond. She was clearly flirting with him, but the grim reference to her dad's suicide threw him for a loop.

"Look, I know that sounds awful and I didn't mean for it to sound like I don't care. I loved my dad more than anything, but I guess, sometimes it's just easier to kill the elephant in the room rather than pretend it isn't there. Know what I mean?"

Before he could answer, she continued, "The reason I wanted to meet with you is because I wanted to apologize in person. I should've done it earlier at the café, but I was too embarrassed." She corrected herself, "No. *Ashamed.* That's a better word for it."

"Ashamed?" Garrett assumed she was referring to the fact she had forgotten about his mother's death but was surprised by her reaction. "Why? Because of my mom? I told you. That was a long time ago and I—"

"It's not just that, Garrett. I should have been nicer to you back in high school. And I'm sorry I wasn't."

He paused, unsure how to respond to this sudden show of emotion. "You weren't *not* nice. You just—"

"Didn't care about anyone but myself. I know."

Garrett shook his head. "I wasn't going to say that."

"You don't have to." Her warm smile put him at ease. "I know who I was back then. And I'm not proud of it."

"That was a long time ago, Lacey. We've all changed since then. Besides, I haven't thought about any of that in ages." Garrett hoped the little white lie would make her feel better.

Her smile faded a little. "Even your mother?"

Before Garrett could answer, the waitress walked up to take their order. It took him a moment to break from his trance and acknowledge her. Since he was clearly shaken, Lacey ordered for them both. Beef Enchilada Montadas. Double beans. No rice.

Lacey turned back as the waitress darted off. "It's what I always get. Hope that's okay?"

Garrett nodded in response, still thinking about his mom and the fact that Lacey had brought her up. He'd like to think people move on and forget, but the gut-wrenching stories tended to linger like a rotten smell. Of course, he was just as guilty. One of the first things he remembered was that her dad lost the family fortune and blew his brains out. Sad how the mind gravitated toward incidents like those and not something better.

Lacey covered his hand with hers again. "You all right, Garrett?"

"You know, we're not too far from where it happened." He shifted a little but was careful not to move his hand, hoping she would keep hers where it was. "The wreck I mean."

Lacey nodded. "Is that why you and your brother got sideways a while back? Over him working for Preston Kaiser?"

As soon as those words came out of her mouth, Garrett felt a little ridiculous. If he was mad at Bridger for dealing with the Kaisers, he might as well be mad at the entire Texas Panhandle. Everybody took Kaiser money in some form or fashion. And the fact that one of their trucks had run his mother off the road over two decades ago didn't change reality. Mescalero was there to stay.

Of course, none of the people who defended the Kaisers were there with him, holding his mother's hand when she lay dying on the side of the road. And none of them saw the truck driver keep going after he'd swerved into their lane, forcing her little Jeep Cherokee off the highway where it rolled four times and landed upside down in a culvert. And they damn sure weren't there to hear Mescalero's lawyers put the blame on her, hammering in the fact that she'd worked a night shift at the hospital, and suggesting to the jury it was *she* who was at fault—not the doped-up truck driver.

Worst of all, nobody saw how Garrett's family looked at him after the funeral, the one who'd walked away with little more than cuts and bruises. They never said it was his fault she'd gone out of the way to pick him up at Sanchez's house after a sleepover when she should have been home in bed. They didn't say it because they didn't have to. If he knew it to be true, they sure as hell did also. There was no denying that his actions, even though unintentional, were a major factor in her death.

But understanding shone in Lacey's eyes. She was once a girl who expected the finer things, and when her father could no longer provide them, he ended it all. Now she lived with the same guilt as Garrett. It was the kind you never shed. Because the person you needed absolution from was not around to give it.

"You know, Lacey, when it comes to the fight with me and my brother, I don't even know anymore. I've held a grudge against the Kaiser family for so long it seems like it's all I've ever known. And the one I hold responsible for my mom's death isn't even alive anymore. Now I'm holding his son to account for no good reason."

Garrett shook his head and laughed. If his own dad had forgiven and forgotten, maybe it was time to let it go. He was starting to feel like one of those Japanese soldiers, still fighting the war decades after it was over.

"I'm sorry if this opens old wounds. It's just that when I saw you, it brought back these feelings I had after my dad died. And I wish I'd been there for you when you needed it. When you could have used a friend. I wanted you to know I'm sorry, that's all."

He smiled.

She was about to say something else when their food arrived. The waitress set their meals before them and gave the obligatory warning. Be careful. Plates are hot.

Lost in the moment, the first thing Garrett did was grab the plate like an idiot. Pulling his fingers back with a yelp, he looked to the waitress who shook her head as she walked away. When he tasted the food, he was glad Lacey had made the call.

Girl knew how to order.

After a good half hour of lighthearted catching up, which mostly included a *where are they now and what are they doing* rundown of everyone in high school, Lacey again turned the conversation to a more serious note. She looked a little nervous.

"Is your brother in some kind of trouble?"

The question set him on edge. "You know Bridger, if there's mischief, he'll find it. Why do you ask?"

Garrett already suspected Bridger had dug himself into something deep, particularly after his conversation with Ike Hodges that morning, which all but confirmed his suspicions that something shady was going on with Renegade.

Garrett figured it best to play dumb.

Lacey looked around before speaking, almost as if scared. "I drove over to Bridger's office the other day to discuss a problem I was having, and a couple of guys were inside. I didn't get a good look, but it seemed like they were up to no good. Harassing him or something. By the time I parked and went inside they were gone. I asked him about it, but he told me it was no big deal and changed the subject. Any idea what's going on?"

"Yeah, he mentioned it to me, actually. Something to do with an old case, but they got it all straightened out, I think. Just a dispute over a payment or something like that."

"Oh, good." Lacey looked relieved. "Seemed like it was about to get ugly."

Garrett shook it off. "Nah, he got it all squared away. No big deal." He narrowed his gaze. "If it's not too personal, do you mind telling me why you were there?"

She raised her eyebrows. "Well . . . I got an offer from Preston Kaiser to purchase our family's minerals." She shook her head in disbelief. "A lump sum of over two and a half million."

Garrett looked at her with a curious expression. "Got to be honest, I don't necessarily see how that's a problem."

"The *problem* is my father lost everything when he went bankrupt. He leveraged all we had, including our mineral rights."

To Garrett, the story was unusual but not unheard of in mineral acquisition. The title chain went back well over a hundred years and could get extremely complicated. An inexperienced land man or even an attorney could have easily made a mistake. Not only that, energy companies were exploring new formations all the time. It was possible her father hadn't lost it all, maybe only existing production or whatever they had under lease. It was possible other zones were open for purchase.

Garrett cocked his head, trying to think through all

the scenarios. He knew a lot about the industry but that was one area where you needed an expert. "If there's anyone who knows his way around an oil and gas lease and mineral law, it's Bridger. But if it were me, I'd get someone else. There's an obvious conflict of interest since he works with Mescalero. I'm surprised he didn't tell you that directly."

Lacey nodded as if she'd already heard everything Garrett was saying. "So . . . that's where it got even stranger. You see, I did go to someone else for that reason. And what he explained was that the offer wasn't necessarily a direct payment as much as it was a type of partnership on future wells. The money would be put into an escrow account to be used when it was time to drill. At which point, we'd divide the expenses and eventually the revenue once the oil wells started producing."

Garrett didn't see the downside other than the fact Lacey wouldn't see a dime until the well was completed and operations were paid in full. There were worse situations to be in. "This seems like good news. Mescalero must be interested in drilling into a zone your family didn't lose during the bankruptcy."

Lacey looked only slightly more cheerful. "Exactly. That's the good news."

"And the bad?"

"Mescalero wants to target formations below what we've already drilled."

Garrett wasn't a geologist but knew going deeper wasn't cost feasible—not without better technology. And not with the price of oil as low as it was.

"Oh." Now Garrett was stumped.

"Yeah, *oh*," she repeated.

"Any idea why they'd want to do this?"

Lacey let out a frustrated sigh as she shook her head. "My attorney had no idea. He said it was a legitimate contract and I could sign it if I wanted to. But it was kind of like . . . waiting for the Oilers to go to the Super Bowl, or something." She looked a little frustrated. "I don't even know what that means."

It meant there wasn't a chance in hell this was going to happen.

"What did my brother say? I'm assuming it's why you went over there. To find out Mescalero's intentions."

"It's *exactly* why I went over. And he didn't really say anything. A bunch of double-talk about how companies buy leases and make deals when the oil prices are low, so they don't get gouged when prices are high."

"What about the formation they were looking at? He had to agree it was crazy. Right?"

She shook her head. "Again, it was just more crap

about how technologies are always changing and how in ten years' time everything could be different. He pointed to the whole fracking revolution to prove his point."

Garrett had to admit, most of it was true, at least the part about new technologies. But Bridger was guilty as sin when it came to muddying waters. His *lawyerese* was legendary. And the truth was that real moneymakers in oil and gas didn't plan in years, they planned in decades. If nothing else, the Kaiser family were experts at turning a profit. That couldn't be denied.

There was a chance Bridger was being vague with Lacey, so as not to be held responsible if she regretted her decision later on. After all, it was her gamble. Not his.

She went on to say, "It wasn't just the way Bridger was speaking, though he seemed genuinely nervous, like he'd rather be anywhere other than having a conversation with me. I felt like he was shooing me out the door."

Garrett couldn't imagine any man not wanting to be around Lacey for any reason, least of all Bridger. He treated beautiful women like diplomats treat foreign dignitaries. He'd have normally rolled out the red carpet, which meant something was off. He was just about to ask when he could see her again when she looked at her watch, startled.

"Oh, gosh! I didn't realize the time. I've got to get back to work."

"Back for the lunch rush, huh?"

Lacey looked a bit confused until it dawned on her Garrett had made an incorrect assumption. "Oh no. My mom owns the café. I just help her out in the mornings and on weekends. I'm an office manager at Renegade."

The revelation hit Garrett like a ton of bricks, but he forced himself not to react. Between Bridger's troubles and Ike's intel linking Renegade to a Mexican drug cartel, it was all he could do not to warn her. Of course, that was assuming she didn't know something already. Sanchez's earlier words crept back into his mind.

Drilling stops and this place dies. Money like that takes care of lots of problems.

Garrett didn't want to assume Lacey was involved any more than he wanted to believe Sanchez was on the take. But reality is harsh when it comes to protecting your livelihood. He'd seen really good people do some really bad stuff for a whole hell of a lot less.

18

Garrett turned his pickup right out of the Chihua's parking lot, stewing over Lacey's revelation about Renegade. He shuddered when his cell phone rang over the truck speakers. It was a 703 area code, common among those living in northern Virginia. Maybe it was DEA headquarters checking in. He clicked the answer button on his controls and was greeted by a familiar voice.

"How was your lunch there, cowboy?"

Garrett was tempted to ask how she knew but didn't want to give Kim the satisfaction. He assumed the CIA was tracking his phone and credit cards. "Delicious as always," he replied casually. "You ever want to come out for some real Tex-Mex, I'll take you there. My treat."

There was a brief pause. "And how is our young friend taking to the local cuisine?"

Garrett paused. She knew he'd been at Chihua's but not without Asadi. Apparently, she wasn't up on everything. "The boy likes burritos and hot chocolate, but who doesn't?" After a beat, he confessed, "He's not with me now. Left him with my dad while I ran a few errands."

Garrett worried she might be angry he'd left Asadi behind, but he also wanted to be honest about it. There'd been no hard and fast rules about anything, only that the boy needed to be kept out of sight, which he was.

"Actually, that's good. I wanted to discuss a few things and I prefer he not be present."

Garrett had assumed she was only checking in, so it made her news a bit disconcerting, as if there might be an issue. "There a problem?"

"Quite the opposite." There was a brief pause and a ruffling of papers on the other end. "We think we've got a bead on who's responsible for what happened in the village and are looking into next steps to take care of it."

Garrett wanted to ask exactly what she'd learned and how the CIA was planning to *take care of it*, but they couldn't discuss classified issues on an unsecure line. "That's good news."

"Once we do what we need to, we'll turn it over to the State Department. They'll work with a host nation to set up a tribunal for the government officials responsible for the massacre."

"What does it mean for our little friend?"

There was a pause on Kim's end. "Means he'll need to come back to testify."

"That really necessary?"

"I'm afraid it is. This has to be public to make it stick. And there needs to be a face for the victims. And right now, it's his."

Given Asadi's fragile state, particularly his awful nightmares, Garrett hated the thought of him having to relive this all over again. He was about to argue when Kim interjected.

"Look, Kohl, I know it's not ideal. But there's some good news in all this. We know he has an older brother, Faraz, and we believe there's a chance he's still alive."

It was all Garrett could do not to shout *Praise Jesus*. The thought that Asadi might still have someone left in the world was too good to be true. He did his best to play it cool, not wanting Kim to know how much the kid was growing on him.

"I can't get into all the details," she added, "but we think the brother was captured during the attack, along with a few others around the same age. We're making every effort to track them down. That means I need you on standby. Ready to get back to Tsavo at a moment's notice if something comes together so we can reunite the brothers. Got it?"

"Absolutely. We'll be waiting."

There was an interruption on Kim's end, and some inaudible whispering until she came back on the line. "Look, I've got to run to a meeting. Hang tight, lay low, and keep your fingers crossed. If things work out, there might be a happy ending to this story after all."

Garrett arrived back home to find the happiest kid in the universe. Grinning from ear to ear Asadi was atop Rascal, the gentlest horse on the Kohl Ranch. Butch was walking alongside them holding a lead rope. After parking his truck by the barn, Garrett walked up to the corral, climbed up on the top rung of the fence, and got comfortable. It warmed his heart to see the boy so at ease.

Butch and Asadi were so preoccupied they hadn't even noticed him watching. The air was still cold and crisp, but the sun beat down hard. Garrett took off his hat to let the rays warm his face. After a couple minutes basking, he called out to the boy.

"Hey, Outlaw!" Asadi's smile grew even wider at the sound of Garrett's voice. "You're making it look too easy!"

Distracted, Asadi lost his balance and grabbed onto the saddle horn. Quickly realizing his breach of etiquette, he let go and looked to Butch. Garrett couldn't hear what his dad told him but saw an affirming nod followed by instructions. Asadi gave the same nod back.

Butch led horse and rider over to where Garrett was sitting. "Did I tell you he was a horseman, or what?"

"You weren't lying." Garrett smiled at Asadi. "He's a natural all right."

"Got Foxy saddled up if you think the boy's ready to venture beyond the corral."

"You tell me, professor. You're the one doing the teaching."

Butch looked at Asadi, conveying his pride. "He's ready for the next step."

"Lead him out of the corral and I'll meet you by the barn."

Hopping from the fence, Garrett walked to the hitching post where Foxy was tethered. She looked less thrilled than Rascal to be out on such a cold morning. He untied her reins from the post, put his boot in the left stirrup, and hefted his right leg over the saddle.

Foxy turned without prompting toward the corral where Rascal was coming through the gate. The two old horses were buddies—had been since birth. Garrett vividly remembered them chasing each other across the ranch in a full lope.

It was a memory he'd carried fondly his whole life. In the army he'd heard the word *freedom* thrown around probably more than any other. But his idea of it rested on that particular image. If there was anything freer than two yearlings kicking and bucking across the wide-open plains, he'd yet to see it.

Garrett rode over to find Asadi looking less confident than he had in the safe confines of the corral. The boy put on a brave face, but he was clearly scared. It was exactly how Garrett had felt the first time he ventured out himself.

Butch handed the lead rope to Garrett, who looped it around his own saddle horn. He made a big show of pulling it tight so Asadi could see he was latched on good. "Like I told you, before, Outlaw. You'll always be safe with me. *Okay?*"

Relief spread across Asadi's face when it was clear he was good and tethered. And Garrett understood. There was something about the open prairie and clear sky before them that was a bit like outer space—nothing to hold you down—as if you might drift forever into the vast emptiness of the frozen white plains.

Asadi was torn. Although he grieved the loss of his family and thought about them nearly every second, there was a part of him that was letting go—just a little. His mother, father, and brother were all dead, but he had never been more alive. Of course, that is exactly what they would have wanted. For him not to be too sad. But it still felt wrong. And it was strange to be so at home in a place so far away from it.

Asadi tried to focus on the task at hand, which was a big one. There was nothing in the world more frightening and thrilling than riding a horse. He was amazed at how much trust he put in this giant beast, but Butch had made sure the two were well-acquainted before the riding even began.

Getting to know Rascal was a leisurely process that involved Asadi holding out his hand for the horse to smell, followed by feeding him a handful of pellets. From there, Asadi groomed Rascal from top to bottom. He imitated Butch's every move, to the point of mimicking the old man's facial expressions as closely as possible, unfurling his brow and letting his lips rise in satisfaction when a task was complete.

Asadi looked left at Garrett, who had pulled the reins, and he did likewise although it wasn't necessary. Rascal followed Foxy's lead and came to a stop.

Garrett smiled, reached down, and untied the lead rope from his saddle horn, then leaned over and unclipped it from Rascal's bridle. "You don't need this anymore. You're good to go."

Asadi's heart raced so fast he could hear it thumping against his chest. He looked all around in panic, at the never-ending white plains that surrounded him, wondering if the horse might bolt at any second. But Rascal stayed planted, then craned his big neck downward and nudged through the snow at a little tuft of grass protruding through the powder. Asadi looked back to Garrett making sure that was okay.

Garrett chuckled at the sight. "Trust me, he ain't hungry. Just bored."

Asadi turned toward the house, barn, and corrals to find them much farther away than he thought. It was amazing how far they had traveled in such a short amount of time.

Garrett turned also and his saddle creaked under his shifting weight. "We better head back, I guess." He nodded at Asadi's reins. "Ready to steer on your own?"

Asadi didn't comprehend the words but understood the meaning. He nodded, making an extra effort to show confidence, even though he had very little.

"Figured as much." Garrett lifted his cowboy hat by the crown, leaned over, and sat it atop Asadi's head, right over the John Deere stocking hat, which made for a perfect fit.

"There you go, Outlaw." Garrett smiled. "Like you were born to wear it."

Garrett spurred Foxy and pulled the reins left, turning her in a circle. Before Asadi could do the same, Rascal was already following. Asadi made the same motions anyhow, figuring he should. By this time, it had become clear there was no danger of his horse running off, which set him at ease and allowed him to really enjoy the ride.

Though still feeling a bit guilty over the fun he was having on the ranch, he wondered if maybe his family was looking down on him from above. And maybe his protection was a gift from his mother, still watching after her little boy from heaven.

To pick up the pace, Garrett leaned forward on Foxy, moved his rein hand toward her mane and squeezed with his calves. He took the briefest of glances to make sure the boy was doing okay but didn't want to make Asadi think he doubted him. Garrett was just about to give Foxy a little squeeze to get her into second gear when the phone vibrated in his coat pocket. He pulled it out and read the text:

Some of them Renegade boys are up here at the bar drunker than Cooter Brown. Want me to see what I can find out? -Ike

Garrett wanted to know everything that was going on but didn't want Ike to put himself in danger. Of course, it was probably a few regular old rig hands just blowing off steam. The only one who'd know if it was Bo Clevenger's gang was Bridger, who'd seen them when they came into his office.

He texted back:

Hold tight. Bridger and I will be there ASAP.

After getting the thumbs-up emoji from Ike, Garrett immediately called Bridger and asked him if he wanted to meet up for a couple of beers out at Crippled Crows. His brother jumped at the chance to knock back a couple like they had in the old days. But it was Garrett's plan to do a little intelligence gathering, find out more about these hotshots and see if he could get

Bridger to spill the beans. Given Ike's tale of the Mexicans up here "doing business," Bridger might be in way over his head.

When Butch came out the back door, he was wearing his old house slippers. His white hair was all tousled, like he'd been napping. "Well, if it ain't the Lone Ranger and Tonto."

Garrett sat deep and pulled back on the reins, stopping Foxy near the porch. "I take it I'm Tonto since he's the one in the hat."

"Yeah, and I expect you're the only Comanche within five hundred miles that ain't parked his ass in front of a slot machine."

Ah hell. Garrett knew better than to linger on that comment lest he get another twice as stupid. "Need to head over to meet Bridger real quick. Mind watching the boy awhile?"

Butch shook his head. "Just tie the horses to the post and I'll get to them later."

Garrett turned in the saddle and looked off into the distance, toward the northeast corner of the ranch where he'd done most of his hunting growing up. "Was thinking about getting up early and doing a little hunting. Saw a decent-size ram in the herd when I was driving in."

The Barbary sheep, more commonly known as aoudad, were introduced to the ranch from North

Africa sometime after World War II and had thrived in the rocky canyons. They were incredibly agile and a challenge to hunt. Most people wouldn't eat them, but Garrett had figured a way to make them tasty using a recipe Sanchez's mom had given him for cooking *cabrito* tacos using garlic, onion, and a certain kind of red *chiles* you could only get in Hatch, New Mexico.

Butch's eyes lit up. Apparently, he was already salivating over the tacos. "I think that's a good idea. If the kid's been through a hard time, as you said, we'll need to keep him busy as possible." He gave a nod. "Hunting usually does the trick for me."

Garrett was amazed by how the old man could follow his dumb comment about the Comanche with one so smart. "Think you can be up before dawn and whip up some pancakes? Boy might need a little incentive to get out of a warm bed."

"My guess is that you might need a little incentivizing too."

Garrett smiled. The old man had nailed that one. And there was one request he'd yet to make since his return home. "A little cowboy coffee won't hurt my enthusiasm."

Butch had a way of making coffee over the fire that Garrett had tried to replicate a thousand times but never gotten right. Cowboy coffee tasted like heaven or hell depending on the cook. And for some reason the old man had just the right touch when it came to the process.

"You got it." Butch tilted his head toward the kitchen. "Saw ya'll coming and whipped up some hot chocolate given the boy seems partial to it."

Since they hadn't died from the twenty-year-old cocoa powder yet, Garrett didn't see any harm. "I'm sure he's worked up a thirst." He turned to Asadi, reached over and plucked his cowboy hat from atop the green stocking cap. "Head on in, Outlaw, there's a cup of hot chocolate with your name on it."

Asadi hopped from the saddle and walked a little bowlegged to the porch. He rubbed his stiff thigh muscles, but it didn't seem to slow his stride. The boy was on a mission and there wasn't a thing in this world that was going to stop him.

19

Garrett walked into Crippled Crows and found Bridger in a dark corner, his back to a wall built from corrugated tin and cedar fence posts. The glowing light from neon beer signs and cigarette smoke created an electric haze that blazed blue like a summer storm. The bar was less depressing packed wall-to-wall—looking less like a hay barn and more like a place you might get stabbed.

"Cherokee Maiden" by Bob Wills was blasting over the speakers and the raucous roar of the Friday night patrons, as their shouting and laughter reverberated off the concrete floor. It reminded Garrett of the cantina scene from *Star Wars*. Replace the aliens with a bunch of cowboys and roughnecks and you'd get an exact replica of the joint.

Garrett nodded at Ike, whose hands were full pouring shots of Crown Royal for a group of camoed-out hunters, then strolled up to Bridger. His brother was sitting under a mounted elk head that was losing its fur. He'd traded his lawyer suit for blue jeans, cowboy boots, and an old denim work coat with a sheepskin lining. There were four empty bottles of Lone Star on the table and a fifth in his hand.

Bridger kicked out a chair that screeched across the floor. "Have a seat and join the party."

Garrett shook his head. "Looks like I'm late."

"This is a rare and treasured occasion for me, Bucky." Bridger hoisted his longneck bottle. "It's not often I get the chance to kick back like I did in the good ol' days."

"Find it hard to believe Cassidy keeps you on a tight leash. Or any leash, for that matter."

Clearly feeling the effects of the fourth beer he'd just downed, Bridger sighed. "She's too good for me, Garrett. She deserves better."

"Humph, I've been saying that for years."

Bridger ignored the jab and signaled the waitress for two more beers. "I mean it. Cassidy and the girls are everything to me. My whole world. I couldn't live without them."

Ah hell. Bridger was getting that look of a weepy drunk, which meant it was time to go. Garrett had turned to find the waitress and cancel the order when he spotted a crew of cowboys and rig hands a few tables over. Bo Clevenger was at the head of the table.

Garrett turned back to Bridger whose contrite look had switched to vengeful. "You got your eye on somebody over there?"

"Oh yeah. I see the two I threw out of my office."

Garrett kept himself from turning around again, just in case they were watching. "How many at the table, you think?"

"Half a dozen or more."

"Think they'll want to start any trouble?"

Bridger shrugged. "Let 'em."

The more Bridger drank, the hotter his blood ran. It had always had that effect on him. And knowing his brother the way he did, Garrett figured at least one or two of those guys were the ones who'd killed Scooter.

"Bridger, I need you to be on your best behavior. I'm not exactly sure what's going on yet and we need to get your ass out of trouble. Not into more. Got it?"

Bridger didn't respond.

The waitress walked up and set down two Lone Stars. "Be anything else, boys?"

Garrett turned to the rail-thin bleach-blond waitress in cutoff jeans and a red tank top. Her shirt was doing its damnedest to wrestle back her aftermarket double D's, but a hard sneeze would've ripped it to confetti.

"We're fine for the moment," Garrett assured her with a nod.

"No, we ain't," Bridger slurred. "How about some shots?"

Her Texas drawl was bigger than the state itself. "Well . . . what'll it be, cowboy?"

Bridger mimicked her thick accent, which she fortunately didn't notice. "Well . . . whatcha got for a special occasion?"

The waitress thrusted out what she considered a hip and planted her hand atop it like a Dallas Cowboys cheerleader. The move looked well-rehearsed. "Depends. What are you celebrating?"

Bridger took a swig of his fresh beer. "A reunion of sorts."

"A reunion?" She was clearly feigning both interest and enthusiasm.

"Yep, my brother's back in town." Bridger paused and added, "And I was never quite sure if we'd ever be sitting here like this again. So, we're celebrating."

Garrett could tell the poor waitress didn't know what to say. She probably had a quip for every bad pickup line known to man, but there was nothing in her arsenal to combat a guilt-stricken brother fessing up to something bad he'd done.

Her voice rose with uncertainty. "Tequila?"

Hoping to end the awkwardness quickly, Garrett answered for Bridger. "Tequila will do just fine, ma'am."

The waitress scampered off, clearly glad to escape. "Okay, Bridger, cut the crap. I know you've gotten yourself into trouble. Now what's going on?"

Bridger took a swig and let out a defeated laugh. "Hell if I know. But it ain't good."

"How do you figure?"

"Exactly that."

"Exactly what?" Garrett looked to the cowboys and truck drivers who were eyeing him then back to Bridger. "Look, I'm trying to help you out here. Either be straight with me or handle this yourself." He rose to leave but Bridger grabbed his arm.

"Whoa, Garrett. Wait a minute."

Garrett eased back down. "You ready to talk for real?"

Bridger was quiet for a moment, but the wheels were clearly turning upstairs. "So . . . some of the deals I did for Mescalero weren't exactly on the up-and-up."

"Okay, spill it. What happened?"

"There's nothing to spill, really. Some of the contracts I was writing up were a little sketchy. And the further I dug, the sketchier they got."

Garrett did a quick glance over his shoulder and lowered his voice. "Sketchy how?"

"Some of the investors I was doing contracts for didn't look legit."

"How'd you know?"

"Years as an oil and gas attorney teach you a few things. And one of those is how to smell a load a crap from a mile away. When I couldn't put real names and real people behind the entities backing the money that was coming into Mescalero prospects, I started to do some courthouse research and made a few phone calls. And I found out that some of the companies investing in Mescalero wells and buying minerals were based out of South Texas. Laredo. Harlingen. Kingsville. At first, I figured they were just investors who'd made money drilling down in the Eagle Ford looking for new opportunities. But the further I dug on the names on these participation agreements, the less I could find."

"What'd Kaiser say about it?"

"Told me not to worry. Said he knew the people involved by reputation and they were so far removed from our day-to-day operations he wasn't concerned."

"You think he knows they're into something illegal?"

Bridger shook off the idea. "No way. Oil money aside, the Kaisers own one of the largest banks in the region. There'd be no point in risking it all for pennies in the bucket. It'd take down everything they've got."

There was no denying that, but Garrett thought back to his conversation with Lacey at the restaurant. Kaiser's business decisions made little financial sense. "Why the hell are they still drilling when no one else can seem to make money at it?"

"Look, Bucky, I'm not his geologist or his CFO. Their drilling operations and portfolio are not my concern. Maybe it's just to keep things running for when things turn around. I don't know. Your guess is as good as mine."

"But it's not just the drilling, Bridger, he's buying up minerals like crazy? Some of the formations they're purchasing won't pay out for decades. Maybe longer."

"These farmers and ranchers are hurting right now with ag commodity prices down. Selling cheap. This energy slump won't last forever, and you know as well as I do that that's when millionaires become billionaires in the oil business. Prices spike and Mescalero and its investors are sitting on a gigantic gold mine. They'll be filthy rich for generations to come."

Garrett leaned back and processed what he was hearing. There was nothing illegal about what they were doing. The question was where in the hell the money was coming from. "Bridger, if you thought this money was coming from somewhere bad, you should've gotten out. It sounds like you could be helping someone launder money."

"*Dammit!* I tried to get out!" Bridger worked to collect himself but looked like he was about to lose it. "That's when Renegade sent the ones who showed up at my office and that whole business with Scooter went down." Bridger reclined in his chair and shook his head. "Now I don't know what to do."

Garrett was about to tell Bridger not to worry, when the busty waitress flounced over with their shots. No salt—no lime—just two full jiggers of yellowish tequila. "Ike says they're on the house." She sat them down but didn't linger.

Before they could take their shots, Ike ambled up to the table and dragged out a chair. "You boys living life to its fullest?"

Garrett laughed. "From anyone else, I'd take that as idle conversation, but from you I expect it's a business proposition of some sort."

Plopping down beside them, Ike cocked an eyebrow. "I'm not one to stand in the way of another man's pursuits. Wherever they might take him." He tilted his head in the direction of three good-looking cowgirls wearing blue jeans so tight they looked painted-on, who were not so subtly staring back.

Although it happened quite often, their smoldering stares made Garrett a little uncomfortable. "*Employees of yours?*"

Ike shook his head. "Nah, just some students from over at Frank Phillips College in Borger." He gave Garrett a nod. "Looking for a real cowboy and a good story to tell, I expect."

Garrett concluded they were probably looking for a place they could drink without being carded, but that was beside the point. Only thing on his mind was getting Bridger out of trouble.

"They'll have to make memories with somebody else. I've got enough on my plate as it is." Garrett gave the customary look around to make sure no one was listening. "You got any intel, I'm all ears."

Ike stared at the oil field crew as he spoke. "Seems Mexicans with the silk suits and pointy-toed boots I told you about are connected to a bandito family south of the border named Garza. Sound familiar?"

In fact, it did. According to DEA assessments, the Garzas were known for weapons smuggling, human trafficking, and the sex trade. But they were pushing hard into drugs as well. Of course, edging out the competition wasn't easy. But what the Garzas lacked in numbers, they made up for in brutality. They'd executed an entire family for allowing a rival drug-trafficking organization to use their apartment for a one-time exchange.

Garrett played dumb. "Means nothing to me." He looked to Bridger who gave a shrug. "Mind if I ask how you came upon this information?"

"A crew of Renegade hotshots were in here earlier whooping, hollering, and raising all sorts of Cane. One of 'em got left behind when he went to take a leak. He bellied up to the bar stumblebum drunk, pissed off, and ready to vent. So, I poured heavy and he spoke freely." Ike leaned forward and spoke a little lower. "Took some coaxing, but the guy told me there's a trigger crew up here helping to run the Garzas' operations. Folks with special operations background. Supposedly, they belonged to some elite unit. Same ones hunted down El Chapo.

"So, we got thugs with skills?"

Ike gave a nod. "Real bad asses to hear this guy tell it. Got all these boys real scared."

To Garrett, the news wasn't all that surprising. Cartels had been recruiting out of military and law enforcement for years. The infamous Los Zetas drug-trafficking organization was founded by former Mexican commandos. He glanced at the Renegade boys, then to Ike.

"Anything else?"

"That pretty much squeezed him dry. And who knows how much is true? What I've learned over the years is that it usually falls somewhere in the middle with drunks."

Garrett took a swig. Embellished or not, that was good intel. This wasn't just some low-level drug-trafficking operation. A cartel was involved, which raised the stakes when it came to Bridger and his family's safety.

"Well, you came through for us, Ike." Garrett turned to Bridger who'd been noticeably silent during the exchange. "Now we at least know what we're up against."

Ike looked over at the bar where it appeared to be getting backed up. "Well, I better get back to work. The community's not going to better itself." He pushed away from the table and stood. "But I'll keep an ear tuned in to anything worth hearing."

Bridger finally spoke. "Much appreciated, Ike."

Ike sauntered back behind the bar.

Garrett turned to his brother. "You sure got quiet all of a sudden. What happened to good-time Charlie?"

Bridger finally got around to downing his shot and gently placed his glass back on the table. "News like that'll make you shut up and think."

"Think about what?"

"Think about how I'm going to get out of this mess. I don't want any trouble with these *Garzas*, whoever the hell they are."

It dawned on Garrett that his brother wasn't used to being this close to real danger. And Ike's story was pretty unnerving, even for him. "Well, Bridger, it sounds like you're involved with them whether you want to be or not."

"What's your take, then?"

"My take is you've gotten yourself in the middle of some kind of money-laundering scheme. And if I was you, I'd be sitting in the Texas Rangers' office in Lubbock first thing Monday morning. You still got the card they left you?"

Bridger gave a nod. "Back in my desk at the office."

"If they were poking around asking questions about Renegade, then it sounds like they've got an active investigation. That's who you want to talk to." Garrett tapped Bridger's phone on the table. "And I'd call Kaiser and let him know what's going on. In fact, you'll probably want to take him down with you. Only way to get out ahead of this thing for you both is to come clean."

"I'll tell Kaiser if I can find him." Bridger shook his head. "The great white hunter doesn't spend much time around here these days. If he's not chasing trophy game in Alaska, he's deep-sea fishing out in the Gulf. He's been a bit of an absentee owner these days."

"Absentee or not, you better track him down. Rangers are going to grill him hard over who these people are and what he knows about them."

Bridger shook his head. "Losing him as a client is gonna hurt like hell."

Garrett was working hard to sound like a civilian, which was hard to do given the dire circumstances. But he needed his brother to understand how deep the crap was about to get. There was a good chance he could lose his law license, maybe even do a little jail time. Still though, it was better than running afoul of the Garzas, who were as vicious as they came.

"Bridger, losing Mescalero business should be the least of your concerns. You need to be thinking like a defense attorney. Start building a case to protect your client, who is *you*."

Staring down at the Lone Star bottle, Bridger peeled at the edge of the label, ripping off a little piece at a time. "I didn't do anything more than draw up the contracts."

Garrett could feel his blood boil. His brother wasn't going to *woe is me* out of this one. "Contracts you knew were garbage, on top of defending the Renegade hotshots doing the trafficking. It sounds a whole hell of a lot like you were fronting for a drug cartel."

DEA would nail a guy like Bridger to the wall and the Rangers would too.

"Bridger, you want out of this, you better go to the feds loaded for bear. Put together all you can on Renegade and these investors. Every contract, tax ID number, phone number, and address. Show the Rangers what you found on these phony companies and how they're tied together. Just tell them what happened, and that you'll do everything you can to help their investigation. It'll show a good faith effort and that you're trying to do what's right. And if you can prove this thing all ties back to Mexico, that'll be the cherry on top."

"*Ah hell*, Garrett." Bridger looked up and shook his head. "You really think I'm involved with some damn *drug* cartel?"

"I don't know, but the Rangers will. All you need to worry about is getting them everything you have. Anything that'll make the case you're one of the good guys."

In truth, Garrett didn't know exactly what to think just yet. But it didn't sound good. He pulled out two twenties, set them on the table, and put his beer bottle on top of the bills. "Let's get out of here. You've got a lot of work to do between now and Monday."

Before Garrett could rise, one of the muscled-up Renegade boys sauntered over all casual and smiled. He stood there a moment rocking a longneck Budweiser bottle between his index and middle fingers.

"Kohl brothers, right?"

Before Garrett could get out, *we're leaving*, Bridger filled the gap with *who's asking*.

The guy was no-necked and square-jawed, with a tuft of black hair like a wide Mohawk plastered to his scalp. His tight undershirt revealed a set of heavy arms covered in a hodgepodge of tribal tattoos and Chinese symbols. Given his cauliflower ears, it was clear he'd done a bit of mixed martial arts, possibly cage fighting at the competitive level.

"I'm Hoyt Anderson. But everybody round here calls me Rocky." He balled his hands into fists as his lips curled into a cocky smile. "Care to guess why?"

Bridger squinted his eyes, looking pensive. "Is it . . . because you . . . look like a squirrel?" He scratched his head, pretending to think on it harder. "No wait. I bet it's because you're best friends with a moose. Is that it?"

The Rocky and Bullwinkle jokes clearly didn't register because he moved right on. "Actually, I'm a *friend* of Bo Clevenger." Rocky gripped his Budweiser harder than needed to flex his bulging bicep. "Said you had an arrangement, and you backed out on the deal."

Bridger took a swig of his Lone Star, set the bottle on the table, and stared down Rocky. "Well, you can deliver a message to your *friend*, that my decision to cut ties with Renegade is final. End of discussion."

Rocky leaned over, planted his palms flat on the table, and turned his massive triceps outward in a show of intimidation. He leaned in close to Bridger. "You don't have any more dogs out at your place, do ya'?"

Garrett knew what was coming but wasn't quick enough to stop it. Bridger had already swiped Rocky's arms from under him, grabbed the back of his neck and slammed his face into the table. The blood had just started spewing from his nose when Bridger shattered a beer bottle over his head.

Garrett pushed Bridger before his brother could get in a whack with his left fist that was already cocked and ready. "Whoa, Bridge! He's had enough!"

The guy slumped to the floor in a heap and Bo and his crew cleared the table, sending nearly every chair flying backward and slamming to the concrete floor. They were on their way over when the music died, the crowd of patrons went silent, and the unmistakable *sheck-shick* of a pump shotgun came from behind the bar.

"Hold it right there, fellas!" Ike walked past the college girls who were no longer having fun and got in between the Kohls and the Renegade boys. "Garrett, you've got two minutes to get your brother out of here. After that, they're right behind you. Understand?"

"On it, boss." Garrett pointed to the door and looked at Bridger. "Git!"

Bridger smiled at the Renegade crew, who were held at bay by Ike's Mossberg pump, then walked the length of the bar and kicked open the door. He disappeared into the darkness of the parking lot laughing like some cowboy version of the Joker.

Garrett didn't say a word, just stepped quickly through the crowd of gawking patrons and made his way outside. He stood in the glow of the fluorescent lights above the Crippled Crows sign until he finally spotted Bridger standing on the hood of Bo's silver F-350.

"What the hell are you doing?"

Bridger's eyebrows rose. "You know when I drink, I like to dance."

"Oh no you don't." Garrett moved to Bridger like he was easing up on a wild animal. "Get your ass down from there. Right now."

"Too late, Garrett. You know I gotta do it."

Garrett turned back to the entrance, knowing their two minutes was half over. And once it was, a half a dozen pissed-off sons of bitches would be flooding out the door.

"Come on, Bridger! We've gotta go! Now!"

Bridger wagged his index finger. "Not before the Texas two-step."

"*Ah . . . hell.*" Garrett turned to the door and back. "Well, go on ahead then if you're gonna do it."

Not really waiting for permission, Bridger broke into a drunken jig atop the truck hood that erupted into a clatter of *thunks, clanks,* and *clunks* of cowboy boots on aluminum. It wasn't much of a two-step, rather something akin to the Charleston that morphed into Riverdance.

Garrett looked back at the entrance knowing they were out of time. "Finish up, moron!"

Bridger bowed to Garrett in a way that was surprisingly graceful, then gave a one-legged donkey kick to the windshield, spiderwebbing the safety glass from top to bottom. He then leapt from the crumpled hood looking satisfied.

No sooner had he landed than the Renegade boys were out the door and running over with Bo leading the pack. Garrett grabbed Bridger by the collar and yanked. "Come with me! You *damn sure* ain't driving!"

Garrett dragged him to his truck, flung the door open, and shoved Bridger inside. His brother was laughing like an idiot, which pissed him off further. "You're gonna get us killed!"

Bridger laughed harder. "Oh, quit being such a little bitch."

Garrett cranked the GMC, threw it in drive, and mashed the accelerator right as the first of the Renegade crew arrived and was pounding his fist on the window. He didn't even try to turn the truck around—just rolled through the culvert and laid on the gas until he could no longer hear the shouting voices.

Bridger was leaning against the passenger door, out of breath, trying to stifle his laughter. "See what you've been missing all these years! Now, that's what I call *fun!*"

"Fun," Garrett huffed. "We'll see how fun it is after they figure out which truck is yours."

Bridger's cackling slowly died off over the next few seconds and he didn't say a whole lot on the way back home. By the time they got there, he was snoring and snorting as loud as Butch in his recliner. The party man had partied himself out and it wasn't even seven o'clock.

20

After dumping Bridger at his office to sleep it off, Garrett made a swing through Canadian to see Lacey. If Renegade was using hotshots to transport drugs on legitimate runs across state lines, there would be a paper trail documenting which drivers made the haul, where they were headed, and who received the shipment in the end.

In the world of criminal investigations, this was about as close to a "silver platter" as it got. Bridger coming to the Texas Rangers with information that could take dope off the streets and put traffickers behind bars would go a long way to getting him out of a major sling.

First though, they needed hard evidence, which meant access to Renegade logbooks and manifests connecting it to the rest of the distribution chain. For that,

Garrett would need someone like Lacey. Could he ask her? Getting her on board would take some finessing.

Of course, there was also the chance she was involved in Renegade's schemes. But his gut told him she was clean. And more important, he was desperate. He'd taken chances on wilder cards than Lacey Capshaw.

He pulled his truck up to her bungalow home and parked out front. Thankfully, when Lacey opened the door, she greeted him with a smile. "Well, look what the cat dragged in! To what do I owe this surprise?"

Opting not to reveal he was there to make her part of a federal law enforcement case involving a violent drug cartel, Garrett played it a little more casual. "I was just driving through town and thought I'd pay you a neighborly visit."

Lacey chuckled, but the furrow in her brow told him she didn't buy his story. "Well, we're not exactly neighbors, but that's all right. Come on in." Taking him in from tail to withers, she fanned her nose. "What the hell happened to you?"

Garrett looked down at his blood-spattered blue jeans from the earlier fight, feigned shock. "Oh yeah. Sorry about that. Met Bridger out at Crippled Crows."

"Crippled Crows, huh?" Lacey gave him another onceover. "Well, I'd ask what happened to you, but the mere fact you made it out of that place alive is all I need to know."

Garrett nodded but didn't elaborate beyond a *yep.*

With a come on in gesture, she turned and walked through the living room. "Well, no reason to halt a night of redneck debauchery on my account. As long as you're wrecking your health, how about a whiskey?"

Garrett took off his cowboy hat and hung it on a coatrack. Lacey walked into the kitchen and pulled out two glasses and a bottle of Still Austin Bourbon. She poured two over ice, then came back and handed him one.

In that brief moment she took her sip, Garrett caught a quick glance of Lacey in full. Her chestnut hair was down over her shoulders and she wore a black denim shirtdress with tights and no shoes. She'd always been stylish, having a knack for combining a high-fashion look with a down-home feel. As usual, her ample curves were the perfect accessories.

Garrett took a sip before she noticed he was staring and glanced around the living room. "Nice place you got."

That was no lie. The Capshaws always had good taste, especially back when they had money. Their multimillion-dollar home just south of Canadian had been a showplace. Garrett wondered what it was like to go from having everything one moment to nothing the next.

Seeing a few kids' toys in the corner he decided to change the subject, lest he bring up an uncomfortable topic like he'd done at breakfast. "Little ones around?" He'd seen neither hide nor hair of them since he arrived. And other than some Lyle Lovett playing in the background, the place was dead quiet.

"No, their dad was supposed to get them next weekend, but he's going out of town. So, he asked if I could swap. Picked them up a little while ago." She smiled. "It's just me."

Garrett cleared his throat. "That's good. Gives us a chance to talk."

Suddenly he couldn't think of a thing to say. Fortunately, Lacey filled the dead air.

"Are you . . . by chance into art at all?"

"Hate it," Garrett said, knee-jerk, before remembering she was an artist. "I mean . . . I don't hate it. Just never had much use for it, I guess."

She looked at him puzzled. "Well, there's not much use for it other than covering bare walls. But some people find that of value."

His skin burned, and he cursed himself for the stupid answer. "Well, I'm willing to give it a chance. It's just that I've never quite understood how a square or a triangle or a blob of paint is a work of art. You know what I mean?"

Lacey laughed, which eased the tension. "Yeah, I know what you mean." She grabbed his hand and led him over to the sofa where they sat. After riffling through a pile of books on her coffee table, she pulled out one that featured the artwork of Charles Marion Russell. "I think this might change your mind."

She sat the book on her lap and scooted close until their knees touched. Then she flipped slowly through the pages of scenes with bronc-busting cowboys, cavalry soldiers, and bear hunters on the frontier.

About halfway through, Garrett focused in on a painting titled *When the Plains Were His*. It displayed a Native American man riding across the frozen prairie. Garrett figured it was somewhere on the Badlands of North Dakota, but it didn't say that anywhere in the caption. He put his hand on the page to keep her from turning it.

"Whoa, wait. Stop here."

Lacey eased the book into his lap and leaned in. "Why this one?"

Garrett stared at it awhile longer before answering. "The way he's sitting in the saddle."

"What about it?"

"Look at him compared to the others." Garrett pointed to the one who looked like the chief. "See how he sits tall while the rest hunker down in the cold."

"Why do you think Russell painted him like that?"

Garrett studied the painting a few seconds longer, finally comfortable with the silence between them. "Because they're all watching. If he bends, they will too. And he's not going to let that happen. This is a man you'd follow to the end. And they probably did."

Lacey studied the image for a good half minute before adding, "I like his face."

"That's the best part." It was another knee-jerk response, but Garrett felt it deeply.

Lacey was clearly enthralled with his reaction. "What does it do for you?"

Garrett remembered his dad's comment from earlier, about how *he* was probably the only Comanche around who wasn't parked in front of a slot machine somewhere. That certainly wasn't true by a long shot, but it characterized more than he wished. And it made him sad, especially knowing how his ancestors lived not that long ago. He'd often daydreamed about going back in time and riding the plains with them.

"Look at his eyes." Garrett traced his finger over them. "There's as much pain as dignity. It's almost like he can see what's beyond the horizon and he knows what's coming isn't good. But he'll keep all that to himself to protect his people. He'll worry so they don't have to."

She turned to him and smiled. "You got all of that from his eyes?"

"Sure." Garrett smiled back. "That and life experience, I guess."

He'd been so occupied with the painting he hadn't realized their faces were just inches apart. He should've been nervous, but he felt as comfortable in her gaze as he had about anything in a very long time. With a quick turn of the head, he scanned the walls to see if any of hers were hanging, but it was mostly family photos. "How about your paintings? Got any I can see?"

Lacey picked up an iPad from the end table and pulled up her web site. She clicked from the home page to the gallery and handed over the tablet. And to Garrett's horror, everything she painted was squares, triangles, and blobs. But before he could even apologize, she was laughing so hard there were tears in her eyes.

After insulting her life's ambition, Garrett figured he couldn't do much else but laugh. He would've felt worse had he not remembered what his mother once told him about *finding your soul mate*. She'd said you'll know you've met her when you laugh till you cry.

By anybody else's standards the evening was a disaster. By his mother's measure he was knocking it out of the park. And since he'd always cared more about what she thought than anyone else, he'd count it as a win. To his recollection, things had never gone so well.

Garrett had just got his laughing under control when Lacey had what looked to be a genuine eureka moment.

"Got an idea." She grabbed her cell phone from the coffee table and took it into her bedroom. After a couple of minutes, she came back with a mischievous smile. "The Citadelle."

The first thing that came to Garrett's mind was the military college in South Carolina. He'd known an officer or two back in the army who were Citadel grads but that was the extent of his knowledge on the subject. "What about it?"

"Remember?" Lacey laughed. "At lunch today, you said you'd never been there."

It took a second but then it all came rushing back. The Citadelle she was referring to was an old Baptist church—turned mansion home—turned world-class art museum.

"A friend of mine runs it, so she's going to open it up for us. We'll have the whole place to ourselves."

When Garrett had told Lacey he'd never been to the Citadelle, it was more of a boast that he'd managed to avoid it all these years than a hint that he wanted to go. But he did like the western paintings she'd shown him. He'd even come to the conclusion that if there was more stuff like that, people wouldn't hate art so much.

"Any Russells over there?"

Lacey shook her head. "No. But there are a couple of other things you'll like." She still looked excited. "Trust me. No triangles. And no blobs. I promise."

Garrett found it interesting that she was so keen on convincing him to go. "Then what are we waiting for?"

They strolled over to the museum, which was just a few blocks away. It was on the same street as the Stumblin' Goat Saloon, which would've been a preferential locale in Garrett's opinion. But when they walked up to the massive iron gates in the fading light of dusk something changed his mind. There was a bit of magic to the place he hadn't noticed blasting past it in his pickup at forty miles per hour.

With eager anticipation, Lacey asked, "What do you think, so far?"

"Impressive," Garrett said and meant it.

Between the redbrick church with its white pillars and the cold soft breeze, the place radiated tranquility in a way Garrett didn't know you could find beyond the great outdoors.

They walked inside to find a place frozen in time. Exactly what time that was Garrett wasn't sure, but it took him back to his childhood. The museum wasn't at all what he expected. There was a warmth to it that felt like a real home.

They stepped into a smaller area and Lacey turned to Garrett. "This is what I wanted to show you." She twirled around and smiled. "They call it 'the cowboy room.'"

Immediately, Garrett knew why. There were several paintings of western subjects that piqued his interest, but the one that impressed him the most was by a Chinese artist named Xiang Zhang. It captured the Oklahoma land rush of 1889, and featured dozens of pioneers on horseback and wagons racing to stake their claim.

The image encapsulated everything Garrett loved about the American West. It was wild, woolly, and wonderful—a place where grit mattered more than wealth or pedigree. He didn't know you could make something come so alive with just a little paint on a piece of canvas.

He turned to Lacey, who was smiling. "All right, all right, I'm impressed."

She didn't have to speak. It was obvious she was thinking—*told you so.*

Without a word, Lacey walked out of the room and Garrett followed. She led him to the old church sanctuary, and it was immediately clear what she was taking him to see. In fact, he knew exactly what it was before he got up close.

"*The Rough Rider*," Garrett said to himself.

The bronze sculpture depicting a rifle-toting cavalryman was about as cool as it gets. For obvious reasons, the original Rough Riders, Teddy Roosevelt's 1st Volunteer Cavalry Regiment made up of cowboys, college athletes, Texas Rangers, and Native Americans, held a special place in his heart.

Lacey beamed. "Figured this one would be your favorite. What do you think?"

He sauntered up to her and smiled. "I think I'm impressed."

"Maybe I am too."

Garrett didn't know exactly what that meant but he was pretty sure it was a compliment. He was still so wrapped up in the night's events he'd almost forgotten his mission. So, before this went any further, he figured he'd better reveal his ulterior motives. And hope she didn't hate him after that.

21

G arrett awoke the next morning to the red glow of the old digital alarm clock he'd had since high school. It read 4:47. Apparently, Butch had been kind and let them sleep in. Asadi was in the twin bed against the other wall covered under an avalanche of sheets and his thick camo comforter, snoring somewhere beneath like a hibernating grizzly.

Forcing himself out of bed, Garrett kicked off his covers and set two feet on the cold wood floor. He was having second thoughts about the early morning hunt until the aroma of coffee, bacon, and pancakes wafted inside the bedroom. He threw on his blue jeans and a thermal undershirt and wandered to the kitchen.

Butch turned from the stove holding a cast-iron skillet with enough sizzling bacon to feed four counties. "Coffee's on the fire. Should be about ready."

Too sleepy to talk, Garrett grabbed a red-and-white Perryton Rangers mug from the counter, walked over to the fire, and pulled the pot off the grate. After pouring a steaming cup, he leaned in close to the flames to warm up. A slight throb from a couple more glasses of the whiskey than he needed had resulted in a gnawing pain in his forehead.

Butch set breakfast on the table, walked over holding his old Texas Tech Red Raiders coffee cup with the chipped rim, and filled it full. "Well, you must've been having a good time. Don't remember you ever staying out that late before a hunt."

Garrett smiled wide. Not only had things gone extremely well with Lacey, he'd managed to convince her to pull a few files from the Renegade office that would no doubt help his brother's case. And managed to pull it off without raising too much suspicion. He didn't want to worry her unnecessarily.

"Yeah, partying before a hunt was always Bridger's MO." There were times when his brother would show up just minutes before sunrise, with bloodshot eyes and reeking of beer and cigarettes or perfume. Sometimes all three. "He never missed one though, did he?"

Butch laughed also. "Not to my recollection."

"Asadi is still in there sleeping like the dead. You wore him out again, huh?"

"He wore himself out." Butch nodded toward Garrett's old recurve bow and quiver on the couch. "Set up some hay bales last night and let him at it. Bet he shot a thousand times."

"How'd he do?"

Butch took a sip of his coffee and smiled. "Took a while but he got the hang of it. Kid was about to turn blue he was so damn cold, but I couldn't get him to quit. Once he sinks his teeth into something, he don't let go easy." He turned to Garrett. "Like someone else I know."

Garrett could tell his dad was proud. "Asadi's got the bug now, huh?"

"Hunting's in his blood, all right. Just like horses." Butch pointed at the stove where he had milk boiling and the cocoa powder sitting out. "But that's his kryptonite there."

"If that's his, I guess this is mine." Garrett hefted his mug of cowboy coffee, took a burning-hot sip, and savored the rich flavor on his tongue before swallowing.

Butch looked a little uncomfortable. "Well . . . there's plenty more where that came from if you ever decide to come back for good."

Garrett looked around the room. "Come back and do what?"

Butch stared at the television, which wasn't even turned on and dragged out a tortured answer. "Might could use a hand around here for starters."

It was a big step for Butch to admit he needed help. It was the old man's version of an olive branch. Putting the past behind and telling his son that he wanted him back in his life.

"Well, it's mighty tempting, Daddy, but then we'd both be broke off our asses."

Butch chuckled and said, "Ain't that the truth of it."

No sooner had he said it than a wild-haired Asadi came stumbling into the living room rubbing sleep from his puffy eyes. He was wearing one of Garrett's old maroon West Texas A&M Buffaloes T-shirts. It was so large, it covered everything but his skinny brown legs.

"Good morning, sunshine," Butch called out, more cheerful than even Garrett was ready for at five AM. "Ready to earn your feathers?"

Asadi walked over to the couch, picked up his bow, and yawned. He faltered when his toe caught the edge of the rug on the way over to the kitchen but caught himself before falling.

Garrett turned to his dad. "Well, that's the look of a cold killer if I ever saw one."

From there, they all took a seat at the table and ate like it was their job. By the time they'd finished, Garrett was stuffed to the point of needing a nap. But by his second cup of hot cocoa, Asadi was pushing him out the door. They went to the barn, saddled up, and by the time the horses were ready, Garrett figured he was probably even more excited than the boy.

Asadi felt like he had barely slept. He nervously tossed and turned for at least a couple of hours before falling asleep. And once he finally went down it seemed like it was only moments later that Butch's pots and pans were clanging in the kitchen. But aside from the cold, the early morning start did not bother him. In fact, he was eager for the hunt—even more so for the ride.

As he sat atop Rascal gazing out at the giant orange fireball rising above the snowy plains, he tried to remember all his hunting instructions from the day before. Target practice with the bow and arrow had gotten off to a rough start. His first shots went wild, landing far beyond the hay bales and out in the pasture. Butch pretended not to mind fetching them, but

Asadi had heard him grumbling as he dug the arrows out of the snow.

Eventually, Asadi got a feel for it and was able to hit the target at thirty yards. But it was one thing to hit a hay bale, and quite another to shoot an animal on the move. The mere thought of it made him nervous all over again. The last thing he wanted to do was disappoint Garrett by missing an easy shot.

It also crossed his mind that his first hunt should have been back home with his father. Of course, neither his dad nor his brother hunted, so it was unlikely to have happened anyway. But the deep joy he felt made it seem like he was doing something wrong— like he was cheating his real family out of a special moment.

Asadi wondered if he would feel this way forever. But even worse, he wondered if the day would come when he did not think about it at all.

Garrett spoke to Asadi just like he would anyone else. The language barrier made giving instructions a little more difficult, but the boy got the hang of whatever he and Butch taught him rather quickly. The old man had said *if a horse can learn English, then why can't an Afghan boy.* It was a weird sort of logic, but it actually made sense.

It was clear to Garrett that Asadi was much brighter than others his age. And the better he got to know him, the more evident that became. According to Butch, the kid had even taken to the bow quicker than he and Bridger ever did. Garrett couldn't verify that with any degree of certainty but didn't see the point in arguing. Asadi was happy and that was all that mattered.

At any rate, Garrett wanted Asadi to learn the basics. The boy was unlikely to make a kill with his recurve bow, but that wasn't the point. The point was learning the craft. And the craft had less to do with the kill and more to do with the hunt.

Spotting a set of animal tracks in the snow, they dismounted and knelt beside them. Garrett whispered *aoudad* and then added the Dari word for goat, the closest thing he could come up with to describe what they were hunting.

Asadi repeated the word and butted his head against his hand like a ram.

"That's right." Garrett made similar tracks to the sheep but with a slight variation. "*Deer.*" He pointed to the leaping deer emblem on Asadi's John Deere stocking hat.

Asadi touched the emblem and repeated the word *dare*, then raised both hands to his head and spread his fingers out like antlers.

Garrett was convinced the boy knew what they were hunting, so they remounted and rode for a good twenty minutes following the sheep tracks across the snowy plains until they came to a crag in the earth that ran about fifty or sixty feet deep. The rocky terrain and steep slopes gave the sheep good protection from most predators. But unfortunately for them, a lifetime of hunting both animal and human in the mountains had made Garrett equally at home.

He grabbed the compound bow from his scabbard and dismounted slow and quiet. Asadi did likewise, seeming to understand the need for silence. Garrett hobbled the horses since there was nothing to tie them to and knelt in the snow. He plucked a little strand of dried grass, let the wind carry it north to south, and sniffed at the air like an animal. After drawing a crude illustration of the canyon in the snow with his finger, he poked several holes at the end. He made two dots to represent himself and Asadi, then drew a line running through the canyon.

Asadi yanked a piece of grass, moved it to the top of the replica, and let the wind carry it down to where they would be sneaking in from behind. He looked up at Garrett and sniffed. Damned if the boy hadn't figured out that they were trying to stay downwind.

With nothing left to do but get moving, Garrett led Asadi down into the draw, moving quickly but quietly. Normally he'd have trod a bit slower, but with the wind blowing hard in their direction, he wasn't too worried about spooking the wild game on the approach.

After walking a good fifteen minutes they came upon a set of tracks in the snow. Garrett knelt, pointed to them and asked in a quiet voice, *"Aoudad?"*

Asadi shook his head and pointed to the John Deere logo on his stocking hat. *"Dare."*

Boy's a natural. Garrett rose and kept on the trail, amazed at how quickly Asadi was catching on. They hadn't hiked another five minutes when they came upon the spike buck who'd made the tracks, nibbling on a tuft of grass in a little grove of cottonwood trees. The aoudad sheep were about forty yards behind him.

Garrett crouched and eased right, putting a tree between him and the spike to break up his silhouette. He turned to Asadi, whose eyes were saucers. Although the spike was a cool find, it was out of season. They'd have to stick to the sheep. The problem was that the deer was highly attuned to the dangers of its surroundings. One wrong move by either him or Asadi would send the spike running and spook the sheep, rendering the whole morning's stalking efforts a complete waste of time.

Garrett squatted, easing to his stomach, and Asadi did the same right beside him. It was cold lying in the snow, but it was their only option. Being downwind was an advantage, but with the wind circling in the canyon there was a good chance the spike would get a whiff of their scent and bolt, sending the sheep on a dead run out of there.

He turned to Asadi to find the boy shivering, his chin turning red where it rested in the snow. His eyes were steadfast though, watching the buck with a hunter's gaze, studying its every move. Even his breathing was controlled and silent—just like Butch had taught him.

A few seconds passed and the spike lifted his head and scampered away on his own. Garrett rose slowly to his feet, took an arrow from his quiver and nocked it. Asadi did exactly the same. Garrett was just about to take his first careful step when he spied the mountain lion creeping down the trail about thirty yards to the northeast.

It was highly unusual to see a cougar out roaming this long after dawn, much less at all. The animal was probably taking a risk because he was hungry. Predators rarely broke their hunting habits, but a few missed meals might've made him desperate. Likelier than not, the big cat would turn and run at the sight of them, but animal instincts were unpredictable. A bony kid like Asadi might look less like a threat and more like a snack.

Garrett looked to Asadi whose eyes were even wider than before, then turned back to find the cat crouched in a pouncing position, ears pinned back, and teeth bared. Then in a lightning flash the cougar sprinted toward them and leapt.

To Asadi the attack felt no more real than a dream. One moment a deer—the next a goat—the last a lion. Images like these had haunted him since the massacre. His mind switched between the faces of his family and the murderers so quickly at times they changed into one.

But this was no dream, it was real and there'd be no running like he had back in Nasrin.

Having already drawn the bow, he aimed at the charging beast with shaking hands and let the arrow fly. He would have kept his eyes open like Butch taught, but it was simply impossible. They clamped shut like a trap and he could not force them open until he heard Garrett's triumphant voice. "You did it, Outlaw! You did it!"

Garrett didn't know where Asadi's arrow had landed, only that it was nowhere near the cougar. Still though, the vibrating *thunk* of his released bowstring was enough to spook the cat, which broke left only feet before them and scampered off into the mesquite.

Although the boy hadn't technically made his first kill, it was close enough. Asadi was a good tracker, a great stalker, and had managed not to piss his pants at the sight of an attacking mountain lion. It was a job well done by any hunter's standards.

None of it would make up for the loss of his home, family, or innocence. But victory over death counted for something. And maybe it would give him confidence in a world out of control. Only one thing was for sure—the kid needed a win and today he got one.

22

Lacey pulled the glass door to the Renegade office shut, snapped the dead bolt from inside, and killed the lights. She made a brisk but thorough sweep of the building only to find a couple of mechanics cleaning up in the shop around back. Everyone else had cleared out after lunch.

Content that it was safe to snoop, Lacey moved to the storage room where she perused row after row of file cabinets, focusing on the mission at hand, which was *borrowing* the Renegade documents Garrett had requested the night before. And Saturday afternoon was the perfect time to do it. On a weekday, the place bustled with rig hands, pumpers, roustabouts, and truckers. But the weekends were sparse, especially now in the late afternoon.

It didn't take long to find the cabinet containing the drivers' logs and the hotshot files she was looking for, but to her surprise it was locked. It was the *only one* that was locked.

If the key wasn't with Bo Clevenger, then it had to be in his office. Bolting from the file room, Lacey moved down the dark hallway and crept into his small work area. But for his messy desk and a whitetail buck head mount on the wall behind it, the room was empty. Easing around his desk, Lacey opened the top drawer and riffled through the junk.

No cleaner inside than on top, she found little more than an assortment of pens, pencils, Post-it notes, and half-empty snuff cans. Lacey had nearly given up when she saw the key. She'd just reached inside when the light clicked on and a low growling voice followed.

"What are you doing?"

It was hard to imagine that a man that big could move that quietly. But Bo had slipped in like a phantom. For some reason, the truth seemed less suspicious than a made-up excuse.

"*Uh* . . . just looking for a key."

Bo eased into the door frame, blocking her in, his enormous body filling all but a few square inches. "What key?"

"File key." She pointed to the wall where the cabinets were on the other side.

Bo didn't look convinced. "Why are you in the dark?"

Lacey gave him the *how stupid of me* eye roll. "Just in a hurry." She giggled the best ditsy girl giggle a non-blonde could muster. "You know. Been a helluva day. Trying to get home and enjoy the weekend."

Bo moved inside and stared her down. "What files you after?"

"Drivers' logs."

His face warped into either confusion or anger. Maybe both. "What for?"

With a shrug and a smile, Lacey dug herself a deeper hole. "Not really sure. Corporate office in San Antonio called me at home asking about government mileage rates. Something to do with payroll reimbursements." She rolled her eyes again. "Said tax laws changed and wanted to make sure everything was how it should be."

There was a disbelieving edge to his voice. "How *should* it be?"

Her pulse now racing, her hands began to tremble. "I beg your pardon?"

"How—should—it—be?"

Lacey didn't know a lot about mileage rates other than that drivers obsessed over them. "I don't know."

She faked another girlish giggle, struggling to conjure up an answer that wouldn't draw more questions. "It has . . . something to do with the IRS, I think."

Wrong move.

Any disbelief on Bo's face dissipated and anger took hold of him as he moved toward her. "What the hell does the IRS want with *our* records?"

He stepped closer, and Lacey shoved the drawer closed as she came around the desk. When Bo didn't move, she tried to ease past him, but he grabbed her arm and yanked her close. Jamming his thumb into Lacey's wrist, he forced her hand open. The key flew out and pinged on the floor.

At nearly the same moment, the air compressor motor in the shop ceased to knock and the machine gave off a shrill whistle of air. If someone was out there, maybe they could hear her scream. Maybe they could help. She was about to cry out when Bo released her.

"Just go on home now and enjoy your weekend." Bo's scowl gave way to a knowing smile. "And I'll make sure folks at headquarters know *exactly* what you were looking for."

23

Asadi had just turned on SpongeBob SquarePants and gotten settled on the couch when Garrett slipped out the front door. He hadn't said much to either Butch or to him, but it felt like something was wrong. It was a look on Garrett's face that Asadi had come to recognize. It was the same look he had the night they arrived.

Asadi had started to move over to the window when Butch came clomping over in his boots. It could mean only one thing. The day's chores weren't over. Asadi would have normally been ecstatic but after the early morning hunt and nearly being eaten by a lion he was exhausted.

Butch tossed over the green hat and his blue-and-silver football coat. "Ain't quitting time yet, Daniel

Boone. Your old buddy Mrs. Shanessy just called. Said she was riding the top of the caprock and seen one of our windmills ain't working."

The name *Shanessy* rang a bell. It was what Butch had called the fiery little woman with the big gun in her truck. Asadi had only understood the curse words, but there was something about her that radiated a mother's warmth.

Butch handed Asadi his bow and quiver. "Keep this handy, son. Need you to watch my back. Never know if a condor might swoop down and try to carry me off in its talons."

Asadi only understood the word *wim-meal,* but that was enough to get him moving. The giant iron structures that belched water from beneath the ground fascinated him to no end. He hopped from the sofa, massaged his stiff thighs, then followed Butch out the door.

After the usual process of letting the truck warm up, Butch put it in drive and maneuvered down a snow-covered road Asadi had never seen. A few minutes later, the big wheel on the structure was jerking so hard in the wind it looked as if it might rip right off and fly away.

Butch jumped outside, opened up a metal box, and took out a few tools he'd stuffed in his pockets. From there, he hopped onto the giant structure and climbed it like a monkey.

"Be back shortly." Butch turned to Asadi, a few rungs up. "Hopefully with good news." He had just made it to the top when an airplane roared overhead.

Asadi watched it clear the caprock by no more than a hundred feet. Shortly after, the plane dipped its left wing, passing a set of metal tanks, and dropped something that looked like a suitcase from the window. In the far distance, a truck made its way across the rim of the escarpment to where the object had fallen.

Asadi looked up to find Butch was already near the bottom of the structure. The old man jumped from the last rung and ran toward the truck. "Get in! Let's see what these fools are up to."

They both hopped in the pickup, Butch started the engine, and threw it into gear. They cut a trail across the pasture to a narrow pathway dug into the caprock. As the truck began the sharp climb upward, it leapt and caught in herky-jerky fits. With its wheels slipping on the steep incline, loose gravel shot into the wheel well with a loud series of pings and thuds. But Butch jammed the accelerator harder and the tires gained traction, sending them onward at a speed too fast for their narrow corridor.

White-knuckled and tense, he turned only slightly. "Hold on to your hat, pardner."

Asadi gripped the armrest below the door handle as his stomach did somersaults. He held on even tighter as the nose of the truck went so high, he could see only the sky above. Half a minute later, it leveled off and they were atop the mesa.

Butch pointed to the other vehicle, less than half a mile away. "We've gotta move. Seems our friends are in a big hurry."

He punched the accelerator and a spray of mud and snow kicked up around the truck as it fishtailed into a right turn. They climbed onto a slight hump under the snow that made a winding path to a place with a couple of small buildings and three large silver tanks. A barbed wire fence surrounded it and there was a big sign with a hatchet on the front.

Butch must have spotted the package also because he popped his knee with his palm and yelled, "Jackpot!"

He veered the truck right and made a beeline toward the fence post, where the package had skidded in the snow before coming to a stop against a post. It was clear whoever'd dropped it from the plane had been trying to make it onto the caliche pad but had come up short.

Butch drove to the fence, grabbed it, and dusted the snow off. It was a plain cardboard box about the size of a couch cushion. He placed it on the bench seat between them, pointed to the label, and snarled. "Property of Renegade, *my ass.*"

He turned the truck around and drove back to the main road, following his own tracks to the caprock cutaway road. They had nearly made it when the vehicle headed their way pulled out front and cut off their exit.

Two men jumped out of the cab and approached Butch's truck in a huff. One man was big and beefy, wearing a scraggly bush of red facial hair that hung below his chin like the beard of a goat. His skin had a red tint, wind-beaten and leathery. The other straggling behind was tall and bony, eyes noticeably bloodshot against his pale skin. He looked around anxiously, moving herky-jerky as a lizard. It was clear he expected trouble.

Both wore the same logo on their gray coats, with the odd-looking hatchet. It was the same as the one on the package and the sign on the fence.

Butch rolled the window down. "Can I help you with something?"

The big one spoke in a mumbling voice, his mouth unseen under the thick matted red beard. "I don't know. Can you?"

Butch looked rattled. "You know you're on private property?"

"Actually, that over there is a *Mescalero* well." The hulking man made a show of surveying the area. "And this right here is an oil field road built and paid for by the company. Per the terms of your *surface lease* with the company," he looked to the thin man, as if he'd said something impressive, "we've got more a right to be here than you do. You see, we've got an *easement* through your property." He stressed the word *eeehzmett*.

Butch spat out a stream of tobacco juice from his window. "I know exactly what's in my surface use agreement, given my son is the one drafted it and I'm the one signed it." He pointed to their vehicle. "And since you know the law so well, tell me what gives you the right to block my path."

Goat's smile broke loose from behind his ugly red beard. "This here road is for oil field operations, which supersede ranch operations. Didn't you know that, old-timer?"

Butch nodded. "And what operations would those be, *junior?*"

"We're checking wells." Lizard bobbed his head in the direction of the large tanks. "You give us that package you took, and we'll be on our way."

Asadi watched as Butch slid his right hand under a pair of brown coveralls lying on the bench seat between them. He rubbed his chin with his left as he spoke.

"You boys are out checking wells, huh? Well, I happen to know the pumper, and his name is Reilly Hobbs. But I can't say I've ever seen the likes of you two. *Ever.*"

As Butch started to drive away, Goat grabbed the handle and yanked the door open. He lunged inside but not before Butch jerked a silver pistol from under the pair of folded coveralls. Asadi heard the *click-click* as the big barrel stopped short of the bearded man's bulbous nose.

As quickly as Goat had made his move, he fell backward and skidded onto his butt in the snow. He scrambled to his feet, red-faced, and jabbed his finger at Butch. "You just made a big mistake, mister! We'll call the law on your old ass! Get a restraining order."

Butch let the hammer down on the gun but didn't lower his aim. "Now, you ain't calling the law and we both know why." With the gun still pointed at Goat, he grabbed the door and shut it. After putting the truck in drive, he eased around the vehicle blocking their way.

Butch turned to Asadi and smiled. "You handled yourself pretty well there, sonny. Between you, me, and our friend Mr. Colt here, I believe we can handle about any trouble comes our way."

24

When Garrett walked into the Stumblin' Goat, he passed the bar and maneuvered around a few empty tables to where Lacey sat alone at the far side of the room. The worry on her face matched the fear in her voice that he'd heard in their phone call. She'd insisted on meeting somewhere public and he couldn't blame her. Her run-in with Bo would've shaken anyone.

Garrett couldn't get out his apology fast enough. "I'm so sorry, Lacey. I shouldn't have gotten you mixed up in all this."

"*Gotten* me mixed up?" She let out a little laugh as he took a seat. "I work for Renegade, Garrett. Kind of mixed up in it already, don't you think?"

"Yeah, but not to this extent."

Lacey pushed one of the two frosty mugs over to him. "Shiner Bock." His surprise must've registered. "Last night, you said it was your favorite."

"I've been looking forward to one of these back at this place for long as I can remember." Garrett smiled as he took the ice-cold beer in hand. "Just imagined the circumstances being a bit different."

Every soldier has *the meal,* and for Garrett it was a Chile Cheese Billy with an order of fried jalapeños. Lacey Capshaw just happened to be the perfect side order to the perfect side order. But given her desperate phone call it was clear all that would have to wait.

Lacey looked a little guilty. "Sorry about what happened."

"Sorry? What on earth do you have to be sorry about?"

"I wasn't able to get what you were looking for."

He couldn't believe what he was hearing. After putting herself in jeopardy, Lacey was worried she'd let *him* down. "I never should've asked you to do that in the first place."

"No, I'm glad you did. Because now I know something bad is going on over there." She looked around and lowered her voice. "The way Bo was acting. It was like he knew that I was on to him. Or on to something. The way he was talking. Grabbed me."

"Whoa, wait." Before the Shiner had even reached his lips, Garrett set it back on the table. "You telling me, he *touched* you?"

"Grabbed my wrist and squeezed so hard I dropped the key. There was a noise outside, and he let go. Had someone not been there, I don't know what would've happened."

The idea of Bo making a woman uncomfortable was one thing. He'd probably done that every day of his life. But grabbing Lacey was another.

"Look, Lacey, Bo's day is coming. And you won't have to worry about him. Okay? We're going to see to that real soon."

Garrett was about to tell her Bridger's plans to go to the Rangers when a half dozen Renegade oil field hands walked in the door. The sight didn't spook him as much as it did Lacey, but when the crew made their way through a restaurant of empty tables and sat right beside them, it was clear this wasn't an accident. Bo's show of force and intimidation was just getting started.

Leaning across the table, Garrett spoke in a voice that only she could hear. "Your kids still with their dad?"

The intent of his question was not at all lost on her. She nodded, fighting a show of fear. "Whole weekend. Why?"

"Follow me back to the ranch." Garrett glanced over at the Renegade crew who were staring at them. "I got a feeling this thing won't hold until Monday. And if it doesn't, I don't want you by yourself."

Garrett was sliding back to leave when his phone buzzed on the table. He answered his dad's call and immediately detected a tone of regret. It was a sorrow he hadn't heard since his mother's accident. It was the way that he spoke when she died.

25

G arrett pulled the truck up to the porch, clicked off the headlights, and shut off the engine. At a glance, there were no signs of trouble, and the chimney was belching out smoke like always. So far, so good. Garrett and Lacey walked inside the house to find a scene about as close to a modern-day Norman Rockwell painting as you'll ever find.

The old man and the kid were sitting on the couch in front of the fire watching television and eating Hungry-Man frozen dinners. Asadi was launching popcorn chicken into his mouth while Butch was sawing away at a rubbery Salisbury steak.

As Garrett walked farther into the living room, Asadi unglued himself from the cartoon just long enough to smile and wave. Butch jumped up from the couch and slid past the boy, almost tiptoeing, so as not to interrupt his program. He was clearly surprised to see Lacey but recovered quickly.

"You must be the girl that put that big smile on this one's face." He reached out and shook her hand. "I'm Butch Kohl."

She reciprocated and smiled. "Pleasure to know you, Mr. Kohl."

"*Mister* Kohl died in '87. I'm Butch."

"You got it, Butch," Lacey said with a laugh. "Hard to believe we're just now meeting after all these years."

"Well, I knew your daddy some." Butch cut eyes at Garrett then back to her. "Don't care for oilmen much, but he was one of the good ones. Maybe the *only* one."

Lacey looked pleasantly surprised. "I didn't know you two were acquainted."

"Not well," Butch admitted. "But we'd see each other over at the feed store now and again. Man had a good eye for horses. Something you don't find too often these days."

Garrett cleared his throat. "Lacey, do you mind if I talk to my dad for a second?"

"No. Not at all."

With a quick glance into the living room, Garrett winced when he saw that *Family Guy* was on. Last thing he wanted was for Lacey to peg him as a deadbeat caretaker.

"Hey, Outlaw!" Garrett called. "Want to meet a friend of mine?"

Asadi popped from the couch, his brow furrowed with purpose as he marched to Lacey and thrust out his hand. "*Nice. Meet you.*"

Garrett had seen sloppier performances by guards at the Tomb of the Unknown Soldier. On top of ranching and horsemanship, Butch had apparently been running a charm school.

Clearly impressed, Lacey turned to Garrett and smiled. "My-my, what a gentleman you've got here. Color me impressed."

Butch was quick to chime in. "That was *my* doing." He thumbed over at Garrett. "When this one's not stuffing the boy full of Bandit burritos, I've been teaching him a thing or two."

Her eyebrows rose with approval and Lacey gave Butch a nod. "Nicely done."

It was about that time Lois Griffin's nasally voice carried over her own. Garrett glanced over at the television to find a scene playing out that was barely appropriate for himself, much less a ten-year-old. Any admiration gained from Lacey was most certainly lost.

In a kind but motherly voice, she asked Asadi, "What are you watching in there?"

"Uh . . . probably something he shouldn't be," Garrett interjected. "Would you mind helping him find something a little more—?"

"Age appropriate." Lacey checked her watch and looked to Asadi. "Looks like it's *Ninja Turtles* time. My son won't miss them." She smiled wide. "You a fan too?"

"He doesn't speak much English," Garrett answered. "But I'm sure he'd love it."

"Turtles it is." She took Asadi back into the living room where they made themselves comfortable on the sofa.

With the two out of earshot and settled into the program, Garrett asked, "You okay, Daddy? What's going on?"

A guilty-looking Butch walked over to the pantry and opened the accordion door. Sitting on the top shelf was a stainless steel .357 Magnum nestled in between the Frosted Flakes and three cans of evaporated milk. The walnut grip of the Colt Python was facing them, positioned for quick access.

Butch pulled the box from beneath a pile of plastic grocery bags and brought it to the kitchen counter. He glanced over at Asadi and Lacey, who were laughing together on the couch.

Butch opened the box, revealing about half a million dollars, street value, of black tar heroin. Maybe more. Garrett spoke low enough not to be heard by Lacey.

"Daddy, where *in the hell* did you get this?"

Butch explained what had happened in almost excruciating detail, from the time he got the phone call from Kate Shanessy to when he pulled his gun. For some reason, the old man felt it important to give every part of the story equal airtime. Garrett was tempted to jump in but didn't want to get his dad so flustered he forgot something important.

When Butch was done explaining though, Garrett couldn't resist asking one important question. "Why *on earth* did you think it would be a good idea to take this?"

There was a hesitation before Butch spoke and Garrett could tell his dad regretted the decision immensely, but he wasn't going to readily admit it. "An airplane flies over and drops something on *my property*, and you think I'm not going to check it out?" He gestured toward the box and the dozens of bags wrapped in cellophane.

As the only one in Garrett's family who actually knew he worked for the DEA, it was rare for his father to even acknowledge his work as a federal law enforcement officer, lest there be some vague reference to jackbooted henchmen whose sole job it was to tear up the Constitution and squash the Bill of Rights. But now that Butch had gotten himself into trouble, he seemed to have finally figured out what his son did for a living.

"*Hell*. Isn't this what you do? They ought to be giving me the key to the city for this."

Garrett raised his hands and made a big show of pointing out the obvious. "*What* city? We're on a ranch in the middle of nowhere, Daddy. And you're messing with some big-time traffickers here. You're lucky they didn't kill you." He turned to Asadi, who was still sitting on the couch engrossed in his cartoons. "*And him.*"

Butch stared at the boy with a look of contrition and did something Garrett had never seen him do before—admit he was wrong. "Look, son, it all happened so fast, I didn't think it through real good." He walked over to the window and stared out at the blanket of snow stretching as far as the eye could see. After a few seconds of silence, the old dog relented and tried another new trick—asking Garrett's opinion. "Okay, how do we fix this?"

Garrett went to stand by his dad. They stared at the prairie in silence. Before anything else, he had to do something about the drugs. Someone somewhere was going to want them back. And when they did, they wouldn't ask nicely.

Under normal circumstances he'd call local law enforcement, but that option had problems. First and foremost, he didn't know who to trust. Even Sanchez was questionable at this point. Whoever owned the heroin was coming for it sooner rather than later. The only viable option was to continue as planned and get the dope to the Texas Rangers down in Lubbock just as soon as humanly possible.

Garrett was planning next steps when his phone buzzed in his pocket.

Quick panicked breathing preceded Bridger's quivering voice. "Somebody's got Sophie and Chloe, Garrett. Took 'em. Said Daddy took their drugs. Is that true?"

"He did, Bridger. But it was just a misunderstanding. We're gonna—"

"Garrett, we got to give 'em back. They said they'll kill my girls if we don't."

Garrett's mind was racing but it wasn't hard to connect the dots. The Garzas were sending a message. And the best way to do that was with someone's children. With the thought of the twins in cartel hands, every law-abiding instinct he had flew right out the window. He'd deal with the aftermath later.

"Hold tight, Bridger. I've got what they want. I'm on my way."

Garrett ended the call and turned to find Lacey and Butch staring at him. "The twins have gone missing."

Lacey's hand flew to her mouth. "What happened?"

"There's just some threats being made right now. That's all." For Butch's sake, Garrett lied. "We've got something they want, and as long as they get it, everything's gonna be fine."

Lacey eyed the package on the counter. "Is that what they want?"

Garrett nodded. "Taking it to them right now. So, don't worry."

Neither Lacey nor his dad looked convinced.

Garrett could tell Butch wanted to say something. "What is it, Daddy?"

Butch glanced at Lacey then back to Garrett. "Your brother. Well, he's capable enough at most things, but . . . with Sophie and Chloe involved now—" He was clearly skirting the issue of Garrett's DEA affiliation, so as not to tip off Lacey.

"I'll be there every step of the way, Daddy. The girls are going to be just fine. I promise you that. So, don't worry about a thing. Okay?"

Butch exhaled and took a big breath. It was as if he hadn't taken one since the moment Bridger called. His big blue eyes were racked with worry—guilt over the fact that because of what he'd done he might never see his granddaughters again. He looked like he might say something but only nodded.

Garrett looked to Lacey, who appeared equally concerned. "You mind keeping an eye on these two for me? Don't expect I'll be gone too long."

Lacey reached over, put her hand on Butch's shoulder and forced a smile. "Of course not. We'll keep busy until you're back."

Garrett could tell that she too wanted to say more but was fighting to keep calm. He grabbed the box from the counter, clamped it under his arm, and walked right out the door.

And in that moment, he turned from lawman to outlaw. His heart sank at the prospect of what he was about to do, even though he knew what the outcome would be if he didn't. He'd seen lives wasted for a hell of a lot less and this was the only way possible to save the girls. There'd be blood spilled over this.

Lots of it.

But there was no blood equal to family.

PART THREE

The coward never starts and the weak die
along the way.

—Kit Carson

26

Smitty quit fumbling with the pack of Winstons and stuffed it back in his front pocket with a shaky hand. His fingers were so numb he could barely work the lighter. He actually hadn't felt like a smoke, just wanted something to distract him from the freezing cold. He looked over at Floyd Boggs, who was standing at the edge of the caprock, eyes trained on the Kohl house about fifty yards below.

Boggs was one of those cock-strong sons o' bitches you couldn't whup with an atomic crowbar—a full-fledged sociopath who hated drug users with a passion. Called 'em cockroaches. And as a recovering addict, Smitty didn't get much sympathy.

Once a tweaker always a tweaker, Boggs would say— usually over some mess-up that could've happened to anyone but only seemed to happen to Smitty when Boggs was watching.

But there was no room for screwups this time. Smitty wasn't going back to his old ways. Not now. Not ever. And he damn sure wasn't going back to prison. He had a wife, a daughter, and a pontoon boat out at Lake Meredith. Life was good, if he could just hold on to it.

Needing some space from Boggs, Smitty moved to his partner's old van, parked a few yards away, and hopped into the passenger seat. He slammed the door, yanked the phone from his coat, and worked on a frantic text to Malek.

Shipment got stolen. Now what?

Waiting for a reply, Smitty hung his arm out the window and yelled over the wind, "See anything yet? Don't want to be here all *damn* day."

"What's your big hurry, cockroach?" Boggs turned back again and smiled. "You got somewheres else to be?" He hopped up from his perch and moved to the van. His puffy face was ruddier than normal.

"Ain't no hurry. Just don't like sitting out here in the freezing cold, that's all."

Boggs stuck his giant head through the window, a golf ball–size plug of Red Man chew swelling his left cheek. "You up to something, ain't ya'?" He leaned in so close Smitty could smell the tobacco juice. "Bo said he seen you talking to somebody up at Locust Grove. Said maybe you done got greedy. Working for the competition."

Smitty shook off the accusation. "Hell no. It ain't like that." He turned forward and stared out the windshield, hoping Boggs would lose interest. "I done explained all that to Bo at the Wagon Bridge. We got it straight."

"Then maybe you back on that dope again, huh?" Boggs smiled wide and pulled his head out of the window. "Once a tweaker always a tweaker." He just stood there, staring. His reddish-blond beard was nearly sideways from the wind. "Might have to put a bullet in your head before this whole thing is over."

Smitty closed his eyes and prayed Boggs would just walk away. Nutjob would kill him as quick as Bo. Maybe quicker. And he didn't need a gun to do it. They'd both done time at the Wynne Unit down in Huntsville, and he'd seen Boggs beat an inmate half to death with only his fists. He was like a psychotic Pit Bull, abused since birth. Didn't think about biting—just bit.

"Look, Boggs, all I'm saying is the longer we sit here, the better the chances we get caught."

"Ain't nobody but us and them Kohls within ten miles of here except that shriveled bitch Kate Shanessy. And Bo's about ready to smoke her old ass anyhow for taking potshots with her rifle at the Garzas' plane."

As Boggs walked back to the edge of the caprock, Smitty jerked the door handle and hopped out of the van. He was eyeing the AK-47 leaning against the tire when Boggs turned back and stared him down. "Don't be getting no ideas there. I see what you're looking at."

Smitty feigned disbelief. "What are you talking about?"

Boggs was just getting that mad dog look in his eyes when he turned suddenly to the house and dropped to a knee. "Shut up. Something's happening."

Smitty crept up and squatted beside Boggs, right as Garrett Kohl's black GMC pulled away, kicking a trail of snow and gravel behind it. "You see the old man and that boy?"

Boggs squinted and craned his neck. "Nah, they're still inside." He turned back to Smitty. "We're going to have to go down there."

"What for?" Smitty stared at the windows of the house but couldn't see any movement. "I thought we were just supposed to let Bo know when Garrett takes off."

"We are. But that boy and the old man seen our faces. Know we work for Renegade." Boggs turned and smiled, a spark in his eyes. "And Bo said Lacey Capshaw's been snooping around up at the office."

"So! What the hell are we supposed to do about it?"

"He told me to gather them all up and tote 'em out to the ranch for Nagual to deal with."

"*Deal with?*"

Smitty could feel the bile rising in his throat. Instead of digging out from under a dead body, he was adding more to the pile. If Malek didn't get back to him soon, there'd be nothing he could do to stop it.

Boggs lumbered over to the AK-47 against the tire and snatched it up. "You got a problem with how the Garzas do business?"

"Well, it's not a problem necessarily. Just ain't my job."

"Your *job* is to do what you're told." Boggs racked a bullet into the chamber and pointed the gun at Smitty. He pulled the trigger twice and there was a *ticktick* of metal on metal since the gun's selector was on safety. "And if that old man screws with me again, it'll be the last time."

27

With his adrenaline pumping ninety to nothing, Garrett stomped on the accelerator and the Duramax turbodiesel engine snarled. With his GMC pegged at over seventy miles per hour, he focused on the far edge of the hydrogen beams that cut into the darkness. His stomach knotted as the pickup thundered over a steel cattle guard and hydroplaned into the pasture.

He tapped the brakes, finessed his wheels back in line, and jammed his boot on the gas where he rolled up to a three-way junction and cut a hard right. Fishtailing onto the county road to Bridger's house, one resounding thought dominated Garrett's mind.

How the hell could he have let this happen?

It wasn't as much a question as it was self-flagellation. Mixing work and family was one of Joe Bob Dawson's cardinal sins—right up there with screwing your female informants and trusting headquarters.

Garrett jerked the Glock from his holster, tossed it on the passenger seat, and pulled his own Nighthawk 1911 pistol from the center console. Taking his service weapon wouldn't be right. Of course, none of what he was doing was on the level—not even close. But the switch from white hat to black didn't mean he had to drag the DEA down with him. Consequences for his actions would be entirely on him.

A quick check of his watch and he turned off the county road onto the winding gravel trail up to Bridger's place. The twenty-minute trip had taken less than ten. Pacing on the front porch of his two-story log home, his brother looked up and sprinted over.

While Garrett was coasting to a stop in the circle driveway, Bridger yanked the passenger door open and grabbed the box of heroin from the seat. "What took you so long?" He slammed the door without waiting for an answer and darted back in the house.

Garrett put the truck in park, shut off the engine, and jumped out. He sprinted inside the house and took a quick look around. At a glance, he noticed some significant upgrades. Like everything else in Bridger's life, the home was a testament to his financial success. Floor-to-ceiling stone fireplace. Elk antler chandeliers.

Top-grain leather sectional. And an eighty-six-inch flat screen.

But what grabbed Garrett more than anything else was the portrait above the fireplace of the twins in their cowgirl regalia. They were leaning against a fence post out at the ranch with a smiling black Labrador at their feet. It couldn't have been taken more than a couple of years ago. About the time he and Bridger had had their big falling-out.

Breaking himself away, Garrett walked up to the dining room table where his brother was yanking plastic baggies of heroin from the box and tossing them in a pile.

"What are you doing, Bridger?"

His brother didn't look up, just kept unpacking. "Making sure it's all here."

His answer made Garrett wonder if Bridger was further into this thing than he'd admitted. "How do *you* know what's supposed to be in there?"

Paying no mind to the accusation, Bridger kept counting. "Guy told me when he called. Said there better not be a single one missing." When the last bag was tallied, he breathed a sigh of relief. "It's all here."

Garrett snorted. "Well, who do you think might've taken something? Me? *Daddy?*"

Bridger looked shell-shocked. "I don't know, Garrett." He shrugged and shook his head. "They just said if they didn't get 'em all back, they'd—" Choking up before he could get the rest out, he held up his cell phone and opened a text message.

Garrett took in the photo. The girls were sitting side by side, knees to chest, their hands and feet bound. They were blindfolded and gagged.

Garrett swallowed hard. "Don't pay any attention to that, Bridger. They're just trying to mess with your head. Make sure you don't call the law. We do what they ask, the girls will be fine. I promise."

The fact that the twins were sitting on the floor of a room and not in a vehicle on their way to the meeting location was a bad sign. But Garrett wasn't about to mention that to his brother. At least not yet. He looked around. "Where's Cassidy?"

Bridger tilted his head toward the bedroom. "Told her about my *not-so-legal* dealings with the investors in Mescalero and her reaction wasn't good. Said I got greedy." He turned and looked Garrett in the eye. "I can't believe I let it get this far. I ought to have known better."

Garrett shook it off. "None of that matters right now. All we need to focus on is getting the girls back. So, I need you to pull it together. Can you do that?"

Bridger took a breath and nodded. He picked up his phone from the table and texted while he spoke. "The guy said to let 'em know as soon as I get the package. He'll text me the location where we meet and make the exchange."

Garrett had seen this scenario play out more times than he could count. Bad guys were vague on meeting times and locations until the very last minute, which made it impossible for law enforcement or rivals to plan ahead or put anyone in place.

A few seconds later, Bridger's phone dinged, and he read the text aloud. "Says get on the county road outside your house and start driving south. Come alone or the girls are dead."

Garrett had planned to go along and make the exchange, but their instructions were clear. Bridger would go alone. He followed his brother to the front door and yanked it open, but before he'd even taken a step outside, machine-gun fire erupted and splintered the door frame.

So much for the plan.

Garrett shoved Bridger back inside and slammed the door as a second barrage of lead shattered a side window and sent them diving for cover. As bullets raked the wall behind them, a burst of glass shards and wood slivers rained down and littered the floor.

Lying prostrate, with his hands over his head, Garrett glanced up to see headlights in the dining room mirror. A vehicle was pulling around back.

Grabbing his brother by the sleeve, Garrett leaned in and yelled over the noise, "Go get Cassidy and stay low!"

Garrett flinched as automatic gunfire ripped through the back of the house, shattering the dining room window and blasting doors off the kitchen cabinets. Another salvo from a side window ripped a lazy trail of bullet holes along the wall until it got the twins' portrait and peppered it to kindling.

Cassidy screamed from the master bedroom and Bridger sprinted to her. He ducked low as a salvo from the front of the house blasted the eighty-six-inch flat screen. It sparked and smoked, then crashed to the floor in a heap of smoldering debris.

Leaping to his feet, Garrett darted across the living room and sprinted upstairs. He turned right into Sophie's bedroom, shoved the heroin under her bed, and turned back at the sound from downstairs of screeching hinges.

Easing to the door, he peeked around the corner, down the stairwell, and into the den. One hitman stepped into view from the left and panned the room with a short-barreled AK-47. He had a stocky build, short cropped hair, and a gray goatee.

The second gunman entering right had his CZ Scorpion submachine gun at the ready. He was tall and lean, with a spiderweb tattoo covering the length of his neck. His inky-black ponytail fell to midback. Both men wore the uniform of the trade—shiny dark suits and pointy-toed boots.

When the one with the goatee headed toward Bridger and Cassidy's bedroom, Garrett slammed his elbow against the wall with an echoing *thud*. An instant later, heavy footsteps rumbled up the stairs.

Garrett got flush with the wall, raised his pistol, and aimed at the doorway.

Leading with his rifle, the one with the goatee made a sharp right turn into the Nighthawk.

Garrett pulled the trigger and the *sicario's* head became a red splotch on the wall.

Stunned by the near headless body, the trailing gunman with the spiderweb tattoo faltered, giving Garrett the half-second edge to lean out and aim. With the barrel of the 1911 at nearly point-blank range, Garrett fired a .45 hollow point into the *sicario's* chest—sending him tumbling down the stairs to land at the bottom in a heap of twisted limbs.

A gunshot rang out from below and Garrett raced down the stairs, across the den to the master bedroom, and threw a shoulder into the door. At the crack of a second shot, he found Bridger by the window, his lever-action Henry X model leveled at a man missing half his head.

Given the *sicario's* additional gut wound, Garrett quickly deduced that Bridger's second shot was done execution style. It wasn't the kind of thing that held up in court as self-defense, but he assumed his attorney brother already knew that. It was the act of a father doling out a little justice of his own.

Before Garrett could say a word, Bridger hurried to the closet, opened the door, and led Cassidy out by the hand. He held her as she sobbed.

Garrett shifted uncomfortably. "Ya'll need to get out of here and go somewhere safe. Cassidy's parents' maybe? Just keep your phone handy and I'll be in touch."

Bridger turned back, his wife still in his tight embrace. "You're not doing a damn thing without me, Garrett. That's for sure."

"Look, I understand you're upset and I—"

"No. You *don't* understand. We lose those girls, we lose everything. You don't make a move without me."

Realizing he really had no choice in the matter, Garrett gave a slow nod. "Okay, fair enough. We do this. We do it together."

Cassidy pulled away from her husband. "Same goes for me." She drew herself up, chin raised, and locked eyes with Garrett. "I'm not going anywhere until my baby girls are safe in my arms. You got that?"

Garrett knew she wouldn't be dissuaded but he looked to his bother in deference anyhow.

Bridger was decidedly resolute. "We live as a family. We die as a family. Whatever you've got planned. Count us both in. All the way."

Garrett moved from the bedroom to the bottom of the stairs and spun the sicario over. Just as he'd done in every raid in his special operations career, he searched for intel, riffling through every pocket but ultimately finding nothing. No phone. No pocket litter. Not a thing to provide a clue to where the girls were located.

Seeing what Garrett was doing, Bridger checked the body up top and Cassidy did the same in the bedroom. Garrett was about to go help her when his brother called down. "Got something."

To Garrett's relief Bridger had found a phone. It was a prepaid device, likely a burner meant to be used only once. Bridger eased down and stood beside Cassidy who'd come back empty-handed.

Garrett flipped the phone open. There were no plugged-in numbers and no history—just a single cryptic text exchange from the same number that had made contact with Bridger.

Incoming:

Girls are here at the house. Kohl brothers?

Outgoing:

Soon.

Incoming:

Call when it's done.

Nobody said a word but they all locked eyes. Bridger gave the nod and Garrett pushed the number. It rang and rang but nobody answered. No voice mail. No nothing. They were back to square one. Garrett was about to look for the *sicarios'* truck keys when the phone vibrated.

It happened so suddenly it gave Cassidy a jolt. After putting his index finger to his lips, Garrett answered and pressed the speaker button. Not a second later, the caller on the other end asked, "*You take care of it?*"

Bridger couldn't have hidden his reaction if he'd tried. The shock and rage burned way too deep.

28

Asadi looked over at Garrett's friend Lacey, who sat rigid beside him—not even laughing at the funniest parts of the cartoons. Unsure what was wrong, he rose from the couch and walked into the kitchen where Butch stared out the window at nothing in particular. His face looked the way Asadi's father's had when the marauders came—the last time he ever saw him.

The old man turned, looking startled. "*Oh,* hey there, sonny." He gave Asadi a playful jab on the shoulder. "You're sneakier than Geronimo."

Butch checked his watch and ambled to the coatrack by the back door. "You wouldn't want to go feed horses now, would ya'?" He tilted his head to Lacey, who was still sitting on the sofa watching television. "Maybe your pretty friend over there will pitch in and help?"

At the word *horses*, Asadi's pulse quickened. It was what he had been waiting for all day. He grabbed his Dallas Cowboys coat and John Deere stocking hat from the kitchen table.

Butch donned his jacket and dusty brown cowboy hat and called to Lacey. "Got a few chores out in the barn. Could I interest you in joining us?"

It took a second for Lacey to realize he was talking to her. "Be glad to, Butch." She rose from the sofa and threw on a coat that was as white and puffy as a marshmallow. "Gotta see those quarter horses Garrett's always bragging about."

Butch looked surprised. "He's mentioned them to you?"

Lacey walked over to Asadi, zipped the Dallas Cowboys coat to his chin, and turned back to Butch. "Talks about those horses more than anything else."

The old man fought back a smile. "Well, he's proud of what we got. But I reckon I'm as guilty. Haven't done a whole helluva lot right in my lifetime but them horses are near close to perfection. Still have folks call me from all over the world interested in our bloodline."

"Doesn't surprise me." Lacey joined Butch by the back door. "I've heard enough jealous ranchers grumbling over at the café to know you've outdone them by a country mile."

Butch blushed at the compliment. He dug into his coat pocket, turned to Asadi, and handed him some cubes. "Lacey and I'll distract the others, so you and your buddy can visit."

Asadi scooped up the sugar cubes, careful not to drop any, and put them in his front pocket for safekeeping. Understanding Butch's plan, he nodded. "*Tenk. You.*"

Butch looked as if he was about to say something but was interrupted by a barking growl from Pato, who had been napping out in the barn. From the look in Butch's eyes, something was wrong. Asadi wanted to stop him before he opened the door, but it was already too late.

Butch hadn't taken even a step outside when a gunshot cracked and the bullet ripped through his shoulder. He slammed the door and clutched his wound as his knees buckled.

Lacey's eyes went wide, she screamed, then rushed to Butch.

Collapsing, he threw his back into the door, reached up and clicked the dead bolt. "Saw two shadows by the corral." He looked to Lacey. "I can hold 'em a minute, but you two gotta run. House down the road. Shanessy place. Get there quick as you can."

"No way, Butch." She shook her head. "*Uh-uh.* We're not leaving you."

"Gun and bullets." He jabbed his finger toward the kitchen, wincing as he spoke. "In the pantry."

Asadi knelt beside Butch as Lacey sprinted to the kitchen. She rummaged through the closet then darted right back with the big silver pistol. "I'll call the sheriff. Maybe they can—"

"Won't do no good." He shook off the suggestion as he took the handoff from Lacey. "It's going down, right here, right now. Gotta take care of ourselves."

Asadi shuddered, his heart jumping, at the sound of footsteps that *thump-thump-thumped* along the creaking planks of the back porch. He scooted nearer Butch who looped his arm around him and pulled tight. "It's all right, sonny. Everything's gonna be fine."

Lacey whispered, "What do I do?"

Butch leaned hard into the door and whispered back, "Go to the bedroom. Lock yourselves in and get behind the bed. Call Garrett and tell him to get here quick as he can."

Lacey glanced up as the steps ceased outside the door. "What about you?"

"Something happens to me," Butch took a deep breath and grimaced in pain. "Hightail it to Kate Shanessy's place. Climb out the window and run like hell. It's the white house," he said, gasping. "Big trees out front."

Butch pressed his bloody hand against the wound and red droplets oozed between his fingers. He gave Asadi a gentle nudge and whispered, "Go on, sonny. Hide real good for me now." He smiled with his eyes and pointed to Garrett's room. "Keep her safe." Butch slid to the side, his back against the wall, and aimed the silver pistol up at the door.

Asadi took Lacey's hand as he trailed her through the living room, down the hallway, and into Garrett's bedroom. The last thing he heard was Butch cocking the pistol. Then Lacey shut the door, turned off the lights, and their whole world went completely dark.

Smitty looked to Boggs and shook his head. The psycho had fired on Butch Kohl without cause and it was clear as day he had no intention of taking the old man alive.

Boggs pointed the AK-47 at Smitty. This time the safety wasn't on. "What's your problem?"

Smitty looked for a place to take cover but there was none to be found. They were out in the open between the back porch and the barn. "I didn't say nothing."

"You got a look though."

In one last bid to save his own life and everyone inside that house, Smitty made a desperate appeal to logic. "Didn't Bo say to bring 'em alive for Nagual to deal with?"

"He said bring 'em. Didn't say *how*."

Smitty gave another shake of the head. "Come on, man. That kind of thinking's gonna get us killed. What if Nagual's got questions? You know how he is. Might want to beat up on that old man for a spell to see what he knows."

Boggs went silent and it was clear he was giving it some thought. "*Ahh*, that coot don't know nothing. If he did, he wouldn't a stole our dope."

"What about Lacey? Bo said she was snooping around the office. Must know something."

Boggs turned the gun barrel away from Smitty and pointed it at the back door. "We'll take her and the boy then." He nodded, revenge in his eyes. "That ought to be good enough."

Before Smitty could argue, Boggs jumped on the porch, walked to the door, and turned the knob to find it locked. Taking a step back, he shouldered the AK and aimed at the hinges.

"Gonna blow it to splinters." Boggs clicked the selector to full-auto and ripped off about fifteen rounds—thirteen more than needed—and followed them with a kick that busted the door wide open. Stepping up all casual-like, he thrust the rifle inside and sprayed until it was empty.

Turning back to Smitty, Boggs grinned wide—proud of his handiwork. "Now that's how you do it right there. Shock and awe, bitch."

Boggs dropped the mag, popped in another, and strutted inside.

Smitty had just stepped on the porch when Boggs hit the deck and belly-crawled out of the house with his big gut dragging along the floor, ducking with each *bam-bam-bam* of the .357 Magnum.

Smitty flew off the porch with Boggs right behind. They tumbled into the snow, scurried to get upright, and leaned their backs against the planks for cover. One bullet lodged in the deck above Smitty's head, cracking the wood and showering him in splinters.

Smitty cringed, stooped lower, and pulled his knees to his chest as two more shots popped at his work boots. He didn't want to kill anybody, but he damn sure didn't want to die. "What we gonna do now, man?"

Struggling to his feet, Boggs grumbled, "That's six. He's out of bullets." He raised the AK to hip level and sprayed full-auto in a side-to-side motion—ripping the walls to shards and busting out windows. With the magazine spent, Boggs ejected it, jammed in another, and leapt onto the porch. "Come get your medicine, old-timer!"

He'd just stepped inside when Butch Kohl swung a wooden chair around like a baseball bat and bashed him across the head. The chair cracked in two, seat and legs crashing to the floor, leaving the old man holding the back. Boggs grabbed his forehead, stumbled, and fell backward.

Asadi flew down the hallway with his bow and a quiver full of arrows but stopped short of the living room in complete shock. Every wall was pocked with bullet holes and the furniture torn to shreds. Among the broken glass and wood shards lay Butch, covered in blood—his eyes half-closed and his body limp.

The bad man Asadi called Goat was unconscious beside him, lying halfway through the back door. And the pointy-faced Lizard was leaning over his friend's body picking up a rifle.

Reaching back over his shoulder, Asadi pulled an arrow from his quiver and nocked the bow. His hands trembling, he drew back, closed his eyes, and let the arrow fly. He opened them again only upon hearing the soft *thuck* of the metal-tipped shaft as it tore through flesh.

Lizard's mouth went agape, in the shape of an *O*. His gasp built into a shriek as he stared down at his impaled left thigh. He tugged at the arrow with his free hand, but the bloody shaft budged no farther than halfway.

Asadi released his second arrow and this time he didn't close his eyes. Instead he took in the entire spectacle. From Lizard dropping his gun, to the cussing and screaming while he jerked at the shaft in his arm.

Beside him, Goat rose on shaky legs, reached for his bloody head wound, and smeared a red streak down to his nose. He scanned the room unfocused until his eyes rested on Asadi. And that's when his bewildered expression turned to a scowl. Goat put one foot in front of the other, arms outstretched toward Asadi as his shuffle built into a lumbering sprint.

Asadi tried to reload his bow but his shaking hands fumbled the arrow. He ducked just in time to escape Goat's grasp, pivoting out of reach as he bolted for the back door.

Leaping from the porch to the ground, Asadi lost his balance and took a tumble in the snow. Dropping his bow and quiver, he scrambled to his feet and looped around the house in search of Lacey, who'd slipped out the window to go to Kate Shanessy's house for help.

Smitty limped after Boggs to keep him from doing something stupid, but it was already too late. The bastard yanked up the rifle, ran to the porch, and blasted away at the snow-covered prairie.

Stumbling around like a drunk, Boggs turned to Smitty and gave him the gimme here motion with his hand. "Need another clip! He's gettin' away!"

"Ain't no more! You shot 'em all!"

Boggs reached up again and dabbed his head. "Dammit!"

Smitty gripped his thigh and blood ran between his fingers. "Kid stuck me clean through, man! Hurts!"

"Old fart whacked me with a Martha Washington." Boggs glanced back inside at the wreckage of the chair. "Split the damn thing in half! You don't see me crying about it, do you?"

Boggs lumbered over, wrapped his arm around Smitty, who was struggling to yank out the arrows, and pulled him into a headlock. "Come here, you little bitch." He plucked the arrows out and tossed them off the porch. "Got a bad enough headache without your pissing and moaning."

Smitty hobbled back inside on his wounded leg and stared down at Butch Kohl, who was unconscious and white as a sheet. His heart sank. The only thing the old man was guilty of was crossing a psycho like Boggs. "What are we gonna do about him?"

"Nothing." Boggs took labored steps up to the door, breathing hard. "That old mummy's as good as dead. Let him suffer." He spit a stream of tobacco juice at Butch that landed shy.

Seeing all the blood, Smitty couldn't help but believe that was true. He'd get a message to Malek if he could, but it wasn't going to do much good at this point. Butch Kohl was a goner.

"He's swung his last chair. That's for sure." Smitty turned back to Boggs. "What about the boy?"

Boggs gazed out over the prairie. "We got a full moon. Nearly bright as day. *And* he's on foot. We ain't. Won't take long to track him."

"And Lacey?"

"She's probably hiding. Check the back of the house where the kid came from."

Smitty walked down the hallway to a bedroom. He flicked on the light and saw the open window. "Girl musta hopped out and ran!"

Boggs clomped up to the door, shook his head. "Don't worry. Cold as it is, she won't get far."

The metal clank of slamming doors sent a shiver up Asadi's spine. An engine sputtered then screeched as it roared to life. With nowhere to hide on the flat open prairie, Asadi ran. Fast as he could—hard as he could—he sprinted to Kate Shanessy's house.

A hundred yards. Two hundred yards. Half a mile. Weary with exhaustion and stumbling over his own feet, Asadi felt he couldn't go another step. But the rumble of the engine from behind prodded him onward.

Headlights flashed all around him—left then right—up then down—until finding their mark. Then the beams went from bright to brighter. Now he heard voices like they were after him on foot.

His breath coming in gasps, Asadi sprinted to the white slatted fence surrounding the house. He glanced back, tripped, and tumbled. The engine roared and he scrambled to his feet, gulping in frozen air as he trudged through powder as high as his knees.

He had just reached the fence, grabbed the top rung, and flung his right leg over when the clomping footsteps caught up to him.

Shifting his weight to the other side, Asadi's coat snagged—not on a board or a nail but in the grip of a fist. Goat's bearded face hovered over him before growling, "Got his ass!"

Dangling like a rag doll Asadi kicked, squirmed, and twisted, flipping and flopping like a fish out of water.

As Kate's silhouette passed by the window, Asadi screamed for help.

Adjusting his grip, Goat lost hold and Asadi fell face-first into the snow.

Popping right up, he sprinted to the light but a shadow darted out ahead of him. Tree to tree, his pursuer dashed spastically but purposefully—a step ahead of his every move.

The shadow, which Asadi knew was Lizard, grabbed his collar and yanked him back. Cold, bony fingers muffled his cries.

Goat hobbled up with his fist cocked, and Asadi neither saw nor felt the blow. His ears rang, he felt nauseous, then everything went hazy. Everything that followed was a ceaseless blur of pain and fear. They dragged him to their van, stripped off his clothes, bound his hands and feet, then tossed him in the back.

As the doors slammed shut, his world went dark. Not since the massacre had he been more afraid or felt more alone.

29

G arrett ended the call the moment he realized who was on the other end. It was a gut reaction but one he trusted. Convincing his brother of this wouldn't be easy. Bridger reached over and grabbed the phone out of Garrett's hand.

"What the hell's wrong with you?" Bridger stared at him in disbelief. "That was Kaiser!"

"That's what I figured. It's why I hung up."

"Have you lost it?" Bridger looked to Cassidy, who was equally dumbfounded, then back to Garrett. "Maybe he knows who took the girls!"

Garrett gave Bridger a moment for reality to sink in. It wasn't uncommon for people to miss the obvious under severe stress, even when the truth was right in front of them. His brother had trusted Preston Kaiser and it turned out the bastard was not only dirty, he was dangerous.

"Bridger, he knows *exactly* who took them because he was behind it."

Bridger shook his head. There was a moment when he looked at a loss, then had so much to say he didn't know where to begin. He could barely get out the words. "But—the Garzas. Renegade. I thought—"

"I know what you thought. I did too. But Kaiser's involved somehow. And it may not seem like it right now, but this is good news."

"How in the *hell* is this good news?"

"Think about it. From the text messages and the phone call, we got a *who* and we got a *where*. That's all I need."

Bridger calmed a little. "Okay, we know they're at his house out at the ranch. I'll give you that. But we should've at least talked to him. Maybe we could've worked things out."

Garrett pointed to the dead body. "Does this look like the actions of a man ready to work things out?" Before Bridger could answer, Garrett interrupted. "What did Kaiser say when you told him about going to the Rangers with all this?"

"He pushed back. *Hard.* But ultimately I convinced him it was the only choice we had."

"You didn't convince him of anything, Bridger. And proof of that is lying right here on the floor. I don't know how or why, but Kaiser's in this thing deep, with the Garzas. And I can tell you there's no reasoning, bargaining, or pleading with people like them. They're out for blood now. And they're going to get every drop of it if we don't handle this thing right."

Bridger stared at the *sicario*. "Things have changed."

"Have they? They've still got the twins, which means they've got all the leverage in the world. But right now, they think we're dead. We can use that to our advantage."

"Kaiser knows we called," Cassidy argued.

"No. He knows *someone* called." Garrett pointed to the dead body. "And until otherwise informed he'll believe it was this guy."

The phone lit up in Garrett's hand as it rang.

Bridger shook his head. "See. He suspects something's off. He's gonna keep calling."

"Let him call. Suspecting isn't knowing. Cell service is poor around here. He'll think his men did their job and they're on their way back."

"And when he gets tired of waiting?" Cassidy asked.

Garrett had that bad feeling in the pit of his stomach again. It was the same one he'd had before the massacre at Nasrin. "He'll send more men. That's why we have to move fast. We gotta get to Daddy's and get the horses."

"Horses?" Bridger looked at him, curious. "For what?"

"The driveway to Kaiser's house off the highway will be under surveillance, gunmen posted up front. Only way we're getting in is through his backyard."

"I don't disagree, but Kaiser's backyard is about sixty thousand acres of the roughest ranchland around. Even on horseback it won't be easy."

"I never said it'd be easy. I said it's the only way."

"Look, Garrett, I'm not exactly sure what you did in Special Forces. And I never asked because I figured I probably wasn't supposed to know. But I can't take any chances with my girls' lives at stake. If you tell me we can do this, then I'll take you at your word." Bridger paused, thinking hard on his options. "But if we've got to get the law involved, so be it. Hell, I'll spend the rest of my life in prison. But losing the twins isn't an option."

"Hear you loud and clear, Bridger, and normally I'd agree. But local law enforcement isn't equipped to handle these guys and the closest SWAT team is over two hours away. By the time they get the go-ahead, come up with a plan, and make it out to the Mescalero Ranch, the girls will be long gone. Maybe even dead.

"More important, we don't know who can be trusted right now. Kaiser's got the whole Texas Panhandle bought and paid for. Someone tips him off, they might kill the girls straight-out just to cover their tracks. I'm telling you, our best bet is to handle this ourselves. In and out. Quick and quiet."

Bridger stared blankly at the wall, an argument playing out in his mind. "You're sure they won't make a swap for the drugs? We've still got what they want."

"Bridger, they *never* intended to honor that deal. In fact, my guess is they care less about the heroin and more about shutting you up for good."

"Then they can have me, *dammit*! Swap me for the girls. *And the drugs!* What the hell do they want with Sophie and Chloe anyhow? They had nothing to do with this!"

Grabbing his brother by the shoulders, Garrett leaned in and locked eyes. "These people don't think like you and me. The Garzas believe you're going to the Rangers and Daddy stole their dope. We took a big swing and now they want payback. That's how cartels operate." He pointed to the *sicario.* "You've seen what we're up against here. There's no making a deal, so get that out of your head. Best we can hope for is to beat them at their own game."

Doubt rested in Bridger's eyes. "You're sure we can do this? Because if we can't—"

"We can do it, but we're wasting time arguing. We need to go. *Right now.*"

Cassidy spoke up. "I told you. You're not leaving me behind. And I meant it."

"Good," Garrett confirmed with a nod. "Only way this'll work is with you and Daddy up on the highway. Once we get the girls, we'll need you ready to exfil us the hell out of there. But none of that's happening unless we slip in through the back of the ranch undetected."

Bridger raised his index finger. "I've got something that'll help." He went into his office and came back holding two cardboard tubes, each about three feet long.

Garrett crossed to the dining room table as Bridger unfurled the contents. "What's this?"

"Plats and blueprints for the ranch and compound. Kaiser had me take a look at the property before he bought it." Bridger laid out the two schematics side by side. "House alone is over fifteen thousand square feet."

Bridger pointed to a room on the northeast corner. "Easiest point of entry. Back door."

Garrett nodded. "All right, looks pretty straightforward."

"At one time maybe, but not anymore." Bridger switched focus from the house blueprints to the compound map. "Folks don't call this place 'Babylon on the Canadian' for nothing. Kaiser's created his own hanging gardens. Man-made lakes and streams. Hedgerows and mazes. Terraced gardens and Roman aqueducts. It's a dream come true in the summer but a frozen nightmare right now. Maneuvering through it is gonna be tricky. Especially at night."

Garrett studied the map. "We've got a full moon. As long as the weather holds, we'll have enough light to travel by."

Bridger dragged the ranch map in front of them and traced his finger along a squiggly line running the length of the Canadian River. It cut south sharply and spoked into multiple oil field roads leading to several drill site locations and tank batteries.

"We can drive to this point and take the horses the rest of the way." He drew a circle around a well location. "Boone 12–25H."

Garrett pointed to a spot closer to the compound. "What's wrong with here?"

Making a curvy line with his finger, Bridger outlined their obstacle. "You've got Tallahone Creek running south. It's frozen over but won't hold a man's weight. Damn sure not a horse. We'll have to cross at this culvert."

Eyeing their launch point, Garrett checked the elevation. "We'll have plenty of mesquite brush for cover right here, but not much farther past the Central Tank Battery, which is wide open." He borrowed Bridger's pencil and drew a line through a shaded area. "Between here and the compound we're fish in a barrel."

Bridger leaned in and studied the map. "Any other way will take us over an hour."

"Then we ride in the open. And we ride like hell." Garrett looked up and locked eyes with his brother. "Soon as they know we're there, the clock starts ticking. Everything after is just borrowed time."

30

S mitty had never seen the Mescalero Ranch this heavily guarded. Kaiser's mansion, which had fake turrets and was designed to resemble a castle, had never looked more authentic. There were four cowboys with machine guns up at the front gate and six more riding perimeter on horseback. And that didn't count the Garzas' Mexican soldiers stationed at every door.

Bo Clevenger lumbered out a side entrance and met Smitty and Boggs in the circle drive. "You got 'em?"

Boggs rolled down the window and spat out a plug of his tobacco. "We got the boy."

Bo laughed, spying the goose egg on Boggs's forehead. "The hell happened to you?"

"Old man put up a fight." Boggs winced as he massaged the knot. "Kid shot up Smitty with a bow and arrow."

"*Bow and arrow?*" Bo leaned inside the cab of the van and gave Smitty the onceover. "Well, you know them Kohl brothers are Comanches way back on their mama's side. Still got kin over in Lawton. Maybe that boy's a cousin or something?" He chuckled to himself, seeming to think on the possibility. "What about Lacey and Butch?"

Boggs shook his head. "Like I said, old man made a ruckus. And the girl ran off."

"*Ran off?*" Any amusement on Bo's face over the arrow incident vanished. "Boss ain't gonna like that." He pulled his head out of the window and glanced over his shoulder at the house. "Let you explain that one."

Boggs shrugged. "Couldn't be helped."

Bo turned back and whacked the side of the van with his thick palm. "Kid in the back?"

"Yeah, you don't worry about that little bastard." A rare grin rose from under Boggs's scraggly beard. "We hit the *pharmacy* on the way over."

"*Pharmacy?*" Bo cocked an eyebrow. "What pharmacy?"

"Parking lot behind the Flying Bandit." Boggs lifted the hypodermic needle he'd used on the kid and gave it a squirt out the window. "Stopped off and got a little ketamine from a guy I know. Should keep the brat docile until the Garzas take him."

Bo gave an approving nod, turned on his boot heel, and gave them the follow me gesture. "Go grab his ass then. We'll lock him up in the library with Bridger Kohl's girls."

Smitty hopped out, went to the back of the van and opened the double doors. He sighed with relief and wrestled back a *Hallelujah Jesus* the kid wasn't dead. As Boggs dragged the boy out, Smitty gathered his clothes, coat, and hat, wadded them into a ball and tucked them under his arm.

He followed Bo into the house and trailed him down a dim hallway. It reminded him of an art museum, like one he'd been to with his foster family back in the sixth grade. The paintings were mostly of nature scenes and wildlife, but he recognized a Jasper Johns and slowed to admire it.

Boggs threw a shoulder into Smitty's back as he was walking by. "Hurry up. Boss wants to see us in his office."

Smitty's heart sank. They'd done their job and all he wanted to do now was go home to his wife and let her tend to his wounds properly. "Mr. Kaiser wants to see us?"

Still following Bo down the hall, Boggs turned and called back over his shoulder, "I'm talking about the *real* boss."

Smitty didn't know all the details, only that Kaiser had run afoul of the Garzas' cartel on a high-dollar whitetail hunt down in Mexico. As the story went, he got coked up out of his mind and beat to death a fourteen-year-old prostitute. But rather than kill him, the Garzas took pictures of the two naked as jaybirds and threatened to release the photos if Kaiser didn't play ball. Since then, the Garzas' man Nagual had been calling the shots at Mescalero.

Smitty followed Boggs into the library and over to where he laid the boy down on an Oriental rug by the fireplace. He knelt beside him and tucked the ball of clothing under the kid's arm. Leaning in close to his face, barely visible but for the glow of the flickering flames, Smitty could tell he was still breathing, albeit shallow.

He took the crocheted scarf his wife had made from around his neck, stretched it out, and draped it over the kid. Worried Boggs or Bo might've seen what he'd done, he turned back. They were already out in the hallway.

With the split second of privacy he checked his phone, but there was still no response from Malek. The son of a bitch was taking his sweet time. Smitty typed another frantic message.

Butch Kohl shot and dying at home. I'm at Mescalero Ranch. Please help now!!!

He'd just hit send when Boggs yelled from behind, "What the hell's taking so long?"

Shoving the phone in his pocket, Smitty turned and saw a shadow move in the corner. It was Bridger Kohl's twins, huddled together in black-and-gold sweat suits. Their terrified eyes glimmered in the fire. Smitty didn't know what to say. He knew what was in store for those kids and none of it was good.

"Boy here's been runnin' around out in the cold. Maybe you could get him dressed." He pointed to the fireplace. "See to it he gets warmed up or something. Could you do that for me?"

When the girls didn't answer, Smitty looked back at the bony kid, unsure if he was going to make it—unsure if he *wanted* him to make it. There were worse things in the world than a quiet death beside a warm fire. And if the boy lived, he'd find out exactly what those things were.

31

Trembling from the cold, Lacey peeked around the thick trunk of a hackberry tree about thirty yards from Butch's house. The van was gone and there was no activity inside. *At least, as far as she could tell.* For probably the thousandth time, she pulled up her cell phone with a shaky hand and checked for service. And like every time before the results were the same: no signal.

Her head and heart were torn. As a mother, Lacey wanted more than anything to run and hide, to live another day and see her own children again. But a young boy and an old man were in trouble. And right now, *she* was the only help they had.

Forcing her stiff legs into action, she stumbled toward the house, her feet frozen numb.

Lacey circled the house once for a closer look, then hopped onto the back porch and eased the door open. Her heart broke at the sight of Butch's body. He was bleeding badly and white as a sheet.

She dashed to the landline in his kitchen, lifted the receiver, but found no dial tone. From there, she grabbed a dish towel, sprinted back to Butch, and pressed it against his dripping wound.

Groggily he opened his eyes and gave her a weak smile. "If you're Saint Peter I ain't disappointed."

Lacey couldn't help but chuckle. Even on the brink of death, the old man could flirt. "Hang in there, Butch. I'm gonna get you to a hospital." She tried to get him off the floor, but he was pure deadweight. "Can you walk at all? I don't think I can carry you."

Butch made an effort to pick himself off the floor, but even with Lacey's help it was no use. He winced, slumped back down, and closed his eyes.

She rubbed his stubbly cheek gently but firmly. "Come on, Butch. Stay with me now." She looked up at a set of headlights in the front window. For some reason she felt it was safer to whisper. "Somebody's coming up the road."

Feeling around for his pistol, Butch opened his woozy eyes about halfway. Once his finger found the gun, he handed it to Lacey. "Know how to use one of these?"

She could shoot really well, but it'd been a while. Her father insisted she practice before going off to college at TCU in Fort Worth. As far as Lacey knew, she was the only Tri Delta in the sorority house packing a nine-millimeter.

Butch slurred out, "Just gotta pull the trigger."

With a nod, Lacey took the pistol and reloaded the bullets from the box beside him. All she could think about was her own two kids and how heartbroken they'd be getting the same kind of devastating phone call she'd received about her father. Determined not to let that happen, she cocked the pistol and pointed it at the door.

Rumbling over the cattle guard, Garrett jammed his foot on the gas, bringing the pickup to up over sixty on the caliche road leading up to the house. He tried Lacey's cell phone again, but nobody answered. Same went for his dad's landline.

He turned to his brother, but before he could speak, Bridger beat him to it. "Something's wrong." He leaned forward with his eyes trained on the house. "Front door's wide open. Looks busted off the hinges."

Dammit! Garrett pounded the steering wheel. Every window was shattered and there were bullet holes everywhere. Looked like a war zone.

He skidded up and threw the truck in park. Yanking the .45 from his belt, he jumped out and leapt onto the porch. Shoulder to wall, he inched to the door. Peering inside he found no threat, just glass shards and wood slivers from what used to be his mother's kitchen.

With his pistol at the ready, Garrett took his first steps inside. Despite his effort to tread in silence, debris cracked and crunched beneath his boots with every step.

At the sound of ragged breathing in the living room, Garrett slowed his pace and inched past the pantry. He had just dipped his head to peer around the corner when the deafening boom of a .357 Magnum sent him flush with the wall. The bullet ripped past and lodged in the ceiling.

"Whoa, whoa! Lacey, it's me! It's Garrett!"

The cocking hammer set him rigid.

He rested his pistol down on the kitchen counter, loud enough for her to hear it. "I'm putting my gun down, okay? And I'm coming over to you now."

He was about to ease his empty hands out for her to see when Bridger stepped up to the door. "What's going—"

Throwing up a palm and pumping the air, Garrett put his index finger to his lips. He turned back in the direction of the living room.

"Lacey, I know you're scared, but I need you to put the gun down, okay? It's just me, Bridger, and Cassidy. We're here to help."

She didn't answer.

"I'm coming around the corner now, so please don't shoot."

Amid heavy breathing, she let out a slight whimper, and then, "*Garrett?*"

He eased out hands and arms first, then let his head trail behind. The massive .357 Magnum was pointing at him. A moment later, Lacey's terrified eyes registered that it was him and she tipped the barrel up to the ceiling.

Garrett rushed over, grabbed the gun, and set it to the side. "It's okay, Lacey. You're safe now." He took her into his arms. "I've got you, baby. I've got you."

She quickly pulled away and looked at him with tear-filled eyes. "It was those Mescalero boys, Garrett. Same ones I saw in Bridger's office."

Scanning the room, Garrett asked, "Where's Asadi?"

"I think they've got him." She shook her head as tears fell. "I snuck out to get help but got turned around in the drifts. And when I came back, he was gone."

Bridger scrambled over with Cassidy on his heels. He knelt beside Butch and scooped his father's lifeless hand into his own. He'd worn the exact same look right before he smashed Rocky Anderson's face into the table. "These sons of bitches, Garrett. I swear to God."

"I know, Bridger—I know. There'll be plenty of time to settle the score. But right now, we've gotta focus on getting Daddy to the hospital." Garrett pulled the cell phone from his coat pocket. "I'll call up Ike. He can have him over to Pampa in no time."

Cassidy knelt beside Butch and ran her hand gently over his thick white hair. "What about a Med-Star helicopter?"

Garrett glanced at his dad who was growing paler by the second. "No time. He's lost too much blood. Ike's just minutes away."

Having done all the explaining he was going to, Garrett instructed Bridger and Cassidy to load up the horses. He dialed Ike and prayed like hell he'd pick up. Remarkably, the barman answered, and accepted the job as casually as Domino's takes a pizza order. He sounded a little drunk though.

After ending the call, Garrett turned to Lacey. "Look, I don't even know what to say."

"You don't have to say anything."

He looked down at his dad for what he hoped wouldn't be the last time. "Take care of him for me, okay?"

Taking a momentary break from caressing Butch's cheek, she applied a fresh towel to his wound. "If anybody knows how much is riding on this, it's me." She glanced up and smiled. "He's in good hands, Garrett."

Garrett couldn't believe how quickly Bridger and Cassidy had saddled the horses and hooked up the trailer. Of course, those were two things both had been doing since childhood so he shouldn't have been all that surprised. What did take him off guard was the fact that in addition to King and Ginger, Sparrow was ready to go too.

"Ah, *hell no.* Not a chance."

Cassidy charged up to Garrett looking ready to take a swing. "You think you're going to stop me from going after my own girls?"

"It's nothing to do with that, Cassidy. Truth be told, I'd rather go in alone. The more of us there are, the likelier it is they'll see us coming."

"I can ride as well as you, Garrett. Maybe better. I may not have been to war, but nobody can beat me on a horse. You know that."

Everything she said was true. Cassidy was as good a rider as God ever put on the face of the earth. And now with Asadi in the mix, he needed an extra horse. He needed her too.

"All right then." Garrett gave a nod. "Plans have changed anyhow."

It was Bridger who took the bait. "What do you mean *changed*?"

"Now that we're owning up to our secrets, I've got a little confessing of my own."

Bridger narrowed his gaze. "What the hell are you talking about?"

"About why I'm back home and who I really work for." Garrett could already feel the weight rising off his chest. "Ya'll get in the truck, I'll tell you on the way. You're going to want to be sitting for this news anyhow."

32

Asadi awoke to warmth, comfort, and the tune of a familiar lullaby. He tried to open his eyes, but they were far too heavy. The rest of his body was the same—arms and legs full of sand and a head swimming in fog. In his mind, he passed from earth to heaven where his mother was waiting with outstretched arms.

Asadi forced his eyes open. Unfortunately, as in every dream since the massacre, the image of his mother disappeared as soon as he woke fully, and he was left with an awful emptiness.

Instead of his mother, the lovely faces of two pretty girls hovered above him. One was singing. The other, holding his head in her lap, stroked his hair. At first, he thought they might be angels, but after a few seconds he recognized them from a photo on Butch's dresser.

The twins had long blond hair and blue eyes and wore identical black-and-gold hoodies, just as they did in the picture. The one singing moved closer. Her forehead wrinkled as she turned to her sister.

"I think he's awake." Her voice barely carried over the crackling fire.

Asadi panicked, remembering the kidnappers had stripped him nearly naked. But with a quick glance downward he found himself clothed again. The shame of realizing these pretty girls must have dressed him caused his face to grow warm. He pushed passed the embarrassment, propped up, and glanced around, taking in the strong scents of leather and varnish from the dark wood tables and plush burgundy chairs. His cloudy gaze moved beyond the furniture, and out to walls made entirely of books—thousands of them—all lined up on two separate levels.

The twin stroking his hair moved her hand to his swollen eye. "I'm so sorry they did this to you."

Asadi was put at ease by her gentle words. He felt safe in the girls' presence, as if he'd known them forever. He tried to speak but produced only gibberish.

The singing twin spoke. "He's trying to say something."

Feeling slightly more in control, Asadi tried again. "*Booch.*"

The one stroking his hair turned to her sister. "Sounds like he said Butch."

"Maybe he speaks Spanish like the men who took us. Ask him and see."

"You know as much Spanish as I do. *You* ask him."

The singer looked pensive, then spoke to him softly. "*Hola. Coma estas?*"

Clearly annoyed, the other rolled her eyes. "*Hello. How are you?* Are you *kidding* me? He's in big trouble, just like we are!"

"I don't know what to say! You say something!"

The one who'd stroked his hair smiled and put her hand to her chest. "I'm Sophie." She pointed to her sister. "This is Chloe."

He patted his chest and forced his words past swollen lips, "*I. Asadi.*"

Chloe sounded out the name, carefully pronouncing each syllable. "*Uh-saw-dee.*" She nudged her sister. "See! I told you it was Spanish."

Wanting to say something, anything to let them know he was a friend, Asadi searched for the right words to explain his connection to their family. "*Booch. Gerwett. Fren.*"

The girls looked to each other in amazement. Sophie grabbed his hand and squeezed. "Did you say . . . Garrett?"

Asadi nodded and patted his chest. "*Fren. Fren.*"

Chloe smiled. "You know my grandpa and uncle?" She thought hard for a moment. "How do you know them?"

Asadi had never wanted to understand so badly. "*Booch. Pease. Hewp.*"

Chloe looked to Sophie. "You think they hurt Grandpa?"

Remembering the condition Butch was in, Asadi rose to his feet. He tried to walk but he was moving far too quickly and immediately felt his head spin. He faltered after his first step but caught himself before falling. "*Booch. Need. Hewp.*"

Sophie grabbed Asadi by the arm and steadied him. "Look. I know you don't feel well, but we're going to have to make a run for it." She pumped her arms. "You know—*run?*"

Asadi made the same motion to show her he understood. If there was a chance to escape, they would take it. "*Run,*" he repeated.

Chloe looked at the door leading out into the hallway. "I wonder if these are the same horrible men who killed Scooter."

Sophie shook off the suggestion. "I'm not sure about anything, Chlo. I just know we have to get out of here or something bad is gonna happen." She glanced up at the sound of footsteps in the hallway. "So, just get ready to run. *Okay?*"

Chloe didn't answer—just stared at the door.

Sophie turned back to Asadi and made the pumping motion with her arms again.

Asadi made the motion back, even though his knees felt like jelly and his stomach was queasy. He was game for anything the beautiful girl told him to do.

The door to the hallway flew open to reveal a chisel-jawed man on the other side. He was tall and broad-shouldered, with yellowish hair swooped back like a lion's mane. He scanned the room until his scowl rested on Asadi. "Where the *hell* do you think you're going, boy?"

He raised a short glass, filled to the rim with a dark liquid, and thrust it out clumsily. Mumbling slowly, he switched his glare to the girls. As the man staggered toward them, Asadi got a better look. With his tan outfit and tall leather boots, he resembled the hunters in Butch's magazines. All that was missing was a rifle.

Sophie spoke with a quivering voice. "You're Preston Kaiser, aren't you?" She took a step back as he turned to face her. "I've seen you around town."

For the first time since he'd entered the room, Kaiser smiled. "No doubt you have, little girl. I *am* the town." He took a few steps forward and stopped. "And I've seen ya'll too." His hungry eyes narrowed on Sophie. "Cheerleaders, right?"

She swallowed hard. "Eighth grade."

Asadi's eyes darted back and forth between the man and Sophie.

"Went to one of your football games last fall. Got a nephew plays quarterback."

Chloe spoke up. "Yeah, we know Duke. He's our friend."

Kaiser shook his head. "He ain't worth a damn." He took a couple of wobbly steps toward the girls. "Enjoyed watching you two though. Almost made it worth my while."

Asadi wished he could understand their conversation. From the tremor in the girls' voices, he could tell they were terribly frightened.

Kaiser took a gulp of his drink, wiped his mouth with his sleeve, and stared Chloe down. "What are you so scared of, honey?" He pointed at the door leading to the hallway. "It's not me you gotta worry about. It's them boys outside you gotta watch out for."

Sophie stepped forward and stood by Asadi. "When my dad hears about this, he's—"

"Your *daddy* ain't gonna do nothing."

Moving over to a silver canister on a table behind the leather sofa, Kaiser scooped out a few ice cubes and dropped them in his empty glass. He poured himself more of the brown liquid, swirled it around. He reached behind his back with his free hand, pulled a black pistol, and let it hang at his side.

"You don't scare us," Sophie said.

Although her words were strong, Asadi could hear the fear in her voice. Something bad was about to happen and he thought she sensed it too.

Kaiser set his empty glass on the end table. "Little girl, you don't know the meaning of the word *scared*. But you will. Trust me, you will. Down in Mexico you'll be introduced to a whole new ugly world you should pray didn't exist."

Chloe said with force, "They'll know you're responsible."

"Well, not necessarily." Kaiser smiled, looking very pleased with himself. "You see, all the evidence points to your daddy being involved with some *muy malo* business partners south of the border. And because of *his* poor choices, you and your family got caught in the cross fire."

Chloe didn't back down but sounded less confident. "Nobody will believe that."

"Doesn't matter what people *believe*." Kaiser locked eyes with Chloe and moved from the table to where she was standing. "What matters is evidence. And I've got people who'll make sure it all points back to your dear sweet daddy." He reached out to stroke Chloe's cheek, but before he could, she let loose a glob of spit that hit his nose.

Kaiser's face registered a look that fell somewhere between shock and rage and he unleashed a back-handed slap that knocked Chloe to the floor. Asadi rushed to help her, but a hard shove from Kaiser sent him tumbling.

Struggling to his feet, Asadi ducked a wild right hook and a clumsy left jab that sent Kaiser stumbling over the rug and face-first to the floor. He was rising to all fours when Sophie snuck up from behind and bashed him across the temple with a brass table lamp. With the humming *clang* still echoing, Kaiser's elbows buckled, and he crashed forward.

Backpedaling, Asadi saw the pistol and bolted for it. He had just grasped the gun when he saw Kaiser's eyes open and settle on him.

33

S mitty leaned against a lion's pelt and scanned the length of Kaiser's trophy room. With its vaulted ceilings and exposed rafters, it looked and felt like a small church chapel. Dark and shadowy. Almost spiritual. The floors and walls were covered in all kinds of skins, heads, and full body mounts, from zebras to rhinos. Their glassy dead eyes flickered in the light of the fire.

Up front stood about a dozen machine-gun-toting *sicarios*, Renegade roughnecks, and Mescalero cowboys—a motley crew of *discoteca* derelicts, oil patch thugs, and Stetson-clad ranch hands. Smitty hadn't seen a nest of crooks this thick since the prison yard in Huntsville.

Nagual paced back and forth before them like some kind of old-world general. Dressed in all black, he had the look and intensity of Che Guevara. It was something about the eyes. He was tall and wiry, built less like a cage fighter and more like a long-distance runner. Despite his slight frame, he was scary as hell. When he spoke, nobody said a word. And that included Kaiser.

Smitty did his best to keep out of sight, slinking between Boggs to his left, and a mounted nine-foot Kodiak bear to his right. Unfortunately, it did no good. Nagual looked to the back of the room and switched from Spanish to his trademark heavily accented English.

"I am expecting a visitor tonight. And that means *you two* will be here to greet him."

Smitty didn't say a word. Just nodded. He prayed his partner would do likewise. Of course, that would've been too easy.

Boggs crossed his arms, leaned forward, and spat a stream of tobacco juice on the Spanish tile floor. "Well, *jefe*, I don't see that happening." He tilted his head at Smitty. "We done our part. Killed that old man and snatched the boy. Far as I'm concerned, the job is done."

Nagual's face tightened. "And the woman?"

Boggs shrugged. "Ain't nothing between her and where she was headed but ice, snow, and a whole lotta nothing. She's a popsicle by now."

Wading through the crowd of Mexican hitmen and Mescalero cowboys, Nagual marched toward them. "And the loss of our shipment?"

"Smitty done told you that old fart ran off with it before we got there. Nothing we could've done." Boggs's lips curled into a smile. "You don't *comprende* too good, do you?"

Smitty clenched his jaw. He'd seen the kind of twisted stuff Nagual had done to people for less than what Boggs was doing right now, and he wanted no part of it. Last fool to cross him was macheted to death and dunked in a barrel full of acid.

Nagual stopped within a few feet of Boggs and bored a hole into him with his eyes. "Perhaps you are just not capable of completing simple tasks."

Boggs unfolded his arms and puffed out his chest. "Let me *splain* your ass something, *jefe*. Our job is *delivery*." He made a motion with his hands as if he was lifting something. It was an over-the-top use of sign language clearly meant to be insulting. "Your job is *supply*." He pretended like he was throwing something on the ground. "If there ain't no shipment when we go to pick it up, then that's *your* fault. Not ours. Your damn pilot missed the drop. Maybe you should talk to him."

"I *have* spoken to him. And I made a very convincing case to his replacement that such an incident will not be repeated."

Smitty knew exactly what that meant. Boggs was about to get the both of them executed right there on the spot.

"Mistakes were made on our side," Nagual admitted. "But why didn't you just take back the package he stole?"

"Coulda done that, but *you* told us don't do nothing without asking first. Just following *your* orders. *Jefe.*"

After several seconds of awkward silence, Nagual's eyes softened, and his lips curled into a smile. "You caught me on a technicality, I suppose."

Nagual turned to his hitmen and translated for them. He shook his head with a contrived look of disappointment. The Mexicans let loose with some nervous laughter and Smitty joined in, just to lighten the tension.

Assuming the laugher was at his expense, Boggs's face turned beet red as he jerked his hunting knife from a hip scabbard and lunged. Smitty didn't know if Nagual saw, heard, or sensed the attack, but he sidestepped the blade with ease.

The knife hadn't hung in the air for more than a half second when Nagual pulled a T-handled push dagger from his belt and sliced Boggs's forearm, then followed with a matching dagger that ripped through the psycho's fleshy paunch like warm butter.

By the time his injuries registered, it was already too late. Boggs made another lunge with his knife, took a wild swing, then lost his balance and stumbled to his knees.

Too terrified to move, Smitty stood like stone. The whole fight seemed to go down in less than a second. In a moment of clarity, realizing he might be next, Smitty took a shaky sidestep as Nagual moved in behind Boggs, gripped his chin, and yanked back.

Nagual dragged his blade across Boggs's jugular and windpipe. The giant fell forward, his body spasming, blood pumping out of him on the shiny tile floor.

Smitty could barely control his bowels. He'd told Malek this was going to happen—warned him this whole thing was crashing in. And now he was going to have to die for it.

Looking from Boggs's quaking body to Nagual, whose glinting daggers looked hungry for more, Smitty shuffled backward a few more steps.

Nagual smiled before asking in a velvet voice, "What about you, friend? Any more *technicalities* I should be aware of?"

His back to the wall, Smitty went stiff. A step either way and those damn little blades would cut him six ways to Sunday. He'd have begged for his life if he could speak. But a vigorous head shake was all he could manage.

34

Asadi's heart sank when he realized they had ended up right back where they started. Spinning around in the dimly lit hallway, he eyed the paintings carefully to be certain. But he was sure of it when he saw the American flag—its bright shining colors still vivid in his mind.

In the face of their failed efforts to escape, the black gun at his side suddenly felt so heavy he could barely keep it in a grip.

Noticing his struggle, Chloe offered to hold it. "We'll take turns," she said with a smile.

A little embarrassed, Asadi handed it over, but felt immediate relief. "*Tenk you.*"

Glancing around the foyer, Sophie whispered to her sister, "We're just going in circles." She scanned the darkness of the formal dining room to their right and spotted a swinging door at the far side. Moving to it with caution, she nudged it open with two fingers and peeked inside.

Asadi and Chloe eased up behind her and peered in also. Beyond the threshold was an industrial-grade kitchen equipped with stainless steel appliances and a big butcher block table surrounded by stools.

The lights were off, but a pale blue glow coming from the far window provided just enough illumination to maneuver by. Asadi eased up behind Chloe, who kept her pistol leveled, sweeping it back and forth in a side-to-side motion.

Spying a door leading to the porch, Sophie moved to it, turned the knob and yanked, but it didn't budge. She rubbed her thumb over the smooth dead bolt. "Locks from the inside." Sophie turned and whispered, "*Now* what?"

Chloe eyed the door leading back to the dining room. "There's no going back. Mr. Kaiser's out there."

"We have to," Sophie argued. "We're trapped in here."

At the sound of approaching voices, Sophie nodded at the spiral staircase in the corner.

Chloe looked nauseous. "*Up?*"

As the voices grew closer, Sophie grabbed Asadi by the sleeve and dragged him up the stairs with Chloe close behind. At the top, they took the first right into a tiny bedroom. By the light of the full moon shining through the window, Asadi and the girls rushed to the closet.

Sophie eased the accordion door open, ducked as she crawled beneath the hanging clothes, and sat with her back flush to the wall. Asadi and Chloe followed.

Once inside, Sophie reached forward, gripped the side of the door, and slid it closed.

In the darkness, Sophie whispered so softly Asadi barely could hear her. "Were we followed?"

"I don't think so," Chloe whispered.

They sat in pitch-blackness for at least a minute with no other sound but their panting. Finally, Sophie spoke again, "Was there a phone out there?"

"I didn't see one." Chloe paused. "I think our only chance is to get to the highway and flag someone down."

"Okay . . . how do we do that without getting caught?"

Chloe had just started to speak when a light switch *clicked*, and a beam flooded beneath the door.

A metallic voice barked and the man standing outside growled, "*Nada.*"

Asadi could hear Chloe's ragged breath and was certain the man outside could too.

A blast of static, the metallic voice again, then the man answered his walkie-talkie, "*Voy para allá.*"

His footsteps thumped away, the light switch *clicked*, and it went dark again.

It was Sophie who spoke first. "That was way too close." She slid the door open and crawled out on hands and knees.

With eyes adjusted to the darkness, Asadi could make out hunting gear around them in the closet— thick camouflage coats and quilted pants. He nudged Chloe and pointed to them.

She rose up, eased a brown fleece pullover off the hanger, and handed it to her sister. Then she gave a coat to Asadi and put one on herself.

Sophie zipped Asadi's coat to his chin and pulled the hood over his head, cinching the cord so tightly it left only his eyes exposed. She turned to her sister who was slipping on a camo beanie she'd found in one of the pockets.

At the sound of shouting downstairs, Chloe stiffened. "*Someone's coming.*"

Sophie grabbed a chair from a desk, dragged it across to the window, and used it as a ladder to reach the latch. She twisted it open with her thumb. "We can jump out the window."

Chloe looked like she was going to be sick again. "From the second story?"

"There's at least a foot of snow on the ground. It'll be soft." Sophie looked to her sister in desperation. "Come on, Chlo! We have to get out of here!"

At the rumble of footsteps downstairs, Sophie yanked the window open. The screech of metal on metal was followed by the *genk-genk-genk* of the alarm system. A blinding strobe in the hallway flashed in unison with the blaring siren.

Asadi looked back to the window, where floodlights outside turned on in sequenced clusters across the compound, illuminating the snow-covered grounds in a halo of white.

Sophie leaned over, surveying their landing pad below. "It's really thick here."

Chloe stepped up to have a look for herself. "Maybe there's bricks underneath."

As a light clicked on in the hallway, Sophie climbed onto the windowsill and made the first leap. Right behind her, Chloe perched precariously, then turned back to Asadi before taking the plunge. "It's okay. Just follow me." Within an instant, she vanished.

Asadi sprinted to the chair, climbed up it onto the ledge and rested there on his haunches, careful not to tip forward. He glanced down but found neither girl, just two dark holes in a fluffy white snow dune.

Hearing heavy footsteps behind him, Asadi leapt, falling for what felt like forever before slamming into the earth with a bone-jarring *thud*.

Below him. Around him. Above him. A frozen cocoon covered his body.

Panic was taking hold when he felt a tug on his coat and was pulled from the mound.

Asadi wiped the snow from his eyes and sprinted after Chloe, chugging through powder as high as his knees. Hurdling icy skeletons of small shrubs and darting around swollen bushes dusted with snow, he ran as hard and fast as he could for at least a hundred yards.

Their flight blocked by the edge of a frozen lake, they hunkered down in a grove of leafless trees to catch their breath. Through a clearing in the woods, a group of men on horseback galloped by, bunched together so tightly it looked as if they were moving as one.

"How many are there?" Sophie whispered to Chloe.

"Too dark to tell. Three. Maybe four?"

Sophie's eyes rested on the pistol in Chloe's hand. "Really think you can use that thing?"

Chloe nodded but did not look confident. "Just aim and shoot. Like Grandpa taught us. Remember that rattlesnake out by the corral?"

"I remember us missing every shot and Grandpa chasing the thing down before it slithered into the barn."

Whatever they were arguing about, Asadi prayed they would figure it out soon. Only minutes outside in the frigid wind and his body was numb. The powdery snow had gotten into his shoes and melted. Now his socks were squishy and freezing.

Sophie sighed, scanned the frozen grounds, and turned to Asadi. She made the running motion with her arms again. "You ready?"

They had just gotten to their feet when a gunshot cracked, and a bullet *whapped* the tree behind them. Nobody said *run*, but they did anyway. Tearing a path through the grove, they dodged skinny saplings and ducked low limbs in a sprint to nowhere.

A snow-covered shrub tripped Asadi but he smothered a cry. He scrambled to his feet and dashed to the girls, who suddenly stopped at the edge of a clearing.

A man on horseback charged toward them, and Sophie grabbed Asadi's coat to yank him the other way. But they were stopped by three more riders coming in on all sides.

With no other option, Sophie turned toward the frozen lake and leapt out onto the ice.

Asadi followed her lead, jumped from the shore and slid until his feet came out from under him. Scrabbling back up with Chloe's help, he tore into a slipping, sliding sprint, then slid to a wobbly halt when he finally caught Sophie.

She crouched low, turned back and raised her finger to her lips. "Quiet," she whispered.

Creeping up from behind, Chloe squatted beside her sister. "You see something?"

Sophie shook her head. "No. That's what worries me."

Stooped beside them, Asadi spun on a heel, surveying the lake's edge. They were about fifty yards from land in every direction.

Chloe glanced back to where they started. "I think they're gone."

Straining his eyes, Asadi searched but found only snow-covered prairie on the moonlit horizon. Then a *crack-crack-crack* of bullets slammed the surface, buzzing and whirring as they ricocheted across the ice and out into the darkness.

With her pistol raised, Chloe spun around, aimed the pistol, pulled the trigger, and a burst of fire leapt from the barrel. There was a short pause as confidence trumped fear and she pulled the trigger three more times.

Asadi squinted hard, looking for movement. There was a sharp *snap*, then a *pop-pop-pop* as the ice split beneath him. He shifted his weight and the fissure grew longer and wider.

"Don't move," Chloe whispered. She took a step, the ice *cracked* underfoot, and she broke into a run. "Go! Go! Go!"

Asadi did his best to keep up, but the girls outpaced him by four or five steps. As he fell farther and farther behind, he imagined the ice caving in beneath his every step, frigid black water lapping at his heels—dragging him under.

Relief washed over him as he hit the edge of the lake, but he was no safer when he dove into a snowbank. Just ahead, a group of riders were galloping toward them— four horses, at least. With the horses bearing down, Asadi looked to the girls for their next move. But the riders' gunfire sent them immediately running.

Each twin grabbed a handful of Asadi's coat and yanked him along. They sprinted a wide loop around the lake dam, leapt a hedgerow and darted across a garden, rising terrace by terrace until equal in height to the mounted gunmen.

They ran as far and fast as they could until coming to a dead-end wall. To the right, one of the marauders galloped up on a black horse and raised his rifle to shoot. But Chloe beat him to the trigger.

As the gunman fell, she shot three more times until the other riders turned and beat a hasty retreat for the cover of the woods.

Sophie screamed, "Keep shooting! What are you waiting for?"

"I'm trying! I'm trying!" Chloe pulled the trigger, but nothing happened. "I think something's wrong with it!"

The top of the pistol locked back like it was hung. *Maybe even broken.*

Sophie grabbed the gun and inspected it. "It's out of bullets!" She tossed it to the ground.

On the other side of the clearing from where they stood, riders dismounted and scurried beneath the shadows of the trees, speaking in hushed voices before suddenly going silent.

And in that moment, Asadi came to a simple understanding. They were no longer being chased—they were being hunted.

35

Hovering through the late-evening darkness in his Hughes 500, Ike pondered all the dumb things he'd done to shorten his life span. Almost dying in nearly every war zone on the planet was his crowning achievement and running a dirty dive bar that catered to scofflaws and cutthroats ran a close second. But flying drunk into whatever trouble the Kohls had gotten themselves into with a Mexican drug cartel was somewhere at the top of the list.

Of course, knowing it was stupid didn't mean he regretted it—not one iota. Ike considered himself a no-account daredevil destined to die a fiery death. His mother once told him he'd end up dead in a ditch, rot to pieces, and turn to dust before anybody could do him the courtesy of a decent Christian burial. It was a story he was apt to believe but he didn't so much care if the buzzards picked his bones, so long as his boots were on while they did it.

Ike always knew God kept him around for a reason. He didn't know if helping Garrett Kohl was his saving grace, but he'd put his neck on the chopping block for lesser men. On top of that, there'd always been a nagging voice in the back of his head that still pricked him raw over Mogadishu, even after all these years. He'd had the good fortune to come home while others hadn't. Since then, he'd tried to make amends.

Finding Butch Kohl's house in the dark wasn't as tough as it could've been. The moon was shining bright and the massive caprock escarpment made for a perfect landmark. All he had to do was follow the ridge to the ranch headquarters and the rest was cake.

Ike circled Butch's house, making a wide swath. He wasn't averse to setting down in a hot landing zone, but if someone was going to be shooting at him, he preferred to know it beforehand. As far as he could tell from his quick reconnaissance, there was nothing to see but a lot of snow and an old white house ripped up by gunfire.

With hardly a window unshattered, the ruined farmhouse sent a chill up his spine.

Nestling into a clear spot between the horse barn and the corral, Ike eased the stick left and lowered the collective. As he hovered in to set her down, a whiteout blasted up from the rotor wash beneath, blinding him momentarily. Not ideal landing conditions, but with no other choice, he rested the skids in the snow by feel and powered his bird down quick as he could.

"Thank God, he's here," Lacey whispered to herself, and pulled the big comforter up around Butch's chin. With the windows gone and the door busted in, the temperature was dropping by the second.

"Just hang in there a little longer, Butch. Help's on the way."

The minutes it had taken Ike to get there felt like hours. Lacey looked down at Butch's ashen face to find it looking different—less determined. The man who wore a permanent scowl, the portrait of grit, was yielding to his injuries. As much as she didn't want to believe it, even a tough old cuss like Butch had his limits.

Lacey had her ear to Butch's face to check for breathing when Ike came flying through the door from the back porch. He rushed over, knelt beside her, and scooped the rancher into his arms like he weighed nothing. And he did it all without a single word.

Lacey grabbed some more clean towels for bandages and bolted out the back door after him. By the time she leapt from the porch Ike was already loading Butch into a black-and-silver helicopter.

She sprinted over and hopped in back with Butch, resting his head on her lap atop a pillow of towels. Ike placed a headset over her ears then ran back to the front and jumped in.

As the motor whirred to life, Ike spoke to her over the headset. "Lacey, you hear me?"

She nodded instead of answering, fixated on how much more listless Butch had become. After a few seconds, Ike spoke again. "You gotta talk into the mike, darlin'."

Realizing her mistake, she immediately answered. "Yes, I can hear you. Sorry."

"No sweat. You've got a lot on your plate back there and you're doing fantastic."

Lacey didn't feel that way, but it was still nice to hear. She leaned down to put her cheek against Butch's nose. "I can barely feel his breath, Ike. I think we're running out of time."

"You don't worry about time. That's my department. Just keep lots of pressure on that wound and change out the bandages soon as they soak through. Can you do that for me?"

She nodded again then caught herself. "Yeah, I can do that."

"What are his vitals?"

She felt his wrist. "His pulse is so low I can barely feel it. He feels really cold, but he's not shivering. Not moving at all, really."

"Okay, there's a good chance he's going into shock. Keep him warm as you can with that blanket. Cover him up with those towels too and elevate his feet. Now if his pulse starts to race and he starts breathing heavy, I don't want you to panic. Just talk to him nice and easy. He may not respond but I guarantee he can hear you. Let him know what we're doing the whole way there. You don't have to lie to him like some kid. Just keep telling him we're close to the hospital and a team is waiting to treat him, which they are. Got it?"

She remembered to answer this time. "Got it."

It was clear to Lacey that Ike had done this many times before, which made her wonder how many shootings there'd been at Crippled Crows.

Ike turned his head slightly. "One more thing I need you to do for me."

"What's that?"

Ike lost the bravado in his voice. "I'm uh . . . probably not on the best of terms with the *Almighty*, so any favors to be asked might get a better reception from you rather than me."

Lacey nearly laughed but she could tell he was being sincere. "Consider it done, Ike."

With his bird zooming toward Pampa at 150 knots, Ike glanced back to see if he could gauge Butch's condition. Lacey was smiling optimistically and speaking to him in a soft voice, just like he'd told her to do. Through the headset he could hear her walking Butch through every step of the process, all matter-of-fact, like they were taking a Sunday drive.

"Almost there now, Butch." Lacey stroked his white hair gently. "You're doing great. Flying over the Hayhook right now. Means we're real close to the hospital."

Glancing down at the massive Hayhook Ranch, Ike determined she was right. He could see the lights of Pampa off in the distance and hoped Sanchez was there waiting for him like he was supposed to be. He'd told the deputy to keep quiet about what was going on, but there was nothing in the world low-key about flying in hot with a gunshot victim in the back of your bird.

There'd be a lot of questions from law enforcement to which he had few answers. And he wanted Sanchez there to make sure he could break loose of any eager-beaver cops, deputies, or state troopers who felt the need to grill him over a bunch of crap he knew nothing about. Last thing he wanted to do was get held up in questioning when Garrett needed him most.

Let 'em be pissed. Wouldn't be the first time.

Circling to set her down, Ike saw a crowd of folks standing around the helipad. It was mostly medical personnel by the gurney, but some lawmen were in the bunch.

Ike pushed the stick left and pulled the collective as he spoke to Lacey through the headset. "You did a great job back there."

A nervous laugh preceded her voice. "I didn't really do anything, Ike."

"You did everything you could do with the tools you had. And you did it to perfection."

"What do I do now?"

Ike throttled back, lining up on the pad. He held the bird steady before landing.

"You stay right there by Butch's side and let him know everything's going to be just fine. And you tell him I'm headed out to the Mescalero Ranch to help his boys. Okay?"

The second the skids hit concrete Lacey's door opened and a blast of frigid air filled the cockpit. Butch was whisked from Lacey's lap and placed on the gurney.

Parting the crowd like Moses split the Red Sea, Sanchez stepped up and opened the front-passenger door. He yelled over the rotors and engine, "Who the hell did this, Ike?"

Ike turned to Lacey, who hadn't moved a muscle. She looked as if she might be going into shock herself.

Willing her to shake a leg, Ike mustered a voice that was both gentle and commanding. "Mission accomplished, darlin'. Now head on in there and take care of our patient."

Lacey didn't look up or acknowledge him. She just sat in stunned silence.

Sanchez yelled again at Ike, this time louder, "Come on, Ike! What's happening? Where's Garrett?"

Cupping his hand over his ear, Ike feigned confusion to give Lacey some more time.

Sanchez leaned in and yelled, "Dammit, Ike! Shut her down!" He tilted his head toward the throng of law enforcement officials behind him. "These boys have some questions!"

Two grim-faced state troopers—thick and solid as chimneys—stepped up behind Sanchez. One reached for his sidearm.

Ike looked back to find Lacey unchanged. She was staring straight down, her eyes transfixed on the blood-drenched towels in her lap.

He spoke to her again. This time with a little more force. "All right, Lacey! You done real good, girl! Now hop on out and go help Butch!"

Her trance finally broken, Lacey flashed a timid smile and stepped out onto the helipad.

Ike looked to Sanchez, who had just leaned in, grabbed him by the collar and jerked him into the cockpit. The stupefied state troopers sprinted forward but not before Ike yanked the collective, shooting the bird off the ground like a bottle rocket.

Sanchez yelled so loud that Ike could hear him over the blast of the rotors. "Dammit, Ike! You crazy-ass son of a bitch! What the hell are you—"

His reaction was the same as anyone who'd been shanghaied while hanging halfway out of a helicopter. But there was no time to deal with that. Ike figured his old buddy Deputy Dawg would understand once he got an explanation. And if not, there was always the door.

PART FOUR

Shoot first and never miss.

—BAT MASTERSON

36

Garrett panned the moonlit horizon for any signs of trouble. But in the fifteen minutes his pickup had been bumping over the Mescalero Ranch oil field roads, he, Bridger, and Cassidy had encountered only a few nasty chuckholes. Roughly the size of Washington, DC, Kaiser's backyard was a colossus of rough country. Towering mesas, deep crags, and rolling sandhills over two stories high covered a snowy landscape of frozen creeks and thorny mesquite.

Garrett wondered if they'd bitten off more than they could chew, but there was no going back now. Decisions were made, and this was happening. No amount of second-guessing would change any of that.

Shaking off the bad juju of pessimism, he cut his eyes to Bridger, who was uncharacteristically quiet. As Garrett expected, his admission to working for the DEA had come as quite a shock. "I know you got something to say, so go on and say it."

His brother didn't look over, but at least he spoke. "You didn't trust us, or what?"

"Not that at all, Bridger. I kept it quiet for your protection and my own."

Garrett was thinking specifically of DEA Special Agent Kiki Camarena, who was horrifically tortured and murdered by drug traffickers down in Mexico.

"But you told Daddy?"

"I needed to designate a next of kin in case something happened."

Bridger finally turned and stared. "So, this oil company work you've been talking about for years was all just a big lie?"

"I was living my cover, Bridger. That's what we have to do. The more real it is to me and everyone else, the more real it is to a narco who might want to lop my head off. Cartels have eyes and ears everywhere. I couldn't take a chance." He turned and faced down his brother. "*Hell,* what's happening to us right now is all the proof you need. Surprised I have to explain it."

Bridger was silent and he appeared to be calming down as he digested Garrett's reasoning. "Still. You could've told me."

Garrett had to think for a second. He didn't know how much he wanted to get into with everything else going on. But it was clear Bridger wasn't going to let this thing go. He glanced in the rearview, hoping Cassidy might weigh in on his side, which she sometimes did, but his sister-in-law looked as eager for an answer as her husband.

"Bridger, our whole lives you've always been *the show*. Quarterback. Rodeo star. Scholarships. Law school. You name the award or trophy, you won it."

Bridger looked over. "What the hell does that have to do with you?"

"Nothing. And that's the point. DEA was all my own. Something you couldn't one-up me on with Daddy."

"One-up you! Is that what you think I've been doing all these years?"

Hearing it out loud, Garrett had to admit it sounded petty. "I know it wasn't intentional on your part, but that's how it played out. Living in your shadow wasn't easy."

"I could say the same," Bridger snapped.

Now Garrett looked over. "What's that supposed to mean?"

"Means exactly what I said. How do you think it felt to be the brother of a big war hero? You really think Daddy was going to let that one slip by?"

Garrett shook off the notion. Bridger was just trying to flip this thing around.

"He never cared about any of that."

"Not to your face, maybe. But believe me, Garrett, I heard plenty. And so did everyone in the whole damn county. When you made Special Forces, it was all he talked about. You were the patriot son. Out there serving God and country. And I was the butt of his lawyer jokes."

Ah hell. Butch Kohl strikes again. That was the old man's MO for sure.

Bridger let out a breath and continued, "Look, we're brothers. And despite our differences, we've always had each other's backs. Had to after Mama died. And that's how I want it to be from here on out. No more secrets. No more grudges. We got a deal?"

Having come face-to-face with the Kohl Code for the second time in forty-eight hours, Garrett nodded and threw out a hand, which Bridger shook. And in true Kohl family fashion the hatchet was buried. Again.

Tapping the brakes at a Y in the road, Garrett looked at Bridger. "Which way now?"

Bridger pulled the map close to his face. "Southeast from here."

As Garrett veered left, Cassidy, who'd been silent for her own reasons, spoke up from the backseat. "How much farther?"

Glancing in the rearview again, Garrett saw her fidgeting, her face tense with worry. "Almost there. Couple minutes maybe." He looked to his brother for confirmation, hoping he'd be the one to do the consoling. "That right, Bridge?"

Engrossed in his map, Bridger didn't answer.

Garrett's iPhone buzzed in his pocket. He pulled it out to see Kim Manning again.

Damn! Four missed calls in an hour.

Clicking it to voice mail, Garrett turned his pickup south at Bridger's command, and tore down a smaller oil field road leading up to an old drill site location. The sign on the fence around the forty-eight-foot pump jack read Boone 12–25H.

Right where it was supposed to be.

Garrett killed the headlights as he pulled up behind a couple of crude oil reservoirs. Turning to his brother he asked, "Still think this is as far as we can make it by road?"

Bridger laid the map down on the center console and clicked on the interior light to confirm. "Afraid so. From here, we cut due west, ride about a mile to this ravine." He made a circle around it with the tip of his finger. "It's a hundred-foot drop in some places, but we can cross at this little gulley."

Shifting into park Garrett glanced at the map. "Central Tank Battery looks hard to miss."

"It is. Every bit of oil and gas on the Mescalero Ranch flows into this spot. There's at least a dozen or so forty-foot crude reservoirs and that's not including all your flow lines, condensers, and separators on the pad. They keep an office out there too. But I doubt anyone's around this time of night."

A trace of Garrett's finger put them where they needed to be. He could tell by the topographic map they'd have the high ground. "Looks like Kaiser's compound will be in plain view from there."

Before Bridger could answer, he was interrupted by a clang of stomping hooves from the trailer. The horses were ready to move.

"Guess that's our cue," Garrett added.

Grabbing their gear, Bridger and Cassidy jumped out of the truck and slammed the doors.

Garrett had just pulled the door handle when he noticed Kim had left a voice mail. He clicked the speaker button and played the message as he pulled his pack from the backseat.

Where are you, Kohl . . . ? Contreras and I put a team together in Virginia and we're headed back to Tsavo. Got the go ahead to "take care" of the problem. Call me ASAP.

Garrett instinctively reached to call back but stopped short. *Where would he even begin?*

After trading his silverbelly Catalena for a black wool stocking cap, he threw open the door and stepped outside. Shuddering as the cold wind slammed him, Garrett couldn't believe how quickly the temperature had dropped in the half hour since they'd left the ranch.

Grabbing the Spiritus Systems Micro Fight chest rig from the front seat, he slipped it over his coat and wrapped a black-and-gray *shemagh* scarf around his neck. Behind him, Bridger and Cassidy were already outfitted in thick camo coats, beanies, and snake boots as tall as their knees. Better still, they were mounted and ready to go.

Garrett opened the back door, pulled his Lone Star Armory TX15 off the seat, and slung the rifle over his shoulder. He turned to find Bridger riding over on Ginger, the roan mare.

Handing over the reins to a muscled sorrel gelding, Bridger asked, "You good with King?"

Garrett gave a nod. "Fastest we've got, to hear Daddy tell it." Thrusting the toe of his left boot into the stirrup, he swung into the saddle and looped King in a circle to face Bridger and Cassidy.

"Got everything? Guns? Extra ammo? Flashlights? Maps?"

Bridger patted the Henry rifle tucked in his saddle scabbard. Cassidy mimicked the gesture, but with Butch's Colt Python tucked into her jeans. With a little spur, Garrett eased King closer to Ginger and Sparrow. Their breath formed one rising vapor cloud.

Harkening back to the old days, Garrett resurrected his sergeant's voice. "Something happens to me, ya'll keep going for the kids. Ride hard, fast, and don't look back. Understand?"

Bridger shook off the order. "We ain't leaving you behind. Might as well get that nonsense out of your head."

"Now, I'm serious about this, Bridger. Don't wait on me. Not even for a second. This thing goes sideways, just haul ass. I can take care of myself."

Bridger didn't reply. He tugged the reins right and spurred Ginger into a trot. Cassidy was right behind him, kicking up a snow cloud in Sparrow's wake.

Garrett panned the flat horizon and nudged King with his boot heels. Eager for the chase, the sorrel lurched forward and dug his hooves into the earth until they built into a gallop.

Within a couple of seconds, the world around them was a blur of white prairie and a ceiling of stars. Beyond the blasting wind and the four-beat pattern of thundering hooves, every other sound disappeared.

It was serenity and chaos—all in a single motion.

But as Garrett charged into battle, his mind wrestled with Bridger's earlier words.

We live as a family. We die as a family.

Smitty figured he'd tromped through the snow for at least a mile and a half. He turned back to Kaiser's compound and admired the luster. With the floodlights blazing, the place looked like a raging fire. After several minutes meandering through the mesquite, he found the Central Tank Battery. In the light of the fluorescents shone a set of stairs and a scaffolding atop the tanks. He hurried up the iron framework, his work boots clanging with every step.

Smitty turned east and detected horses galloping in from the back side of the ranch. In the darkness they were silhouettes, but he recognized Garrett Kohl by the long hair. With his scarf-wrapped face and strapped down with ammo, he looked like some outlaw gunslinger from *The Magnificent Seven*.

Smitty fished the phone from his coat pocket to find there was still no response from Malek. Instead a call came in from Kaiser.

"All right, Smitty, cameras picked up the Kohls at the 12–25H. Got three coming on horseback your way. You see 'em yet?"

"Not yet," Smitty lied. "Maybe they went in another direction."

"Not likely. Straightest path to get here is down the CTB road. Right beside you."

Smitty kept a careful eye on the Kohls, who were still at the edge of the canyon. "I'll keep a good lookout for them."

"You'll have to do more than that. Those Comanche brothers get the drop on you and there'll be hell to pay. You heard what they did to Nagual's men, didn't you?"

Smitty swallowed hard. "Yeah, I heard. Killed 'em all dead."

"I'll send Rocky and the Mexicans to back you up."

"How long?"

"Few minutes at the most." There was a pause on Kaiser's end. "And, Smitty, you let them slip past, then you'd better put a bullet in your own head. Those brothers don't kill you, I sure as hell will."

Before he could respond, Kaiser ended the call. Hoping he'd get a text from Malek telling him help was on the way, Smitty checked his phone again. Nothing.

Smitty looked out over the ravine as the Kohls trotted up to the ledge. If he murdered them in cold blood, he'd be no better than the Garzas. If he didn't, Kaiser would kill him straight-out. He shouldered the AK-47 and put the sights on Garrett, praying desperately for an option that was somewhere in between.

37

G arrett had traveled no more than a mile, but he was just about frozen solid. Still, it was good to be back in the saddle. The rhythm between horse and rider had no equal. There was a mutually recognized cadence, a union of spirits where everything faded but the ride itself.

Pulling up behind Bridger and Cassidy, he stopped at the ledge of a gully. At first glance, the area below the ridge looked like a dark abyss, but after his eyes adjusted, he estimated the drop to the bottom of the gulch was about fifty feet.

On the other side was Mescalero's Central Tank Battery—a complex about half the size of a football field. With its two thirty-foot pipes flaring natural gas, the facility looked like something out of *Mad*

Max. The steel fortress basked in the light of a flickering orange glow.

Nudging King in between Ginger and Sparrow, Garrett shouldered the TX15 and scanned the facility with his Vortex scope. There were twelve steel cauldrons, each forty feet high, and one mobile home office flanked by halogen lamps on poles.

"This is it." Garrett turned to his brother. "You ready?"

"Hold on a second. Need one last look." Bridger pulled the map from inside his coat, clicked on a small flashlight, and studied a folded section. "Once we cross here, we head due south. There's a road leading straight up to Kaiser's compound." He swapped the ranch map for his blueprints. "Kitchen entrance is on the north end."

Panning the snow-covered mesquite brush, Garrett studied the tank battery for a third time, finally satisfied it was secure. "And what if the kids aren't around when we get there?"

"Then we find somebody who knows where they are and start asking some serious questions."

Garrett hated to grill his brother over simple objectives, but in his experience, direct-action assaults were never pulled off without a hitch or two. Their crash course in close quarters battle wasn't ideal, but it was better than nothing.

Pulling up his rifle, Garrett panned the tank battery again. This time a silhouette dashed across the yellow scaffolding above the oil tanks. He had just gotten the shadow in his crosshairs when a muzzle flashed, and a bullet cracked overhead.

Damn! So much for coming in under the radar.

Garrett yelled, "Go, Bridger! Go! I'll catch up!"

Tugging the reins left, his brother spurred Ginger into a gallop along the lip of the ridge with Cassidy close behind on Sparrow. About thirty yards out, they found a switchback trail leading down into the gulley and turned onto it.

Adrenaline pumping, Garrett jerked the rifle to his shoulder and clicked the selector off safety. With eyes on optics he searched the top of the tanks and saw a shadow move. Multiple muzzle flashes followed as the gunman kept firing.

Resting his crosshairs on the erratic light bursts, Garrett pulled the trigger twice and the *thenkthenk* of his suppressed rifle echoed in the ravine below. Sweeping the platform, Garrett caught movement at the bottom of his reticle. He dropped the scope and found the gunman hurtling down the stairs—taking three steps at a time.

Garrett fired again, but the shooter cut left and the bullet sparked off a handrail.

Working to reengage, Garrett trailed his target, but the crosshairs were always a sliver behind. The gunman took cover behind a maroon shipping container and the shot was lost.

With a lull in the action, Garrett snuck in a quick breath to get his head in the game. He lowered the scope and took in the tank battery with his naked eye.

Beneath the licking flames of the gas flares, every shadow moved, and every pipe was a gun. He'd just focused in on the Conex box when a rifle hung around it and fired full-auto.

Garrett ducked as supersonic rounds ripped the air overhead and spooked King into a panicked fit of snorting, rearing, and bucking. Nearly thrown from the saddle, he gentled the horse with some sweet talk and a scratch between the ears.

When the rodeo ended, Garrett loped his horse in a counterclockwise circle, building momentum into a gallop as he steered toward the ravine.

Leaning back in the saddle, Garrett thrust his full weight into the stirrups as King leapt from the ledge and they plunged in a near vertical free fall.

One.

Two.

Three seconds passed, until hooves caught again and thundered on the downslope.

The bounding sorrel let out a shallow breath as he picked up speed and tore across the straightaway of the valley floor.

Spotting a cattle trail, Garrett moved the reins right, nosing onto the path. He leaned forward, head beside King's as they traversed up the ridge.

Once they'd crested it, he gave his horse the spurs and galloped the length of the tank battery, pulling up behind the shipping container where he had last spotted the shooter. But all that was left were spent casings and fresh tracks.

Sucking in frigid air, Garrett dismounted and followed the trail that twisted and turned on the narrow concrete pathway through the towering steel cauldrons. The odor of methane hung heavy in the air, catching his attention, as did the startling sight of a red flammable gases sign.

Ignoring the warning, Garrett shouldered his rifle and switched from optics to offset iron sights. Finger by the trigger, he crept forward.

Beyond the oil tanks, twenty yards ahead, a gun barrel swung around a blue compressor unit and opened fire.

With bullets sparking off steel, Garrett dropped to a knee and found flesh in his sights. His shot ripped the gunman's hip and spun him off his feet.

Garrett hopped up, sprinted forward, and kicked the rifle out of reach.

The gunman rolled to his back and threw up his hands. "Don't! Please! I wasn't trying to hit you!"

"If your plan was to shoot at me and miss, you need to rethink your strategy."

"I swear it!"

Garrett leaned in and read the name patch on the guy's Renegade coat: *Ray Smitty.* Remembering him from the Wagon Bridge, he jammed a boot on his chest to keep him pinned as he tried to squirm away.

Smitty clenched his eyes. "Look, I been hunting all my life. I had a clean shot from the tower. If I was going to hit you, I'd a hit you, man. I just wanted to run ya'll outta here!"

Remembering where Smitty was positioned on the tower, Garrett realized it could've been true. Country boys like him had hunted since birth. If the guy had missed them, while they were standing still, no less, he was either the worst shot in the world or Smitty was telling the truth.

Garrett pressed the barrel of his rifle against Smitty's forehead. "You know why I'm here, Ray. Where are the kids?"

"They're gone, man! Gone!"

Garrett's blood ran cold. "What do you mean *gone?*" He slid the rifle down and jabbed the muzzle into Smitty's cheek.

Confusion spread across Smitty's face. "Just ran off! That's all!"

Garrett rested only slightly easier. Cold as it was, they wouldn't last long. "Ran off where?"

"Hell if I know! They whacked Kaiser with a lamp and tore off with his gun! Everybody's out searching for them!"

Praise Jesus, they're still alive. Garrett took a relieved breath. "The kids are all right, then? Nobody's been hurt?"

"Somebody done whupped up on that boy, pretty good." Smitty pointed back at the compound. "Probably Kaiser that done it."

Glancing around again Garrett noticed approaching headlights. "Who's on the way?"

"Nagual's crew, I reckon." Smitty shook his head. "Whatever you got cooked up, man, it ain't gonna work. They seen you coming in on a security camera. Whole place is on lockdown."

Garrett turned back and scanned the horizon. Given the elevation, he could see the lights of Kaiser's sprawling compound nearly a mile away.

He pulled out his phone to warn Bridger or Cassidy.

No answer.

Dammit!

Garrett sprinted back through the narrow passageway between the steel cauldrons to find King. The dutiful horse was waiting behind the shipping container right where he'd left him. Swinging into the saddle, he gave the sorrel a nudge, galloped away from the pad about thirty yards, and took cover in a clump of hackberry trees.

If Kaiser wanted a war, he was damn sure going to get one—blood, bullets, and more.

38

Preston Kaiser hopped in the copilot seat of his blue-and-white Bell JetRanger 206 and placed the headphones over his ears. His head was spinning from the half bottle of Balmorhea whiskey he'd downed and he was still seeing double from getting whacked with the lamp. He looked to the normally loudmouthed chopper pilot who hadn't said a word.

Chaz Zuma, no doubt a ridiculous alias, was a leather-skinned blowhard from Panama City, Florida, who never shut the hell up about his flying exploits. He claimed to have honed his piloting skills working for an offshore energy company in the Gulf of Mexico. Only thing Kaiser knew for sure was that he'd done a stretch in an Alabama state prison for drug trafficking.

Once situated in the cockpit, Kaiser chambered a round in his Colt Canada C20 rifle, equipped with a Trijicon REAP-IR thermal scope. His Bell was retro-fitted with multiple gun ports on the front and back doors. He'd originally had them done to hunt coyotes and feral hogs, but tonight they'd do just as nicely for killing Kohls.

Kaiser opened the midport, thrust the rifle barrel outside, and swept it across the frozen landscape. The howling winds would make firing from a helicopter like shooting from a roller coaster. He nodded to Zuma and the Bell slowly lifted, never climbing more than a couple hundred feet off the ground.

As they hovered over the lake, Kaiser lowered the optics and took in the scene with his naked eye. The kids were hunkered down on an eight-foot garden ter-race running the edge of the lake. Huddled together behind a hedgerow so tightly, they looked like a clump of bushes.

Bo and his cowboys were fanned out in the snow about fifty yards in front of them, below the kids' po-sition. Their rifles were ready, but nobody moved or fired.

Kaiser gave Zuma the swirling motion with his index finger. "Circle around. I want to see what the hell is going on down there." He picked up his phone and texted Nagual, who was directing operations below:

What's the holdup?

Nagual replied:

Children have a gun.

Kaiser jabbed the keys on the phone and mashed send.

SO WHAT??!!

There was a short delay, then:

They killed one of your men.

Kaiser was about to respond when Nagual added:

Do you have a shot at them?

Leaning forward, Kaiser raised the scope and scanned upward toward the lake. In the glow of the viewfinder, the kids' faces were looking up. His crosshairs found them with ease, but with his Bell bucking and bobbing he couldn't hold a good aim.

He turned to his white-knuckled pilot and barked, "Can't you hold this thing steady for two damn seconds?"

Fighting the stick, Zuma's panicked eyes darted from the controls to the windscreen. "Ain't easy, boss. Wind's slamming us at over twenty knots."

Kaiser readjusted the rifle and jammed it against the bottom-right corner of the port window for stability. "Gimme some left pedal, dammit!"

As the pilot brought the tail around, Kaiser scanned left and found the kids. He put the crosshairs on one of the Kohl girls.

Hopefully, it was that bitch who'd whacked him.

But the Bell suddenly dipped, knocking him off target.

He worked hastily to find them again and drew favor with the wind. A quick lull, Kaiser readjusted, and found one in his sights.

Resting the crosshairs on the boy's face, Kaiser pulled the rifle tight to his shoulder, and braced for recoil.

From the hackberry grove, Garrett watched the white Ford one-ton drive onto the tank battery. The flickering flames of the gas flares illuminated gunmen inside the cab and several in the bed. Looked to be six in total.

They pulled up around behind the oil tanks and Garrett lost visual. The brakes squealed, and the engine died to a muffled rumble.

Allowing them a few seconds to disperse, Garrett spurred King into a gallop, crossing the flat and leaping onto the pad from behind a compressor unit. He'd just shouldered his rifle when he came within ten yards of a guard standing by the office door.

The startled *sicario* yanked up his AK to fire a half second too late. Garrett's irons were already center mass. Pulling the trigger twice, he landed a double tap to the chest. The gunman stumbled backward and collapsed in the snow.

Garrett scanned left, then upward, following a heavy knock of gunfire. On the scaffolding above the tanks, a shooter sprayed wildly, taking no time to aim.

After firing two low shots that sparked off the grated scaffolding, Garrett raised his rifle, canted from irons to optics, and eased the crosshairs between the yellow bars of the handrail. A squeeze of the trigger and his bullet caught the gunman in the right thigh.

The *sicario* wavered but kept firing.

Garrett adjusted aim and took a headshot. The gunman crumbled and somersaulted down the stairs with a reverberating *clang*.

Spurring King into a trot, Garrett scanned right to the Renegade truck where he glimpsed a muzzle flash. Inside the cab a pistol barked twice, and its rounds cracked overhead.

Rotating his rifle just a fraction, Garrett switched from optics to irons, found the gunman inside the window, and put three rounds in his chest and neck.

Garrett spun. Saw the backs of two deserters taking cover in the mesquite brush.

There was panicked shouting, followed by the distinctive knock of AK-47s as they fired back blindly. Seconds passed, the gunfire subsided, and the gunmen fled the scene.

Dismounting on the fly, Garrett jogged between the oil tanks where he'd left Ray Smitty. The wretch had propped himself up on his elbows and was moaning like a wounded animal.

Garrett knelt beside him. "Got any smokes?"

Smitty reached inside his coat with a shaky hand and pulled out a crunched pack of Winstons and a red Bic lighter. "This ain't like my last request or something, is it?" He chuckled nervously as he handed them over.

"Oh, don't worry about that." Garrett pulled a bent cigarette from the pack, clamped it between his pointer and middle fingers, and placed it on his lower lip. "My guess is stupidity will kill you long before I do."

"While you're at it." Smitty eased his bloody hand up. "Wouldn't mind one myself."

Garrett lit the cigarette, took a deep drag, and tossed the pack and lighter back to Smitty. Eyeing the oil and gas separator, he asked, "About how fast can you run?"

Preoccupied with Garrett's question, Smitty lost interest in his cigarettes. "What the hell are you talking about, man?"

"I *said*, how fast can you run?"

"Not too fast," Smitty whined. "You done shot me in the hip and that Indian kid stuck me with an arrow. Cain't even feel my feet no more I'm so damn cold."

"Well, I wouldn't worry too much about that last part."

Watching the glowing tip of the cigarette, Smitty's eye went wide. He scurried to his feet and hobbled toward the ravine.

Garrett walked back to the idling Renegade truck, put it in gear, and drove over to the oil and gas separator unit. He put it in park, hopped out, and took the plastic jerry can full of gasoline from the bed. Unscrewing the lid, he tipped the can over inside the cab.

Giving it a few seconds to gurgle out onto the floor-board, Garrett took several big drags off his cigarette, then flicked it inside and slammed the door.

Sprinting away he heard a *whoosh* then a *whump*, and not a second later the ice-covered mesquite flickered like amber diamonds. The natural gas line exploded and flames from the first oil and gas separator rose sixty feet in the air.

Garrett jumped into the saddle and got King into a gallop just as the first cauldron blew. The shock wave nearly knocked him from his saddle. Fighting for balance, he turned to see a tempest of orange flames and a rolling mushroom cloud of billowing black smoke.

At a safe distance, Garrett turned back and watched with a smile.

The destruction.

The chaos.

This multimillion-dollar bonfire was about to get some serious attention.

With his crosshairs set on the boy, Kaiser rested the pad of his finger on the trigger and was about to pull when panicked shouting erupted in the cockpit. He'd turned to give Zuma a good ass-chewing when the domino explosions at the Central Tank Battery superseded his plans.

"*What—the—*" Kaiser's eyes went wide at the *whump, whump, whump* of exploding steel cauldrons both felt and heard in the air from a half mile away.

"Get us over there! *Now!*"

A squeamish-looking Zuma pushed the stick left, raised the collective to get some speed, and made a straight shot to the Central Tank Battery. The bluish glow from the full moon that had bathed the white landscape gave way to a hellish red blaze emanating from the twisted steel flow lines and towering reservoirs of burning crude.

As Zuma made a couple of wide passes around the fiery wreckage, Kaiser spotted the burning hull of the white Renegade truck and two dead bodies atop the pad. About to make a third pass around, Kaiser caught a glimpse of movement in the ravine.

He tapped the pilot on the shoulder and pointed to the writhing body. "Take her down. We've got a live one."

Maneuvering into a clearing, Zuma dropped the skids with a jarring thud. Snow whipping up from the rotor wash circled the Bell in a blinding white whirlwind.

Kaiser opened the door, shouldered his rifle, and jumped out. With the sharp bite of snow and ice stinging his face, he ducked low and sprinted out of it. He followed the pathetic moan that ultimately led to Ray Smitty.

On his back, looking near dead, Smitty lay with cheeks glistening in the leaping flames from the tank battery atop the ridge. "Oh, thank God, man! Thank God!"

Kaiser lowered the C20 and knelt beside him. "What *the hell* happened?"

Smitty looked as if he'd seen a ghost. His state of consciousness was somewhere between delirious and dying. He eked out the words, "Shot me."

Gripping Smitty's face between his thumb and fingers, Kaiser pointed to his blazing facility. "Not to you! I'm talking about up there! *What. Happened?*"

"That Green Beret is what happened. Blew everything all to hell."

"I can see that, you idiot!" Kaiser let loose and watched as Smitty struggled to push himself up. "*How?* I sent Rocky and Nagual's men to back you up." He looked up and surveyed the top of the ridge, wondering if Garrett was up there now. "I warned you, didn't I? I warned you not to let him slip by."

He swung his leg back and kicked Smitty in the ribs. "Every bit of oil and gas I've got on this place is going up in a *damn* ball of flames because you couldn't handle a simple job!"

Drawing back for another kick, Kaiser stopped short, fighting like hell to calm down and collect his thoughts. "Did you *at least* see where he went?"

Smitty raised a shaky arm and pointed to nowhere. "Went after Rocky and Nagual's boys on horseback." His voice was low and raspy. "Tore off after 'em like he was tracking a deer."

Kaiser looked down and kicked a boot full of fresh powder in Smitty's face. "This is all because you and that Boggs couldn't get the dope from an old rancher. Now this crap's *really* gonna get messy."

Smitty tried to push himself up but his arms gave out. "I need a doctor."

Kaiser laughed. "Well, you'd better get a move on then. Closest hospital is in Gray County. And that's a good twenty miles."

"Please. You gotta fly me out." He pointed to Kaiser's helicopter and croaked out his plea. "I'll die out here."

"Go on and die." Kaiser turned and marched away. "Doubt anybody'll miss you."

Remembering Smitty had a wife and kid he felt a tinge of guilt. But not enough to waste a trip to Pampa. Back aboard, Kaiser donned his headphones and turned to Zuma. "Take her up."

Zuma pulled the collective and the Bell lifted off the ground. Once they were up about a hundred feet, he turned to his boss. "Where we headed?"

Hatred burning in his eyes, Kaiser stared down at the inferno below, watching as his tank battery warped into a pile of molten rubble. "We're going to find the man responsible for this. And when I'm done, there'll be nothing left of him to bury."

39

When Garrett got to the edge of the mesquite brush, he brought King to a halt, jerked his TX15 up, and scanned the flat horizon. Two of the runaways he'd tracked from the Central Tank Battery were kneeling behind a concrete feed bunker about seventy yards out. The tops of their heads were barely visible above a windswept pile of powdery snow.

He spurred the sorrel into a full gallop and made a wide loop on the gunmen's flanks. Forty yards from the first shooter, he lined up his iron sights and popped off a shot. His aim wasn't perfect, but close enough. The bullet ripped through the *sicario's* belly and doubled him over.

Galloping past the bunker, Garrett ducked as a bullet snapped by. He tugged the reins left, making a sharp pivot, and leveled his rifle at the remaining *sicario* who fired wildly.

With a quick squeeze of the reins, Garrett set the crosshairs on the shooter's midsection and let off a round that sent him tumbling over the bunker and into a snowbank.

Lowering his rifle, Garrett spied a third hiding gunman behind a fallen hackberry tree forty yards to his right. As the guy darted into the mesquite thicket, Garrett popped three quick shots. He pulled the reins right and gave King a little spur.

They loped across the plains until they arrived at the edge of the undergrowth, where Garrett slowed King to a trot. The moonlit sky provided just enough light to see the gunman's trail.

The tracks, sinking deep in the snow, appeared to be made by work boots. Kaiser's man for sure. And a big one at that.

Garrett followed the prints to where they dead-ended at a frozen creek beneath a rickety bridge made of old railroad ties. Unsure if the gunman had gone over or under it, he leapt from the saddle, shouldered his rifle, and eased up slowly.

He was almost convinced the guy had vanished when the barrel of an AR-15 slid around a concrete piling and fired.

Startled, Garrett dove prone, aimed at the leaping flames of the gunman's muzzle, and pulled the trigger rapid fire.

Then, as suddenly as it had started, the shooting stopped. And the guy leaned out for a look.

With a quick breath and careful aim, Garrett put a round through the gunman's shoulder.

Unfortunately, the bullet was little more than a nuisance. The guy barely flinched. He just popped in another magazine and went back to firing.

Garrett emptied his own rifle, dropped the mag, and jammed in another. He was chambering a round when the shooter blitzed, barreled over, and slammed him to his back.

Pinned beneath the weight, Garrett absorbed the first blow from Rocky Anderson's meaty fists with his face. The punch felt like a sledgehammer but the second was even worse. Pissed off and thirsty for blood, the cage fighter was well on his way to getting his fill.

Zuma yelled through the headset, "Over by the bridge!"

Right where they were headed, Kaiser observed two men fighting near the creek's edge. It *had* to be Garrett Kohl.

"Get on top of them and gimme a good angle."

Zuma nudged the cyclic forward and spun around to get Kaiser in position. The pilot fought the stick, but the chopper still bucked with every gust of wind.

Kaiser edged the C20 out of the gun port. "That's Rocky. Bring her around and keep steady."

Kaiser brought the scope up to his eye, but with the wind blasting, he couldn't keep the brawling figures in frame. He turned to Zuma and snarled, "Thought you were the big hero pilot. Flew into a hurricane and rescued some rig hands or fisherman or some crap."

For once Zuma had no response, just kept working the pedals.

Kaiser took out his phone and texted Nagual.

We found Garrett Kohl. You got the kids yet?

Nagual texted back:

Soon.

Kaiser replied:

Good. Send me some troops. We take out Kohl, this thing is over.

Turning to his pilot, Kaiser pulled the rifle in from the gun port. "Just go ahead and land. I'm gonna go out there and end this for good."

With each jarring blow, Garrett faded. He gave a hard shove, but Rocky held tight, cocked a fist and raised it for leverage. Mustering what little strength he had left, Garrett thrust his knee upward, catching Rocky square in the balls.

The cage fighter groaned, his body seized, and Garrett threw a left cross to the chin.

Dazed but not done, Rocky lunged for Garrett's throat, but was met with a solid right that smacked his jaw. His eyes rolled backward, he swayed left, and collapsed like timber.

Garrett gasped for air, drawing in a blizzardy breath from the chopper's rotor wash. Light-headed and weary, he scuttled to his feet on shaky legs, and spun in search of the helo.

A full woozy circle and he found the Bell not thirty yards out, settling into a clearing behind some mesquite. Its skids had just touched the ground when Garrett ripped the Nighthawk from his holster, took aim, and fired.

Kaiser had just reached for the door handle when Garrett's bullets peppered the windscreen. Throwing his forearms in front of him, he braced for the shock of incoming rounds. But it was the *wope-wope-wope* of the Ground Proximity Alarm that really woke him up.

The high-pitched shriek was soon overcome by a grinding buzz like a chainsaw on iron. The tail rotor was churning through mesquite.

While the fuselage bucked to forty-five degrees, he turned to the pilot and clutched a fistful of sleeve. "Pull it together, dammit!"

Zuma pushed the cyclic and worked the pedals like mad. With a pull of the collective, the bird climbed, and the alarm went silent. As they rose above the swirling blizzard from the rotor wash, blasts of frigid air whistled through tiny bullet holes into the cockpit, knocking the already low temp down a few degrees.

Zuma jerked the cyclic left to get them the hell out of Garrett's bead as he frantically checked his controls. Remarkably, there was no other damage.

"Dammit, Mr. Kaiser! We're lucky he didn't knock us out of the sky!"

"*The sky?*" Kaiser pointed at the ground. "We're a hundred feet up!"

Realizing that Zuma was rattled enough already, Kaiser took a deep breath and spoke calmly. "Now listen to me closely. Sooner you give me a shot, the sooner we're back on the ground."

Zuma didn't respond but gave the bird some left pedal to turn them back in the right direction. Despite the cold, his brow was dripping sweat.

Satisfied that his pilot was halfway under control, Kaiser slid his rifle out the port and searched with his scope. "Get lower so I can see him."

"*Lower?*" Zuma huffed into the mouthpiece. "We're clipping the damn treetops as it is."

Scanning the area with his optics, Kaiser saw nothing below but a bunch of spent cartridges and an unconscious Rocky Anderson.

Garrett Kohl and his sorrel were nowhere to be found.

40

Asadi's excitement bubbled over as he watched two white pickups roar across the prairie, racing toward the thundering blaze in the distance. He had no idea what had exploded but had an idea who was responsible. It was the man who had saved him in Nasrin, the cowboy who had promised—*you'll always be safe with me.* With a big smile, Asadi turned to find Sophie.

Leaning in close, she whispered, "Come on! Now's our chance!"

Keeping his head below the snowy shrubs, he scurried behind the girls for about fifty yards until they arrived at the end of the hedgerow. Sophie sat on her haunches and turned back. "Think it's safe to cross?"

Chloe leaned around her sister and eyed the garden terraces between them and the mansion. Each one glowed under a towering floodlight.

"I don't know, Soph." She shot her sister a skeptical look. "I think they'll see us."

Sophie rose and peeked over the bushes. "They might. But we have to chance it. If someone is coming to our rescue, we have to be where they can find us."

Chloe pointed to a building about forty yards down an incline to the right. It had rock walls, a steepled tin roof, and massive plank doors. "What about that place?" she asked. "Looks like a barn or something."

Sophie's eyes lit up. "If there are horses we can ride out of here."

Asadi could not follow what they were saying but heard the word *horse*. And it did not take a genius to understand what they were planning.

Chloe turned to him and made the running motion with her arms. "You ready?"

Asadi nodded and Chloe scrambled to her feet, sprinting from the hedgerow with Sophie on her heels. Immediately, gunfire erupted like a thousand fire-crackers at once.

Scared to move, but too terrified to stay, Asadi sprung from the bushes, bounding through the powder like a jackrabbit. He raced across the courtyard, ducking each time a shot screamed past. When he finally reached the barn, his heart pounded as he gasped for breath.

Sophie reached the door first, yanked it open and held it for Asadi and her sister. They all rushed in and Chloe secured the lock.

Before Asadi had even gotten a good look around, he knew exactly where they were. The tangy smell of alfalfa hay was a big hint. So was another less pleasant odor. But his heart sank when he turned to find row after row of empty stalls.

It was obvious the girls felt the same way. He could see the disappointment on their faces. Chloe looked past the stalls and the tack room, to the other end of the barn. Above a pile of feed sacks and a folded metal chair hung a dusty black telephone.

With the heavy thump of the helicopter's rotors fast approaching, Garrett spurred the sorrel from under the snow canopy of the willows. Bearing down in the saddle as they raced across the prairie, his body was in sync with the four-beat pattern of the rumbling hooves.

Fifty yards from the perimeter wall, the Bell 206 roared over, broke right, and circled around. He took aim at the helo and raked its fuselage until his rifle was empty. At the rumble of a truck engine from behind,

Garrett twisted in the saddle to locate the threat. Grabbing a new mag from his chest rig and reloading, he spotted the second white pickup not forty yards out. It was dipping and bounding as it rumbled toward him at well over seventy.

Garrett fired three rounds, but the truck didn't waver.

With both an air and ground assault under way, Garrett worried that he was pushing King beyond the limits of his luck.

Reluctantly, he leapt from the saddle, gave the gelding a little whap to the rear, and watched as his old friend trotted out of the line of fire.

Desperate for cover, Garrett dashed to what looked to be an old bison wallow, dove in, and scurried to its earthen edge. He had just settled into the prone shooting position when he remembered the words of Joe Bob Dawson. He said if you're in danger of being overrun, it all boils down to four simple words:

Kill everything that moves.

Garrett took three quick shots at the approaching pickup then flipped over and pulled the trigger rapid fire at the hovering Bell, raking its underbelly until his TX15 was empty. While the helo bucked and veered left, he popped in a fresh mag, chambered a round, and was about to set his sights on the truck when it roared overhead.

Dropping the rifle, Garrett rolled out from beneath it, narrowly missing the pickup's skidding back wheels as they plowed a trench through the snow-filled wallow.

Bo Clevenger's silver F-350 slid to an abrupt halt when the front wheels rammed the berm. A cowboy flung the back door open and blasted at Garrett with a Kel-Tec KS7.

The shooter was quick, but Garrett's aim was truer. Jerking the Nighthawk from his belt, he sank three center mass and pivoted left as the driver leapt out firing a pistol.

His ammo spent, Garrett sprinted to the back of the truck and dove behind the bumper. Reloading on the move, he turned back just as the driver flew around the bed.

Garrett dropped the slide, pulled the trigger, and put a single round in the gunman's chest.

At the screeching of a door, Garrett scrambled on all fours to the end of the bumper, hung his pistol around the side, and fired twice. The .45 hollow points sent the gunman tumbling backward.

Garrett clambered to his feet, dashed to the passenger side, and dove in. He'd just climbed into the driver's seat when the helo buzzed over, rotated left, and hovered in front of the pickup.

Caught within the cyclone of snow and ice kicked up by the Bell's rotor wash, the cab went completely dark. Seconds later a bullet *thwacked* the windshield.

Gripping the steering wheel, Garrett threw the truck in drive and stomped on the gas. It rocked forward a few inches, then the engine whined and the tires spun. He slammed it in reverse, with the same results.

Another round cracked the windshield and slammed the center console.

With the compound floodlights less than forty yards to his left, Garrett flung the door open and bolted for the cover of the perimeter wall. He'd barely made it a few steps when the Bell circled in from behind, and rounds snapped past, popping at his feet.

In a dead sprint, twenty yards from the safety of the stone hedge, a bullet grazed his right shoulder and sent him tumbling prostrate into the snow. With his momentum halted, out in the open, and several yards from cover, there was little left he could do.

Garrett rolled over, looked up, and braced for the kill shot.

41

Ike knew he'd done right to trust his gut when he saw through the green glow of his night vision goggles (NVGs) that Garrett was on the ground taking heavy gunfire from the Bell 206 hovering above. He blasted past, looped back around, and spoke to Sanchez through the headset.

"How's our boy?"

There was a brief pause as Sanchez stared out the copilot window and scanned the grounds with his NVGs. "Chopper has him pinned flat."

"Then let's give him some breathing room."

Sanchez turned to the pilot. "What the hell are you thinking, Ike?"

"Thinking you'd better hold on to your ass."

Before Sanchez could object, Ike pulled the collective and pushed the cyclic, launching them toward the Bell. At fifty feet, he lowered the collective and yanked hard on the stick, exacting a quick stop maneuver, and flipped on his spotlight.

Immediately, the Bell tilted, veered left, and bugged out. It made a circle over the grounds, giving Ike's Hughes a wide-ass berth.

As Sanchez hurled a slew of profanities, Ike yanked the collective, blasting them into the air.

Sanchez turned, infuriated. "Where we going, Ike? Fight's down there."

Watching his altimeter, Ike got to ten thousand feet and slowed to a hover. He looked below to find the Central Tank Battery blaze was now the size of a campfire.

"That bird's gonna stay on Garrett's ass unless we get rid of it."

"How you gonna do that from up here?"

Ike turned and smiled. "Who do you think is shooting at us?"

"Probably Kaiser. It's *his* chopper."

"You're damn right." Ike smiled wider. "And that arrogant son of a bitch won't like the stunt I just pulled one bit. After he's done scooping the crap from his britches, he'll come after us."

"You better be right or Garrett's a dead man."

Ike took a hand from the stick and pointed down. "Look back and tell me what you see."

Still looking skeptical, Sanchez glanced out his window. "Blinking lights."

"Bingo. Kaiser's as cocky as his pilot is stupid. Heard enough of that loudmouth to know the only thing he's good at is talking trash."

Sanchez smiled for the first time since the flying circus act began. "So, what's the plan?"

Ike paused before answering. "You really want to know?"

Now the pause came from Sanchez. "Probably not."

"Smart boy." Ike pushed the cyclic forward. "Time for a little *follow the leader*."

"Whatever you have in mind, Ike, just remember one thing."

Ike could tell his friend was cooking up something good. "What's that, pardner?"

"You kill me, you better hope you die too."

Ike laughed into the headset. "Let me guess, if God don't take me out Silvia will."

Sanchez flicked up his NVGs. "*Hell* . . . you won't get off that easy. We got mouths to feed. She'll knee-cap your old ass and take your bar as condolence pay."

"Well, there's no need to worry about any of that, Deputy Dawg."

"And why is that?"

Ike turned and smiled. "Because you're *ridin'* with the best there is."

Sanchez laughed and mumbled an inaudible response.

Ike pulled the collective to generate some thrust and pushed the stick forward, approaching the Bell 206 from the rear. He flipped his NVGs back in place and watched the Bell circle, trying to spot him.

When the bird quit spinning, Ike flipped the strobes on. "Over here, dumbass. We're right on your tail." He tapped the goggles on Sanchez's head. "Need you as my eyes."

Ike pushed the stick left and pulling the collective, he added, "This Zuma ain't worth a damn, but he'll stick with me out of spite. Pilots can be a cocky bunch."

Sanchez chuckled through the headset. "You don't say?"

Ike had walked right into that one. "Just let me know what's happening out there."

Sanchez turned, looking nervous. "Where we headed now?"

"Higher."

"Higher?" Sanchez looked down at the earth below. They were so high they could see the lights of Pampa over twenty miles away. "Think they'll follow us?"

"It'll be so slow and gradual they won't even know what's happening."

Sanchez looked across the cockpit. "I see lights. They're coming."

Ike pushed the right pedal to give Sanchez a better view. "Now what's happening?"

Sanchez jerked right. "Muzzle flash! They're shooting!"

No sooner had he called out the warning than a bullet tore through the window and lodged in the roof of the cockpit. Ike mashed the left pedal to even up and put the tail between them and the shooter.

Sanchez yelled through the headset. "This part of your *brilliant* plan, Ike?"

"*Hell no!* You ever heard of a plan where the objective is to get shot?"

The truth of the matter was that it was working exactly as Ike had hoped. Kaiser had thrown common sense out the window and was flying angry.

Kaiser knew it was a mistake to pursue the Hughes but was not about to turn back. If there was any hope at all of taking down Garrett and the others, he would have to get rid of his white trash buddy, Ike Hodges. One clear shot would put an end to the barman's flying theatrics.

He kept a careful watch on the strobe lights, and when the moment finally came, ordered Zuma to get in position. "Move in on his left! Close as you can without hitting the rotor!"

Zuma raised the collective to get more speed. They were thirty yards off the Hughes on his eight o'clock position.

Kaiser kept watching the flashing strobe on the tail rotor. "Get in there! Faster!"

The pilot pushed the stick left and increased torque. They were even with the Hughes, seventy-five feet on the left. Kaiser opened the portal and a sub-zero gust rushed into the cockpit.

Pushing past the sting of the wind, Kaiser forced the barrel of his rifle out the small portal and looked into his optics to find them clouded over. He pulled the rifle back and worked with frozen fingers to defog the scope. "Hold steady, dammit!"

"I'm trying!" Zuma whined. "My damn hands are froze!"

With the optics ready, Kaiser thrust the C20 out and quickly lined up the crosshairs on the pilot's window. "Little closer! Just an inch!"

With the Bell moving in on his nine o'clock position, Ike knew Kaiser was lining up for a shot. He checked his altimeter and vertical speed indicator. They'd been at such a gradual climb that the other pilot either hadn't noticed or was too pissed off to care.

Ike turned to Sanchez. "You like roller coasters, don't ya'?"

Sanchez shook his head. "Hate 'em with a passion. Even when I was a kid."

"But you trust me, right?"

"Nope. Wish I was ridin' with the other guy."

Ike laughed, figuring this was all the buy-in he was going to get. He looked to his left and could see that the other bird was about thirty yards out. Realizing it was now or never, Ike made his move. He decreased collective power and jammed the stick forward, nosing downward from a ten-degree climb to a sixty-degree descent.

With his stomach in his throat, Ike could only imagine what Sanchez felt. The poor bastard would've probably cussed him a blue streak if he weren't trying to keep from puking his guts out. Ike spoke to him in the calmest voice he could muster.

"Sanchez, I need my eyes."

No response. Ike turned toward the window to find

Sanchez gritting his teeth. Other than fighter pilots, not many could handle the g's they were pulling and keep their wits.

In mid-dive, Ike gave some right pedal to give Sanchez a better view and asked again, "What do ya' see back there?"

"Lights," Sanchez groaned, struggling to get the words out. "Behind us."

Ike yanked the collective and pulled back on the cyclic to level out. "Okay, I'm taking her back up again. Keep your eyes open and make sure they're following."

Sanchez didn't answer but Ike knew why. He was feeling the effects of the g-force too, experiencing a bit of tunnel vision himself. "Hang with me, buddy. Almost there."

A few seconds later they were back up, at which point Ike leveled off again and turned the bird for a better view. He was just about to ask for an update when Sanchez spoke over the headset between rapid breaths. "Lights still behind us."

Ike was happy to hear the Bell was still trailing but honestly a bit surprised. Maybe Zuma deserved more credit.

"Okay, Sanchez, tell me when they're close. And I mean right up on our ass."

Ike hit the right pedal and waited for what seemed like an eternity. When there was no report from Sanchez, he wondered if Kaiser had given up and gone back down. As he prepared to recalibrate, Ike heard the words he'd been waiting to hear.

"Forty yards out and approaching fast, Ike."

Ike continued a gradual climb and gave it some right pedal to give his copilot a clear view of the bird at their six. Growing impatient, he was just about to ask for an update when Sanchez yelled into the headset.

"Right behind us!"

Ike dropped the collective and drove the stick forward, pushing his bird into a ninety-degree vertical plunge. Mid-nosedive he nudged the cyclic left, spinning until the Hughes went into a barrel roll. He yelled into the headset, "Sanchez! You with me?"

No response. Sanchez was incapacitated.

Watching the ground coming fast, Ike yanked the stick and pulled the collective. He was fighting to level out at about a thousand feet when the Bell screamed by them and slammed to earth in a booming explosion of smoke and flame.

With his bird under control, Ike flipped up his NVGs and hovered a minute to make sure his body was back in good order. He gave a little left pedal to turn the Hughes in the direction of the crash. There was nothing left of the Bell JetRanger but a blazing pile of rubble.

Ike leaned over, flipped up Sanchez's NVGs, and patted his cheek. "Wake up, Sleeping Beauty."

When Sanchez fully came to, he looked ready to hurl. "What happened, man?"

"Good guys won! That's what happened!"

Sanchez shook his head and took a few deep breaths. "We did it?"

"Yeah. We did it." Ike chuckled. "Not too bad for a jarhead, I suppose."

Sanchez wore a look of disbelief. "What the hell kind of stunt was that?"

"That was right from the manual, son."

"Manual?" Sanchez looked unconvinced. "What manual?"

"I call it Rotors for Rednecks," Ike said proudly. "What do you think?"

Sanchez just shook his head. "Trust me, Ike. You don't want to know."

42

Lacey stood at the vending machine looking back and forth between a honeybun and a pack of powdered doughnuts. She wasn't even hungry, just needed the distraction. A nurse had been kind enough to bring her a Styrofoam cup of coffee she'd yet to try. The problem was that her mind was racing, focused on about a billion other things, most of which were put there by the state troopers, police officers, and sheriff's deputies who all had questions she couldn't answer.

At first she'd been treated like a hero for surviving the ordeal and keeping Butch alive, but the officers' tone soon changed when they concluded she was stonewalling. Garrett had prepared her for this, giving her clear instructions not to say anything.

Law shows up and the kids are dead.

His last three words played over in her head like a skipping record. But for some reason it was the image of her own children that resounded. It was the first thing she'd guiltily thought of after hearing about Cassidy Kohl's twins.

What if this happened to me?

Her own children were safe with their father in Amarillo, but for all she knew the Kohl kids were dead—and so was Garrett. Tears formed in her eyes.

Lacey would've welcomed any distraction but the one walking down the hall toward her.

Hemphill County sheriff Ted Crowley was in every way a bad stereotype of the crooked country lawman—down to the bulging paunch that lopped over his oversize belt buckle.

"How are we doing now, Miss Lacey?" Crowley removed his cowboy hat and placed it over his heart like he was standing graveside. A few gray strands of his comb-over drooped onto his forehead. "I know you've been through quite an . . . ordeal."

"Fine, I guess, Sheriff. Given the circumstances."

He set the hat back on his head, the brim high on his forehead. "That was a fine job you did with Mr. Kohl. *Real fine.* He was lucky you were there."

Lacey nodded politely. "Wish I could've done more."

Crowley jerked his thumb over his back at the group

of state troopers circled by the doors leading to the intensive care unit. "And I'm sorry about them boys over there. If you've ever dealt with highway patrol, you know they don't have the sense of humor God gave a Doberman."

He laughed at his own joke and took a look around to make sure nobody'd heard him.

Lacey just shook it off. "It's okay. They're just looking for answers I don't have." She stared at the troopers, who were watching her also. "Guess I'd be frustrated too."

Crowley donned a phony-looking smile—the same one from all his campaign posters. "Well, see, the problem is they're used to folks lying at 'em all the time. Makes 'em pissed off and mean." He eyed her intently. "Of course, nobody likes a liar, I suppose. Do they now?"

When she finally realized it wasn't a rhetorical question, she stuttered out her answer. "Oh. Oh—no. Of course not."

"Then how about we revisit your story. See if we can't remember some things maybe you . . . *forgot*." His smile returned. "It's expected given the stress you've been under. But that usually fades with time and folks start to remember all sorts of stuff."

Her pulse raced at the veiled accusation. "I really don't know anything, Sheriff." All of a sudden, she felt like a sixteen-year-old caught at a keg party. "When we got to the house, Butch was unconscious, and whoever shot him was long gone. Garrett called Ike immediately and then went to look for anyone else who might be hurt."

"Anyone else?" He looked at her curiously. "Who else would've been there?"

She shrugged.

"And you say Garrett never came back?"

Lacey just shook her head, feeling more comfortable not having to say the lies out loud.

Crowley cleared his throat. "Why did he call that barman and not 911? Seems peculiar."

"He said it would take too long for Lifestar to get there. Ike was just down the road."

"Uh-huh. But why not call *us* as soon as you could?"

"I did," Lacey lied. "I mean, I tried to call but I didn't have cell service out at the ranch. And the landline was dead." She paused and added, "You can check."

She regretted adding that last part which made her sound guilty.

"I will." Crowley glanced around again at the troopers then back to her. "And you don't have any clue who did this? Garrett never mentioned anything *at all*? Not a name? *Nothin'?*"

She shook her head again but this time her reticence seemed to make him angry. She could see it on his face. His phony smile faded away.

Crowley looked around before asking, "You have a couple kids, don't you?"

His sudden switch of topic startled her. "What about them?"

"Where are they?"

"Why does that matter?"

Crowley donned a satisfied smile. He'd struck a nerve and knew it. "No need to get defensive now. I'm just asking as a matter of *security*. Didn't know if they were alone."

The accusation made her bristle. "My children are eight and five, Sheriff. Of course, they're not alone. What kind of mother do you think I am?"

"Well, now, I thought maybe you might've left them in a moment of . . . haste. Emergency situation and all." He pointed to a deputy leaning against the wall, twirling a cigarette in his fingers. "Could send a man by the house if you need someone to check on 'em."

"Sheriff, my children are perfectly safe. They're with their father."

"In Amarillo?"

"What does that have to do—" Lacey was about to keep going when she stopped herself. "Their father took them out of town for the weekend." She added the lie, "Skiing in Red River."

Crowley glanced over his shoulder at the other law enforcement officers then back at her. "Listen, I'm trying to help you here." He lowered his voice. "The Kohls are into something bad. Working with a drug cartel, we think. Found a big stash of dope and three dead bodies out at Bridger's house this evening."

"I'm sure there's an explanation," Lacey snapped back.

"Yeah, there is. And it starts with Bridger Kohl acting as conduit between a Mexican cartel and Renegade hands running heroin all over the country. How's that for an explanation?"

"Bridger Kohl is a prominent attorney. He does quite well on his own." Lacey shook off the idea like it was nonsense. "I highly doubt he's involved with the people you're describing."

"He's very much involved," Crowley argued. "Defended that Renegade oil field trash in a court of law. Look it up if you don't believe me."

"If Renegade is at the center of this, then search no further than Preston Kaiser. I know firsthand he's into some shady dealings with them. Look *that up*, if you don't believe me."

Crowley let out a huff. "Now, you can't go throwing around accusations like that. The Kaisers are a respected family. That just won't fly."

"*Respected?* Maybe by you, kowtowing for their blessing and campaign contributions."

"Now, you listen here." The sheriff was close to losing his cool when the doctor approached. He'd been the first one to look at Butch when they arrived. He must've thought Lacey was family since she was the one who brought him in.

"Sheriff, may I have a moment with her in private?"

Crowley murmured something under his breath about police business but walked back toward the group of law enforcement officers waiting for the elevator. He put his pudgy hand on the shoulder of a state trooper and made a lame joke resulting in his own howl of laughter and courteous chuckles from the others.

The doctor shook Lacey's hand. "Mrs. Kohl, I'm Dr. Yaza. My apologies for not introducing myself earlier, but I wanted to get him into surgery immediately."

Lacey considered correcting Yaza's assumption that Butch was a relative but opted against it. She was the closest thing he had right now. "Thank you, Dr. Yaza. How is he?"

Yaza's grave expression told her much of what she was about to hear. "Critical but stable. He's lost a lot of blood. In fact, most would have died before they even got here. But—" His face softened. "He's a tough one, Mr. Kohl. Of course, I'm sure you know that."

Lacey smiled, nodded, but didn't elaborate. The less said, the better.

"Well, I expect you would like to visit him."

As Dr. Yaza led her back to the ICU, he took her hand and patted it gently. "For now, we've done as much as we can do. In the meantime, he needs to hear encouraging words." The doctor stopped mid-step and looked her in the eyes. "Do you understand? He needs hope."

Lacey again nodded. She did understand. The prognosis wasn't good.

Sheriff Crowley, who unfortunately hadn't left with the others, called out in a voice slightly above a whisper, "Miss Lacey!"

Lacey kept her gaze straight ahead and quickened her step. She was already through the electric double doors leading into the intensive care unit and past the big No Unauthorized Visitors beyond This Point sign when she heard him again.

Crowley called louder, "Lacey! We're not—"

A nurse the size of a refrigerator stepped out from behind the desk and stopped Crowley in his tracks,

repeating the sign's clear message verbatim. "No unauthorized visitors beyond this point." She added with
disdain, "Not even you, *Sheriff*."

"But she's not—"

As the nurse chased Crowley back into the hallway,
Lacey walked to Butch's bedside along with Dr. Yaza.
At the sight of him hooked up to tubes and a respira-
tor, she nearly broke down in tears. Without his Texas
armor of Wrangler blue jeans, work jacket, and wide-
brimmed Resistol, Butch Kohl was just a regular old
man fighting for his life.

Yaza started to say something but didn't. Lacey took
it as another bad sign. "I need to check on a patient
downstairs." He flashed her a consoling smile, then
turned and walked out.

Spotting a rolling chair just outside the curtain she
brought it in and positioned it next to Butch. She sat
down and held his limp hand in hers. He had the rough
calluses of a real rancher—the kind that were too few
and far between these days.

"Mr. Kohl." She corrected herself, per his earlier
instructions. "*Butch*, you gotta hang in there for us,
okay?" After looking around to make sure no one was
listening, she continued. "I know what it's like to lose a
father and—" Tears formed in her eyes as she spoke. "I
know Garrett will never admit it, but he's still broken

up over his mom." She swallowed hard. "And losing you would be too much to bear."

The next part was almost too embarrassing to utter, but if *hope* was the answer, then *hope* she'd deliver.

"My dad taught me horses, but I don't know a thimble of what he did. I thought maybe if things worked out between me and Garrett that you could teach my kids. The way he would've." Her lips curled at the thought. "Now that's between you and me, old man." She gave his hand a light tap.

Lacey doubted he heard a word but imagined that he'd like the idea. She was just about to continue when the electric doors leading to the ICU whirred open and an echoing tap of boot heels followed.

Crowley is relentless.

With the nurse no longer standing guard, Lacey would have to fend for herself. She sprang from her seat, eased up to the plastic partition, and peeked out. A fireplug of a man in a black leather overcoat stood in the entry. He was dark-complected, with a smooth-shaven head that shone under the fluorescents. Alerted by a chirp from Butch's monitor, he looked over.

Jerking back, Lacey said a silent prayer as the reverberating *tock-tock-tock* of boots on vinyl tile got closer and closer.

43

G arrett thanked the good Lord above that he'd made it across that field alive. Somebody up there was looking after him, and it wasn't just his guardian angel. The only son of a bitch crazy enough to play chicken with another helicopter was the old Night Stalker pilot himself—Ike Hodges.

Out of breath, out of gas, and frozen out of his mind, Garrett yanked the *shemagh* scarf from his face and huffed in frozen air. With adrenaline waning and the aftershocks of the beating from Rocky Anderson taking their toll, he felt the temptation to give up and give in. But his mother's words came to him just when he needed them.

She'd always said, *It's not what you want. It's what you can't live without.*

Unable to bear the thought of losing those kids, Garrett struggled to his feet, stumbled to the perimeter wall, and clambered over. He forced one foot in front of the other, trudging toward the mansion through snowdrifts as high as his knees.

Garrett thrust a frozen hand into his coat pocket, pulled out his cell phone, and tried to call his brother. He again got no answer.

Keeping a sharp eye out for more trouble, he maneuvered across the outer grounds until coming upon an open courtyard where he found a small blessing.

A weapon.

As luck would have it, the guard standing watch some ten feet below the garden terrace was carrying a tactical model Mini-14. Garrett recognized him from the Crippled Crows. He'd been sitting at the table across from him and Bridger, wearing the same black coveralls and bright orange stocking cap.

Garrett crept to the ledge and dropped in from behind, knocking the gunman off his feet. The startled guard dropped his rifle, rolled left, and popped up. But before he could locate the Ruger, he came eye to eye with Garrett's Nighthawk.

Rigid with fear, the roughneck threw up his hands. "Wasn't gonna do nothing, Kohl. Just trying to scare you off. That's all."

Garrett had to laugh at the bald-faced lie. "Bullets flying at my head tell another story."

"Wasn't me. That was Nagual's crew. I swear it."

"Nagual, huh? Where's he now?" When he got no reply, Garrett eased his .45 into the guard's forehead. "This ain't no time to go defending your buddies."

"He ain't my buddy and I ain't defending no one." Considering his options, he took in a stammering breath. "But Nagual will kill me, sure as the world, if I rat him out."

Garrett pressed the muzzle into flesh. "I'll kill you if you don't."

Narrowing his eyes, the guard pointed to a spot about fifty yards beyond the house. "Thataway. Out by the lake. Took off after them kids with his rifle."

Garrett surveyed the frozen landscape between him and a thick grove of cottonwoods, finding a layout of hedgerows, statues, and water features all brightly lit under halogens.

Nagual could be behind any one of those, lining up the kids in his sights.

With enough intel to get moving, Garrett turned and pistol-whipped the guard, knocking him to the ground. He moved to pick up the rifle and found himself staring down the barrel of Bo Clevenger's 12-gauge.

"Well, well, if it ain't the big badass Green Beret." Bo looked exceptionally pleased with himself. "Drop that pistol nice and easy, why don't you?"

Slowly and carefully, Garrett set his Nighthawk in the snow, then stood, hands raised. Hearing the shriek of jet engines in the distance, he glanced over at Kaiser's airport. From the high elevation of the compound, Garrett got a full view of the six-thousand-foot runway, hangar, and massive tarmac.

Bo stepped forward with his Remington 870 trained on Garrett's head. "Oh yeah, Garzas sent us some backup. Just in case."

"In case of what?"

"In case I didn't get to fill you and your brother full a buckshot."

Garrett snorted. "That your big plan, Bo?"

"Too bad for you. *It is.*"

The reverse thrusters of the landing jet forced Garrett's attention back to the airstrip. "Well, then I'd get started if I were you."

Bo had just opened his mouth for a smart-ass retort when a *whirring* from behind caught his attention. He jerked around about a half second too late. The loop of Bridger's rope was already beneath his chin. With a swift yank, the lariat cinched tight and the line went stiff.

Bridger coiled the rope on his saddle horn, gave a palatal click, and Ginger shot backward, whipping Bo off his feet and slamming him on his back with a thud. His eyes bulged, neck veins swelled, and face burned beet red as the noose tightened around his neck. He dug in his boot heels but gained no purchase. Bo's thrashing was little contest for the champion roping horse.

Images of Bo Clevenger killing innocent animals and threatening Lacey flashed through Garrett's mind. And the temptation to rid the world of this nuisance was a powerful one. But summary execution wasn't part of the plan. At least not yet.

After a good thirty feet of dragging, Garrett called to Bridger. "He's had enough!"

With a slow nod, Bridger uncoiled the rope and whipped out some slack.

Bo yanked the noose free and jerked it from around his neck. His massive body quaked as he gasped for air—coughing and hacking, then struggling to his knees to dry-heave.

Garrett picked up the shotgun, considering whacking Bo in the head, but he knew it'd probably kill him. Instead, he pumped the action on the Remington to eject all the shells and hurled it into the bushes.

Bridger rode over. "We gotta move!"

Garrett moved to the unconscious guard, picked up the Ruger, and yanked four extra magazines from his belt. By the time he got loaded, Cassidy was trotting up from behind.

Bridger threw out a hand and pulled Garrett into the saddle behind him. "Kids just called. They're at the horse barn. Told them to stay put until we get there."

Cassidy pointed west as she shoved the map back inside her coat. "Quarter mile that way. Other side of the lake."

Garrett had a million questions, but before he could fire off a single one, Bridger spurred Ginger into a lope across the grounds. With his brother at the helm, Garrett could do little but hold tight and pray. Dodging bushes, ducking limbs, and leaping hedgerows was a whole hell of a lot less fun when you couldn't see them coming.

After the moment it took to get into the rhythm, he looked over Bridger's shoulder to find Cassidy in the lead. But when she stopped suddenly, Garrett knew something was wrong.

Bridger pulled Ginger up alongside Sparrow. Both horses snorted and stamped, clearly eager to carry this thing across the goal line.

About forty yards ahead stood the Mescalero horse barn. The singular stone-walled structure with its steep-pitched roof sat in a clearing surrounded by a grove of willows and cottonwoods.

In the glow of the fluorescent lamps, two Stetson-clad Mescalero cowboys eased along the wall with rifles at the ready. They stooped low, keeping their heads below the windows.

Cassidy yanked the scarf below her mouth. "They're moving in! We gotta go!"

Beyond the barn's halogen lamps, an unnatural clump moved in the dark periphery.

Garrett raised a hand. "Hold on, Cassidy. We rush in now, and they'll cut us to pieces."

"Can't wait," his brother argued. "They're nearly at the door."

Damn! Turning back, Garrett saw Bridger was right. He slid off the saddle and looked up.

"You ride in. I'll be on overwatch. Smoke anyone brazen enough to show his head."

Bridger turned to his wife. "I go down, you keep on. Don't stop until the kids are safe."

Tears welled in Cassidy's eyes. "Same goes for you."

Bridger reached down to Garrett. "See you when it's over."

Garrett took his brother's hand and gave a single pump. "See you when it's over."

Bridger spurred Ginger and they were off in a lope.

Cassidy gave him a couple of seconds head start and did the same. As they rode in hot, Garrett chambered a round on the fly, turned to the clump he'd seen earlier in the open area between the cottonwood grove and the stable's dim edge. He rested his finger on the trigger and waited for movement.

Garrett saw a flash and ducked as the bullet snapped past, missing his head by only a hair. Rolling right, he popped up and sprinted along the tree line, keeping low as a flurry of rounds shredded limbs around him. About thirty yards out, Garrett took cover behind the thick silver trunk of a lone cottonwood. He had just leaned out for a peek when a bullet *whapped* the bark inches above his head.

The shooter was good. A professional. It had to be Nagual.

His heart racing in hope of rescue, Asadi hurried to the window, stood next to the girls, and stared at the shadowy edge of the tree line. With the guns' leaping flames and echo of gunfire off the barn's stone walls, the idea of being saved was as terrifying as it was thrilling.

"Look! Horses!" Chloe turned to Sophie. "I think it's Mom and Dad!"

Sophie's eyes lit up at the sight of the approaching riders. "It's them! I'm sure of it! That's Ginger out front!"

As the girls dashed to the door Asadi followed closely, careful to avoid looking at the dead men on the walkway. He looked out at the woman instead and realized he recognized her from one of the photos in Garrett's bedroom.

Leaping over the lifeless body by the door, Sophie ran to her parents, waving her arms wildly. "Mom! Dad! Over here! Over here!"

As the two riders flew up to the barn and halted their horses, Asadi smiled at the sight of Ginger and Sparrow. It felt like seeing old friends.

Chloe took Asadi's hand. "It's okay." She patted her heart. "They're family."

Recognizing the word *family*, he pointed to them. "*We go. For ride?*"

Chloe smiled and nodded as she mimicked his words. "*We go for ride*. That's right." She pointed to her mom. "You hop on with her. Okay?"

With her head and face covered, the woman atop the horse looked a bit intimidating. But her eyes shone with a mother's warmth. "It's okay. I promise." She lowered her scarf and smiled. "Time to go, big guy. Not out of trouble yet."

As more gunfire erupted, Sparrow whinnied and stamped. The woman reached out and Asadi took her hand.

In the blink of an eye, she yanked him into the saddle and Sparrow lurched forward. Within seconds, they blasted across the snowy flatland, bounding over bushes and swerving to miss trees.

Nearly bouncing off the saddle, Asadi squeezed the woman with an iron embrace. At first he closed his eyes, but eventually he peered out, feeling the burn from the frozen wind.

Just out front, rifles erupted, and bullets buzzed past them.

Keeping his body pressed tight against the woman, he ducked below her left elbow. With eyes trained forward, he searched in vain for the twins and their father. They had pulled out ahead and were no longer visible.

At the pop of gunfire, they veered right in a wide circle, only to be met by more bullets, then cut left, desperate to evade the shooters. But with guns blazing in every direction, Cassidy pulled Sparrow to a halt.

Asadi swiveled in the saddle in search of an outlet, his breath coming in panicked gasps, but it was clear they were completely surrounded. Chance of escape was hopeless.

In Nagual's crosshairs, Garrett burst from his cover and low-crawled to the closest tree. With a popping trail of machine-gun fire in his wake, he scurried to his feet and sprinted to Cassidy and Asadi, surrounded by Garza reinforcements.

Midstride, Garrett tripped, dropping his rifle. He scrabbled beneath the snow and felt the cold steel in his palm. Jerking the Ruger to his shoulder, he aimed at the gunman nearest Sparrow and pulled the trigger. His heart sank as he heard the telltale *tick* of an empty mag.

But in nearly the same instant the gunfire intensified, and the *sicario* was felled by another bullet. Searching for muzzle flashes on the outskirts of the moonlit battlefield, Garrett came up empty. But one thing was certain. He hadn't heard several of those distinctive sounds since his Special Forces days in Iraq and Afghanistan.

One of them was the *thuck–thuck* of an M-203 grenade launcher. The other came from an M-249 Squad Automatic Weapon. Whoever was wielding the SAW used controlled bursts from the belt-fed machine gun to obliterate any bad guys not already decimated by the bombs.

Garrett observed with pleasure the panicked frenzy as the SAW's ceaseless stream of bullets tore the cartel fighters to shreds. Then as suddenly as he first heard them, Garrett's saviors materialized like phantoms from the snow-covered brush, and began hunting down what was left of the Garza gunmen as they fled for the safety of the hangar.

Given their distinguishing look, this unit could have been from any of the U.S. military's elite cadre of fighters. But these were no everyday special operations soldiers.

Why in the hell Carlos Contreras's Ground Branch team was on the Texas High Plains, Garrett hadn't a clue. And he really didn't care. All that mattered was that the *eyes in the sky* were on him. And the CIA had done what it does best.

Make some hellacious craters.

Feeling elation beyond any he'd ever known, Garrett rose to his feet, spying the Dragon Queen herself, Kim Manning, running and gunning with her paramilitary officers. With the exception of the H&K MP7 in her grip, she looked a bit more snowbunny than spec ops soldier. But never in his life did Garrett think he'd be this happy to see anyone.

He had just taken his first step toward her when the bullet from behind ripped through his abdomen and sent him face-first into the snow.

His ears rang.

His body shook.

His sight went blurry.

The warm wetness of his draining stomach wound soaked his hand. He sucked in a quick stinging breath through his teeth while swirling pain seared its way through his body.

As the cloudiness engulfed his mind, he was tempted to give in and let the darkness take him. But of course, that would mean never meeting Nagual face-to-face.

And there wasn't a chance in hell he was going to let that happen.

44

As the steps grew closer, Lacey felt the urge to panic. If she screamed, it would give them away. And if she ran, Butch was dead. Her only option was to fight. She had just thrown her back against the partition when she saw the gunman's black boots under the aqua curtain. She saw the shadow of something in the man's hand on the other side of the curtain. *Could that be a gun?*

Mind racing and heart pounding, Lacey rushed the assassin with such force it ripped the plastic curtain from the grommets. The pistol barked and punched a hole in the wall, missing Butch by only a sliver. The gunman blasted another wild round that went high as he fended off Lacey, then leveled off on her to fire. But suddenly someone else was shooting and they caught the gunman before he could get off another shot.

Whether it was five or fifteen rounds, Lacey wasn't sure. She only knew that Sheriff Crowley didn't quit until the gunman stopped moving.

Seconds later a mammoth state trooper rushed in and knocked the silver pistol away from the gunman on the floor. The trooper flipped him over and cuffed him even though he was probably dead.

The trooper gave Lacey the onceover. "You hurt, ma'am?"

"Don't think so."

Lacey went over to Butch to make sure he hadn't been hit by an errant round.

Crowley walked up behind her. "Is he okay?"

Lacey looked over at the heart rate monitor which kept a steady beat. "It's a miracle."

Crowley took a few more steps inside. "And you?"

She couldn't be certain, but thought he looked disappointed.

Crowley pulled the magazine from his pistol and popped in another. He donned his campaign smile again. "Guess you're lucky I got here when I did."

She wanted to ask how the gunman slipped into the hospital in the first place but was careful not to start raising questions here. Crowley seemed unnerved. Like something had gone wrong.

The sheriff dropped his smile. "Now, you're sure there's nothing you want to tell me?" He pointed back to where the EMS crew was loading the gunman on a gurney. "Could be more folks at risk. Don't want that on your conscience, do you?"

Crowley was edging toward her when a man in boots, a blue blazer, and a silverbelly Stetson entered the room. He was a bit on the tall and lanky side.

Flashing his Texas Rangers badge, he turned to Crowley. "Got it from here, Sheriff."

"A day late and a dollar short. As *usual*," Crowley said.

"Cade Malek, ma'am." The man ignored the comment and moved closer to Lacey. "I'm going to need you to come with me."

Lacey put her hand on Butch's shoulder. "I'm not leaving him here alone." She looked right at Crowley when she said it.

Malek gave a slow nod, an obvious signal he understood. "Only my men will be watching him." He stared down the sheriff. "From now on, he'll be in good hands. I promise."

"What are you looking at me for?" Crowley's face reddened. "Case you haven't heard, I'm the one saved the day here."

"Yeah, and we all appreciate you doing your job, Sheriff." Malek reiterated his initial statement with more force. "But like I said, *we've* got it from here."

There was something about the man Lacey trusted. He was leading her out when Crowley blocked the door.

"I think you got your facts mixed up, Malek." Crowley patted the badge on his chest. "You got questions, you talk to me."

"Oh, don't worry about that. We'll be talking to you plenty." Malek pushed past Crowley and escorted Lacey out into the hallway where two other Rangers were waiting. "See that the sheriff finds his way out." Under his breath he added, "Been watching him for a while."

Malek turned right instead of left and walked Lacey toward the back exit. "I've got strict orders not to let you out of my sight."

Lacey glanced over her shoulder to make sure Crowley was gone. "Where are we going?"

Malek popped the door open and ushered Lacey down the stairwell. "I've got an informant out at the Mescalero saying the Kohls made a raid on the place."

"Are they okay?"

"No idea. I just flew in from Weslaco and when I got off the plane, I had a bunch of frantic text messages and phone calls saying Butch Kohl was shot and

Bridger's kids were abducted by the Garza cartel. Got here as quick as I could."

"Is anyone helping them now?"

"Got a deputy I trust out there." He turned to her, curious. "You know Tony Sanchez?"

Lacey nodded, thinking it odd that he and Garrett were best friends. She wondered if this connection had something to do with the secrets he was hiding.

"I know Tony, but not well. We went to school together and I see him at our café."

"Sanchez has been helping me on the Renegade investigation. Started over a year ago down in South Texas and I followed the trail up here. It's what led me to Sheriff Crowley and Preston Kaiser. We were about to move in a Ranger Reconnaissance Team on the Mescalero Ranch when my captain got a call from the chief, who got a call from the governor telling us to stand down. Said another organization was taking care of things."

Lacey got the impression Malek knew more than he was saying. "But someone *is* helping them out there?"

"That's my understanding." He opened the door leading back to the helipad and a gust of frigid wind nearly stopped Lacey in her tracks. There was a waiting black-and-white helicopter with the Texas Department of Public Safety logo on the side. A man in black military fatigues jumped from the copilot seat as the rotors started to spin and the engine whirred to life.

Malek stepped in, took Lacey by the hand, and helped her into the helicopter. He raised his index finger to the pilot, swirled the air, and got a nod in return. As the bird slowly lifted, she affixed the headphones to her ears just in time to hear Malek's voice over the intercom.

"You ready?"

Lacey would have asked, *for what*, but she wasn't quite sure she was ready to know.

45

G iven the line of work he'd maintained through-
out most of his life, Garrett always knew death
was stalking him. But up until now he'd never been this
close. It had struck by surprise, while his guard was
down and the world had seemed right. He was elated
beyond belief that Kim and the paramilitary officers
had shown up to even the odds, but his saviors were
over a hundred yards out and chasing the enemy in the
opposite direction.

Garrett needed their help and he needed it now. The
crosshairs were on him, and Nagual likely was creeping up from behind to confirm his kill.

Facedown in the snow, Garrett mustered every bit
of self-control to keep from quivering, as his wound

burned, and he struggled to breathe. He was right at the limit of his pain threshold when he heard the *crunch* of cautious steps.

When they finally ceased, Garrett innately knew the rifle barrel was hovering above his head. He could almost hear Nagual's finger grazing the trigger—feel his body clench as it braced for recoil.

And as the muzzle drew closer, an angel whispered softly but firmly.

Move. Now.

Garrett spun right, yanking his bowie knife from its sheath and raking it across the gunman's calf—slicing to the bone.

The shocked assassin fired, lost his grip on the AK-47, and bent to retrieve it.

Quick with his blade, Garrett thrust the knife into the shooter's outstretched arm, ripping a gash across his bicep.

The *sicario* staggered back, escaping the next slash and gripped his bloody arm.

Drawing on the last fumes of his reserve strength, Garrett clambered to his feet and crouched in a fighting stance. He extended the bowie knife in his right hand and cupped his dripping gut wound with the left.

With an aching curiosity, he asked, "You Nagual?"

The cartel commander gave a single nod, pulled two T-handled push daggers from his belt, and replied in a thick Latin accent, "You the soldier?"

Given his roguish appearance, Garrett had to smile. "Do I look like a lawyer to you?"

Nagual didn't respond, just limped forward. The razor-sharp blades jutting from his fists glimmered in the moonlight.

Garrett took a few steps back, feeling more light-headed by the second. Hoping to buy a little recovery time, he tried to bargain. "I'm guessing you know this already, but Kaiser went down in that chopper. And your whole crew is wiped out. This thing is over, Nagual. Finished. No sense in dying for a lost cause."

Nagual marched forward. Then, without warning he charged—punching and swinging with daggered fists. *Left-right-left-right. Uppercut-hook.*

Garrett bobbed and weaved, then parried and struck with a stab to the ribs.

Despite his wounds, the hitman kept up the attack—jabbing and ducking like a professional boxer. He lunged with a groan but lost his footing and stumbled to one knee.

Garrett seized the opening and thrust his blade into Nagual's shoulder, then pulled back for another blow.

But Nagual popped up and landed a solid front kick to Garrett's gut wound.

In a shock wave of blinding pain, Garrett stumbled back and hurled his knife. He caught his balance and braced for the daggers. But when his vision cleared, the fight was done.

Motionless, Nagual stared down at the knife jutting from his sternum in a state of pure disbelief. Reaching up with his right hand, he jerked the stag handle until the blade slipped out.

A mere distraction for Nagual, but it was all Garrett needed. He jerked his pistol and drilled a .45 hollow point through the assassin's forehead.

With nothing left to give, Garrett collapsed where he stood. He didn't know if it was shock, blood loss, or the fact that he was just plumb worn out, but he couldn't move, not even to raise his arm when Bridger called his name.

His brother rushed in, knelt beside him, and checked his wound. "Let me get a look here." Pulling a flashlight from his coat, Bridger clicked it on and ran the beam across Garrett's body. "*Ah hell*, I've seen hangnails worse than this."

Bridger's cheery words didn't match his worried eyes, and Garrett wondered how many of his friends had seen that same look on his own face right before they died.

He turned his head slightly at the sound of shouting voices in the distance. "Kids okay?"

Bridger pulled off his coat and started cutting material for a makeshift compress with his pocketknife. "Cold as hell and scared out of their minds. But no worse for the wear. Your little buddy took a thump to the eye, but he hasn't stopped grinning since we put him on the back of a horse. Took that to mean he'll be all right."

Garrett smiled a weak smile. "Boy loves horses." He raised his head and looked over his chest, wondering if Asadi was nearby. "Don't let him see me like this. Please."

"See you like what? *Ugly?*" Bridger set the dressing on Garrett's wound and pressed. "Afraid it's too late for that."

"Don't joke." He laughed and coughed out his words, "Hurts too much."

"Quit your bellyaching then." Bridger turned back at the sound of a landing helicopter. "Ain't but a damn scratch."

Garrett couldn't help but laugh again. Bridger was

treating the gunshot the same as he would a skinned knee during a backyard football game. Some things between brothers never changed.

"Thanks for the sympathy."

"Told you a million times, Bucky. Sympathy is for soccer players." Bridger looked over at the clearing where Ike's Hughes 500 was landing. "Ready for the latest and greatest in trailer park triage?" He turned to Garrett and smiled. "Probably fly you over to Crippled Crows. Let our old waitress, Nurse Knockers, fix you up with some Wild Turkey and duct tape."

Garrett laughed again, but this time it didn't hurt as much. He thought about Ike using that nasty old bar rag to clean his wound. "Just put me down before that happens."

His brother chuckled but Garrett recognized that look of doubt. It was one he himself had worn many times before. With the loss of blood making him woozy, Garrett had to get a few things off his chest. "Listen, Bridge, I gotta tell you something."

Bridger looked back at the helicopter. "What's stopping you?"

"That boy I was looking after. Asadi. Doesn't have family anymore. And I want someone to take him in. You and Cassidy, or Daddy if he lives. Just want him to have a good home."

"*Daddy? Good home?*" Bridger gave a skeptical glare. "Hang with me now. You're talking crazy."

Garrett coughed out a laugh. "Believe it or not, those two are thick as thieves." When Bridger didn't answer, he pressed. "You'll do that for me? Make sure someone looks after him?"

"*Yes*, I will do that for you, Garrett."

Bridger looked uncomfortable and Garrett couldn't blame him. He'd had more than a few fatalistic conversations on the battlefield, making promises to blown-up soldiers just like himself. It was a miserable affair. And more than a few times he'd wished he was the one dying.

Bridger kept looking back at the chopper. Voices were moving closer. "Anything else, while I'm at it? Want me to adopt Daddy too? Give him a kidney? You name it. I'll do it."

Given the way Bridger was frantically making bandages, Garrett could tell the situation was getting worse. His pain was easing, and he was drifting off. He mustered a smile. "One more thing."

Bridger leaned in. "What's that?"

Garrett grabbed Bridger's sleeve. "I'm sorry for what happened to Mama."

Bridger looked up. "What the hell are you talking about *sorry*? Sorry for what?"

"For everything."

Shaking his head, Bridger's eyes went glassy with tears. "Garrett, that wasn't your fault."

Garrett hesitated before answering. But he knew he had to get this off his chest. "Yeah. But everybody always acted like it was. And I don't blame them."

Bridger looked out over the snowy plains bathed in the moonlight. "I know, Garrett, and that wasn't right." He turned back and looked Garrett in the eye. "But let's be clear on this. You did nothing wrong. For better or worse, the world just *is*. It's cruel as hell and incredibly unfair sometimes and that's a *hard* thing to accept."

Garrett thought about the fact that Kaiser was dead, but it wouldn't change a thing. His mother was still gone, and his death wouldn't bring back the saint of all saints.

As Garrett's world grew dark, Garrett himself was loaded onto a gurney, the hands of the paramedics tearing at his clothes, checking wounds, reading vitals. Their faces were a blur and words muddled in his ears but the alarm in their voices was crystal clear.

Closer and closer to the thundering blast of the helo's rotors, Garrett forced his eyes open to find loved ones around him. Asadi, the twins, Cassidy, and even Lacey were waiting. Softly uttered prayers covered him like a quilt and one hand touched his as he was loaded inside.

The door closed, the medical team went to work, and the bird rose high into the night's sky. And at that moment the moon had never been closer nor shined so brightly. His Texas stars were more plentiful than they'd ever been.

It was either a parting gift or a welcome home to Glory—he didn't know which. Garrett only knew that everything had changed. And whatever the outcome— life or death—he was ready to accept it.

The world just *is*.

Asadi had not even had the chance to say good-bye. He'd merely touched Garrett's hand as they carried him off and loaded him onto the helicopter. Then the golden-haired woman named Manny had wrapped Asadi in a scratchy wool blanket and whisked him away from the scene.

At first he thought she was trying to warm him, but it was clear the covering was more of a shield—a way to hide him from the others. Seeming nervous about the police cars, ambulances, and fire trucks, Manny hurriedly ushered Asadi to one of the big black vehicles, opened the door, and helped him into the backseat.

He turned in every direction, looking for the twins, but could not find them. All around were flashing lights, sirens, and the commotion of people. Standing guard outside were the men who had come to their rescue. The soldiers.

There was a time when these hulking men, with their big machine guns, would have frightened him. But not anymore. He was a soldier now too.

Asadi had not run from danger the way he had in Nasrin. He had stood up to the lion, held his ground, and fought ferociously. Maybe his nightmares were over. He would always weep for his family and especially his mother but knew in his heart she was with him, protecting him and those that he loved.

Watching the helicopter take Garrett away, Manny pulled him close and spoke in broken Dari. "Are you warm?"

Asadi smiled and nodded even though he wasn't.

She smiled back, looking as though she was struggling for the right words. "You hungry?"

He should have been starving but had no appetite. He shook his head. *"I-okay."*

Manny laughed and squeezed his leg. "On top of teaching you some English, I can see Garrett's been feeding you well." In Dari she added, "More meat."

Knowing what she meant, he answered in English, "*Pamcates.*"

"Pamcates?" Her brow furrowed then she asked again, "*Pan-cakes?*"

Asadi wondered if it was a dish served only in Texas. He repeated more slowly to help her understand. "*Pam-cates.*"

Manny rolled down the window and called to a guard standing just outside the door. "Carlos, they make any MREs with pancakes in them?"

The dark-skinned soldier frowned. "They've got 'em. But you don't want 'em."

Rolling the window back up, she turned to Asadi. "Well, we'll see about getting you some real *pamcates* back at Tsavo." She let out a sigh. "We'll have to see about a lot of things."

Asadi noticed her eyes were a little misty and wondered what was wrong. She seemed sad or scared. Maybe both. He reached up and rubbed her back in wide circles just like Garrett used to do when he had a bad dream. "*You safe. With me.*"

His words didn't have the effect he had hoped for. She turned her head away so he couldn't see her.

Asadi rubbed her back a little harder and made wider circles, just like Garrett had done when he was impossible to console. But her body still trembled.

"It-okay. It-okay."

Manny brushed her eyes with the back of her hand, looked back, and smiled. "I'm going to make sure everything works out for you." She furrowed her brow, then told him in Dari, "Your future. Good." After some more mental digging, she added, "Promise."

Her words made him feel slightly warmer, but Asadi had no idea what was going to happen to him. Everyone was gone and nothing would be the same. He may have escaped death, but there was little to look forward to. And despite any promises of a *good future*, he could not imagine a world after the death of his real family that did not include Garrett and Butch.

46

Three days later . . .
Pampa, Texas

Blinking away the cloudiness, Garrett turned to the window, wondering if it was dusk or dawn. From his third-story hospital room he studied the sky and guessed it was evening. Given the pinkish hue, it had to be sunset. His heart sank at the prospect of another long, sleepless night. The last thing he needed was more time to think.

Letting his gaze drift from the windowsill to the nightstand, Garrett found a new addition to the many flowers and gift shop balloons. It was a six-pack of Shiner Bock beer with a yellow Post-it note sympathy card attached to the carton.

Deputy Dawg said you do have a flavor. Drink up. Get well. Expect a hefty tab. -Ike

Garrett marveled at how quickly he'd managed to rack up an insurmountable debt in the few short days he'd been back in Texas. Chuckling at the thought of what he owed Ike, his thoughts turned to Lacey, Sanchez, and inevitably Kim Manning.

Not unlike Hodges, they'd laid it all on the line. And for that, he was eternally obliged.

The knock at the door came so gently, he wondered if he'd imagined it. His response sounded more like a question than an answer. "Come in."

Lacey eased her head in and greeted him with a voice so soft it bordered on a whisper. "Good morning, sunshine. Open for business?"

Morning. Not night. Praise the Lord!

Garrett smiled back. "For you, I am."

Lacey tread so lightly she was almost tiptoeing. Given her trademark faded Levi's, white V-neck, and New Balance running shoes, she was already back to work at the café. With Renegade under indictment, Henry's would be her only source of income for a while. He patted a spot beside him on the bed for her to sit.

"No rest for the weary, huh?"

She moved to his bedside, sat gently, and took his hand into hers. "Farmers don't farm, and ranchers don't ranch on empty stomachs. Somebody's gotta keep this place going."

"Guess that's true." Garrett squeezed her hand, fumbling for the right words. He'd rehearsed them a million times but now that she was here, nothing he said could fully express his gratitude.

"Lacey, I heard what you did for Daddy. I don't even know how to begin to thank you."

She shook it off. "Didn't do much. Ike gave instructions. I followed. Pretty simple."

"No. I'm not just talking about tending to his wounds. I mean after. With the gunman. You risked your life." Garrett found himself choking up. "How can I repay you for that?"

Lacey squeezed his hand back. "First of all, you don't have to, Garrett. You would've done the same for me. And second of all, there's something you have to understand."

Her glassy eyes found the window.

Garrett pulled her hand to his chest. "What is it, Lacey?"

She turned and smiled. "I see so much of my father in Butch. When all that went down, it was kind of hard not to feel like I was saving my dad. I know that sounds crazy. Maybe even a little selfish. But in that moment, I saved a part of me too."

It didn't sound crazy or selfish. Lacey had joined the ranks of Ike, Tony, and himself, who sought to assuage their survivors' guilt, which for combat veterans was as common as bad backs and bum knees. And at the end of the day it was all about surviving—not just the bullets and bombs, but the spiritual and mental toll of lifelong second-guessing.

Garrett had taken it for granted that civilians were immune. But he wouldn't make that mistake again. Watching Lacey go to that dark place, he changed the subject.

"Speak of the devil. Have you seen Daddy yet? Bridger said he's recovering just fine."

She smiled and laughed. "Yep. When I asked him how it felt to cheat death, he just shrugged it off. Told me *the Reaper* needed to get to work or get gone because he was bored as hell and ready to go home."

Garrett couldn't resist a good belly laugh, even though it stung like fire around his stitches. "That's him all right. Old man would rather be dead than twiddling his thumbs, I guess."

Lacey glanced back at the door. "The nurse was insistent I stay no longer than a couple of minutes, so I'd better skedaddle."

She loosened her grip on his hand, but Garrett didn't let go. "Only if you promise to return."

With a smile and a nod, Lacey squeezed back. "It's a deal." She got up and turned to the door but stopped short before leaving. "Oh, that reminds me. You have another visitor." Her attitude went from sweet to bitter in a heartbeat. "A *blonde*?"

At first, Garrett assumed it was a nurse or doctor. There'd been a passel of specialists in and out of his room for the past couple of days. But then it hit him. *Kim Manning.*

"She kind of a . . . tiny thing?"

"Very petite. Gray pinstripe. Hermès attaché case." With a little contempt she added, "A bit busty for her size."

"That's my . . . uh. *Boss.* The woman I told you about who asked me to look after Asadi."

"Ah, yes. The one you're doing the *favor* for?"

Sheepishly, he answered. "That's the one."

Lacey dispensed with the doubtful expression, replacing it with a playful smile. "I'll tell your *boss* to come on in." She spun on a heel and stepped out of the room.

The door hadn't fully closed behind her when Kim charged in. Unlike Lacey's, the Dragon Queen's steps were less tiptoe and more double-time march. It was the first time he'd seen her in anything other than 5.11

tactical pants, Merrell hiking boots, and an Under Armour polo.

She was all business. And she wore it well.

When she stopped at the edge of his bed, Garrett prepped himself for both a flaying and a beating. He mustered his most charming smile.

"Figured you'd be back at Tsavo, Kim. You didn't have to hang around on my account."

"Oh, but I did, Special Agent Kohl. I certainly did."

She didn't elaborate.

"Take it there was a fair amount of cleanup to do, given my uh . . . adventures."

She drummed her fingers on the black leather bag slung over her shoulder. "*Adventures*. That's a good word for it."

Kim was uncharacteristically taciturn, which made Garrett wonder if she had something worse than the scalpel or mallet in mind. Since it seemed she wasn't in the mood for banter, he got right to the point.

"Well, what's the verdict? Termination from the DEA? Prison time?" To lighten the tension, he took a stab at a torture joke. "The whip? Iron maiden? A good keelhauling, maybe?"

She shook her head, seeming to drink in his fear with pleasure. "Any of those would be letting you off easy, Kohl. And I don't plan to do that."

Racking his brain for something worse than prison or torture, he finally came to one unpleasant conclusion. Hoping like hell Kim wasn't going to see to it that he just *disappeared*, Garrett queried with pleading eyes. "What are you thinking, then?"

"I'm thinking . . . conscription."

"*Conscription?*" He took a moment to consider what that could mean. "Like recruitment?"

Kim flashed a game-show host's smile. "More like . . . indentured servitude."

He was just about to launch the first of many questions when she cut him off cold.

"Nope. Uh-uh. This isn't a negotiation, Kohl. This is option A, B, C, and D, which is *all of the above*. To get you *and* your brother out of a whole lot of trouble." She lowered her voice. "Including felony fraud for certain and potential murder charges. I'm going to have to convince some very high-ranking government officials of some very untrue things."

Garrett pondered her list of grievances. Most of what he had done could be argued as self-defense. But a whole helluva lot couldn't. There wasn't much defense for a rogue agent.

"All right, what's the official story? Just tell me what to say and where to sign."

"The official *story* is, you were working a joint op with CIA involving a terrorist threat, SA-24s, and the illegal trafficking of these weapons across the Mexican border by the Garzas." She paused, allowing it to sink in. "This coming together for you?"

Garrett nodded. The mere mention of surface-to-air missiles inside the United States would scare any politician to death. They'd approve anything to keep that from happening. And her story was plausible too.

Their connection at Tsavo.

His money for missiles mission.

And to top it all off, deep-cover experience with Mexican cartels.

Because of Executive Order 12333, Agency operations are restricted on American soil. Kim needed a law enforcement officer as her domestic conduit. And who better to fill the role?

Damn. The CIA was good at being bad.

Kim's plan was as devious as it was brilliant.

"I'm in." Garrett threw out a hand. "But where does that leave me?"

"Leaves you hat in hand before the woman at your bedside."

When she didn't shake on it, he gave her the gimme here sign. "Just toss it over."

"Not that easy. There's still a lot of sweeping up to do with the Garzas." She reached into her satchel, pulled out a business card, and handed it over. "So, here's your broom."

Beside the big gold star on the card was printed the name CADE MALEK—SERGEANT—TEXAS RANGERS. His office was in Amarillo.

Garrett looked up curiously. "What's his connection to the cartel?"

"A very *personal* one."

"Personal how?"

"Involves the death of another Ranger and a connection to some local loser who got mixed up with the Garzas."

"Who?"

"Guy recovering in the room next door." Kim tilted her head left. "One of Bo Clevenger's low-level flunkies. A *Ray Smitty.* Name sound familiar?"

Shocked as hell that the guy was still alive, Garrett wrestled back a smile. "What does he have to do with a dead Texas Ranger?"

Kim's face revealed she was holding back. "I'll let Malek fill you in on that one."

When she elaborated no further, Garrett let it go. He only had one real concern.

"Kim, I know I don't have a lot of standing to ask for a favor but I'm going to anyhow."

Her mouth went slack. "You have to be joking."

"No. I'm not." Wincing, he rose in bed as much as he could. He wanted to make sure he had her full attention. "Has to do with Asadi."

"What about him?"

"I know my future's uncertain. But his doesn't have to be. And I want you to know that Asadi has a home here. My family will take good care of him. Treat him like one of their own."

"Garrett." It was the first time she'd ever used his first name. "I'm an illusionist, not a miracle worker. It's one thing to cover up your mess and quite another to uproot a child and plant him—" She raised her hands to her sides and looked around. "Wherever the hell this is."

The heat rose on Garrett's neck. He didn't care if he owed her his life. She could have it. But she couldn't take Asadi back to Afghanistan if there was nothing for him to go back to.

"Look, if you tell me he's got family waiting for him, that's one thing. But if you're dumping him off at an orphanage that's another. I won't allow it."

"Won't allow it?" Kim laughed. "You're not in a position to make demands, cowboy."

"Well, call it a compromise then."

"In case you haven't figured it out, you're leveraged to the hilt. You'll be lucky if I can dig you out of the trouble you and your family are already in."

Staring glumly out the window, Garrett noticed the snow on the ledge was starting to melt. He racked his brain for anything left he could offer. "Well, there's gotta be something. Anything. You name it, it's yours. I just can't let him go now."

Kim leaned over to get his full attention, which she did. Her face softened, as did her voice and demeanor. "Garrett, you may not believe this, but I do care what happens to Asadi. And as far as family goes, other than his brother, Faraz, who may or may not be alive, the boy has no one left in the world. He's on his own back there."

Garrett smiled. "So, he can stay then."

"*Temporarily.*" With a heavy sigh, she added, "I'm not comfortable with him back in Afghanistan just yet, anyhow. Not until he testifies at the tribunal."

Garrett hated to think Asadi had to return at all. But if that's what it took to make the government officials behind the massacre pay for their crimes, then that's what they'd do. And he'd be by the boy's side every step of the way. Although it wasn't the fix he wanted, Garrett would take what he could get.

"And after he testifies, you'll look into a permanent solution?"

"Not making any promises. But I will say that if I *do* get this done, you need to understand one very important thing."

"What's that?"

"Next time I need a bull in a china shop, *you're* my first phone call."

Garrett didn't ask what that meant because he already knew. *Conscription* was a *no questions asked* kind of deal. Kim had plans to make him a domestic operator, her black bag soldier back in the homeland. It wasn't just bending the rules, it was shattering them to pieces. But to save Asadi from the hell to come he'd do that and a whole lot more.

Apparently, Garrett had more in common with Ike Hodges than he cared to admit. Given his newfound arrangement with the CIA, he was willing to accept that the law could be a little *hazy* sometimes, particularly when the lives of loved ones were concerned.

Kim's demeanor relaxed further with her next question. "You want to see him?"

He didn't even have to answer, his expression said it all.

Kim moved to the door, ducked her head out, and waved Asadi inside. His first steps were a bit timid, but when he saw Garrett, a big smile crept across his face. He ran to him so fast he nearly lost his balance and slammed into the bed.

Garrett winced a little as the skinny arms flew around his neck, but he didn't mind it at all. Every bit of the boy's warmth and affection was worth the pain.

In three days' time, Garrett had gone from white hat to black hat, until settling on a nice shade of gray. He'd always been partial to a silverbelly anyhow, so the look was about right.

In Asadi's tight embrace, Garrett pondered what on earth would possibly come next. But among the many uncertainties, one thing was for sure. On top of making this boy his own, he'd devote himself to blood, soil, and paying back his debts. Ghosts be damned. This cowboy was home and he intended to stay.

Acknowledgments

Many believe writing a novel is a solitary endeavor. While there are long, lonely hours, the reality is that it's far from a solo affair. To my friends, family, and mentors who've been there every step of the way, I offer my deepest gratitude.

To my agent, John Talbot, I will forever be grateful for your faith, guidance, and vision, without which, none of this would be possible. To my editor, David Highfill, I thank you and William Morrow/Harper-Collins for inviting me to join the most talented authors in the world. I'm honored and humbled to be on your team.

To esteemed writers Bruce Edwards, Linda Broday, and Jodi Thomas, without your mentorship and guidance I would not be here. Not only are you the best critique partners a writer could ask for, I'm proud to call you my friends. I also want to thank authors John R. Erickson and Bethany Claire. Without your encouragement and advice, I would not have taken this great leap of faith. Thank you to all above for your belief in me as a writer.

To pilots Jason Abraham, owner of the Mendota Ranch, and CW4 Boyd N. Curry (Ret.), U.S. Army 160th Special Operations Aviation Regiment, thank you for your expertise on helicopters. By pushing some boundaries, we definitely came up with something fun, unique, and exciting.

To my longtime friend Cade Browning, I thank you for both your legal and equine knowledge. To friends Sam Pender, Sergio Alcantera, and Ed Hesher, I appreciate your petroleum and geological expertise.

For ensuring historical accuracy, I thank Alex Hunt, Vincent/Haley Professor of Western Studies, Director of the Center for the Study of the American West (CSAW), West Texas A&M University; and William Elton Green, Curator of History, Emeritus, Panhandle-Plains Historical Museum (PPHM) for their efforts. Both CSAW and PPHM do a fantastic job preserving and showcasing the region's rich heritage and we are very lucky to have them.

To the International Thriller Writers and the ThrillerFest staff and volunteers, thank you for representing our genre and for putting on one of the best events in the business. I can't express how much ThrillerFest has meant to me as a venue to grow, network, and cultivate lifelong friendships.

To the military, intelligence, and law enforcement personnel who will go unnamed, I thank you for helping me to create an authentic experience for the reader. More importantly, I thank you for your service and sacrifice for this great country.

To my parents, Robert and Holly Moore, and my sister, Allison Jensen, I offer my sincerest thanks for a lifetime of love and encouragement. Thank you for a wonderful upbringing and helping me become the man I am.

It is to my beautiful wife, Diana, and our precious children, Bennett and Maddie, that I owe the biggest debt of gratitude. Without their trust, support, and sacrifice becoming a novelist would still be a dream. Diana, you and the kids are my inspiration, my greatest blessing from above, and my reason to reach for the stars. My love for you is beyond measure.

HARPER
LARGE PRINT

We hope you enjoyed reading
our new, comfortable print size and found it
an experience you would like to repeat.

Well – you're in luck!

Harper Large Print offers the finest in
fiction and nonfiction books in this same larger
print size and paperback format. Light and easy to read,
Harper Large Print paperbacks are for the book lovers
who want to see what they are reading without strain.

For a full listing of titles and
new releases to come, please visit our website:
www.hc.com

HARPER LARGE PRINT